TAD
WILLIAMS

THE HEART
OF WHAT WAS
LOST

A Novel of Osten Ard

HODDER

First published in Great Britain in 2017 by Hodder & Stoughton
An Hachette UK company

First published in paperback in 2017

2

Copyright © Tad Williams 2017

A CIP catalogue record for this title is available from the British Library

Paperback ISBN 978 1 473 64665 0

Printed and bound by Clays Ltd, St Ives plc

Hodder & Stoughton policy is to use papers that are natural, renewable
and recyclable products and made from wood grown in sustainable forests.
The logging and manufacturing processes are expected to conform
to the environmental regulations of the country of origin.

Hodder & Stoughton Ltd
Carmelite House
50 Victoria Embankment
London EC4Y 0DZ

www.hodder.co.uk

Dedication

The Osten Ard books have been incredibly important to me and also to lots of readers, so writing a sequel to the original story after so many years away has been a daunting and even occasionally terrifying project; but it has also been a joy.

This book, *The Heart of What Was Lost*, starts the journey back to Osten Ard by filling in an important piece of history left out of the last volume of "Memory, Sorrow, and Thorn"—namely, the tale of the Norns after the Storm King's War ended in their defeat.

I honestly never planned to return to Osten Ard, at least not in any major way, and it wouldn't have happened had it not been for all the kind people who asked me over the years, "But are you ever going to go back to Osten Ard?" and "What about those twins and their birth prophecy? Come on, you can't tell me that wasn't setting up a sequel!"

After enough readers asked, I started to think about it. A story finally came to me that I wanted to tell; so now, with this small volume and much more to come, I return to those lands I thought I'd left behind. Thus:

This book is dedicated to the readers who always wanted to know more about Osten Ard, about Simon and Miriamele and Binabik and the Sithi and the Norns, who wanted to know more of the history of Osten Ard before the first books began and also the history that followed the More-or-Less-Happily-Ever-After of the first story's ending. Your love for the characters and the place was something I never expected. I finally gave in, and I'm glad I did. Thank you all for your support and kindness. I'm doing my best to make you glad you encouraged me.

Welcome back! And for those of you who are new to Osten Ard, I paraphrase one of our heroes, Simon Snowlock, as he greeted an ally at the end of the first story: *Come and join us. You have a world full of friends—some of them you don't even know yet!*

Acknowledgments

Getting back to the land of Osten Ard after all these years and exploring old and new parts of it has been a huge and sometimes daunting task. I couldn't have managed without the help of many people.

My wife and partner, Deborah Beale, worked hard to make all the good things happen. Thanks, Deb!

My publishers, Sheila Gilbert and Betsy Wollheim, who are also my award-winning editors, also worked diligently to make this the best book possible, as they have with the whole of my return to Osten Ard. Josh Starr of DAW has also done a great deal to make this book possible. Thanks, Betsy and Sheila! Thanks, Josh!

Copyeditor Marylou Capes-Platt always brings the smarts and has improved every book of mine she's worked with. This book is no different. Thanks, Marylou!

My excellent agent Matt Bialer worked his own magic over the project as well, for which I am always grateful. Thanks, Matt!

Lisa Tveit has been a rock of support for a long time now with her work on the TW webpage and in many other ways. Thanks, Lisa!

I owe special debt of gratitude for this book to Ron Hyde and Ylva von Löhneysen, who have been titans of fact-checking and priceless sources of Osten-Ard-iana, not to mention being such enthusiastic fans of the original books that it makes me feel like I have done something useful with my working life. That alone is a gift beyond thanks, but they've given me much more. Thanks, Ron and Ylva!

And of course, I want to acknowledge the support I've had from so many of the people associated with the *tadwilliams.com* website, including Eva Maderbacher, who offered some very useful opinions on the first draft of *Heart*. The other early readers of the series will be thanked properly and personally in the opening volume of the new trilogy, *The Witchwood Crown*, which many of them read in manuscript. But for now, I just wanted to say: Thanks, friends! Because no author has ever had nicer or more supportive readers.

Author's Note

You can find a cast of characters and an index of other names at the end of this book. You will also find a short essay (by one of the characters) titled *An Explanation of the Fairy People Known as Sithi and their Cousins the Norns*, which those new to the land of Osten Ard might find helpful and might want to read before starting the book.

Tad Williams
October, 2016

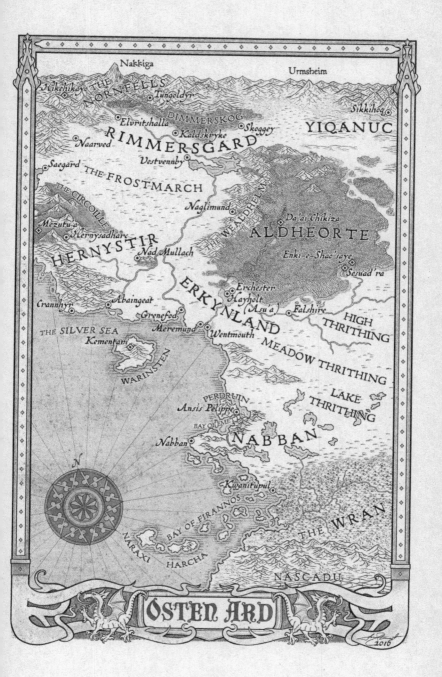

Part
One

The Ruined Fortress

At first, in the flurrying snow, he thought the soldier stumbling in front of him, through the icy mud of the Frostmarch Road, had been wounded, that the man's neck and shoulders were spattered with blood. As he steered his horse around the hobbling figure he saw that the blobs of red had a regular shape and pattern, like waves. He reined up until the soldier was limping beside him.

"Where did you get that?" Porto asked. "That scarf?"

The soldier, thin and several years younger than Porto, only stared up at him and shook his head.

"I asked you a question. Where did you get it?"

"My mother wove it for me. Piss off."

Porto settled back in his saddle, amused. "Are you really a Harborsider, or is your mother a bit blind?"

The younger soldier looked up at him with a blend of confusion and irritation: he thought he was being insulted but wasn't sure. "What do you know about it?"

"More than you do, as it turns out, because I'm from the Rocks and we've been drubbing you lot at town-ball for centuries."

"You're a Shoro—a Geyser?"

"And you're a Dogfish, dim as can be. What's your name?"

The young foot soldier looked him over carefully. The two waterfront neighborhoods—*setros*, as they were called in Ansis Pelippé, the largest city on Perdruin—were ancient rivals, and even here, hundreds of leagues north of that island's shores, it was obvious that his first impulse was to brace for a beating. "Tell me yours."

The man on the horse laughed. "Porto of Shoro Bay. Owner of one horse and most of a suit of armor. And you?"

"Endri. Baker's son."

At last, and as if he had been holding it back, the youth smiled. He still had most of his teeth and it made him seem even younger, like one of the boys who had run beside Porto's horse waving and shouting as he made his way through Nabban, all those months ago.

"By the love of Usires, you're a tall one, aren't you!" Endri looked him up and down. "What are you doing so far away from home, my lord?"

"No lord, me, just a man lucky enough to have a horse. And you're freezing to death because you can't walk fast enough. What happened to your foot?"

The younger soldier shrugged. "Horse stepped on it. Not your horse. I don't think it was, anyway."

"It wasn't. I'd have remembered you, with your Harborside scarf."

"I wish I had another. I'd even wear one in damned Shoro blue. It's so bloody cold here I'm dying. Are we in Rimmersgard yet?"

"Crossed the border two days back. But they all live like mountain trolls up here. Houses built of snow and nothing to eat but pine needles. Climb up."

"What?"

"Climb up. First time I ever helped a Dogfish, but you won't even make it to the border fort like that. Here, take my hand and I'll pull you up to the saddle."

When Endri had settled behind him, Porto gave him a sip from his drinking horn. "It was terrible, by the way."

"What was terrible?"

"The beating we gave you lot this year on St. Tunato's Day. Your Dogfish were weeping in the streets like women."

"Liar. Nobody wept."

"Only because they were too busy begging for mercy."

"You know what my father always says? 'Go to the palace for justice, go to the church for mercy, but go to the Rocks for liars and thieves.'"

Porto laughed. "For a sniveling Harborsider, your father is a wise man."

"This is a true story, if words can be true. If not, then these are only words.

"Once upon the past, during the preserve of the queen's sixteenth High Celebrant, in the era of the Wars of Return, our people, the Cloud Children, were defeated by a coalition of mortals and the Zida'ya, our own treacherous kin, at the Battle for Asu'a. The Storm King Ineluki returned to death, his plans in ruins. Our great Queen Utuk'ku survived, but fell into the keta-yi'indra, a healing sleep nearly as profound as death. It seemed to some of our people that the end of all stories had arrived, that the Great Song itself was coming to an end so that the universe could take its next age-long breath.

"Many, many of our folk who had fought for their queen in a losing cause now departed from the southern lands with thought only of returning to their home in the north ahead of the vengeance of the mortals, who would not be content with their victory, but would strive to overthrow our mountain home and extinguish the last of the Cloud Children.

"This was the moment when the People were nearly destroyed. But it was also a moment of extraordinary grace, of courage beyond the proudest demands we make upon ourselves. And as things have always been in the song of the People, in this, too, even the moments of greatest beauty were perfumed with destruction and loss.

Thus it was for many warriors of the Order of Sacrifice when the Storm King fell, as well as those of other orders who had accompanied them to the enemy's lands. The war was ended. Home was far. And the mortals were close behind, vermin from the filthiest streets of their cities, mercenaries and madmen who killed, not as we do, regretfully, but for the sheer, savage joy of killing."

—Lady Miga seyt-Jinnata of the Order of Chroniclers

"I had hoped you might be exaggerating," said Duke Isgrimnur. "But it is worse than I could have guessed."

"An entire village," said Sludig. "No sense to it." He scowled and made the sign of the Holy Tree. Like the duke himself, the young warrior had seen terrible things during the war just ended, things neither of them would forget. Now another dozen bodies lay sprawled before the tithing-barn in a chaos of mud and bloody snow, mostly old men and a few woman, along with the hacked carcasses of several sheep. "Women and children," lamented Sludig. "Even animals."

At Isgrimnur's feet the body of a child had been half-buried by snow, the blue-gray fingers still reaching for something, the arm stretched like a trampled flower. How terrible it must have been for these villagers to wake in the night and find themselves surrounded by the deathly white faces and soulless eyes of the Norns, creatures out of old and terrifying tales. Duke Isgrimnur could only shake his head, but his hands were trembling. It was one thing to see the mortal ruin of a battle, to see his men dead and dying, but at least his soldiers had swords and axes; at least they could fight back. This . . . this was something else. It made his gut ache.

He turned to look at Ayaminu. The Sitha-woman had been standing a little apart from the duke's men, gazing at the muddle of footprints and hoofprints beginning now to disappear beneath a fresh sifting of white. The steep, golden planes of her face and her long, narrow eyes were alien and unreadable as she examined the ugly work of her people's Norn kin-dred, different from her only in the color of their skin. "Well?" he de-manded. "What do you see? I see only murder. Your fairy cousins are monsters."

Ayaminu's inspection continued for a long moment. She seemed to make little distinction between disturbed snow and tumbled bodies. "The Hikeda'ya were stealing food," she said. "I doubt they would have both-ered to harm anyone, but they were discovered."

"What of it?" Sludig was barely containing his anger. "Do you make an excuse for them because they are your kin? I don't care what you call them—Norns, White Foxes, or Hiki . . . what you said. Name them as you like, they are monsters! Look at these poor people! The war is over, but your immortal fairy cousins are still killing."

Ayaminu shook her head. "My kind are *not* immortal, only long-lived. And as recent battles have shown, both my folk and our Hikeda'ya cousins can die. Thousands of them have done so in the past year, many at the hands of mortals like you." She turned to stare at Sludig, but her face was all but expressionless. "Do I excuse this murder? No. But if the Hikeda'ya were hungry enough to steal from a mortal settlement, they must have been very hungry indeed—to the point of madness. Like my own folk, they can survive on very little. But the north has suffered from the Storm King's frosts a long time."

"We Rimmersmen have suffered from this endless winter too, without needing to destroy entire villages!"

Ayaminu gave the young warrior a bemused look. "You Rimmersmen who came out of the west a mere few centuries ago and killed thousands of my people? And just this year brought death to so many of your Hernystiri neighbors?"

"Damn it, that was not us!" Sludig was trembling. "That was other Rimmersmen under Skali of Kaldskryke—Duke Isgrimnur's sworn enemy!"

The duke put his hand on Sludig's arm. "Quiet, man. That argument has no ending." But at this moment, with his insides knotted by the sight of the dead villagers—*his* dead villagers, the people God had given him to protect—Isgrimnur could not look on the Sitha-woman with any kindness. But for the golden hue of her skin, the fairy-woman could have been one of the Norns, the corpse-white creatures whose murderous work lay all around him. "Remember that our memories are not as long as yours, Lady Ayaminu," he said as evenly as he could manage, "and neither are our lives. I gave you leave to come along with us at the request of your Lord Jiriki, friend of our king and queen—but not to pick fights with my men." In fact, it had only been the strong urgings of the newly crowned Simon and Miriamele that had convinced Isgrimnur to let the Sitha-woman accompany them at all, and he was still not certain he had made the right decision.

He looked down the hill, where his men waited in disordered ranks stretching half a league back down the Frostmarch Road. They were Rimmersmen for the greatest part, along with a few hundred soldiers from other nations who had missed most of the fighting in Erchester but had been hired to reopen the empty forts along the northernmost borders between the lands of the royal High Ward and the defeated Norns. If any of them had expected the White Foxes simply to slip harmlessly back across the border, they were now learning otherwise.

"This village was Finnbogi's." Bulky, shaggy-bearded Brindur, brother of the thane of Skoggey and an important thane in his own right, had survived the final battle at the Hayholt but had left a great deal of blood and most of one of his ears behind. His helmet sat oddly over the bandages. "I saw him die just outside the castle gate, Your Grace. Had his head torn off by a giant who threw it over the Hayholt wall."

"Enough. And enough of this place, too." Isgrimnur waved his hand in angry disgust. "God preserve me, I can still smell the foul creatures even through all this blood—as though they were here only a moment ago."

"It is not likely . . ." began Ayaminu, but fell silent at the duke's violent gesture.

"We should have rounded up all the White Foxes when the battle ended," Isgrimnur said. "We should have taken their heads, prisoners or no, like Crexis when Harcha fell." He looked to the Sitha. "That works for fairies as well as for ordinary men, doesn't it? Cutting their heads off?"

Ayaminu stared at him but did not answer. Isgrimnur turned his back on her and crunched away through the drifts, back to his waiting soldiers.

"Your Grace, a rider is coming. He bears Jarl Vigri's banner!"

Isgrimnur blinked and looked up from his map to scowl at the messenger. "Why do you shout so, man? There is nothing strange in that."

The young Rimmersman colored, though it was hard to see against his burned-red cheeks. "Because he does not come along the eastern fork of the road, from Elvritshalla, but the western fork."

"Impossible," said Sludig.

"Do you mean from Naarved?" demanded the duke. "What nonsense is that?" He stood, bumping the makeshift tabletop with his belly so that the stones meant to represent armies jiggled and jumped. "Why would Vigri be in Naarved when he's supposed to be protecting Elvritshalla?" Vigri was one of the most powerful Rimmersmen lords after Isgrimnur himself. He and his father before him had been some of the duke's most steadfast supporters. It was impossible to believe that the jarl, as earls were called here in the north, would wander away from his sworn duty. Isgrimnur shook his head as he pulled on his fur-lined gloves. "Thank the Ransomer my Gutrun is still safe with our friends in the south. Has everyone in these lands run mad?" He pushed his way out of the tent with Sludig close behind. The Sitha-woman Ayaminu followed, quiet as a shadow slipping along the ground.

The messenger and his horse were wreathed in the plumes of their frosty breath. Beyond them the immensity of the Dimmerskog forest covered the eastern side of the road in snow-blanketed green, the trees silent as sentries frozen at their posts, rank upon rank until they disappeared into white mist.

"What do you have for me, fellow?" the duke demanded. "Is it truly from Vigri? Why is he not at Elvritshalla, defending the city?"

The dismounted rider did his best to bend a knee, but he was clearly almost too cold and weary to stand. "Here, Your Grace," he said, holding out a folded parchment. "I am but the messenger—let the jarl himself speak."

Isgrimnur frowned as he read, then waved to his carls. "Give this man something to eat and to drink. Sludig, Brindur, Floki—we must have words. My tent."

Inside, the men crowded around the duke, anxious but silent. Ayaminu had come in as well, but she stayed to the shadows as ever, still and watchful.

"Vigri says that the White Foxes have been returning north through our lands for over a' month, mostly in scattered handfuls that stayed far from our towns and villages," Isgrimnur began. "But one large group, well-armed, and many of them mounted, were too big to ignore. This one traveled slowly. Vigri says they are carrying the body of a great Norn leader back to *Sturmrspeik*—perhaps even the queen of the Norns herself."

"A body?" said Ayaminu from her place near the doorway. "Perhaps, but it is not the queen's. Utuk'ku Silvermask is not dead. She has suffered a terrible defeat but we would have known if she had perished. And although her spirit was present at Asu'a—the place you call the Hayholt— her bodily form never left Nakkiga. She still waits inside the great mountain."

Isgrimnur frowned. "Well, it is some other notable of the White Foxes whose body they carry, then. It doesn't matter. Vigri says this group have kept together in a small army, and because of that they plunder broadly as they go. They did great damage along the outskirts of Elvritshalla, so Vigri came out to challenge them with much of the city's strength, several thousand men. The Norns fought fiercely, but at last he drove them away into the wilderness. Once he had done that, though, he did not feel he could simply let them escape." He glanced down at the letter, frowned again. "Merciful Aedon grant us good luck, he says he has trapped all those White Foxes—hundreds of them—in a tumbledown Norn border fort on the very outskirts of their land, at Skuggi Pass."

"Their old Castle Tangleroot," said Ayaminu. "It can be no other."

"Vigri left most of his soldiers to protect Elvritshalla," Isgrimnur went on. "He says the men he has are too few to press a siege in such an open place and he fears the Norns will escape again. He asks us to bring our forces and hurry to his aid."

"The castle may be falling down," said Ayaminu, "but the passages beneath it are deep and vast. The Hikeda'ya could hold it for a long time."

"Not if we drive them out like rats," said young Floki, "with fire and black iron." His broad face told how greatly that idea cheered him.

"Let the corpse-skins hide there until Doomsday," Brindur said. "Our men have fought hard and long. Many of them have been away from Rimmersgard for more than a year, and many who came with us now lie buried in Erkynland and foreign lands even farther south. What does it matter what a few hundred Norns do? Their power is broken."

"Their power is never broken while their murdering queen still lives." Sludig bore no title yet, but was certainly due for advancement: he had been one of Isgrimnur's most trusted housecarls even before the war, and had done great deeds in the struggle against the Storm King. "This might be the last of their generals and nobles, trapped in a ruin far from their home. I think Floki has the right of it, Thane Brindur. This is our chance to stamp on the whiteskins like baby snakes found under a rock."

Isgrimnur did not much like either choice. "There are no words for the hatred I feel for those monsters," he said slowly. "For what they did to my son Isorn alone I would kill every last one of them, man, woman, and child." He shook his head, as though it were almost too heavy for his neck to bear. "But Brindur is right, our people are weary. I do not want to see any more good men die fighting the fairies."

"Fight them today or fight them again soon," Sludig said, slapping at one of the axes on his belt. The young Rimmersman had taken the death of the duke's son Isorn almost as hard as Isgrimnur himself. Even now, Sludig's hatred of the Norns ran hot and strong through his blood. "When they have recovered enough to attack our lands again, my lord, we will surely wish we had dealt with them once and for all in their time of weakness."

Isgrimnur sighed. "Let me think, then. We have already made camp so we have this evening, at least. Leave me alone for a while."

As the men went out, Ayaminu stopped at the tent's doorway, her eyes gleaming like golden coins in the reflected light. "Do you wish me to stay, Duke Isgrimnur?"

He snorted. "You wished to come along to listen and watch, and since that was the will of our new king and queen, I said yes. Never did I say that I would let you give me advice."

"That is no surprise, I suppose. Elvrit's race was always stubborn and bloody-minded. Perhaps the days of Fingil Red-Hand are not as far in the past as you would like to think."

"Perhaps not," said Isgrimnur sourly.

"Already slowed by the coffin containing the body of their great warrior, High Marshal Ekisuno, one of the largest troops of the People was soon joined by more Hikeda'ya fleeing the southern defeat. Their swelling numbers now impeded their progress even more.

"Duke Isgrimnur of Elvritshalla, the leader of the Northern mortals, pursued them with a great army of his race, but the People were also harried by one of the duke's strongest allies, Jarl Vigri of Enggidal. Caught between these two cruel enemies, a mixed party of Cloud Children, most of them from the Order of Builders, along with a few Sacrifice warriors and those of other orders, were forced to take refuge in the abandoned fortress of Tangleroot Castle, where it seemed certain that the only conclusion would be their honorable and inevitable deaths."

—Lady Miga seyt-Jinnata of the Order of Chroniclers

Although the roof and most of the upper floors had long ago collapsed, the great hall beneath *Ogu Minurato*, the Fortress with Tangled Roots, was the least damaged part of the ancient, tumbledown castle. It was here that the rubble had been cleared to make room for the great funeral wagon, whose wheels were almost as tall as Viyeki himself. They had to be, because Ekisuno's mighty witchwood sarcophagus was too heavy to be carried by any smaller cart: the various Celebrants now praying around it seemed no larger than children.

Viyeki was disturbed to see how quickly things had fallen apart here outside the sacred protective walls of Nakkiga. Only a few mortal centuries gone and the natural world had all but swallowed Ogu Minurato, eating away at its walls and foundations, replacing them with its own substance, so that a sea of roots now covered the stone floors where the queen's Sacrifices had once drilled. It was a reminder that the greater world lived at the same hurried pace as the mortals—that it was Viyeki and the rest of his Hikeda'ya kind who were forever out of place.

This world knows its own, he decided. After all, the Cloud Children were exiles from the sublime Lost Garden and could not expect any other place to fit them as well.

"We live too much in the past," said a voice behind him, as if contradicting his thoughts.

Caught by surprise, Viyeki turned to see his master Yaarike watching the scene. Viyeki made a gesture of respect. "All praise to the queen, all praise to her Hamakha Clan," he said in ritual greeting. "But I beg your pardon, High Magister. I do not understand what you mean."

"Our love of the past impedes us, at least in this situation," Yaarike said.

By looks alone, Viyeki and his mentor could almost have been brothers. The skin of the High Magister of the Order of Builders was smooth, his face as refined as his noble ancestry, but subtle, almost imperceptible tremors in his hands and his voice revealed his age. Yaarike was one of the oldest of the surviving Hikeda'ya, one who had been born even before the fabled Parting from their Zida'ya cousins—the ones the mortals called Sithi.

"How can we live too much in the past, Magister?" Viyeki asked. "The past is the Garden. The past is our heritage—that for which so many of us have fought and died."

Yaarike frowned slightly. His hair was down; it hung beside his face on either side like fine white curtains. "Yes, of course, the past defines us, but the simplicity of your response disappoints me." He made a flicking gesture with his long fingers that was halfway between irritation and fondness.

"I am shamed, lord."

"You are the cleverest of my host foremen—I should not have to explain myself. But I meant that we are suffering here and now because of our own overconfidence, Viyeki-*tza*." In such moods, his master's endearments often sounded like belittlement. Viyeki waited silently.

"Remember what you first learned when you entered the Order of Builders so long ago? When you discover a flaw in stone, do not examine only the flaw, but how it formed, what it will do if left alone, and how the stone around it has responded. Do not neglect what beauty may have been created—if there were no flaws in order, life would be immeasurably poorer."

Viyeki nodded, uncertain of what this had to do with overconfidence. "Please help me see how to examine this flaw, Master."

"That is a better response." Yaarike nodded. "Ask first how many centuries have we planned this campaign against the mortals? The answer is, for almost eight Great Years—five centuries, as our enemies reckon it, since the Northmen first took mighty Asu'a from our kind. On that day Asu'a and its Zida'ya king, Ineluki, both fell to the enemy, and the precious witchwood groves were burned. So many mourning banners were flown when the news came that all Nakkiga was draped in white."

"I remember, Master."

"Mad with grief," the magister continued, "the people cried, 'Never such loss again!' But now we have been defeated once more."

"Surely not all this could have been foreseen, Master."

Yaarike shook his head. "I do not criticize our Sacrifices, who gave their all, and of course I could never find fault with the Mother of the People—to criticize the queen is to doubt the most sacred of truths. No, it is not our plan of battle I criticize, but our overconfidence. And here we see one perfect example." He gestured to the immense coffin atop the wagon. "I cannot help but think that an army, even one with so distinguished a leader as High Marshal Ekisuno, should not be carrying such impediments as the marshal's casket along with them when they go into battle. If we had won, then whether Ekisuno had lived or not, it would not have been an issue. But since we lost, we are now forced to carry him with us—and as you no doubt noticed, we have been somewhat slowed by the great warrior's corpse in its monstrous, weighty coffin."

In the hush of the ruined great hall, the only noise beside the murmur of the funeral Celebrants repeating their death-prayers was that of the wind keening in the broken ramparts above. Viyeki wondered why his master would say such a thing, especially about a personage as important as the late Ekisuno. It seemed almost a sardonic joke, but it was never possible to be certain with the order's high magister, who was deep as the innermost chasms of Nakkiga. All Viyeki could do was nod and hope that he did not offend.

"Ah. I am glad you agree, Viyeki-*tza*," Yaarike said. "And here is Commander Hayyano and his men, no doubt come to discuss how we may all sell our lives to protect Marshal Ekisuno's lifeless body."

Now Viyeki was almost certain that his master was speaking in some satirical fashion, although he still could not understand why: Ekisuno had not only been the supreme leader of the queen's armies, he was also a descendant of the great Ekimeniso, the queen's long-dead husband. If there was anyone whose corpse should be protected from profane mortals, surely it was Ekisuno.

Hayyano stopped before them and briskly made the several appropriate signs. He had been one of the less effective league commanders of the Order of Sacrifice during the battle for Asu'a, which may have been a reason he had survived, but he had learned the trick of looking busy and important. "How many of your Builders do we have, High Magister?" he demanded before he had even reached them. "We will have need of their engineering skills to defend this place."

Yaarike was silent for several moments, long enough to remind Hayyano that he was outranked not just by Yaarike himself, but even by Host Foreman Viyeki. When Yaarike saw the realization finally cross the commander's face—a subtle but unmistakable flash of unease—he waited a moment longer, then said, "We have enough Builders to make this place secure for a while, perhaps, League Commander, but not enough to defend it against a long and serious siege."

"But there are many tunnels beneath us, Magister!" Hayyano said with poorly hidden surprise. "That is why this place is called Tangleroot! They will never be able to drive us out. And we will kill ten for every one we lose."

"I was aware of the reason for the castle's name, Commander." Yaarike's words were dry as dust. "And if we have no other choice, then yes, each of us can sell his or her life very dearly. But even if we kill twenty for every one of our fallen, we still will not survive long, and we will be little help to those who await us back at Nakkiga. Is that not our greater duty?"

Hayyano drew himself up. He may not have been one of the queen's most successful officers, but he was a handsome, powerful figure and Viyeki knew him to be brave. Talk of duty had brought back his confidence. "My men and I are of the Order of Sacrifice, Lord Yaarike," the commander said. "Our death-songs are already sung. Whatever the outcome, we will make the queen proud of us."

"Certainly. If the queen lives, that is—as we all so dearly pray she will."

Viyeki saw the Sacrifice commander react in shock to old Yaarike's words. "May the Garden preserve her from harm—of course she will survive!"

"As we all pray." Yaarike made the familiar sign that meant *May the queen live forever.* "But in the meantime, we ourselves have two great responsibilities."

"Protecting the body of Ekisuno, the queen's most noble general," said Hayyano promptly.

Yaarike's nod was perfunctory. "Yes, of course. But also the lives of the queen's living servants—my hundred and more Builders, and your three dozen or so Sacrifices, as well as the mixed two or three dozen from other orders, most of whom will be little use in a real fight."

"You would not expect the Celebrants to fight beside Sacrifices, would you?" said Hayyano, looking uneasily at the funeral priests gathered around Ekisuno's coffin. "In any case, they have their own work to do."

"If the choice is between all of us dying like rats and the Celebrants taking a moment between prayers to swing a sword or throw a large rock, then yes, I think they should fight." Yaarike's face was emotionless, but Viyeki knew the magister well enough to hear the anger in his voice. "And as the highest noble within this refuge, I expect my word to be obeyed."

"Of course, High Magister," said Hayyano quickly, but his face suggested he was suppressing more argument. Viyeki thought the commander seemed helplessly transparent. Small wonder that despite high birth, he still held only middling rank.

"Good. Then I want you and your soldiers to make a survey of how we may best defend this place, Commander. We will put my Builders to work shoring up the most needful spots. The mortals who have besieged us—what are they doing?"

"At the moment, not much of anything," said Hayyano. "They seem to think Ogu Minurato is already theirs and that all they have to do is wait."

"They are not entirely wrong," said Yaarike. "We have little to eat and the well is full of rocks. That at least is a task my Builders can begin now. Go, League Commander Hayyano. We will meet again when the First Lantern appears in the sky."

"Yes, Lord Magister." Hayyano crossed his forearms over his breast in ritual acknowledgment, then led his Sacrifices out again.

When he was gone, Yaarike shook his head. "I am glad that the Singers here with us have a field commander like Tzayin-Kha," he said. "She at least is clever and thinks before speaking. What is the Order of Song doing at this moment?"

Viyeki did not like the Singers. Like most servants of the other orders, he distrusted the spell-wielders and was terrified of their great master, Akhenabi, Lord of Song, the most powerful person in Nakkiga but for Queen Utuk'ku herself. "Tzayin-Kha said she would send her followers out in false skins to look upon the enemy's numbers and disposition. And that they would light the fires of unease among the mortals."

"Good. I am glad to hear they are occupied."

For a moment, Viyeki thought he could see the weariness behind his master's immobile face. "I will occupy our Builders as well, Master," he said. "With your permission, I will go and see that the well is cleared of stones."

Yaarike nodded. "Yes, do so, Viyeki-*tza*. Shoring up the defenses of this place will be thirsty work."

He bowed. "It will be done before the Lantern is on the horizon."

"So if you don't want to spend the rest of your life soldiering, what *are* you doing here in the coldest part of the north, little Dogfish?" They were sharing Porto's horse, and the older man was trying to keep Endri distracted. The young man had gone pale when the Northern thane in charge of the mercenaries had given them their orders, and in the two days' riding since then Endri's thoughts had been spinning again and again through the same dismal eddy. "Why aren't you home helping your father make seed cakes?"

"I wanted to see something of the world."

Porto laughed. "And you succeeded! This is certainly something."

"Something dreadful." The youth suppressed a shudder. "Honestly, it's an old story, Porto—too foolish to tell. It was a girl."

"Ah. Her stomach grew large and you began to feel the urge to travel."

"No!" But the young man seemed almost pleased by the idea. "No, not like that. She chose another man. Didn't want to be wed to a baker's son. Didn't want her pretty hands to turn red and sore kneading bread all day, I suppose. I couldn't . . . I didn't want to see her. Her family lived just across from us. So I followed Lord Halawe to Erkynland—to the fighting at the Hayholt."

"Where Lord Halawe was eaten by dirt-goblins, if I remember correctly."

Endri winced. "I didn't see it, but I heard about it." He made the sign of the Holy Tree. "God rest him. He was a good man."

"I've heard that."

"And God preserve us all." Endri made the Tree again.

Porto made the Tree as well. "So all this is just to avoid seeing a girl who threw you over?"

"I didn't think I would end up here, that's certain." A moment later he brightened. "But you, Porto? Do you have a girl back home?"

Porto nodded. "My wife, Sida, may the Aedon bless her and keep her. And our little son who was but a babe in arms. The Lord only knows when I'll see either of them again."

"You'll see them again." When his mood shifted, Endri could be as cheerful and confident as a child. It reminded Porto of his younger brother Andoro, dead ten years or more, and gave him a pang in his chest. "We will come out of this," the youth said, as though Porto had been the worried one. "You'll see."

His attempt at distraction successful, Porto smiled. "I'm sure you're right." But he knew that the deep silent woods and the gray sky would drag the young man back into worry again before too long. "*Heá*, do you know any songs?" he asked.

Endri laughed. "*The Gallant Men of Harborside*, of course. I know all the words, even the part about laying the Dogfish low."

"And me stuck in the saddle in front of you, unable to escape." Porto rolled his eyes. "Go ahead, then, you ungrateful wretch. Make me regret all my kindness."

Endri's singing had ended hours earlier, and conversation had ended not long afterward. As they rode deep between brooding hills, the cold grew and silence settled like a fog over the ancient road.

They first saw the ruins of the castle from the base of the pass, a dark tumble of oblong shapes nestling close to the snow-flecked summit. As they drew nearer, hour by struggling hour, and as the walls of the pass rose higher and higher on either side, plunging them into mist and deep shadow, Porto began to feel he was being dragged helplessly toward the ancient fortress, as if it were some great mill whose stones would grind him to powder.

"I don't understand," said Endri suddenly, his voice startling Porto out of the long quiet. He made the sign of the Tree for perhaps the dozenth time in the last hour. "Sweet Elysia, why did we have to come to this dreadful place? Look at that! Why would Duke Isgrimnur bring us here? He said we were going to a border fort."

"Stop your sniveling, Southerner," called a young Rimmersman riding near them. "You shame us all." The rider was thick as an ox, with a bristling reddish beard that covered much of his broad face; on his shield was painted a red eagle, which told Porto this must be Floki, Thane Brindur's son.

"That *is* a border fort," Floki said. "It just happens to be one of the enemy's, that's all."

"Very clever," said Porto. "But my friend's right. We didn't join for this. We came for a post on the Rimmersgard border."

"Six coppers and food every month," said Endri.

"One silver, four coppers for me," Porto said. "Because I have my own horse."

"But I never said I'd fight the Norns!"

Porto could feel Endri shivering against his back, and knew it was from more than the cold.

"I want to go back," Endri said.

"You didn't think you'd fight the Norns?" brayed Floki, his laugh loud and harsh. "What did you think you'd be doing in a border fort at the edge of the Nornfells?"

"I didn't know we'd go so far," said Endri. "—that we'd . . . that they would . . ." He trailed off into silence.

"Don't let this one discourage you—we'll get back home again," Porto told his young friend, but he was not as confident as he tried to sound. "I'll take you with me, Endri. You'll like the Rocks. My wife's father is a dyer, a wealthy man. He'll give you a place, you'll see."

"He certainly won't give that one a place as a soldier," said the Rimmersman. "Not the way he moans."

"Shut your mouth, Northman," said Porto. "I'm beginning to hate the sound of your voice."

Brindur's son brought his horse closer, and for a moment Porto was afraid he'd have to fight him, but the Northman seemed to have noticed Porto's unusual height. "You'll feel differently about me when the White Foxes are at you, you southern milksop." The bearded youth put his heels to his horse's ribs and raced ahead of them. "Then you'll be crying out for *me*, not your little catamite here," he called back over his shoulder. " 'Floki, come save me from the *Vit Refar*!' That's what you'll say."

"I pray that I lose my voice before my tongue ever shames me." It was an old Perdruinese saying which Porto had uttered many times, but he had never meant it more.

"He's right, though," said Endri. "I am no soldier. I'm frightened."

"I fought beside the great Sir Camaris himself when he led Josua

Lackhand's army in Nabban. I was afraid then, I'm afraid now. There is no shame in that."

"I don't care about shame, Porto. In all truth, I just want to go home."

Isgrimnur's men reached Skuggi Pass and made camp on the slopes beneath the ruined castle, beside the army Vigri had brought from Elvritshalla. The meetings of men who had not seen each other for many long months gave the gathering an air of festival, despite the cold and the flurrying white flakes.

Although the addition of the jarl's soldiers had more than doubled their numbers, Duke Isgrimnur still did not feel entirely at ease. Again and again his gaze was drawn to the broken walls at the top of the pass and the eyes he knew were watching there. He had more experience with the White Foxes than any of his men. Even a small troop of Norns could create chaos in opposing armies, and they were harder to kill than angry bees.

He looked over to Vigri's large campfire, where short, stocky Vigri sat surrounded by his thanes, all drinking and laughing. Vigri saw Isgrimnur and waved for him to join them. The duke raised his hand to say, *soon*. He was not quite ready to take his leisure.

Best to follow the hunt while the trail is new, as my father always said. He turned his attention back to the Sitha-woman Ayaminu, who sat across from him. She was carving a walking stick out of a long ash tree branch and seemed as composed and heedless of the falling snow as a statue.

"Why is it still so bloody cold here in late Yuven-month?" he growled. "I thought the Storm King was gone for good."

Ayaminu did not look up. "Ineluki sang up many great storms. They will not go away again so quickly simply because his influence is ended. Besides, it is always cold here."

Isgrimnur brought his hands close to the fire again. "We have a large troop of the Norns that attacked Erkynland trapped in these ruins," he said more quietly. "If you sent your people a message, Ayaminu, would they come? Would they help us to finish this once and for all?"

She returned a look that he could not interpret. It was always difficult with the Sithi, whose emotions and even ages were largely a mystery to

mortals. He knew Ayaminu was venerable among he
ancient, but to look at her she seemed scarcely dif
younger Sithi women like Jiriki's sister Aditu. Per
ner, her movements less robust—there were times w
fragile, like a woman once considered a beauty but rece
from a long illness. Her golden eyes, though, were as bright as h
Gutrun's angriest stare, fierce as a hunting hawk's.

"No," the Sitha said at last. "As I told you before, Duke Isgrimnur, my
people will not come. The Zida'ya fought as allies to you Sudhoda'ya—
you mortals—but that does not mean our paths will always lead the same
way from now on. We will not help you destroy our kin."

"Then why are you here? Why travel all this way simply to watch?"

She turned the long staff she was working on this way and that to examine it in the firelight before putting blade to wood again. "You speak
as though watching and learning have no value in themselves."

Isgrimnur shook his head. Talking to the Sithi often felt like arguing
with drunkards or children—not that they spoke foolishly, but the conversation always went around in circles until he forgot where it had begun.
Perhaps she meant what she said—that she was only here to observe—but
the duke did not trust it. *Do Simon and Miriamele understand how unlikely it
is that we will be able to live comfortably beside such strange creatures as these fairies? We will sooner make partnership with the birds of the air, I think. They are
just too different from us—nor do they think we are worth the trouble of honest
explanations.* "Please do not muddle me with tail-swallowing words, Mistress Ayaminu," he said. "Of course learning has value, but so does fighting to protect ourselves."

"The Hikeda'ya are retreating to their own land." The Sitha's voice
was mild, as though she merely proposed another interpretation.

The duke struggled to keep his temper. "Yes, after pillaging and murdering all over the north—and through Erkynland too. After trying to
throw down the mortal kingdoms and set their dead master over all of us."

She might have been amused, but he could not be sure. "So you will
teach them not to do that by doing the same thing. Blood for blood."

Isgrimnur shook his head. "Simon and Miriamele, the new king and
queen in the Hayholt, bade me only make sure the retreating Norns can
do no further harm. But without help from your people, I think I have no

choice but to ensure their good behavior by ending their race pletely—that is what I think, more and more."

"And you wonder why my people will not help you."

"I wonder less, now that I have spent time with you, Lady Ayaminu." Despite his best efforts, the duke was finding it hard to keep anger at bay. "It's clear that you think nothing your Norn cousins do is worth punishment."

"No, that is not true. But that is because I know the Hikeda'ya will punish themselves—are already punishing themselves—more deeply than you can understand."

"Enough." Isgrimnur rose in disgust. "Where I come from, we do not let murderers choose their own sentences." He left Ayaminu to her carving and headed to the larger fire where Jarl Vigri and his thanes were passing a skin bag. The sun was down, and the crags behind the White Foxes' castle gleamed like crooked teeth in the last light.

"You are back, my lord!" shouted Vigri. "The ale-feast has its guest of honor!" Vigri of Enggidal was a short man about whom it was an old joke to suggest there might be trolls in his family tree, but he was burly and strong. More than a few arguments at the jarl's own supper table had ended when, offended by something, Vigri had picked up one end of the great oak trestle and flipped everything on it to the floor of the dining hall, often tumbling a few guests into the straw at the same time. Isgrimnur was glad to have Vigri beside him again. He was a steadier, more trustworthy lieutenant than Brindur, who blew hot and cold, or Brindur's son Floki, who blew only hot.

Vigri and his carls seemed surprisingly drunk for so early in the evening, but the duke and his men had only just arrived and Isgrimnur knew it must have been difficult for Vigri's soldiers to wait for reinforcements in an enemy land, especially a spot as gloomy as this, a place so ill-omened that Rimmersmen never ventured here, though the Norns had deserted the crumbling fortress centuries earlier. Vigri and his men would likely have spent the last several days praying for the arrival of Isgrimnur's troop and hearing and seeing evil spirits in every shadow. Small wonder if they celebrated now. "I had to see to a few things. My men are not happy. Most of them expected to be at home in Elvritshalla by now."

"My men feel the same, my lord," said Vigri. "They heard a fortnight ago that the war was over, and not much before that, they learned that Skali Sharp-Nose is dead. We have won, so why are we still fighting?"

"It is one thing to win," said the duke. "It is another to convince your enemies that they have lost."

Vigri grinned. "Killing them is a good way to do that."

Isgrimnur made a sour face. "Killing Norns is never as easy as it sounds. How many of them are here, and how are they disposed?"

"It is hard to say, Your Grace. They move in and out of the shadows like cats. Also, they look so much alike that it might be one Norn soldier seen in a dozen different places."

"Then give me your best guess."

"Perhaps as few as four score or so, perhaps as many as three hundred. But we have seen no giants among them."

"That's something to thank the good God for, at least." Isgrimnur looked around the fire. "And what of us? Most especially, how many archers do we have? I know the White Foxes too well to charge in. We will pick off as many as we can."

"I have a troop of Tungoldyr bordermen who can do what is needed with a yew bow," Vigri said, and waved for the skin once more. "I would put them against any archers in the south, even the Thrithings-men."

Isgrimnur nodded. "And I have my crossbowmen who were with me in Erkynland—those that survived, God save the rest. Those bolts will put a pretty hole even in that damnable witchwood armor." The duke leaned and began to scratch with a stick on the snow-spattered ground. "So what does that make it? I brought a company of paid men for the forts, most of them foot soldiers, but a few lances as well. Most of them are untried, though, and new to the north. I also have a company out of Hringholt, as well as Tonnrud's brother Brindur and their Skoggeymen. What does that make?" He scratched a few more times, frowned. He had not brought anywhere near as many men back from Erkynland alive as he would have hoped, and it pained him deeply. "With yours and mine we must have twelve hundred soldiers altogether, Vigri." He felt a little better, and this time he reached out his hand for the skin as it went around. After a long swallow, he wiped his beard with the back of his hand, then took a second sizable gulp—he had given Vigri and the others a long head start on the drinking, after all. "And the siege machinery we passed on the road?"

"That is what I ordered sent from Elvritshalla, a few stone-flingers and a great iron battering ram to knock down gates and walls—the biggest one we've got."

"Is it the Big Bear?" asked the duke with a smile. "I haven't seen that snarling monstrosity for years. No wonder there were so many horses hitched to the wagon—that thing is heavy as a mountain!"

"Yes, it's the bear. But if we want to use it, we will have to find a tree trunk big enough and strong to mount the head on."

"We will not need the ram here, I think," Isgrimnur said. "There is hardly wall joined to wall in that tumbledown place."

"Better safe than sorry," Vigri said. "Especially with the White Foxes. They are tricksy as weasels."

Isgrimnur nodded. "By all that is holy, you are right about that. I wish we fought men. God grant that at least it all goes quickly. Damn me, where has that sack of ale gone?"

"Why is it always so bloody cold these days?" Endri asked sadly. "It's supposed to be summer!" A tattered rag, dropped by some other soldier, had joined his woolen scarf; with both wrapped around his skinny neck, Porto thought the young Harborsider looked like a turtle. *But,* he thought, *a turtle would be better protected.* Endri's aged chain-link armor had more than a few links missing.

"It's the north," Porto explained.

Endri shivered again. He stared up the hill at the ruined castle, then made the sign of the Tree. "I just wanted to earn a few coppers."

Porto could not help pitying this young man, so far from all that was familiar. "Have you never fought before?"

"In an army? Not really. By the time I joined the prince and Camaris, we were on our way to Erkynland. We were some of the last onto the field at the Hayholt."

"Even the last onto the field must have seen some fierce fighting. I was there."

Endri shrugged, but he looked shamed. "I was near the back. No one ever tried to kill me. I swung my sword at a few of the Norns as they ran past after the tower fell, but I didn't hit any. Too fast. Like swinging at shadows. Or at flying bats. And that was the only fighting I've seen."

"I killed a Norn at the Hayholt," said Porto, and in that moment, beneath dark skies and battered by the wind, it might have just happened. "Or rather I was fighting him when he died. It was when the tower fell, Angel Tower or whatever it was called—were you close when it happened? All around the storms were raging and thundering, but there was fire in the sky, too. The world seemed upside down." He fell silent for a moment, uncertain how much he wanted to remember. "Where I stood," he said at last, "the tower went down with a great groan and roar, like a living thing. The ground jumped beneath me and knocked me down. Snow, dirt, water, all thrown into the air in a great spout, like a whalefish's breath, then they began to fall back to the earth. For a moment I could not see anything at all, mud and stones tumbling down all around me, then something rushed out of the flurry and knocked me over again. Before I even had a chance to make the holy Tree, something swished past my head and a hand grabbed at my arm. Someone was trying to kill me—that was all I knew—and I pulled out my dagger and jabbed and jabbed. I was lucky. I hit something and it collapsed on top of me. As we fought I realized that blood was splashing on me—not dripping, Endri, splashing, as though I lay in the course of a stream. Whatever was on me sagged off then, and I got to my feet. It was one of the White Foxes, and my knife had cut deeply into its belly, but it was also missing part of its head."

"What do you mean?" Endri's eyes were wide, like Porto's younger brother when he had told him ghostly stories in their childhood bed.

Porto shook his head at the memory. He did not like remembering that bloodied, death-pale creature, here, so close to those ruins at the top of the pass. "Perhaps a part of the tower had fallen on him, lad. I can't say. But his helmet was gone and part of his head was dinted in. His one good eye was filming over. I do not know how he fought with me even for those few moments. No mortal could have done it with all his brains out that way."

"Do they not die?" Endri sounded terrified.

Porto silently cursed himself for making things worse. "Nay, nay, of course they do. This one had already died by the time he fell off me. For the love of the Aedon, man, most of his blood was out! The White Foxes are canny fighters, strong and crafty, but when people call them immortals they mean only that they have long lives. They may go on for centuries, as it's said, but with a yard of steel in their guts they will die like anyone else, trust me."

Still, his tale did not seem to make the younger man feel better about the upcoming struggle. Porto decided he would be more careful telling stories in the future.

"While the Order of Echoes sent their calls out upon the dreamwinds, Lord Yaarike the Magister of the Builders employed the Singers led by Tzayin-Kha, who would become one of the revered martyrs of those final battles. Her Singers went secretly among the enemy, traveling on mirror-courses. Undetected, they spread fear among the mortals, but they were too small a force and too weak after the destruction of Ineluki Storm King to do more than sow confusion and bring back knowledge of the enemy.

"The stories they carried gave Yaarike and his lieutenants no solace. The People were greatly outnumbered, and Isgrimnur of Elvritshalla and most of his mortal troops were battle-hardened.

"Lord Yaarike Kijada and his advisors knew that without the protection of Tangleroot Castle, however degraded that fortress had become, their forces would be quickly overcome. Many of the defenders under him believed that the only choice left was to sell their lives as dearly as they could, but others believed just as strongly that they should abandon the stronghold by night, when the mortals were hampered by darkness, and hope that at least a few of the People might make their way back to Na-kkiga, where a proper defense could be mounted.

"But Lord Yaarike knew that to abandon Tangleroot Castle in secrecy and haste would mean not only a shameful retreat, but an even more shameful desertion of the body of the martyred hero, High Marshal Ekisuno . . ."

As Viyeki made his way into the interior of the ancient ruin, the echoes of the funerary priests chanting prayers for General Ekisuno's voyage back to the Garden made the place seem almost homelike. Back in Nakkiga, their city in the mountain, the air of the public places was usually sonorous with the voices of Celebrants, and in the great martyr-temples of the queen's family and other noble dead, the chanting for the departed never ceased.

Only the walls of the old keep still stood intact, though its roofbeams were long gone and the stars now its only ceiling. Viyeki made a ritual obeisance as he skirted the huge casket and its circle of murmuring clerics, then discovered his master standing by himself near the wall in an attitude of meditative contemplation. As always, Magister Yaarike looked to be the very essence of calm, but Viyeki had served the lord of the Builders for more than three Great Years, through times both bad and good, and he had learned that his master was never as unmoved as he appeared. Viyeki treasured the fact that he knew his master so well, but considered such insight to be his secret trust. *We owe correct outward behavior to our inferiors,* his mother had always told him, *but even more to ourselves. When we* think *of what is right, we can* be *what is right.* Warmed by the memory of her, Viyeki sat beside his master and waited.

No little time passed before Yaarike finally spoke to him. "I am beginning to think that the only acceptable tactic is to try to break through the ring of black iron with which the mortals have surrounded us. Not tonight, when they would be expecting us to do so. Tomorrow when the sun comes back they will attack this hill and these inadequate walls. We will have to hold them off at any cost, then be prepared to try our escape when darkness returns—when the mortals will be tending their wounds and expecting us to do the same."

Viyeki was more than a little surprised, but he knew better than to think Yaarike simply wished to run from a fight. "Will you share your reasons, High Magister?"

His master made a small gesture of annoyance. "Have you given up thinking for yourself, Viyeki-*tza*?"

The idea that he had failed his master even in such a small thing burned like fire. "Forgive me, my lord. I understand that you believe our deaths can achieve more somewhere else. But I cannot see that it makes any difference whether we fall here or farther up the pass, or even fleeing toward the outer walls of our city. It is not as though we will be close enough when the mortals catch us for any in Nakkiga to see us die."

"Ah. I sense the misunderstanding." Yaarike nodded. "You are thinking of only where our deaths will be most appropriate or most useful. But I have another puzzle for you to consider, just as I used to set you problems of engineering when you were an apprentice. What if we do not die?"

"I don't understand, Magister."

"It is too early to start considering an honorable death, Host Foreman Viyeki. In fact, an honorable death is only a suitable alternative when death cannot be avoided. But even the most fanatical of the Queen's Teeth or the Sacrifice Elite know that their first responsibility is to stay alive and perform their duties as long as possible. Did you see the great iron ram the mortals brought? The one lashed to a wagon bigger even than Ekisuno's caisson, pulled by three teams of oxen?"

"Yes. It is made of black iron and shaped like a bear's head." Viyeki frowned. "I think it is foolish. Like a child's toy, however huge it may be."

"You would not say that if you saw it knocking down the walls around our innermost preserve—or even Nakkiga's great gates themselves."

"Impossible!"

"Why?" The magister's eyes were bright, his face unusually animated. "What do you think will happen after we are dead here, our lives tidily but honorably laid down in a hopeless fight?" Viyeki had never seen his master like this, showing what looked like actual anger. "I will tell you. With us gone, the Northmen will proceed through the pass and march across our lands. Soon they will reach our outer walls, the very walls that Akhenabi and the rest convinced the Queen—may she live forever—not to repair. We would need ten thousand Sacrifices to defend that ruined barrier now against even a small army like this. We have not a tenth of that number of warriors left in all Nakkiga, I feel sure. Do you hear my song, Host Foreman? Do you apprehend its melody?"

"I'm . . . I'm not certain."

"The Northmen will be at the very doors of our mountain. And the few of our troops that are not scattered across the south trying to struggle home, or have not already bravely and foolishly given their lives here with you and me, will be all that stands between Nakkiga and the revenge of the mortals. Do you know who waits at the base of the hill right now, staring up at us this very moment? Isgrimnur, the Duke of Elvritshalla, descendant of the same Fingil Red-Hand who slaughtered our kind all over the north, who threw down the holy stones of Asu'a itself and burned a thousand prisoners as demons. What do you think will happen when that great, black iron bear-head knocks down the Nakkiga Gates and Isgrimnur and his savages storm into the city?"

That was impossible, surely. Viyeki found that for a long moment he could not even speak. "But they couldn't—!"

"Couldn't they? Who would stop them? The leaders of the Order of Sacrifice are dead and rotting in the meadows of the south. Our queen has fallen into the *keta-yi'indra*—that deep, deathlike sleep of preservation and recovery. You felt her fall just as I did, just as every single Hikeda'ya felt it. We call it 'the dangerous sleep' because our people are leaderless while she slumbers." He leaned closer. "Who will rule in her absence, Host Foreman Viyeki? The Order of Song, that is who. Akhenabi and Jikkyo and the rest of that bloodless fellowship. And if the gates of Nakkiga will not hold, the Order of Song will take the survivors and flee deeper into the mountain, to places the mortals cannot follow." Yaarike shook his head. "And that is what our people will become—creatures ruled by sorcerers, slaves who never see the light of day, who hide in darkness and can be said to live only in that they have not yet died. The Garden that was our home will not even be a story anymore—or, if the tales still exist, Akhenabi and his order will teach that our people lived in darkness there, too, surrounded by stone and ruled by the masters of Song." The magister paused, as if he had realized how strange and desperate his words had become. He looked around quickly, but they were still alone except for the silent guards and the even more silent coffin. "So tell me, Host Foreman, do you still want only to sell your life as honorably as possible here?"

Before Viyeki could answer—although he had no idea of how to reply—Yaarike waved him away as if he had failed some test.

"Go now, Viyeki-*tza*," the high magister said. "If your engineers have finished clearing the well of stones, find some other useful task to keep them and yourself occupied. Let me think. It is nearly the only weapon that has been left to me. But remember what I have said, and remember your family and clan who wait for us back home. Most of all, remember

that what is an honorable death for you might mean the destruction of
your people."

Porto barely slept. The night was full of odd shadows and the wilderness
rang with cries that might have been wolves or the ghosts of weeping
children, but there was more to his unease than fearsome sounds. He could
not shake off the feeling that though the duke's forces far outnumbered
their enemy, and their troops were fresh where the Norns were hungry
and exhausted, somehow they did not have the upper hand. Lying beneath
the distant, uncaring stars, he felt as though he and all the other mortals
were in a brightly lit room in the middle of great darkness, being watched
by countless unseen eyes.

From time to time his gaze was drawn to the broken walls of Tangleroot
Castle and the lights he sometimes saw flickering there. They were nothing
wholesome, not the familiar glow of candles, rushlights, or oil lamps, but
shimmers of ghostly fire in foul colors, marshy green or a cadaverous yellow
that nevertheless caught his eye and seemed to pull him closer, though his
body never moved. At last he rolled over to face away from the top of the
pass, hoping to find better rest, but then was presented the sight of young
Endri trapped in evil dreams, moaning and twitching through his own
shallow slumbers, shivering in a cold that no scarf or cloak could keep out.

Dawn finally came, but the morning sun barely made its presence felt. As
Porto and Endri and the rest broke their fast on what flatbread the field
kitchens managed to turn out, the mists rose as high as the surrounding
hills but then stopped and hung, so it seemed as if a great, gray cloud had
drifted down from the heavens and fallen across the pass. Although the
wind had eased, a river of cold air still flowed down from the heights,
making all the men feel heavy and old in their bones, paining the southern
soldiers even worse than the Rimmersmen.

"I feel like I will die today," Endri said.

"Don't be foolish." Porto gave him a shove, but the younger man only
took it as though it were his due, as a slave might take a beating. "I won't
let you."

"You're a good friend, Porto. How did you manage to get born in the Rocks with all the thieves and beggars?"

"Don't ask me, ask my mother. And don't be so fearful. You and I are not even supposed to go up the hill toward the castle. We'll be protecting the donkey—the arbalest. That's what the commander told me."

He and Endri were in position before the sun made its way above the eastern side of the pass. The engineers they guarded made sure the stone-throwing machine was ready, talking warmly and confidently of how soon they would knock down this wall of ancient stone or that one, as though the battle were no more than a tournament, some sort of contest with prizes for the winning troop.

"Like town-ball," said Porto.

"What?" Endri's eyes had a haunted look.

"Town-ball. This, the waiting before it starts. You know that feeling."

"I never played."

"A strapping, strong fellow like you? Why not?"

Endri looked shamefaced. "Too slow." His face brightened a little. "Did you?"

"Play at the proper game, on festival days? Once or twice, before I went to soldiering. It is good to have long legs when you're running, not so much when people are kicking your shins."

Endri smiled. "At least being tall like that keeps your ballocks up high in the air where people aren't as likely to kick them."

Porto shook his head, glad to see the youth's spirits lift a bit. "Don't forget, there's only a small difference between them being too high to kick and them being low enough to punch. I swear by all the saints, it hurts just as much."

Somebody blew a horn. It echoed along the hillside like a sudden shriek. The color drained from Endri's face. "What's that?"

"It's only the stand-ready," Porto told him. "Don't fear. We'll come through this all right."

It is always dreadful, waiting for the fighting to begin, Isgrimnur thought. But it was much worse when the enemy was as unknowable as the Norns.

As he stood watching sunrise color the sky above the pass, Isgrimnur remembered the first time he had waited for a battle to start, long ago—so long ago! Could so many years truly have passed? His father Isbeorn had led a company of dalesmen against Fanngrun, King Jormgrun's rebellious cousin. Isbeorn had not wanted to fight, but Fanngrun had chosen to march through the thane's family lands in the Hargres Dale on his way to attack the king in Elvritshalla, and the king had made it very clear that if Isbeorn and his carls did not dispute Fanngrun's passage across their lands, then they were traitors, too.

As they had stood waiting, on a morning not much brighter or more pleasant than this one, Isgrimnur's father had seen his young son's look of poorly hidden fear.

"Do you know what the worst thing about fighting is?" Isbeorn asked.

"What, sire?"

"There's a good chance we'll live."

Isgrimnur, all of thirteen summers old, though a good size for his age, hadn't known how to answer to that. His father was not a man given to jests, even grim ones. At last, he said, "You say we'll live?"

"The odds are good. It is not our job to stop Fanngrun's army, merely to show ourselves willing—to prove to the king that we are his men. That is best done not by fighting Fanngrun's Vattinlanders face to face, but by harrying them through our land as quickly as possible. They outnumber us greatly."

"I still don't understand. You said we'll probably live. Why is that the worst thing?"

His father grinned, teeth gleaming in his grayshot beard. "Because if we're killed, we go straight to Heaven, don't we? Doing our king's bidding and defending our home in the name of the True God against unbelievers."

This was far beyond Isgrimnur's youthful understanding. "But our King Jormgrun is an unbeliever, too. So are most of his court!"

"God only cares about His soldiers and what they do. So if someone happens to put a spear through me, don't worry—I'll be on my way to Heaven like a stone out of a sling. They can only kill your body, son. Your soul is beyond any mortal harm. If we survive this day, it means we may have to wait another sixty years or more before we can stand before the Lord's great throne."

Isgrimnur had never felt as reassured by the explanation as his bluff, pious father likely meant him to, but it had set things in a different light.

I wish it were true now, he thought. *I wish we had nothing to fear but death.* But fighting the Norns was different: thinking of their dark, empty eyes and their ghostly faces, the duke could not help feeling that his soul *was* in danger—that there were powers that could not just keep him from Heaven but also drag him away to wander in darkness forever. And Isgrimnur was by no means the only one who felt that way: a few enterprising Rimmersgard soldiers had emptied the font at an abandoned church they had passed weeks ago, in their march north, and were now selling the holy water at a brutally high price. Soldiers were rubbing it on their faces and other exposed skin, even drinking it, in the hope of somehow protecting themselves not only from the blades of the White Foxes, but even from the immortals' very existence.

The dawn light was strong enough now to touch the weathered gray stones at the top of the ruined castle's highest tower, a building whose odd, thorny shape and unfamiliar construction whispered that its makers had not been human. The air was chilly but not as bitter as it had been. That was something. Too much cold sapped the strength from a man's limbs.

Isgrimnur ignored the pounding of his heart and the sourness of his stomach as he looked to his captains, then turned and pointed to the catapult men.

"Let fly," he called. "Knock down those walls. Push the whiteskinned bastards' faces into the mud." He turned back to his captains. "With your men, now. We will soften them up a bit, first with stones, then with arrows. Then it will be fieldwork, men—all hard graft until we drive them out."

The first catapult arm leaped forward with a hum and a loud clack. A stone flew through the air and knocked an edge off one of the freestanding walls.

"Soon!" Isgrimnur shouted. "Captains, keep your men at the ready. Soon we will pay them back for Naglimund and the Hayholt!"

Except for a few Sacrifice sentries and the chanting Celebrant priests around Ekisuno's coffin, most of the Hikeda'ya survivors who crowded now into the root-tapestried hall were of Viyeki's own Order of Builders, several score of battle-trained engineers resting quietly or moving like shadows in that ancient place, illuminated by gray morning sky, the ruin's only roof. They could all hear the battle noises from the hill outside the tower, but could do nothing except wait to see if the Order of Sacrifice's defense failed. If it did fail—and Viyeki thought that likely—they would all have to retreat to the tunnels, then sell their lives down in the dark in hopeless resistance against the victorious mortals. Viyeki should have been frightened at what lay before him, at the thought of never seeing his wife or home again, but he was too angry. The more he thought of it, the more he felt certain that Yaarike was right: the Order of Sacrifice as well as Akhenabi and his Singers had been foolishly overconfident, with no plan made for retreat and no attention given to any outcome except victory.

As if he had guessed what his host-foreman was thinking, Magister Yaarike made a gesture of summoning. Viyeki went to him.

"Yes, Master?"

"Let us walk a little ways apart. What I have to say—and show—is not for these others."

Viyeki followed him to the emptiest section of the great hall. The broken spiral columns in each angle of the sixteen-sided room showed him that the tower had been built back in the era of either the fourth or fifth Royal Celebrants. He knew that even now, so many years after Viyeki had left the academy behind, Yaarike would be annoyed with him for not remembering which.

Even in his despair and fury at their situation, Viyeki could not help being excited that his master had so often singled him out on the retreat from the south, treating him almost as an equal. Magister Yaarike was more than the head of an order, although that would have been honor enough to assure a place among the tombs of the greatest; he was also the oldest member of Clan Kijada, a family that had been powerful long before the Hikeda'ya and their kin had fled the Garden and come to these lands. Viyeki's own parents were distinguished enough, a justiciar and an admired court artist, but his Enduya clan had never been of much importance—a middling noble house whose children mostly became palace clerics or low-ranking Sacrifice officers.

But Magister Yaarike had always looked beyond Viyeki's indifferent family heritage, and for that the host foreman was extremely grateful. He doubted any other magister of the Builders would even have given one of such middling birth a position of importance: Yaarike was one of Nakkiga's few leaders for whom "unconventional" did not always mean "untrustworthy."

"I wish to ask you a favor, Viyeki-*tza*," Yaarike said when they were far enough from the others for private speech.

"Anything, Master."

A slight frown. "Do not make broad promises without knowing what you are promising, Host Foreman, or what may happen in the Song of Fate after you have sworn. Remember the old saying, 'When one finger bends, none of the others can stay perfectly straight.'"

Viyeki bowed. "Apologies, High Magister. I should have said, 'Tell me and I will do all that I can.'"

"Better." Yaarike turned his back on the rest of the room, shielding the two of them from view with the wide expanse of his magisterial robes, then reached into his tunic at the neck and carefully drew out something that gleamed even through his cupped hands, as though he held a live coal. "See." Yaarike raised the object, still keeping it close to his body, and lifted away his upper hand. What he held seemed not just to reflect the sparse light but to contain some inner fire of its own: the magister's pale face was warmed to a ruddy sunset color by its glow.

Viyeki half-closed his eyes as he leaned toward it, the object's beauty too much to take in all at once. "It is magnificent," he said at last. "What is it, Master? Something very unusual indeed, I think. And very old."

Yaarike nodded. "Your eye is good, Host Foreman. It is indeed a thing of great age. Here, take it. Feel its weight."

Viyeki accepted the chain and its dangling pendant, shielding its glow as he had seen his master do. It was surprisingly heavy, but it was typical of the high magister that he should have worn it so long without a word of complaint. The chain was thick and plain, and even in the poor light of the hall Viyeki could see it was made of some strange metal too pale to be copper but too pink to be gold or anything more ordinary. The pendant was the size of his palm, shaped like a rounded triangle hanging pointdown. At its otherwise featureless center glimmered a large oval stone of a sublime red-orange color.

"What am I holding?" Viyeki asked at last.

"It is called The Heart of What Was Lost," the magister said. "My forefather Yaaro-Mon brought it from our people's ancient home in Venga Do'tzae when we left that place."

"This truly came from . . . from the Garden, Master?" He had heard of such artifacts, but other than those that Queen Utuk'ku wore for festivals, he did not think he had ever seen one, let alone held it in his hands.

"The gem did, yes. You know the tales of Hamakho Wormslayer, of course."

Viyeki nodded. He could not imagine any of their people who did not know Hamakho, the ancient hero and founder of the queen's clan.

"When Hamakho was dying," the magister said, "he drove his great sword Grayflame into the stone threshold of the Gatherer's Temple in the very heart of the Garden. But when the time came to board the ships, no one could pull Hamakho's blade from the threshold, so it was left behind, another sacrifice to the Unbeing that claimed our homeland. But my forefather Yaaro-Mon prised this gem from the sword's pommel. Here, hold it up and I will show you something marvelous." So saying, Yaarike reached into the sleeve of his robe and produced a small crystal sphere known as a "cleric's lamp." With a brief stroke of his fingers it smoldered into light. "Come closer—I do not want to make too bright a glare and attract attention. Look through the gem with the light behind it."

Viyeki had to turn the heavy pendant on its back and look through it sideways to see what Yaarike meant, then could not help making a small sound of astonishment. For the first time in days their situation, the fighting outside and the implacable mortal enemy, slipped from his thoughts. "It is beautiful, Master! Someone has carved the interior!" Inside the hemispheric gem some careful hand had delineated a city of tall, graceful towers standing upon the cliffs above a great ocean. With Yaarike's lamp behind it, the whole artful scene was colored by the gem itself, so the miniature city seemed to bask under bright vermillion skies. "Who made such a wonderful thing?"

"Yaaro-Mon himself. The carving depicts great Tzo, our beloved city on the shores of the Dreaming Sea, lost with all the rest to Unbeing when the Garden fell. Like your own father, Viyeki-*tza*, my great-grandfather was an artist, and the voyage from the Garden to these lands was a long one. But now it serves as a reminder of all that the People left behind—all that makes us who we are." He nodded gravely, as if in answer to some question, but Viyeki had not asked one. "I will take it back now, before one of the others notices my light and comes to intrude on us." Yaarike accepted the heavy pendant and hung the chain around his neck again, sliding the necklace down into his tunic until it was invisible.

"I am honored that you showed it to me, Master."

"I do nothing without reason, Host Foreman. I showed this to you because I want you to make me a promise about it, but also because I want to make a promise to you." Yaarike shook out his robes until they hung correctly again. Even in such terrible circumstances the magister was correctly dressed at all times: despite months of hardship and bloody battle, he looked as composed as if he stood in his own home. "If I should fall here or somewhere else before we reach Nakkiga, Host Foreman Viyeki, I wish you to take the Heart of What Was Lost and carry it back to my family. It will belong to one of my children or grandchildren if they return from our defeat in the South, may the queen's eye watch over them. It is Clan Kijada's most precious heirloom. Will you accept this charge?"

"With pride and gratitude, Master. Your trust is an honor to my whole family."

"Do not let it go too much to your head," said Yaarike, amused. "If the Heart becomes your responsibility, that will be because I am dead."

Viyeki's face almost went slack with dismay, but he managed to conceal it. "I spoke without thinking, Master. I beg your forgiveness."

Yaarike showed him a thin smile. "Granted. And now my promise to you. I have watched you a long time, Viyeki sey-Enduya. Over the years I have been impressed by your skills with tools and plans but even more with the way you think for yourself, which it grieves me to say is rare among our people in these fallen days. Thus, it is my wish that one day you will follow me as High Magister of the Order of Builders, and I have written a letter to the Queen's Celebrants to say so. That letter is among my effects. If I do not survive this adventure of ours, when you take the Heart, take that letter and others you will find in my possession as well and carry them all to Nakkiga."

Viyeki stood as if thunderstruck, unable for a moment to find his voice. "Truly, Magister? You wish me to be your successor?"

The magister showed a hint of a mocking frown. "If I did not, this would be an oddly complicated and impractical jest, Host Foreman."

Viyeki dropped to his knees. "I will struggle all my life to live up to the honors you have heaped on me."

"And may that life be a long and useful one, Viyeki-*tza*." But before Yaarike could say more, hoarse shouts echoed from somewhere nearby, clearly the triumphant cries of Northmen. The crowd of Builders in the ruined hall murmured uneasily and pressed closer together facing the doorway, weapons raised.

"Well, it seems that the time to make dispensations for the future is over." Yaarike took Viyeki's elbow, and for a moment seemed to need the support. "Let us stand with the others and be ready to fight. The present is all we have—or whatever remains of it."

Isgrimnur had done his best in just a few days to instill some kind of wider discipline into Vigri's men. Unlike the soldiers Isgrimnur had brought back from the south, they still liked to fight in the chaotic Northern style, attacking and falling back individually or in small groups, as the mood struck them. Even with a huge advantage of numbers, this kind of brawling was a bad idea against an enemy as crafty and patient as the Norns, and the duke had set Sludig and several other trusted lieutenants to work trying to teach the rudiments of the more ordered fighting style of the Erkynguard, but within moments of the attack beginning it was clear that the lessons had not really taken. Eager for glory, young Floki and a dozen of his father's bondsmen did not stop at the first set of broken walls to wait for the rest of their comrades, but hammered through the first Norn defenses and rushed uphill toward the round tower where the Norn commanders were presumed to be. Immediately afterward a shower of arrows sealed the way behind them.

It was impossible to know whether Floki and his followers still survived or had been cut down. Isgrimnur could only be grateful that Brindur was on the far side of the field and had not seen what happened to his son: He would have taken his best men and charged after Floki, compounding the mistake.

So this is what it comes to. I do not tell Brindur what has happened to his son for fear of something worse happening. Usires save me, command is more often a curse than a blessing. Isgrimnur certainly understood Floki and the rest—just the sight of the enemy's rigid, corpse-pale faces was enough to raise a red mist of hate before his own eyes—but he could not concern himself with the fate of one mere man or even a dozen, not when the fate of thousands hung on his decisions.

No matter, he told himself, and waved another line of men up the hill. *There will be time for regrets later. There is always time for regret.*

As the day went on the sun should have burned through the fog, or at least so it seemed to Porto on the slopes below the ruins. Instead the mists grew thicker, swirling on the cold breeze until it was almost impossible to see the valley walls or even the old castle. He and Endri hung back to defend the catapult-gunners from counterattack. Black arrows whistled down from the hillside, and occasionally, when the mists cleared for a moment, Norns could be seen peering from the shadows like the unburied dead, but the White Foxes never left the cover of the ancient walls.

The catapult men kept busy, flinging stone after stone at the great tower near the top of the hill, but although they struck it time and again they could not bring it down. As the day lengthened, mists began to swallow up the scarce afternoon light entirely, so that it seemed that night would arrive long before sunset. Determined to break the resistance before dark fell, Duke Isgrimnur and his captains led a troop carrying siege ladders in an attack on the central tower, the last whole piece of the age-old castle. Now the Norns finally came out, and although Porto and Endri were not part of the struggle, it was clear that the fighting was terrible and bloody.

Then, in the middle of the assault, a great braying sound came echoing down from the ridgetop above the castle. Recognizing the horns that had blown at the commencement of battle in the morning, Porto thought a second force of Rimmersmen had made their way up into the valley heights and now meant to attack the castle from above, and his heart filled with hope.

But the blare of horns came instead from a party of scouts hurrying back from farther down the valley. The Northmen up on the ridge were shouting and waving their arms, and in only a few moments Porto went from cheering to mouth-gaping silence as he listened to the growing thunder of something rushing toward them along the valley floor.

The mists began to boil, then a host of armored riders appeared out of the tatters of gray fog at the bottom of the pass, thundering up the valley toward them. The newcomers were all in white or black, riding horses and even stranger creatures.

"Good God!" Endri cried. "What are they?"

"More Norns." Porto had been worried already, fearful of the battle and of this strange place, but now he felt his insides turning to ice. The oncoming Norn troop seemed big enough to roll through the entire valley like a floodtide, sweeping them all to death or worse.

Porto pushed past fleeing catapult engineers to grab Endri and drag him away from the great machine. All around the base of the hill Rimmersmen broke their lines and scattered, many scrambling upslope to join with their fellows who had surrounded the tower, but the Norn riders were among them in mere moments, stabbing and slashing with weird, angular blades. Some of them rode goats tall as horses, unnatural creatures with eyes yellow as sulfur; but the rider who caught Porto's attention was the leader, a horned figure with a terrible, inhuman face. The apparition wore white plate armor and rode a huge white horse.

At his first panicked glance, as the newcomer dealt death with a long, silver-gray sword to any mortal unlucky enough to be caught within its reach, Porto thought the horned figure some kind of demon summoned by the fairies, a creature straight from Hell. But as he dragged Endri out of the path of the oncoming troop and the leader galloped by, he realized that the demonic face was only a helmet in the shape of an owl's head.

It was all Porto could do to fend off the blows smashing down on him from above, but he held his shield up and managed to keep Endri behind him as he backed out of the path of charging Norns. He took a hard swipe to his helmet, and although it almost knocked him down, he stayed on his feet; a moment later the greater part of the Norn troop had ridden past him and up the hill into the ruins. A quick look showed him that Endri seemed to be unhurt.

To Porto's astonishment, the Norn reinforcements barely engaged with Isgrimnur's besieging force at all but crashed through, killing a few of them and losing a handful of their own. Then they continued upslope where they met reserves from inside the tower who helped to protect the entrance until the Norn riders could get inside. After what seemed only a few dozen racing heartbeats after Porto had first seen them appear from the mists, the new troop of Norn soldiers had disappeared into the tower.

The hilltop was strewn with bodies, but most of the Rimmersmen who had fought were still standing, faces sagging with surprise, as the Norns forced the gates closed behind them, sealing the tower once more.

The general lifted off her helmet. Her braided white hair had come undone in the charge and hung across her face until she swept it aside. She had the long chin and narrow nose of the oldest Hikeda'ya families and an expression as stern as some ancient tomb effigy. "Who is the master here?"

"That would be me, General Suno'ku—Yaarike sey-Kijada, High Magister of the Builders." Viyeki's master made a carefully calibrated gesture of welcome. "You arrive hoped-for but unlooked-for. We had thought ourselves beyond the reach of any reinforcements. Our Echoes received no reply to their calls."

"It could not be helped," she said, offering the scantest of ritual salutes in return. "The mortals have one of the Zida'ya with them, and she carries a Witness. We could not risk breaking silence."

Viyeki stared at this savior that had arrived seemingly from nowhere, like a hero out of the oldest tales of the Garden. He knew of General Suno'ku, of course—most Hikeda'ya did. She might be no higher in the Order of Sacrifice than Viyeki was among the Builders—a subordinate of the ordinal leader—but because of her family blood she moved in much higher circles than Viyeki could ever dream of joining.

As he watched her, fascinated, Suno'ku turned to one of her lieutenants. "See to the wounded. Make them well enough that they can ride."

"What about those who are too badly injured?" the Sacrifice asked.

She only stared at him, her expression flat as a frozen pond, then turned back to Yaarike. "How many are you here?"

"Perhaps two hundred left, more than half of them Builders," the High Magister said. "We also have the Celebrants you see with the general's body, half a dozen Singers under Tzayin-Kha, and a few Echoes. The rest are Sacrifices and now fall under your command."

"But you stand over us all, High Magister," the general said. "I would not flout the Queen's sacred ranks." Which was only barely true, Viyeki knew. Suno'ku was of the Iyora, the Owl Clan, in the male line of the legendary Ekimeniso himself, Queen Utuk'ku's long-dead husband. The Iyora were all but co-equal with the queen's own Hamakha clan, and both of them were as far above even Yaarike's noble family as the uppermost peak of the great mountain stood above the squares and public markets of the Nakkiga floor. Among the noblest clans, family blood always outweighed the hierarchy of the orders, even the most powerful, like Sacrifice and Song.

Viyeki's thoughts and Suno'ku's quiet conversation with Yaarike were both interrupted by the arrival of League Commander Hayyano and a troop of his warriors leading three mortal prisoners, all with their arms bound behind them. The largest of the captives, a young, muscular, yellow-bearded Northman, was bellowing in his crude tongue. Like most Builders, Viyeki did not speak a word of any mortal language, and he thought the hairy one sounded more like a bear than any thinking creature.

Suno'ku's lips twisted a little at one edge. "How I hate the sound of their barbaric yapping. Magister Yaarike, may I kill them all so we can have some quiet?"

Yaarike shook his head. "No, General, not yet. Hayyano brought them at my request. Will you question them about their numbers? I do not have the skill to do it myself."

Viyeki could not help wondering at this, since his scholarly master spoke the mortals' common tongue better than almost anyone in Nakkiga. He assumed Yaarike was testing the Sacrifice general in some way.

Suno'ku repeated Yaarike's questions in the mortal's own speech, then shared the answers. "He says that he is Floki, son of the great thane Brindur Golden-Hair," she explained. "He says that if some of his men had not turned coward and fled, he would already have taken all our heads by now and the fighting would be over." But the prisoner would not tell them anything else, not the numbers of the Northmen waiting outside nor any other useful information.

When she had tried several times and could get nothing further from the red-faced mortal or his brutish companions, the general unsheathed her sword, a slender span of silvery witchwood that seemed almost too long for her. The mortals could not look away from it, their eyes so wide the whites showed all around. "I suggest it is time to use more direct methods, Magister," Suno'ku said. "I scarcely blooded Cold Root today, and it still yearns to drink mortal ichor." She then produced her poniard, long and wickedly sharp, and held both blades before the Northmen. "Or if my lord Yaarike wants the conversation to pass more slowly, I can use Cold Leaf, which will remove smaller pieces." She leaned close until she was only a hands-breadth from the prisoners' faces. "Either way, I will make the enjoyment last as long as I can."

The mortal who called himself Floki began bellowing again, but this time there was a tone of terror in his voice that had not been there before.

"Your famous weapons will not teach them what they do not know, General," said Yaarike in a tone of regret. "I fear we have learned all we can from these."

Suno'ku kicked out, knocking the one called Floki to the stone floor. Viyeki heard what sounded like the mortal's shin breaking. The bearded soldier clutched his leg, rolling back and forth, gasping in pain.

"Whether they had told us more or not," Suno'ku said, sheathing her weapons once more, "it would not have changed the nature of our problem. You have two hundred here, Magister. I have scarcely twice those numbers myself. I mustered every last able Sacrifice in Nakkiga and could find and mount less than four hundred to bring with me. But it matters not. What we must do now is prepare to escape."

"Escape?" Yaarike was clearly surprised, something Viyeki had seldom seen. "How? The tunnels below us lead nowhere."

She shook her head. "Tunnels? No. We shall ride from here—smash our way free if we have to. I did not come so far and so fast to die here in an obscure border fort. I have a more important task."

Yaarike nodded. "You came for Marshal Ekisuno's body, of course. Your foreparent—your ancestor."

Suno'ku showed him a harsh smile. "No, High Magister. I came for you and your Builders. Because without you, Nakkiga will be overthrown by the mortals. Your clan, my clan, they will all be slaughtered in dark holes, like rabbits."

Unsure of what was happening, the yellow-bearded mortal began to shout again, bellowing threats. Suno'ku gave a sign and one of her Sacrifices drew his sword and struck him hard on the head with the pommel. He did not make another sound, but lay on the floor twitching and drizzling blood from his scalp.

"I will kill that one myself in a moment and enjoy it like a good meal," Suno'ku said. "But our time is short, so first we must make our plans."

As the general conferred with Magister Yaarike and the plainly overwhelmed Hayyano, who could only gaze at Suno'ku in awe, Viyeki watched with an interest that almost made him forget their terrible situation. He had never seen Suno'ku before, but of course he knew of her. The general was famous for her bravery, and although a few other female officers held equally high rank in the Order of Sacrifice, none of those commanded either the loyalty or the fascination that the ordinary Sacrifices felt for Suno'ku.

The general had weirdly light eyes, so pale and gray-shot that they seemed like twilight skies compared to the purplish midnight of most Hikeda'ya. She was tall for her sex, but not unusually so—both Yaarike and Hayyano were taller—and her movements were swift and almost impossibly graceful. She was like a bright flame, Viyeki thought, drawing the eye each time she moved.

"But only a few of the mortals were destroyed during your arrival," Hayyano said. "They vastly outnumber us still. Surely we should wait and let them wear themselves down. They are far from home and their supply lines are vulnerable."

"And what if there are more of them coming, Commander?" asked Suno'ku. Hayyano blinked; he might as well have flinched. "While we are pinned here in the wreckage of Tangleroot Castle, the outer walls of Nakkiga are in ruins and the mountain gate in the City Walls at Three Ravens is all but undefended. Did you not see that great ram of black iron the mortals have brought? Where do you think that is to be used?

Not on these old, decrepit stones. That is for knocking on the very door of our home. They will be breaking into the queen's own chamber before the summer months have ended, may the Garden preserve her always." She shook her head. "No. We must break out of this ring now and make our way north as quickly as we can. High Magister Yaarike, do you agree?"

He looked at her for a moment. "Yes. If it must be so, then let it be sooner rather than later."

"Good." Suno'ku put her helmet down on a broken stone pillar rounded by centuries of rain. "Then call all the chieftains and their troops here, leaving only sentries. If a chieftain has died during today's fighting, Commander Hayyano, appoint one who will do what he or she is told. Do you understand?"

"But what of your ancestor's body and its coffin?" asked Yaarike. He pointed to the massive wagon where the chanting Celebrants still knelt. "How will we manage to carry that away while still putting distance between ourselves and the mortals?"

"We won't," said General Suno'ku flatly. "Leave it behind."

Yaarike was clearly astonished. "You will desert your great-great-grandfather's body?"

She shook her head. "No. That weighs but little. It can be carried on the back of someone's saddle, and I will offer prayers of regret and penitence to my foreparent for the dishonor. But the sarcophagus itself—that is useless. We will not be weighed down by it. Break it to pieces to keep it from the grubby paws of the mortals."

Viyeki was watching the yellow-bearded mortal still writhing in pain between the other two staring prisoners. The murderous invaders showed no bravado now, Viyeki thought. Beneath their hairy pelts these Northmen seemed to hide the hearts of terrified children.

A thought came to him then, but he waited until both Yaarike and Suno'ku had paused before lifting his hand in submissive request. "If my master and the general will permit me . . ."

Yaarike turned to look at him. "Yes, Host Foreman Viyeki?"

"Did I hear you say that Host Singer Tzayin-Kha survived the battle?"

"Yes," said his master. "I have seen her. What of it?"

"If I do not offend by putting myself forward," Viyeki said, "I may have an idea."

The campfires of the duke's army had been kept small, especially those closest to the ruins. Porto and Endri had been left to guard the catapult, which loomed above them in the flickering light like a watchful dragon.

"But where did all those White Foxes *come* from?" Endri asked for perhaps the dozenth time.

Porto had given up trying to answer him. He poked the fire and then pushed his hands as close as he could without burning them.

"Are they ghosts? How could they get so close without our scouts hearing them?"

"Oh, sweet Aedon, they are *Norns*, not ghosts!" Porto felt as though something inside him wanted to escape, but if it did it might tear the world to pieces with its teeth. This hellish place was driving him into madness. "Fairies can be killed. Did you not see the bodies lying in the snow? Did you not see the blood? Red, the same as ours. And when it runs out of them, they *die*."

"You heard that soldier! He put three arrows in one not an hour ago, but the creature took no hurt from it! Just vanished away. If that is not a ghost, what is?"

"God's Blood, man, will you stop this? They are tricky, the Norns. Everybody who was at the Hayholt knows that. They make shadows and cast their voices—but shadows cannot hurt us."

"But, still . . ." Endri was almost breathless and could not let it go. "Where did they all—?"

The fire before them suddenly blazed as if a strong wind had fanned the coals. But instead of the flames bending they grew upward until they danced higher than men's heads. All around the other campfires were also erupting into wavering pillars of flame. Startled Northmen scrambled on their hands and knees. Porto, who had tumbled backward at the first fiery billow, sat sprawled on the freezing ground while Endri stared in bulge-eyed terror. Some of the soldiers were so frightened that they cried out for God or their mothers, or let out simple, incoherent cries of terror.

And then a face appeared in the flames in front of Porto—and not just in his campfire, but in every single one throughout the sprawling camp. This fiery mask rippled and billowed like something seen in deep water; the face was female but also not entirely real. Where the eyes should be and in the open mouth, nothing showed but flames.

"It's the queen!" someone shouted in fright. "The queen of the White Foxes! She has come back!" Men scrambled away from the fires and began to run in all directions, like animals.

"Mortals!" The voice rolled out from every fire, from every circle of men, as chill as the ice that had crystallized on the tent ropes. *"You will die in these lands! We will take back what is ours!"*

Porto could not tell if the dreadful voice was in the air all around or came somehow from inside his own skull. He saw Endri stumble to his feet and managed to grab at the younger man's leg as he lurched past, bringing him down heavily into the snowy mud. Porto had no idea what was happening, but he knew if he let him go Endri would run like a maddened beast into the freezing night, never to return. Endri fought back like a terrified child but Porto hung on, even as the apparition in the fire melted and the flames fell back to what they had been. A moment later the fires sputtered and went out entirely, plunging the camp into darkness.

With that horrible voice still ringing in his thoughts, Porto did not understand at first what else he was hearing, but then he heard men shouting in pain and surprise—brief cries, swiftly ended—and felt rather than saw a flock of swiftly moving shadows sweeping down toward the camp from the ruins atop the hill. Men were suddenly dying all around him at the hands of near-invisible enemies, but Porto could not get free of struggling Endri to unsheathe his blade.

"They are here!" he hissed into his friend's ear. "The Norns are here, trying to kill us all! Damn you, man, get up and fight!"

Endri suddenly stopped struggling, and for an instant Porto thought one of the invisible attackers had stabbed and killed the youth right in Porto's arms. Then a glare of red from the top of the hill revealed Endri's face staring up toward the ruins, mouth stretched in a gape of tortured disbelief. Porto turned to find where this new light came from and saw a great blaze at the edge of the ruins, a pillar of flame higher even than the bespelled campfires, almost to the height of the surrounding trees. Now the burning object began to roll down the hill toward the camp, slowly at first, bucking and jouncing over the stony slope, but picking up speed with every one of Porto's racing heartbeats. Its wheels were as tall as a man.

It's a wagon, was his first, confused thought, *some kind of giant war-wagon*, and that was true enough, but there was also something more. Atop the wain's vast bed lay a sarcophagus, a huge thing, but its lid was partway off and the insides were aflame so that a tail of fire streamed behind it, marking its hastening career down the hill. And even as Porto stared in astonishment, a screaming figure lurched up out of the monstrous, burning box, knocking the lid aside. The writhing figure wore a mask and was itself aflame. Burning bandages turned the thing in the casket into a wildly gyrating torch that flailed the air and shrieked and shrieked—the most inhuman noise Porto had ever heard, an unending, whistling scream without words. Any men who had held their ground during the first onslaught of shadow-warriors from the ruins now turned and ran stumbling downhill from the blazing, howling corpse atop its battle wagon.

The besiegers made no pretense of resistance, but fled the apparition as though one thought controlled them all, raw southern recruits and battle-hardened Rimmersmen alike. Many were struck down by arrows Porto could not see, or surrounded in the darkness by deeper shadows, after which they lay silent in the snow with throats slit or guts spilled.

Something crashed against Porto's face, stunning him. It was Endri, who had lashed out in his desperation to escape and was now half-crawling, half-staggering down the slope away from the ruins, mad with fear.

Porto did not know what to do. The camp was overrun with shadows, and already dozens of his comrades were dead, the rest scattered—he could hear some of them lost in the trees, shouting for God to save them. It had all happened so fast, as if a great wind had blown their army to pieces in an instant.

He crawled to his feet and ran after Endri. He could do nothing else. He had no one else to save.

Her song completed, the Host-Singer Tzayin-Kha fell to the uneven floor stones in the central hall of the ruined fortress where she lay gasping like a landed fish, her starvation-shrunken limbs twitching. Viyeki moved to help her.

"No! Do not touch her!" Yaarike cried. "The fire spirit still flows in her. Look."

As Viyeki watched, several more of the red-robed Order of Song moved toward Tzayin-Kha as cautiously as if she were a sleeping dragon. One put a stick beneath her and rolled her over. Viyeki recoiled. The Singer's face and hands, the only parts of her flesh he could see, smoldered with light beneath the skin, as though she herself had no more substance than a wax candle.

"Will she live?" Viyeki asked his master quietly. "She is the best of her order that we have."

"And she was the only one who could have made the fire speak," said Yaarike, shaking his head. "That was a magister's trick, but she managed it. I am impressed that she still lives, although that may not be true for long. Still, even if she recovers she will be useless to us until she can be healed from this effort back in Nakkiga." He turned to the Singers now lifting Tzayin-Kha's body and wrapping it in a heavy blanket. Viyeki could feel the heat still coming off her at several paces' distance. "Go, now, all of you," Yaarike told them. "Get her away while the mortals are still in confusion. Thanks to Tzayin-Kha's efforts, General Suno'ku has carved us an escape route, but it will close very quickly."

As the Singers hurried out, carrying the steaming body of their leader like a holy relic, Yaarike nodded to Viyeki. "Now that all our Builders are out, we must go, too," he said.

As they made their way up the narrow stairs toward the ground level of the roofless hall, Viyeki marveled at his master's balance. Neither of them had eaten at all, or slept for more than a few moments in days, and Yaarike was old enough to have been alive when the Hikeda'ya first took Nakkiga Mountain for their own, but he climbed like a youth. Viyeki could only hope to have half his master's vigor when he reached the same age. If he reached a greater age at all, which had seemed unlikely for some time now.

"Your idea was clever, Viyeki-tza," Yaarike said from the near-darkness above, his voice pitched low. "I thought Suno'ku would balk at it, but she is rare for her order, and even more for her age. I admit she surprises me—I was impressed that she would abandon that cumbersome wagon and her ancestor's coffin." He laughed quietly. "Even better, though, your idea amused me."

Yaarike rarely handed out praise. Even though they were now only a few paces away from angry mortals with arrows and axes, Viyeki was full of pride. "Thank you, High Magister." Still, he was puzzled, too. "I only meant to frighten the Northmen. You say it amused you?"

"It is one thing to win a battle that you should lose. It is another to pour salt in the wounds you inflict. It is scant compensation for the Storm King's failure, but I wish I could have seen the mortals' faces as the sarcophagus came down on them. Do you think they thought it was General Ekisuno himself, come to burn them all—?"

Viyeki heard the soft rustle of the magister's garments suddenly cease. He reached out a hand to touch his master's elbow, letting him know he was behind him.

The magister turned and took his hand. He made the finger-sign "*Silence*" against Viyeki's palm, then the brushing symbol that meant "*Wait.*"

A moment later Yaarike said, "They have gone out of the castle again. By the Garden, those mortals are as noisy as cattle. How did they ever defeat us in the past?" He led Viyeki up the crumbling steps and into the night air, his tread slow and cautious.

"Should we not hurry, Magister?"

"There will be no escape at all if we are caught. Save your haste until we need it." Yaarike struck out toward the far side of the ruins, heading at an angle toward the hilltop that towered over the Tangleroot Castle ruins.

Viyeki could hear the shrieks of wounded mortals from the slopes below and was filled with contempt. Foul brutes. Could they not even bear their injuries with dignity? "Do we know where to join Suno'ku and the rest?" he asked.

Yaarike did not turn around, already leaning into the rising slope. His voice fluttered back to Viyeki, soft as a moth in flight. "It will be easy enough, Host Foreman. Suno'ku is her ancestor's heir, and more. We need only follow the trail of dead mortals."

—‡—

"By Dror and Aedon and all the rest, *what is happening*?" Isgrimnur stamped toward the group of men standing around the wreckage of the fiery wagon that had killed more than a dozen of his soldiers in its downward progress and had terrified at least ten score more into running headlong into the blind night. He feared that many who fled had already been killed by the Norns, but prayed that he would be able to find and bring back any survivors when the sun was up. The night had been a disaster, and now the Norns had escaped the ruins and were heading north again.

Isgrimnur sniffed the air and felt his stomach turn over at the tang of burned flesh. As he neared the gathering, he raised his voice again. "I said, what is happening? Why are you men huddled here? Sludig, is that you? I see Brindur's horse—where is he? I told him to follow those damned, sneaking creatures. We must not let them get away. We must hound them through the wilderness until every last one of them is slaughtered."

"Jarl Vigri went after them with his bowmen," said Sludig from the darkness, but his voice sounded hoarse and strange. "Brindur is . . . he is . . ."

Isgrimnur felt his heart and innards go cold. He hurried forward, ignoring the pain of several bleeding wounds. "Oh, sweet Usires, is it Brindur? Is he . . . ?"

It was only as he reached the circle of men that Isgrimnur could see faces. One was Sludig's long, mournful countenance, and the rest seemed to be Brindur's Skoggeymen. But the man who was kneeling next to the smoking wreckage of the cart and the huge, upended coffin, Isgrimnur was surprised and relieved to see, was Thane Brindur himself.

A black, charred shape lay half in and half out of the scorched sarcophagus. Here and there a bit of pale flesh, a few grinning teeth, or a spot of unburnt bandage gleamed through the ash. Only a single arm protruding from the blackened, shriveled mass remained whole. Around its wrist was a thick gold bracelet.

Brindur glanced up, his eyes red in the torchlight and his face suddenly looking decades older. "It is his." Brindur lifted the arm so that the bracelet caught the light. "He won it at Kraki's Field against the remnants of Skali's army just half a year ago." Isgrimnur must have looked like he still did not understand, because Brindur blinked and said, "This is Floki. My son. They burned him alive and rolled him down the hill to frighten us like children." Brindur shook his head slowly. "God curse them. God curse them!" When he spoke again, it was more quietly. "Telling his mother—that will be the foulest part."

"There is nothing worse," said Isgrimnur. "As I know myself." Sludig leaned over and touched the duke's arm, reminding him that there was much to do. "You stay here for now, Brindur," Isgrimnur said. "Bury your son—and the others. Break camp and follow us when you can."

"And so it goes on," said Brindur.

Isgrimnur didn't like the sound of that, and was almost glad he was leaving the thane behind for now. Brindur was a good man, but perhaps this had been one blow too many. Still, Isgrimnur understood the man's pain. "We will all remember your son," he said. "May God take him swiftly to His bosom in Heaven. Their tricks, the form of his death, they mean nothing—just more cruelty in the cruel war these bastard fairies have forced on us. Floki was captured in battle and died a hero. It is as simple as that."

"If you say so, Your Grace." Brindur let go of his son's arm.

Isgrimnur did not want to see the burned body any longer: it looked as though something ancient and inhuman was trying to will itself into human shape. "It is the truth, Brindur."

The thane of Norskog's face was as still and empty as stagnant water, but his voice had something ragged in it that Isgrimnur had never heard. "I don't doubt it. But are you not tired of seeing so many of our sons turned into heroes before their time, Isgrimnur? I would rather have seen him live and make sons of his own."

The duke had nothing left to say. He could not even let himself feel true sadness now, because he knew it would make him weak when he needed to be strong and move swiftly. He and Vigri had to catch the Norns in the open before they could find another bolt-hole—or, worse, slip back to the safety of their city under Stormspike Mountain. He let his hand fall on Brindur's shoulder, then nodded to Sludig to follow him as he left the thane to grieve.

Part
Two

Three Ravens Tower

"As all Hikeda'ya know, when the children of our nobility reach the proper age, they are submitted to Yedade's Box, and the way in which they escape the box or the way that they fail determines their path in life.

"When she was put to her test, the young Suno'ku seyt-Iyora broke free so swiftly that none present could remember any other child who had performed the feat so well.

"Thus it was later for Suno'ku as general: When no one else could have broken the siege at Tangleroot Castle, she led a small force there to save those trapped in the ruins and then fought her way out again, scattering the Northmen before her like chaff before a reaper's blade. The rest of the besieged followed her, awed by her courage and skill, and when the trap was behind them she led them all north toward the shelter of the City Walls.

"The walls had been built during the time of our greatest power, when the Zida'ya still held Asu'a, when much of Nakkiga still existed outside the great mountain and the North was ours.

"But as our numbers diminished and the Northmen came across the cold sea and began their career of destruction through the lands of the Keida'ya, at our great queen's order we fell back into the sheltering fastness of the mountain and eventually Nakkiga-That-Was stood deserted. Slowly the trees and grasses and the fierce winds began to take back the outer city. The great walls, a vast ring of stone that stretched for leagues around our mountain, fared little better. In the time of Sulen, the

Thirteenth Celebrant, the Order of Sacrifice removed the last guards from the walls, calling them back to the city to better protect Nakkiga itself and the irreplaceable person of Queen Utuk'ku.

"So it was that Suno'ku and the rest of her charges, fleeing ahead of the mortal invaders, came at last to the Tower of Three Ravens and found it in a pitiable state, the tower itself gutted and long empty, the great walls it guarded now perilously weak. Although Lord Yaarike, Magister of the Builders, was with her, there was little his small number of workers could do to make repairs with the Northmen so close behind. Still, the Hikeda'ya were determined to make a stand there, trusting in Suno'ku's generalship to keep the mortals from the mountain and from Nakkiga itself as long as could be managed.

"In the city, nothing was yet known of General Suno'ku's mission, and after she took the largest part of the surviving warriors with her, the caverns of Nakkiga were silent with foreboding, the queen's subjects fearful of what might come next if the invaders continued unchecked.

"They were right to fear."

Overburdened with the duke's own considerable weight, his horse nearly lost its footing on the steep track, sliding back a short distance in a flurry of gravel and scree. Isgrimnur reined up, eyeing the looming cliffs on either side with distaste.

"Tell me again how you know they are not lying in ambush for us," the duke said.

The scout nodded. "There has been no movement that we've seen, Your Grace. I think the fairies are too few now—they're all hiding in the tower, I'd say. Come, my lord, it's just a little way more to the spot where we will make camp."

Isgrimnur snorted. "Too few fairies? Don't ever assume that, lad. Especially when we've followed them into their own lands."

"My men and I found high ground to keep watch, my lord; we can see beyond this wall, all the way to their cursed mountain. This time, we would see any reinforcements long before they arrived. Just a little farther, my lord."

Isgrimnur looked back on the line of mounted men making their slow way up the pass behind him, Sludig nearest, following like a faithful hound, then Brindur and his Skoggeymen, with Vigri and the Elvritshalla men close behind leading a train of foot soldiers. Two thousand able-bodied men left, at most. Could he really take such a small force into the forbidden lands of the Norns and hope to come out again in one piece?

But that doesn't matter, does it? Isgrimnur thought. *What matters is that we leave none of the fairies alive to threaten our lands again. If we can manage that, whatever befalls us, it would be a sacrifice worth making.* He thought of his wife Gutrun, waiting for him not at Elvritshalla but far to the south, in the devastation of the Hayholt. She would be busy, he knew, with wounded men and women to care for and the new king and queen in need of her counsel and wisdom. At least she would have something to distract her from their lost son. Isgrimnur himself had spent too many nights under these cold, starry northern skies too pained to sleep, trying to think of ways things could have been different, that they could have beaten back the enemy without losing his son Isorn.

Wars don't end, he thought suddenly. *They become stories, told to children. They become causes that are taken up by those who were not even born when the war started. But they don't end.*

We are a fierce race, we men. We will give up even our short, precious lives for revenge—no, for justice. No wonder the immortals fear us.

The steep track angled to one side, following the line of the pass. As they came out from behind a massive cliff wall, Isgrimnur could suddenly see all the way to the top, to the darkening sky and the great, dark wall that girdled all of the Norn lands. It stretched thirty ells high across the top of the pass, a thing of monstrous black slabs laid flush one on another as though by the work of some gigantic mason.

In the middle of the pass, squarely above the climbing road and a gate that had long since been filled in with even more stone, a tower bulged out from the wall. The entire structure seemed oddly proportioned to Isgrimnur's eye, but the tower's crown was one of the strangest things he had ever seen, with three beak-like projections, the middle pointing forward and the others angled to either side, each one hanging out ten cubits or more beyond the wall. He thought the tower looked more like some huge weapon than a mere building, a battle mace for a sky-tall giant.

"Sweet Elysia, Mother of Mercy," he said.

Sludig had reined up beside Isgrimnur; he looked as though he had bitten into an apple and discovered half a squirming worm. "This is an evil place."

Another voice said, "Evil is in what mortals—and immortals—do. The place itself is but a place." Ayaminu the Sitha-woman rode up beside them on her own horse, which despite its fine-boned slenderness seemed to have less trouble with the cold and the steep climbs than the Rimmersmen's mounts, bred in cold northern lands. "Once it was a point upon the teeming earth like any other."

"Does this abomination have a name?" asked Isgrimnur.

"That?" She made one of the barely perceptible gestures that passed for a shrug among her kind. "It is called Three Ravens Tower. You see the beaks, of course. They allowed the defenders to drop stones, or hot oil, or other even less pleasant things upon anyone trying to take the wall."

Isgrimnur had not come to like the Sitha-woman's company any better during the sennight they had pursued the Norns from Tangleroot Castle. He had found all the Sithi he met difficult to understand and even more difficult to parley with, and he found their reluctance to engage with their murderous cousins even more frustrating; but if the immortals Jiriki and Aditu had been frustrating, and their mother Likimeya close to maddening, Ayaminu made those three seem easy company. Despite accompanying the duke's troop and offering an occasional bit of information, Ayaminu seemed otherwise unconcerned by the doings of the mortals or even their deaths, and did not seem to care at all whether they ever caught the Norns who had brought so much ruin to her own people as well as Isgrimnur's. Many times he had wondered whether they harbored some kind of spy in their midst, though the men he had set to watch her had seen no evidence of any treachery.

"Do you think the Norns are guarding it?" he asked now. "Or are they hurrying back to Stormspike Mountain?"

"They will defend this pass," she said. "They have no choice. Do you see what has happened to the wall on the right side of the tower?"

Isgrimnur squinted, but in the fading twilight it was hard to make out much beyond the high wall's shadowy, massive presence. "No. My eyes are not like a Sithi's. Speak plainly."

"A very few years ago, just before the beginning of the Storm King's war, the earth shook here—a great writhing of the ground that threw down many parts of the wall around Nakkiga-That-Was, including that section beside the tower. If you look closely, you can see that the tower itself tilts slightly to one side."

"I see no sign of the wall having collapsed."

"Because repairs were done—but they were hasty. My people sent a number of our families to help them. This was before the Hikeda'ya moved openly against us, but Queen Utuk'ku still refused our offer. We know, though, that the repairs were over-swift, most likely because the queen's eye was turned southward to the lands of men."

"Over-swift? What do you mean?" This was Brindur, who had joined the impromptu council. "I may not have your damnable fairy eyes, but they look solid enough to me."

As always, Ayaminu seemed unperturbed by insults. "Yes, the stones were piled up once more with as much skill as could be rendered, but not all the rituals were observed or the proper things done. The queen was keeping her holy Singers busy then, preparing the way for the Storm King's return. We can all be grateful they failed at that, but also that they were so gravely occupied by it, because the Words of Binding and other necessary cantrips were not sung here. The wall is weak. It can be breached with nothing but force."

"What else would we use?" Brindur demanded. "Trickery, like your accursed breed?"

Isgrimnur spurred his mount between the furious Rimmersman and Ayaminu. An argument with their one source of knowledge was a bad idea, and the Sitha-woman had seldom offered this much help before. "Please, explain," Isgrimnur said to her. "What do you mean?"

"Just what I said. You have force. You have implements of war and siegecraft like your great battering ram. The wall is weak there, and the rituals that would have made it all but impervious have not been performed. The tower itself was damaged by the shaking earth and the wall was badly weakened." She looked up the pass to the spiky shape of Three Ravens Tower. "You will lose men. The Hikeda'ya will fight fiercely.

But if you wish to pass the walls of their lands, this is the place it can be done."

"And why should we trust you?" Brindur snarled. "You have not seen fit to offer such useful advice before. Why now? And why could you not have told us that another Norn army was coming down upon us at the ruins?"

Ayaminu only looked at him blandly. "I knew nothing of that army. The Hikeda'ya are aware of my presence, I promise you, Northman. They take pains to keep their plans hidden."

Isgrimnur was not to be distracted from the matter at hand. "But are you certain now? Could they be keeping something else from you?"

"Of course. But what I tell you is true—you could ride along this wall until the season changed and not find a more vulnerable spot."

"You see my dilemma, don't you?" Isgrimnur frowned. "I have the safety of several thousand men in my hands. Can you promise me success?"

Now the Sitha showed emotion for the first time, a faint twisting of the lips. "I can promise you nothing, Duke Isgrimnur. Many men will die. So will many Hikeda'ya. Any one of us may suffer that fate at any time, and a battle between desperate enemies will not make the chances less. But if you wish to pass the wall and enter the lands around Nakkiga—if you truly mean to take the city itself—then you can find no better spot. That is all I have to say. The decision is yours."

"Look, we have reached the camp. Endri, did you hear me? We are here." The younger soldier had not been badly hurt during the Norns' escape, but like Porto himself he had been overwhelmed with a terrible, pressing weariness afterward and had spent most of his time on the back of Porto's horse sliding in and out of troubled sleep. "Endri?"

"Can we stop now?"

"Yes, that's what I said. See, the fires are lit—in fact, I smell food cooking." The sun, unnaturally late in the sky this far north, had only just disappeared, although midnight was surely not far away. The camps, set up well out of range of even the strongest bowshot from the looming walls, nestled in the shelter of the thick, snow-mantled pines on either side of the steep canyon. As Porto reined up he took a brief look at the beaked tower, which squatted against the purple-blue sky like some horrid heathen idol from the primeval days before the Ransomer was sent to Mankind. "Come on, lad," he told his companion, deliberately turning his back on the tower. "We don't want to miss whatever supper is left—I am famished." For the last stretch of the climb Porto had been forced to watch the tower loom larger with each moment, and despite his words to Endri, he found that the thing he wanted just now more than food or even drink was to find a spot where he could not see the tower at all until night finally hid it from view completely. It seemed to be watching them. He could almost imagine that their puniness, their mortal insignificance, actually amused it.

When they had found a fire, and were scooping the last congealing bits of stew out of the cooking pot, Endri suddenly looked up. "Porto?"

"What, lad?"

"I can't remember the way home."

"What do you mean?"

"I can't remember the roads we took, or how we got here. I couldn't find my way back again. Don't leave me."

Porto looked at the other men around the fire, mercenaries from Nabban and Perdruin and a scrawny, hard-muscled veteran of Josua's Erkynlandish army, wondering what they would make of the young man's neediness. Not one of them even looked up from their bowls. "What do you mean?" Porto asked him quietly. "I'm not going to leave you, lad. I promise."

"I can't even remember the road to my own house. You remember it, don't you? You've been to Harborside. I know you have."

Porto shook his head. "Been there? I've been trying to rid myself of that memory for years," he said, hoping to jolly the younger man out of his mood. "You should thank the saints to have lost it. Dreadful place. Not a patch on the Rocks."

"No jokes, Porto." Endri was staring intently at him now, his eyes showing a touch of panicked white around the edges, made all the more eerie by the flickering firelight. "I don't want jokes. Promise me that when it's over you will show me the way home."

"We will go together." Porto did his best to keep his voice light, though he was almost as beaten down by these dark, frightening lands as Endri. He sometimes thought that if he did not have the boy to watch over he might already have deserted to head back south, risking wolves and wild giants and all the other dangers. "We'll all go home then—you, me, these fellows here, and old Duke Isgrimnur leading the way. People will line up along the roads to cheer us—*'The men who finally defeated the Norns!'* they'll shout. And you won't need anyone to show you the way because your people, my people—my wife and son—they'll all be waiting to welcome us home."

Endri stared at him for a long moment without saying anything, his face still wild. Around his neck was his red and white Harborside scarf, grimy now with mud and matted with pine needles. The young soldier reached up and touched it and his expression softened, his eyes blinked. "Of course," he said. "Of course. Thank you. You are a good friend."

"If I am a good friend, then why are you letting the wineskin sit by your knee while I die of thirst? Pass it here."

Endri handed it over, and Porto took a long draught. It was sour and tasted strongly of oak, from one of the last and smallest of the barrels the army had carted north from the Yistrian Brothers' vineyards, but at the moment it was all he wanted. It tasted like salvation. It tasted like home.

A feeling of something close to security had stolen over Viyeki since he and the rest of the Hikeda'ya had reached Three Ravens Tower. He knew it was foolish—in truth, the danger grew greater by the moment, not just to themselves but to their entire race. If some miracle beyond foresight did not occur, the mortal army outside would follow them to Nakkiga if it could, take their race's last city, and destroy Viyeki's people, murdering every last man, woman, and child as though they were vermin. But even with the knowledge of the horrors that were surely to come, he felt better than he had since the terrible moment when the Storm King had been defeated and the great tower had fallen in Erkynland, crashing down in smoke and dust and the last flickers of magical flames, taking with it all the People's hope of making the land theirs once again.

In fact, at this instant Viyeki felt almost ordinary, as though the last horrible months had not happened. It was largely the sturdy stone of Three Ravens Tower that reassured him, the way it wrapped around them like the protective mantle of the mountain Ur-Nakkiga itself. The ruins of Tangleroot had never felt like more than a broken place, suitable only for a desperate, doomed resistance to the inevitable. Resistance here was no less doomed, Viyeki knew, but unlike Tangleroot Castle, this tower still had a roof. Just sheltering in the starless dark beneath it reminded him of his mountain home. It had been a long time since the Hikeda'ya had felt safe beneath open sky.

But there was another factor of reassurance, one that he was only beginning to understand, and she stood before him now, conversing with his master Yaarike. General Suno'ku still wore her battle-stained armor, but despite the fierce fighting she had sustained only a small cut on her neck; the line of dried blood made a wandering stripe down her throat and disappeared into her breastplate like a road on an antique map. Her pale eyes showed no trace of the exhausting week passed, the numerous skirmishes fought with Northmen scouts as she led the survivors to Three Ravens Tower. Viyeki had a beautiful, clever wife back in Nakkiga, but he had never felt anything quite like the fascination that Suno'ku evoked in him. Just listening to her firm, quiet voice he felt as though half their problems were already solved. Viyeki's master, however, seemed less convinced.

"But we still have most of my Builders," Yaarike told the general. "It is true we cannot perform the spells of Binding—not with the strongest of our Singers in such condition." He gestured to Host-Singer Tzayin-Kha, who lay senseless on a makeshift pallet a short distance away, tended by two of her acolytes. Her pale skin had darkened into bruised shadows around her eyes, temples, and throat, and her every ragged breath sounded like it came with terrible effort. "But what Tzayin-Kha and her order cannot do by songs of Binding, mine can do by skill and application."

"No. It is pointless trying to defend this place for long," said Suno'ku. "We must return to Nakkiga as quickly as we can."

"Nakkiga?" Yaarike allowed himself a tone of measured irritation. "You said there were no Sacrifices or other fighters left in Nakkiga, General. That means our only choice is to hold this part of the wall until the mortals give up and go home. A few months at most. The winter will drive them out, even with the Storm King banished to the lands beyond the veil of death."

Viyeki wondered how they would feed themselves. The fields between the Wall and the mountain were empty, burned by years of frost and neglect. Some of their people had not eaten in weeks. But he said nothing aloud.

"The problem remains," Yaarike continued. "You command the last of our warriors, General. There is no defense for the innocents in Nakkiga if we fail or falter."

"I said there were no fighters in Nakkiga when I left, High Magister," Suno'ku said. "But they were trickling back. The survivors were scattered widely after the Storm King failed and are returning by many routes, some very long and arduous. I myself took three hundred Sacrifices and members of other orders out of Erkynland and back through the coastal hills of Hernystir, fighting angry mortals all the way. Others are doing the same." She smiled, but it was no more than a slash in her pale skin, a bloodless wound. "No, we must return to Nakkiga. Word of our defeat in the south has given the human creatures courage. These Rimmersmen may be the first to come against us, but they will not be the last." She made a gesture of negation. "Now, attend me closely. If we try to hold this wall, we will fail. But at the same time, we *must* hold it, at least for a little while."

Viyeki did not understand her. Neither did his master, it seemed; the magister narrowed his eyes but spread his fingers in the sign that meant, *"I am listening."*

"We must hold this wall long enough for most of those with us now to return to Nakkiga," she said. "Nakkiga is where we must make our stand, with whatever forces and weapons we can assemble. Even though the queen slumbers in the grip of the *keta-yi'indra* and cannot defend us, you know as well as I that we have not entirely exhausted our resources. There are things in the lower levels—dreadful things . . ."

Yaarike cut her short with another gesture. "How can we accomplish it, General Suno'ku? I admire your Order of Sacrifice, but this tower is meant to be held by a garrison of a hundred, at least. In time of desperation we might halve that—it is said that the great Ruzayo held Midwinter Sun Tower and the wall against an army of giants with but two dozen

Sacrifices—but with all due respect, none of us here are Ruzayo Falcon's-Eye, nor even the mettle of his Twenty-Four."

"I will task each Sacrifice I leave behind with remaining alive until they have taken the lives of at least ten mortals," the general said. "With the help of a dozen or more of your Builders, I think this tower can be held until the rest—"

A strange, croaking sound interrupted her. Suno'ku turned, as did Viyeki and his master Yaarike. Tzayin-Kha, the Host-Singer who had given her all to make the fires speak at Tangleroot Castle, was now struggling to sit up.

"Mistress, no!" cried one of the Singers who had been tending her. He bent to help Tzayin-Kha lie back again, but the Host Singer grasped his arm and flung him away with such astounding force that he spun halfway across the tower chamber, hit the wall with a terrible, muffled crack, then lay still.

Tzayin-Kha slowly rose, clumsy, tottering, her limbs as stiff as alder branches, but it was her face that drew Viyeki's startled attention: her eyes had rolled up until only a crescent moon of white showed in each, and her jaw was working up and down soundlessly, chewing at the empty air.

"I will bring help!" shouted the other Singer. "She is having a fit."

"You . . . will . . . do . . . nothing," were the words that came from Tzayin-Kha's gnashing mouth, each syllable thick and misshapen. Viyeki recognized that grating, deep voice. It did not belong to the dying Host Singer at all, but to someone far more frightening.

Suno'ku drew her great sword, Cold Root, and leveled it at the thing's breast. The blind, upturned eyes could not possibly see the gray blade, but Tzayin-Kha's slack lips suddenly curled in a smile that made Viyeki feel ill.

"My, but we have grown important and impressive," said the scraping voice. *"I always knew you had the seed of greatness in you, Suno'ku seyt-Iyora."*

"Speak your piece, thing of the outer darkness." The general raised her witchwood blade as if to keep the stumbling, loose-limbed Singer at bay. "Then be gone. You sully the body of one who gave her all for her people."

Viyeki was astonished. Despite his master's favor, Viyeki was still an outsider compared to a high noble like Suno'ku, but even he knew the voice of Akhenabi, Lord of Song when he heard it—Akhenabi, second in power only to Queen Utuk'ku herself. How could the general not recognize it?

"*Upstart! I speak for the queen!*" rasped the voice out of Tzayin-Kha's slack mouth. "*You and the others are to hold your position! Under no circumstance are you to return to Nakkiga! You will defend Three Ravens Tower to your last breath!*"

Suno'ku lifted Cold Root high, took a sudden step forward, and crashed the pommel of her famous sword against Tzayin-Kha's forehead. The Singer's knees buckled, then she dropped like a sack of winter meal.

In the shocked silence that followed the acolyte who had been tending Tzayin-Kha scuttled forward with a look of helplessness on his face, as if all his training had been burned away in an instant. He turned the Host Singer over, but whatever had animated her had now fled. The center of her forehead was pushed in like a broken eggshell.

"You . . . you have killed my mistress!" he said in wonder and horror. "Tzayin-Kha is dead!"

"A regrettable result." General Suno'ku sheathed her sword and bent to examine the body. "I used more force than I intended. But perhaps it is a blessing. The thing that possessed her could not have been driven from her dying body any other way."

"What *thing*?" The acolyte Singer had lost more than his discipline, Viyeki decided—he had all but lost his mind if he thought he could defy an armed superior. "Did you not hear the voice of our master? Of Lord Akhenabi himself?"

Suno'ku gave a pitying shake of her head. "You were fooled by a dark spirit, Singer. Look at your comrade." She gestured to the Singer Tzayin-Kha had flung away, still lying in an awkward, broken-necked sprawl at the base of the chamber's stone wall. "Do you mean to tell me that Lord Akhenabi murdered one of his own Singers for no reason?"

The acolyte's mouth worked, but for a moment nothing came out. Viyeki was fearful that this one too would begin speaking with that terrible, scraping voice, but at last he managed to mutter, "I do not know what to say, General Suno'ku."

She turned to Yaarike and Viyeki. "Do you think it a coincidence that moments after I revealed my strategy, something slipped into the body of Tzayin-Kha to demand we not return? High Magister Yaarike, am I wrong?"

Yaarike again wore a strange expression—Viyeki could almost imagine his master was hiding amusement—but all the magister said was, "I can see no fault in your reasoning, General."

Commander Hayyano and several of his Sacrifices now hurried into the room. All but Hayyano stopped short, staring at the body of Tzayin-Kha. "What has happened here, General?" he asked.

"A deadly trick," she announced. "Perhaps the work of the Zida'ya traitor who travels with the mortal army. But it has failed. Assemble all of your men except the sentries and those on active patrol. With High Magister's Yaarike's permission, I will speak to them."

Hayyano looked to Yaarike. He was better at masking his confusion and doubt than the acolyte Singer had been, but his hesitation was clear to all.

"You heard your general," said Yaarike at last, all surface now, his private thoughts once more hidden behind a wall that needed no sentries to keep it inviolate. "Of course you must follow your orders."

More than two hundred Sacrifices from almost a dozen different troops had crowded into the great, high-raftered hall of Three Ravens Tower. They stood straight, ignoring their many wounds, faces set in masks of resolve. Two torches at either end of Marshal Ekisuno's makeshift bier cast the only light except for the summer star Reniku, burning in the center of the hall's high window like a diamond shining from the ashes of a fire.

"My foreparent Ekisuno lies before you," Suno'ku began, pointing to the marshal's shrouded, unmoving form. Though the general's voice seemed soft, it carried to all parts of the chamber. "He was of the blood of great Ekimeniso himself, our queen's consort, and like his ancestor, Ekisuno was a mighty warrior. He spent his long life fighting the queen's enemies before he died at the fall of the tower of Asu'a, as did so many others. You know what happened. All of you were there."

The torches reflected the gleam of hundreds of pairs of dark eyes, watching her.

"Less than one hundred Great Years ago the first mortals came into our lands, savage, dangerous creatures in numbers ever swelling. But when we would have scoured them from our soil, our cousins the Zida'ya prevented us, saying, 'They are but few, and the land is big enough for all.' You know the tragedy that came from their foolish forbearance. You know how mortals killed Drukhi, the son of our great queen. And that was only the first of the outrages they have visited upon us. They were the wedge that split the two kindreds of the Keida'ya, and although, for a time, we both lived in uneasy peace with the newcomers, it did not last.

"During the lifetimes of most of you here, the first of the bearded ones came over the sea with weapons of black iron and hearts full of hate. Like locusts they devoured all that they touched, destroying even their own kind in their bloodlust and fury. Then the Zida'ya learned to their sorrow the folly of their patience with these short-lived, swift-breeding animals. The last of our people's great cities fell when Ineluki of the Zida'ya was destroyed trying to defend Asu'a against the invaders. Only mortal kings, their hands red with blood—*our* people's blood—have sat on Asu'a's throne ever since."

Here the general suddenly stopped and fell silent, as if some new thought had occurred to her. The assembled Sacrifices, their myriad gazes following her as one, stared raptly at the slender, bright shape in silver-white armor. "Did I say the last city of our people?" Suno'ku asked. "That is not true. One great city remains—one refuge of the People of the Garden. And that city is Nakkiga, our home.

"Beyond this tower, just outside the boundary walls of our land, waits an army of mortals. And not just any mortals, but the very same bearded Northerners who destroyed Ineluki and Asu'a, who laid waste to Hike-hikayo and drove out the last of our people there, who left a trail of our blood across all the lands that once belonged to us. Now they mean to bring down these walls, too. They will swarm in their thousands all the way to Nakkiga itself, now all but undefended after our defeat in the southern lands."

The Sacrifices were stirring, still following Suno'ku's every word and gesture. It felt to Viyeki as though he stood in the middle of a hornets' nest and someone had begun to shake it.

"Will we hold the wall?" she asked. "The answer is, we must, if only for a short while. But we cannot hold it for long. The shaking earth of a few seasons back has weakened it, and if every single one of us laid down our lives here, still we would hold back the mortals for only a short time. In a few days or weeks, a changing of the moon's face at most, our defense would fail before their numbers and they would sweep past us to great

Nakkiga itself. And what would they do there?" Suno'ku's voice became quieter but no less forceful. "When they took Asu'a the first time, a horror that is within the memory of most here today, the mortals killed every living thing within its walls. Nor were those deaths swift and merciful. Do you think they will do any different if they take Nakkiga?"

Now the Sacrifices were openly murmuring, some clenching and un-clenching their fists. Viyeki was astounded—the discipline of the fighting order was legendary, and General Suno'ku had broken it in moments. For the first time in his life, Viyeki wondered if his people's eagerness to be ruled by a greater power than themselves might in truth be a sort of weak-ness, in the same way that over-hardened witchwood lacked flexibility and thus was more easily broken.

"Make no mistake," Suno'ku continued, her noble face as grim as her words. "The mortals will rage through our city like a giant in the Field of Stone Flowers, smashing everything. They will destroy every monument to the Lost Garden, every precious memorial to our sacred martyrs. But what they do to the living will be worse. Your families and clans will fall before them like sheep caught by a pack of raving wolves. Your daughters and wives will be raped and then murdered. No one will be spared. When they have finished, Nakkiga will be a fit place only for bats, beetles, and helpless ghosts." She spoke slowly, each word a painful spite. "They will pull the queen herself from the *keta-yi'indra*, where she lies helpless after the last battle in the south, and they will take her and burn her. The mother of us all will die in agony, and the last living memory of the Gar-den will disappear from the earth. Because we cannot hold this wall. We are not strong enough. The fortifications are not strong enough. And there is no help coming from Nakkiga. We are alone." And slowly, deliberately, Suno'ku turned her back on the warriors and hung her head as if in final defeat.

The murmuring died away, but for a few noises that might have been strangled sobs. Then, out of the silence, a single voice spoke. It was Hayyano, and the rage and pain in his words made even Viyeki, who thought little of the commander, ache inside. "Is there nothing we can do, then?" Hayyano demanded. "Nothing at all? Why do you tell us this, General? Why do you set our hearts afire and then leave them to burn?"

A moment—a long moment—and then Suno'ku made the gesture for attention. It was only for effect, Viyeki knew: all eyes were already on her. "Yes, there is one chance. One unlikely chance."

"Tell us!" cried Hayyano, and although no one echoed him, it was clear from the shuffling and hand-signs of agreement that he spoke for all the Sacrifices gathered. Viyeki could feel their desperate fury—a rage that now made the very air tremble as if a storm was imminent.

"We cannot in any case hold this wall or this tower for long," she said. "But if enough of us can make it back to Nakkiga, especially the Builders here, it is possible we can shore up the mountain's defenses sufficiently to keep the mortals from victory. The great gates of Nakkiga have never been breached by mortal or immortal—even the queen herself could not take it by force when she first came there, but had to be welcomed in by its citizens. The gates of Nakkiga are strong and we can make them stronger still. But we need time. Can you do that?"

"For our queen, for the Garden, we can do anything!" Hayyano shouted, and at last a chorus of agreement broke from the ranks. "Tell us, General! Tell us what we must do!"

She stared at the eager throng for a moment as if considering. Moved despite his moments of doubt, Viyeki found himself leaning forward, half-hoping she would ask him to join the warriors in sacrificing themselves to save their queen and city. "High Magister Yaarike," the general said at last. "Will you choose a dozen of your engineers to remain behind and help with the defense? They will not return to Nakkiga, but they will be promised a place of glory in the tales of this time—and I promise this time will be remembered as long as the Garden itself is remembered."

Yaarike wore his most solemn face. "I will ask for volunteers, General Suno'ku, but one way or another, you will have your dozen."

"Thank you, High Magister." Suno'ku looked to the assembled Sacrifices, who had grown almost downcast when she turned away, but who were now all attention once more. "And what of you, my warriors? Which of you will offer your lives here and now for the chance that Nakkiga may live? I need a hundred volunteers to stay, and each must give me his or her sworn vow to send at least ten mortals into the darkness before the end comes. How many will do this? Which of your names will be told and retold until the sun itself is consumed by the black emptiness at the end of time and the great song finally ends? *Show me your swords!*"

More than two hundred blades leaped from their scabbards as one, a chiming scrape of witchwood and bronze so harsh and loud that Viyeki nearly put his fingers in his ears. Every Sacrifice had lifted his sword.

"I expected no less," Suno'ku said, nodding. "The queen, were she here, would smile to see her brave children." She turned to Hayyano. "League Commander, you will take charge of the garrison. Choose one hundred Sacrifices, favoring those who are older or without families. And do not insult those now standing guard upon the walls by excluding them from the chance to fight this glorious fight."

"I hear you, General," said Hayyano, his narrow face flushed at cheek-bones and temples as if he had run a long distance through the cold. "We will hold this wall to our last beating heart. We will make you proud."

"You already have," she said. "Your death-songs were sung long ago. The Celebrants have already written down all your names. Now you can give those deaths in perfect glory, for our queen and our race. And I prom-ise you in return that those of us who must go to defend Nakkiga will give every last breath we have to honor your sacrifice and save our people. For the Garden!"

"For the Garden!" echoed hundreds of voices, including Viyeki's own. He was surprised to discover that his eyes were brimming. He did not even know when the tears had begun.

Frost made the roof sag, and the wind kept the sides of the big tent rip-pling. The cold seemed to creep in and bite Isgrimnur with sharp little teeth that pierced even his clothing. The duke thought he had never, not even through the worst of the fighting at the Hayholt or even in the foul, brackish Wran, longed so deeply for a chair before a warm fire in a warm room in a stern, safe castle.

Elysia, Mother of Mercy, I am weary of cold, he thought, then dragged his attention back to the matter at hand.

"So what you are saying, man, is that we are winning," growled Brin-dur. "That in a matter of a day or two we will have the wall down and our hands on the throats of those corpse-skinned creatures." But as he talked, Brindur did not even look up from the sharpening of his sword. Since his son's terrible death it seemed the only thing he did. Isgrimnur knew that look of disinterest and feared it, for he had seen it on other men and they had never lived long. *"Already looking to the next world,"* his father had said of another battle-mad warrior. What they had lost here in the Norn lands already was bad enough. Brindur was a man Isgrimnur relied on, had always been one of the most dependable of his thanes: but he did not know this Brindur at all.

"No, that is not what I'm saying!" Sludig's voice was tight-strung with anger, but after receiving a pointed look from the duke, he took a breath and tried again, this time speaking directly to Isgrimnur as though Brindur and the others were not inside the tent with them. "What I am trying to say, my lord, is that we should not be winning *this way*. Yes, the Bear has all but knocked down the wall. Yes, the Norn archers in the tower have killed or wounded only a few of the men wielding the ram. But there were several hundred Norn fighters in the group that escaped from us at the ruins. Why do they not fight back as we knock down their wall? Such mildness does not signify. Nothing lies beyond these walls but their stronghold in Stormspike itself!"

"Nothing that we know about," said Isgrimnur. "But our ignorance is as big as my belly. Is he right, Ayaminu? Is there nothing else between us and the Norn mountains? And is my man right to suspect that something else is going on that we do not see?"

"It depends first on what you mean by 'nothing,'" she said. "The lands between the wall and the mountain you call Stormspike are no longer inhabited, and most of the city that was built there long ago is in ruins now. But that does not warrant they will not be waiting in ambush, or that forces from Nakkiga itself will not meet you before you reach the gates."

"We will have more talk about these gates later," said Isgrimnur. "But now we must consider what is immediately in front of us. Sludig, could it be that the Norns simply have no arrows left, no weapons they can hurt us with until we close with them in actual combat?"

"I await that hour," said Brindur, still sharpening. "I wait for nothing else."

"You will have a sword that is little more than a dagger if you keep scraping away at it like that," the duke told him. "But that isn't my chief concern. Is there anything else that makes you worry, Sludig?"

The younger man shook his head, his forehead and brows drawn together in frustration. "Only feelings, my lord—the smell of the thing. We have fought them many times now and the Norns are nothing if not subtle. They brought many strange weapons against us at Naglimund, both during the siege and later, and just as many tricks in the last battle at the Hayholt. Poison powders. False gates. The dead made to walk. Giants summoned like tame hounds, crushing and rending everything they could reach. But where are these things now? Since their escape from the ruined fort they have managed only noises and shadows, which the men have grown used to, which no longer strike fear in any heart. As for actual fighting, we have seen only a few stones and a few arrows from the tower's three beaks and that weak spot on the wall, aimed at the siege engines and the ram. A few of our men have been downed—by chance as much as anything else." Sludig's frown deepened. "And so I must ask myself—are they truly so weak?"

One of Brindur's Skoggeymen, an older warrior with gray-shot whiskers, spoke up. "The fairies are few now, Duke Isgrimnur, whatever Sludig may think. They have lost the war and we carry it to their own land, as we should. Soon we will destroy them all so they cannot trouble us again. Why make a mystery out of weakness?"

Sludig scowled. "Because when you suppose that an enemy is weak, Marri Ironbeard, you only realize you were wrong when they've killed you."

"Perhaps you have lost your taste for this kind of fighting," Brindur said, briefly raising his eyes to give Sludig a hard look. "Or perhaps your friendship with trolls and fairies—yes, I have heard about you, Sludig Two-Axes—has made you reluctant to pursue them. Or even afraid."

Sludig's hand dropped to one of the bearded hand-axes in his broad belt. His eyes narrowed. "My lord, did you not grieve the loss of your son, as we all do, I would demand you to prove that charge with your own hand, man to man."

"Enough!" shouted Isgrimnur. "No accusations. Brindur, you insult Sludig for no reason. His loyalty is beyond doubt. I too have conversed with, and even fought beside, trolls and fairies. If you question his loyalty, you question mine!"

Brindur shrugged. "I take nothing back, but I did not say he was guilty of treason, merely asked him if he had the heart for this fight."

"This is only what our enemies would wish, to have us arguing and biting each other's backs. Enough!" Isgrimnur was furious. "I asked Sludig a question, Brindur, and he answered me—before you needlessly insulted him. I ask you the same question. Do you believe that the Norns are as weak now as they appear?"

Brindur tested the edge of his blade with his finger, then sucked the blood from his fingertip and spat onto the packed, icy ground in a place the rugs didn't cover. Outside the wind had risen again, rattling the duke's tent so that the cloth hummed like the wings of a monstrous insect. "Yes, the White Foxes are fierce fighters. Hard to kill. I do not make the mistake of thinking otherwise. They surprised us with reinforcements at the ruined fort, but we have seen no signs of any more coming. We killed enough of them there that I doubt more than ten score or so of those reinforcements survive, and they had scarce enough fighters in the first group. So I think they are spent and have but little strength left. Our own men are hungry enough in this blighted, frozen place, and we have brought food for ourselves out of Rimmersgard. The Norns were already hungry weeks ago, and whatever tricks they have, I doubt they can feed themselves on air or they would not have attacked so many villages for grain and other supplies. So my wits tell me Two-Axes is only jumping at the same shadows and strange noises that he himself talked about."

Another petty, pointless sting. Before Isgrimnur could shape a reply, a figure, half-obscured by a crust of snowflakes, pushed in past the quivering fabric of the tent door.

"I crave pardon, Your Grace, my lords," the soldier said. "I bring a message from Jarl Vigri. He says there are pieces falling from the wall after the last blow of the great Bear. He thinks it is about to come down."

Brindur's dour mood dropped away in an instant. "Ha! By God," the thane said, climbing to his feet, "If the wall is coming down, I will not be the last to paint my blade with fairy blood!" He turned to one of the younger Skoggeymen. "Fani, you fool, where is my helmet?"

Isgrimnur still had things he needed to discuss with Brindur and the rest, including the letter that a messenger had brought him only this morning, but he would never keep their attention now. As he watched the thane and his Skoggeymen scrambling for their weapons, he thought briefly of trying to make their rush toward the wall more orderly, then decided it

would be better to bow to the inevitable. Even if the wall was badly damaged it might not fall for many more swings of the battering ram, and even
the most anxious Rimmersgard warrior could not come to grips with the
enemy until that moment. In the meantime, letting Brindur and the rest
vent their impatience on an immense weight of black stone might just be
a good idea. His other news could wait.

Two of Isgrimnur's house carls were standing outside the tent, one
with his battle-helmet and his White Bear and Stars standard, the other
holding the duke's large and patient horse. Isgrimnur heaved himself into
the saddle, not without help, then spurred upward after the others.

The battering ram, close against the wall but well to one side of the
three-beaked tower, was just about to make another stroke as Brindur and
the rest reached it. Like Vigri's soldiers who were already crouched on either side of the massive device, they held their shields above their heads to
ward off arrows from the tower or wall, waiting for their chance to attack.

The ram's sloping roof, which protected the men beneath it from defenders' arrows, was the length of a tithing barn, though much narrower,
and so large that it had to be assembled in sections like the bear-headed
ram itself. Snow had been piled high atop the ram's roof as a protection
against flaming arrows, but Isgrimnur saw no sign of Norns now and little
evidence of defense or defenders at all.

The ram's overseers chanted loudly and beat their drums, competing
with the war-cries of Brindur and his party. The sweating, grunting ram-
handlers drew the great log back as far as its heavy chains would allow;
then, at the chief overseer's command, let it go. The Big Bear's grinning
iron muzzle swung forward and smashed into the already weakened wall
with a loud crunch. The wall still did not collapse, but it shifted and
bowed inward where the ram had struck, causing a shower of stone chips
when cracks between the unmortared stones widened.

"One more time!" shouted Brindur hoarsely. "One more time and
they're ours!"

Isgrimnur rode closer, but still held his distance, keeping his eyes on
more than that one spot: Brindur and even the usually cautious Vigri
seemed blind to anything but the stretch of wall before them. Isgrimnur
looked up to the three protruding beaks of the tower as a few arrows came
hissing down from the battlements. Although some of these shots found

their way between the soldiers' upturned shields, the rest of the ramparts were still all but empty of defenders. Surely the Norns realized that their damaged wall could not hold much longer. Had they turned from their defensive positions and fled toward Stormspike? Or was something else going on?

The ram was pulled back again, the groans of its handlers and the pounding drums mixed with the battle-chants of the waiting Rimmersmen, but the bloodthirsty excitement of his countrymen no longer touched Isgrimnur. Something truly did seem wrong. His men had driven hundreds of Norns to this spot, and although a few of them had been killed on the walls by Vigri's Tungoldyr archers, Isgrimnur knew those had only been a fraction of the enemies that should be fighting to keep mortals from crossing into their lands. *By the Holy Ransomer*, the duke thought, *if Sludig is right, what are they planning?*

The chains creaked as the ram reached its farthest backward point. A moment later the drum fell silent, then the overseer cried, "*Now!*" The ram swung forward and the bear took another crunching bite.

A goodly chunk fell from the middle of the wall where the iron head of the ram had struck; a moment later another piece fell from above it. Then, with a rumble like thunder directly overhead, the great stones began to tip and slide. The troops around the ram, arrested in mid-cheer, scrambled back—some of the stones were bigger than a man.

Once it began, the cascade of black stone could not be stopped. The whole center of the wall before the ram tottered and then fell in on itself with a grinding crash. Huge stones began to cascade on either side, throwing flurries of snow and mud into the air, scattering men in all directions. A moment later the collapse was over: all but the bottom few cubits in the wall's center had toppled, leaving a gaping wound in the great structure like an upturned horseshoe. The Rimmersmen quickly reformed their ranks and began to surge through this opening, climbing over the remaining stones like ants swarming a fallen loaf of bread, screeching and bellowing in their gleeful frenzy to get at the enemy who had evaded them so long.

A moment later the attackers discovered that another wall stood behind the first. It was only barely taller than a man, obviously hasty work by the defenders behind the great wall's weakest spot, but as the first Rimmersmen made their way over the rubble, they found themselves climbing into a hornet's nest of arrows: most of the rest of the castle's defenders were hidden there, waiting patiently for the chance to fight back that had now arrived.

"No fear! They are only a few!" shouted Vigri, his short legs straight in the stirrups as he waved to his troops. "On, now, Northmen! Show them what iron tastes like!"

But even as the jarl's Enggidalers and Brindur's Skoggeymen forged into the gap, Isgrimnur heard another cry. It was only another voice in the chaos of many, but this one caught his attention because it came from a different direction.

To his left and behind him, a good distance back from the breach, stood the catapults that had been pelting the walls with large stones to divert any remaining defenders from the ram. These siege engines were mostly guarded by the mercenaries from the south, men of unknown quality that Isgrimnur had not trusted in his front lines, and now he saw one of these southerners waving his arms and shouting, trying to get the attention of the Rimmersmen fighting near the ram. Isgrimnur could not make out what the man was saying through the noise of the assault, but he followed his wild hand gestures and looked up to the high peaks that framed the wall on either side of the pass. His heart lurched. About halfway up the slope on Isgrimnur's left hand a huge boulder had somehow worked its way loose from the soil and was beginning to move ponderously downward. The massive chunk of stone seemed to be alternately skidding and rolling right toward the Rimmersmen as they fought to get over the collapsed wall through the flurry of Norn arrows.

Isgrimnur shouted a warning, but of course no one could hear him. High above, the irregular boulder slowed for a moment, its flattest side down, and the duke felt a moment of hope that it had stopped; an instant later the great chunk of stone slid over the small level spot that had slowed it and began to roll, big as a three story house in the wealthy merchant's quarter of Elvritshalla, careening toward the base of the hill.

Isgrimnur spurred his horse forward, shouting a warning as he headed toward the hole in the wall the ram had made.

"Forward!" he bellowed with all the strength he had in his great lungs, trying to drive the rest of the waiting troops through the gap. "Forward or be crushed! 'Ware! 'Ware!"

The huge stone smashed the corner of the wall as it scraped past, sending monstrous black shards flying like pebbles but slowing the stone not at all.

The collapsed section of wall lay before him, then his horse was leaping and sliding on the piled stones as men threw themselves out of his way.

"No, forward!" he cried. *"Forward if you want to live!"*

And then a powerful wind nearly blew the duke out of his saddle as the great boulder struck just behind him, grinding men and stones and the mighty bear-headed ram itself into an unrecognizable clutter, with a noise like the end of the world.

Porto, from his position beside the catapult known as the Donkey, had been watching the Rimmersmen waiting to attack with a mixture of admiration and disbelief. As the wall wavered he thought they looked like a pack of dogs, their beards bristling, teeth bared, howling and even singing as they waited, and all he could think was, *Are they really going to charge through that hole into the teeth of whatever defenders are left?* Because surely the Norns were aware of the widening cracks spreading between the great stones. Even a blind man could hear the shifting of tons of rock as the wall slowly began to give way.

Although the catapult had been loaded and wound again, it had not been fired: two of its crewmen lay on the snowy ground with Norn arrows in them and their hammers lying beside them, one man already dead and the other shrieking for God to help him. Several of the long iron stakes that held down the front of the war engine had worked their way loose on its last shot, but Hjortur the catapult master did not seem to have noticed in the confusion of battle. Porto knew that if the front was not anchored the release would not just miss the target, but might throw its stone into the Rimmersmen's own ranks, so he hurried around the wooden frame. As he lifted the heavy maul the dead man had dropped, he heard a sharp, excited cry from the soldiers at the wall as the great Bear was released again and crashed into the heavy stones.

"Endri!" he shouted. "Damn it, man, grab the other hammer and help me knock these stakes in!" Even as he said it, Porto lifted his own maul and swung it, but as he brought it down he was almost knocked from his feet by a tremendous rumbling impact as the great wall that sealed the valley finally collapsed.

He turned and saw the Rimmersgard soldiers scrambling forward over the tumbled stones of the wall. They were bellowing like wild things, and he was so taken by the sound of it, the way it murmured in his bones and made his heart race even faster, that for long instants he did not hear Endri's warning. The young man was leaping up and down, shouting at him and pointing upward; Porto saw a movement at the corner of his eye and turned away from the spectacle of Isgrimnur's soldiers charging the gap just as the first of them began to fall back, sprouting arrows.

Something was tumbling toward him down the slope at the side of the valley. Something very big.

For a brief instant, as Porto tried to understand the size of the shadowy mass skidding downward toward them, he thought, "Dragon!" his mind ready for any kind of madness the Norns might be able to summon. Then he saw it for what it was, a slab of rock the size of a village church. Even as he watched, it tipped and began to tumble.

Porto dropped his heavy maul to run, but because he was still looking back at the huge stone as it grew bigger by the instant, he tripped over the dead man he'd taken the hammer from. The man's face was right below him, mouth sagging open, and for an instant as Porto fell it looked as though the corpse was warning him. Or perhaps taunting him: *You think staying alive is easy?*

Porto hit the icy ground hard, felt a brief spray of cold snow, then struck his head so roughly that his thoughts shrank to a narrow tunnel of light in a field of black emptiness. Even the boulder that was about to crush him seemed far away, without meaning, though its thunderous approach seemed to drown all other noise. *No matter,* he thought absently. Everything was over. Over.

And then he was yanked away, scraped face-first across the rough, stony soil and its layer of snow, heat and chill and bright white pain all battling for his attention—but Porto had no attention to give.

It had not been the great stone that had hit him he realized an instant later, floating in dreamy detachment. He saw its shadow slide past and heard it smash the Donkey into splinters, then he watched the great catapult arm bounce away, end over end like a spoon thrown by an ogre's child, until it finally stopped, leaning upright against the base of Three Ravens Tower.

Endri stood over him now, the sky a swirl of pearl bright light and dark clouds. Porto could only stare up at his friend in wonder. He knew something had happened, but his thoughts seemed to be at the end of a long string, and although he pulled at it, all he was doing was reeling in more and more string.

"The catapult is gone!" Endri cried, as if that should mean something. The young man's eyes were so wide Porto thought it must be painful.

"Now the ram, too. I think the Norns found a way to push that rock down on . . ." Endri paused with a look of confusion. Still puzzled, he turned to look behind him, as though someone had tapped him on the shoulder while he stood in a deserted place. A moment later the youth dropped to his knees, far more slowly than the great stone had traveled down the mountain. Then, equally slowly, he toppled forward onto his face. His chain mail gave a single soft clash as he hit the ground, then Endri lay still and silent, a black arrow quivering in his back.

Duke Isgrimnur did not want to look back at the damage the monstrous stone had caused in its fall, but he could not help himself. The head of the iron ram was intact beneath the rubble but the great log, a single trimmed pine trunk more than thirty paces long, had been crushed to splinters, and he could see broken bodies in the pile of shattered stone and wood. Then an arrow whickered past his helmet, and he hurriedly turned back to what lay before him.

Fewer Norns had been lying in wait behind the small, hastily built second wall than Isgrimnur had feared at first; the fairies had saved their arrows and put them to deadly use, although most of his men had been shot in the first instants of surprise. Though many Rimmersmen fell in the first charge, their comrades had pushed forward after them, climbing over the dead to reach the second wall. Brindur himself had led his Skoggey kinsmen over the top, shouting the name of his dead son Floki, and within moments was among the Norns on the other side, howling with mad glee as he hacked at his enemies. Vigri's men quickly followed. The Norns were deadly fighters, but they were outnumbered by more than a dozen to one, swarmed as though beset by hunting hounds. Within an hour Isgrimnur's forces had taken control of the wall.

A few more White Foxes tried to hold the tower, but its portals had not been fairy-magicked and Rimmersgard axes soon splintered the doors and knocked them from their hinges. Terrible fights took place in the darkened stairwells and in the uppermost chamber between the great beaks, but at last the final Norn died, pinned against a wall by several spears. The besiegers dragged the pale creature's body to the hole in the bottom of the beak and shoved it through. It spun slowly down the long drop to the ground and bounced when it struck, like a discarded fish head.

Thane Brindur had sustained many wounds but none of them were mortal. He licked his lips and grinned as one of the barber-surgeons cleaned and stitched the worst of them. "I told you," he growled. "Fairies can die like anyone else once you shove a yard of iron into them."

Isgrimnur, who in his time had killed more than his share of Norns, did not bother to reply to Brindur's comment. "The rest of the White Foxes are gone. That was but a token force. I counted only a few score corpses. The rest have fled back to their city."

"So?" Brindur rubbed his finger along a freshly sewn cut that extended from his wrist to beyond his elbow, then he examined the blood. "That is only another hundred that we will kill later rather than sooner."

Jarl Vigri approached with several of his thanes. "The scouts are back from atop the cliffs, Your Grace. Yes, that boulder was the Norns' work— the tools are still there where they dropped them. But looking out across the lands beyond the wall, the scouts say it is still several days' march to Stormspike from here. Those who escaped may be waiting for us in ambush along the way."

Brindur wiped his bloody finger on his already muddy, blood-spattered surcoat. "Slaughter them in droves like the beasts they are or kill them one by one—it makes no difference to me as long as we destroy that foul nest in the mountain."

Isgrimnur frowned and tugged at his beard. "We are already in territory that no mortal armies have entered in centuries. We have lost a quarter of our army in two or three small skirmishes on the outskirts of the enemy's lands—what makes you think they will not fight even harder to defend their home? The Bear is smashed, as well as two of our catapults, so how do you propose we enter Stormspike, Brindur, even if the Norns are too few to defend it? Which is by no damn means certain."

"It is certain," Brindur said. "If they had reinforcements a day or two away, do you think they would have let us break down their wall and walk into the Nornfells without a fight?"

"I do not call it 'without a fight' when more than a hundred of my men are killed," Isgrimnur growled.

Brindur spat on the floor. "This is war, not the squabbling politics of court. If we do not destroy these creatures in their final hole we have wasted those dead."

Vigri cleared his throat. "I do not say that Brindur is right, my lord, but I do not say he is wrong, either. We came to finish with these corpse-skins once and for all. If you set out to burn the wasp's nest, you must finish the job or they will just make more wasps."

Isgrimnur snorted. "These are not wasps. These are not beasts. These are ancient creatures more cunning than we are, and they are certainly not cowards. Do you think we have seen all their tricks?"

"They are running out of feints," Brindur said as flatly as he might have said "the sky is blue," or "blood is red." "We saw no faces in the fires this time, no shadows or ghostly voices. Just arrows and stone walls."

"And a very large rock which destroyed our catapults and our ram," said Isgrimnur. "As well as killing a dozen or more of our men. But we will miss the ram more than any of the rest."

"The Bear is not dead," Brindur declared. "His iron head still wants to bite. There are plenty of trees here. We will build him a new body and knock down the fairies' front door."

Isgrimnur turned to Vigri, since it seemed as if the jarl and Sludig were the only sane voices left. "What do you think?"

Vigri looked weary. His armor was almost as bloody as Brindur's. "What do I think? That this is a dreadful chore, my lord. But we have taken it on and we cannot leave off yet. That is what I think."

Isgrimnur sighed. "I suppose you are right." He reached for the bowl of ale one of his carls had set out on top of a wooden chest and felt the letter that he had thrust into his belt earlier, now scratching against his belly. "Ah! Of course! I have some news that slipped my mind in the clamor. Good news, at that."

"Praise Usires!" said the jarl. "Pray do not keep it to yourself, my lord. That is something we need more than food or drink."

Isgrimnur nodded. "When first I heard from you, Vigri, telling of the siege you had begun, I sent out messengers to the nearest thanes, Alfwer of Heitskeld, Helgrimnur Stonehand, and several others, asking help from everyone within a fortnight's march."

"*Alfwer,*" said Brindur, and although he did not spit again, he might as well have.

"Never mind Alfwer," said Isgrimnur with a tight smile. "I have not heard back from him anyway—doubtless he is busy counting his cattle. But the messenger to Helgrimnur came back just this morning." He paused to take a drink.

"Please, Your Grace!" said Vigri. "What good news? You are tormenting me."

Isgrimnur could manage only the weariest of smiles. "I beg your pardon, my friend. Helgrimnur writes to say that he had already mustered men to send to Erkynland, but when they were not called for, he released them for the spring planting—or such as it was this year, with the fields all frozen." He opened the letter, smoothing it on his knee. "Yes, here. But when the Norns began to make their way through the nearby lands, he summoned his warriors back, clever fellow. He has half a thousand men under arms, ten score of them experienced fighters. Now, the happiest part—he is sending them with his sister-son, Helvnur, who also leads nearly a hundred mounted men. The messenger said Helvnur and his men are only a few days behind him. They did not expect to find us already so far north."

Vigri clapped his hands together. "Aedon be praised—that is excellent news indeed!"

"I would rather it were ten times that many, but it will surely help." The duke smiled again and raised his ale bowl in a toast. "By my beard, Helgrimnur is a good man, and I will not forget it!"

"Is there a chance that we may hear back from any others?" Vigri asked.

Isgrimnur shook his head. "Not before we cross into the Norn lands, I think. But Helgrimnur's muster makes up for the numbers we have lost so far."

"As long as these new folk don't get between me and the creatures I'll be killing, they are welcome," said Brindur. "I have a mind to lay my hands on the queen of the fairies herself. Maybe she'll grant me a wish before I strangle her."

Isgrimnur hurriedly made the sign of the Tree. "Trust me, Brindur, you don't know what you're talking about. She would freeze the marrow in your bones if you met her."

"We'll see," said Brindur. "In any case, my sword needs sharpening again. Fairy armor makes a blade dull, and fairy bones are worse."

"Even with more fighters, the next part will not be easy," Isgrimnur warned. "God save me, none of this has been easy."

"You think too much, my lord," said Brindur, and it was hard to tell whether he meant sarcasm or honest reproof. "See the enemy. Kill the enemy. That is the whole of our task."

"Ah, such simple bloodlust reminds me of an old friend," Isgrimnur said, half-amused, but a moment later the memory turned sour. "The White Foxes killed him in Aldheorte Forest."

"I hate to disagree with you, Thane Brindur," said Vigri. "But I would like to add another task to your list: Return alive."

"I hold to an older tradition, my lord," said Brindur. "I would like to live, but I would rather see our enemies dead. I will look down happily from the feasting halls of our ancestors if I take enough of the whiteskins with me."

Isgrimnur had heard enough. He had men to bury, if the living had managed by now to make a big enough hole in such icy ground. He reached for the ale and took a long draught, then took another before wiping his mouth with the back of his hand. "God grant us victory," was all he said.

Endri was not dead, but there were moments now that Porto could almost wish the Norn arrow had killed him outright.

One of the Rimmersgard surgeons had cut deep into the young man's back to remove the black dart, and sluiced the wound with strong spirits. At first it seemed that Endri would recover, because the arrow itself had stuck in his shoulder blade instead of slicing through to his lungs and heart, but whether because of the foul airs of the Nornfells or some poison on the arrowhead, the wound did not heal. At first it was only obvious by the fevers that shook his body and the pains that made him cry out as he slipped in and out of restless sleep. But by the time a full day had passed Porto could see a black stain beneath the skin that had spread outward from the original arrow wound into a blotch bigger than his hand. It was hot to the touch, and the skin seemed almost lifeless beneath Porto's fingers.

"Can you feel my touch here?" he asked as he probed at the lumpy area around the wound.

"Yes. But it's no worse . . . than any other part of me. I hurt all over. God help me, Porto, it feels like my blood is on fire in my veins!"

"You should not have risked your life for me," he said, then regretted it.

Endri tried to sit up but failed, slumping back. The light of the camp-fire made the whites of his eyes seem as yellow as a wolf's. "No!" He struggled to take a deeper breath. "You are my only friend. Don't . . . don't be foolish. You would have done the same . . . the same for me." The effort of speaking had exhausted him, and he closed his eyes again. His chest moved up and down in little jerks.

What are we doing here? Porto wondered. *What are we doing in this cold, empty place, out at the arse-end of nowhere? It would be different if we were fighting for Ansis Pelippé, to protect our own folk.*

As if he had heard Porto's thoughts of home, Endri opened his eyes. For a moment he looked around wildly, as if he did not know where he was, but when he saw Porto's face he calmed. "I want to go back," was what he said. "Back to Harborside."

"You will, I promise. Just rest. Here, drink a little of this." He lifted the cup of melted snow to Endri's lips and steadied it while the young man sipped. "You will be well again. We will go back to Perdruin together in triumph." He looked at Endri's dull, listless face and added, "And who knows what booty we will bring? Gold from out of Stormspike itself, maybe, or jewels from some fairy princess's wardrobe. Even a Norn sword or battle helm will bring a pretty price in Ansis Pelippé, you can be sure of that. We will be rich men. Famous, too—the heroes who fought the Norns."

Endri shook his head, eyes closed again, but this time he smiled. "That is why you are my friend, Porto. You tell such pretty lies. And the Geysers and the Dogfish will celebrate together too, and no one will fight."

"Quiet now. Sleep is the best cure."

Endri's smile shrank but did not entirely disappear. When he spoke again, he seemed to be a long distance away. "Don't worry about me, my friend. I will have plenty of time to sleep soon."

Porto pulled the youth's cloak up beneath his chin to keep out the chill. Now that they were on the far side of the pass, there was nothing to block the icy wind that knifed down from the heights. Finished, he turned away from Endri and pretended to stoke the fire, because it was becoming obvious that the freezing drops that stung Porto's cheeks were nothing to do with the fluttering snow.

Part
Three

The Nakkiga Gate

It was hard to see anything except the great cone of Nakkiga; it dominated the center of the uneven plateau like a brooding, robed figure.

To Viyeki, their sacred peak had always meant many things—a refuge, a parent, a stern and disappointed teacher. Now, as it grew larger before them, hour by hour, he felt his sense of shame grow as well, knowing that he and the other children of the Garden were returning to the mountain in such disarray, not as saviors and barely as survivors; drowning men washed up on a beach only after they had given up hope.

General Suno'ku led the procession, riding ahead of the catafalque bearing the makeshift wooden coffin of her foreparent, Ekisuno the Great, hero of a dozen battles but now only one more corpse, another victim of the mortals' hatred. Viyeki could not help thinking of The Heart of What Was Lost, the ancient jewel that hung around his master Yaarike's neck, hidden inside the magister's garments.

Is that all our people have to show in the end? Viyeki wondered. *More losses? Is this tattered army we bring back, a few hundred out of all the thousands who went south, just another display of our ultimate fate, as pointless as a gem commemorating the vanished Garden? Is all we have—all we are—only a memorial of what we failed to save?*

Viyeki could see nothing else ahead for his people, even if they survived this terrible failure. *We retreat. We hide. We diminish. Eventually we will disappear except in old stories. And they will not be our stories.* Alone among her peers, only General Suno'ku seemed to believe differently. Only Suno'ku had given him anything like hope. But now they were home again, and the only real truths were failure, regret, and loss.

He looked to his master, wondering if Yaarike was thinking similar thoughts, but as usual the magister's face was as enigmatic as a stone weathered smooth by centuries of wind and rain. Viyeki could only wonder how he could hope, one day, to replace a leader of such depth and subtlety.

I am not enough, my great queen, he thought. *You need heroes not mere Builders. I am not enough.*

The small procession wound through the ruins of the abandoned city of Nakkiga-That-Was, picking its way across the pocked and uneven surfaces of a road that had once been the Royal Way. Only a few stones remained from a thoroughfare so wide that a dozen riders could make their way along it side by side without touching. The rest of the paving had been plundered long ago for the city inside the mountain when the Hikeda'ya had turned inward, withdrawing from the hostile world the mortals had created.

But the old city still remained in the tumbled ruins and rings of stones that showed where the great buildings had once stood. The high Gyrfalcon Castles that had once clung to the side of the mountain itself were gone, but their telltales remained, at least to Viyeki's practiced eye. The Sky Palace was only a field of rubble and dead frozen grass, but once, its open dome had framed the night sky in glory for the observers below. Here the Moon Festival Canal and its tributaries had wound through the city like rivers of quicksilver. Delicate boats had carried soldiers, courtiers, spies, and lovers to their various destinies.

For a moment it seemed as though Viyeki could see these pathetic remnants and also the glorious city that had rivaled Asu'a itself—both the arches of the solemn Queen's Gallery as it once stood and the long-collapsed pillars of today; the graceful curves of the Bridge of Exodus and the trample of icy mud that marked all that was left. Where the delicate, high houses of lords and ladies had stood, poems in stone and sky, only a few protruding rocks still remained, broken teeth in a skeletal jaw, the mansions' owners long gone into the Elder Halls in the Silent Palace beneath Nakkiga. The only thing that remained of all that glory was the mountain itself, and the tall gates that offered darkness and safety to those they welcomed.

We come out into the sun only to fight now, Viyeki suddenly realized. It was an idea that, once it entered his mind, would not go away. *We call darkness our friend, but when the elders tell us stories of the Garden, they talk of the holy, unending light that was there. How did shadows become our only dwelling?*

As they crossed the rocky, frozen mire at the mountain's foot that had once been the Field of Banners, the great marshaling ground of the Sacrifice order, Viyeki saw that Nakkiga's tall gates stood open. For an instant, all his thoughts fled away in fear that they had come home too late—that the mortals had somehow beat them here, that nothing would be left to greet them but blood and death. Then he saw the thin line of armored Sacrifices drawn up on either side of the massive witchwood doors and his heart slowed. The mortals had not yet come. The people of Nakkiga were waiting to welcome them home.

As they rode up the slope between the waiting Sacrifices, Viyeki could not help noticing that most of these warriors were too young or too old for proper service. Mortals might not be able to tell the difference between one Hikeda'ya and another, but Viyeki saw the tight-stretched skin of the old and weary and the over-straight backs and gleaming eyes of the young, who did not understand yet how many defeated armies had returned through these gates over the years, each time in smaller and smaller numbers.

As General Suno'ku steered her mount between the honor guard, a crowd of Singers stepped out of the great gate, led by a rider on a great black horse. The rider raised his palm in salute, and even from a distance Viyeki could see that his face was covered with a mask of translucent dried flesh.

Viyeki felt his heart grow cold. It was Akhenabi, the Lord of Song. He had returned from the south before them. Viyeki knew he should have been overjoyed that such a powerful figure still lived, but instead he remembered the possession of Tzayin-Kha at Three Ravens Tower and felt instead a choking fear. General Suno'ku had ignored Akhenabi's orders and then killed the Lord of Song's minion, Tzayin-Kha. What would come from that—and would it come only to Suno'ku, or were the rest of them tainted by her disobedience, too? Viyeki had heard enough stories of the Cold, Slow Halls to know that he would rather face the executioner's cord and rod a hundred times than be handed over to the pain-masters of Akhenabi's order.

Although his voice was as harsh and commanding as ever, the Lord of Song offered only pleasantries: "You return to us, General Suno'ku. I see you bring back the remains of your glorious ancestor Marshal Ekisuno as well. He will lie in state in Black Water Field before he goes to the Silent Palace, so that the people may thank him for his sacrifice."

But to Viyeki's astonishment, Suno'ku said, "No. You are kind, High Magister Akhenabi, but my foreparent's body will lie in the dooryard of the Iyora clan-house instead, as is our custom."

Akhenabi was surprised by this refusal, as evidenced by a moment of stillness before he spoke again. "Ah, but such things should not be discussed here, as if you were strangers on the doorstep. I come on the queen's behalf to welcome you home. There is much to discuss."

"Is the queen awake?" asked Suno'ku. "After her valiant efforts were undone by the mortals, I thought she would still be deep in the *keta-yi'indra*."

"Yes, of course," said Akhenabi with just the faintest trace of stiffness; nobody any farther from the conversation than Viyeki and the other surviving nobles would have recognized it. "The mother of us all still sleeps the *yi'indra*, regaining her strength. I speak on her behalf, only. We have suffered a great catastrophe and Nakkiga was in disarray. Someone had to take the reins of governance." He stopped abruptly, aware that he had been connived into defending himself. Viyeki thought that even where he stood, several paces away, he could feel the Lord of Song's cold rage.

"And, as always, Nakkiga is grateful to you, Magister Akhenabi." Suno'ku turned to the Sacrifice soldiers still waiting in their silent lines. "And to you, true Sacrifices all. We have fought the more bravely because we knew you were here, protecting those we hold dearest." She turned back to Akhenabi and his crimson-robed flock of Singers. "Let us enter now, my lord. We fly just before the storm, and there is little time to waste."

Akhenabi waved his hand and the Singers cleared the doorway; but as Suno'ku rode through, the Lord of Song tugged on the black horse's reins and turned so that he rode beside her. Viyeki felt a moment of helpless envy: Like the Lord of Song and the general, High Magister Yaarike was entering Nakkiga mounted on a fine horse, the property of a Sacrifice who had died at Three Ravens Tower. He and Yaarike had been almost equals while they were on the run in mortal lands, but Viyeki was still on foot, and it would be a long, weary walk to the center of the city for him and the rest of the returning Hikeda'ya.

Did I put too much stock in the favor Yaarike showed me while we were in danger together? He did say I would be his successor. He said it so clearly I could not be mistaken.

As they moved into Nakkiga, Viyeki discovered to his surprise that the city's broad Glinting Passage was lined with hundreds of their people, mostly ordinary Hikeda'ya from the lowest castes. Like the guard of Sacrifices, they seemed mostly very young or very old. All were ragged and hunger-thin, but when they saw Suno'ku they cheered as though she were the queen herself. Nor was it only the lower castes that had come to see the spectacle of their return: other Nakkigai were watching the procession from the balconies of noble dwellings far above them, and many of these were also cheering Suno'ku and her Sacrifices.

Viyeki hurried forward until he caught up to Yaarike, who rode last in the line of returning nobles. "Lord Akhenabi looks unhappy, Master," he said quietly. "*He* has never been celebrated this way."

"Nor does he wish to be." Yaarike sounded out of sorts. "The Lord of Song works best in darkness and quiet. It is not the trappings of power he desires, but power itself."

"But he cannot be happy with how the people cheer for Suno'ku."

"Neither am I." Yaarike made a gesture to forestall his underling's question. "Remember what I tell you now, Host Foreman Viyeki—the enemy of your enemy is not always your friend." He said no more, but spurred his horse ahead. Viyeki was left to wonder at his master's words.

At last they reached Black Water Field, the vast common square at the foot of the cascading Tearfall, where the great stairs led from the main part of the city up to the dwellings of the nobility on the second tier and beyond that to the houses of the dead and the queen's palace on the third tier. The crowds had followed them but the cheering quieted as they moved deeper into the city, where the gaunt faces of the citizens watched as though waiting for some revelation. Suno'ku directed the bearers to carry General Ekisuno's body up onto the great stone platform, a monument commonly known as Drukhi's Altar in honor of the queen's dead son, although in truth it had been built as a memorial to all the martyrs of Nakkiga's wars.

When the catafalque was set down, Suno'ku stood over the simple coffin for a moment, as if in silent conversation with her foreparent, then turned and walked to the front of the platform to face the gathered throng, her silver owl helmet under her arm, her pale hair shining in the torch-light. When she stopped at the edge of the platform it was impossible to miss that she had placed herself between Lord Akhenabi and the people gathered below.

"Hikeda'yei!" she said, her voice loud and clear and tuneful as a battle-trumpet. "Go to your orders now, all you of noble castes—there is much to do to prepare for this coming siege. The rest of you, fear not! You will have work to do as well in the days to come, and your share of the glory will be no less. We will triumph *together*, first against the army that comes to destroy us, later against a mortal world that no longer fears us. Because we will change that. We will *triumph*. For the Garden!"

The general did not wait for the cheers to die down this time but signaled for the bearers to lift her foreparent's catafalque and follow her back down into the square. Viyeki, like many of the other nobles, could only watch in amazement as she and her guards made their way through the throng, so close to the people that many on either side reached out, trying to touch her as she passed. Some even threw flowers, and not just onto Ekisuno's coffin but onto Suno'ku herself, pale blooms of snowsun and everwhite stolen from the offering-vases of long-dead heroes. Others called out her name and begged her to save them. Viyeki had never seen the lower castes so moved by anyone but the queen herself.

The general and her closest followers moved like a wave through the gathered Hikeda'ya until they left the common square and mounted the stair to the second tier, to the great clan compounds and the order houses where the common people could not follow her. A trail of flowers lay on the steps behind them.

After Suno'ku had gone the people finally began to disperse, but they left slowly, reluctantly, as if someone had awakened them from a happy dream they did not want to relinquish.

Despite the great age and degraded condition of the Norn road, the journey from Three Ravens Tower into the Norn lands was the least of Porto's problems. Endri, weak and feverish, could no longer ride behind him, so Porto set him on the front of the saddle as though he were a child and rode with one arm holding the wounded man upright.

The snow continued to flurry, and what was left of the old road quickly became a roil of icy mud as Duke Isgrimnur's army wound its way between the lesser peaks of the Nornfells, headed always toward the ominous, upright bulk of the great mountain that mortals called Stormspike. Nobody was singing now, and the soldiers kept even their speaking voices low, awed to be trespassing in a land that had for so long been the stuff of tales to frighten unruly children. The cloudy, slate-gray sky hung low, like the ceiling of a humble crofter's hut. Porto, like many others, felt as though he was being watched from above, as though tall Stormspike itself had eyes.

Can they see us yet? he wondered. *With their magic tricks? What are they thinking?*

"Is that you, Porto?" Endri asked, each word an effort.

"I'm here, lad."

"I want to go home now. I'm cold."

"I know. We all want to go home." He could feel the younger man shivering, although the day was warmer than most had been since they crossed the Rimmersgard frontier. "We have one more thing to see to, that's all. Then I'll help you get back to Ansis Pelippé—back to Harborside."

"Is it still summer?"

Porto was heartened. Endri hadn't talked this much in days. He hoped it meant that the blackened place in his back was actually beginning to heal, but every time the wind changed direction he could smell the corruption of the young man's wound. "Yes. Still summer."

Endri was silent for a while. "They'll be having the race, the harbor race," he said at last. "My uncle . . . won it once. He had the biggest arms I've ever seen. Like a wrestler. He drowned."

"How could he win the race if he drowned?" Porto leaned forward, hoping to see a smile, but the gape-mouthed emptiness of Endri's face was like that of a dead man. *And God save me, I've seen too many dead men*, Porto thought. *I want to see people I know again. I want to see my Sida, alive and smiling and far, far away from this cursed, freezing place. Thank the Holy Ransomer for Count Streáwe, who kept Perdruin out of the worst of this dreadful war.*

"Uncle didn't . . . drown then. That was another time." Endri sighed, but it turned into a cough that Porto could feel rattling the frail chest through both their armor. "It was all another time," he said when he had his breath back, so softly that Porto had to lean forward again to hear him.

Endri did not say any more and soon his head sagged in sleep as the horse continued to pick its way over the bumpy track that had once been a road as large and as magnificent as the Avenue of Triumph leading to the Sancellan Mahistrevis palace in Nabban. Porto did not know enough about the Norns to guess how long the road had lain like this, all but unused, nor had he heard of a time when the white-skinned northern fairies did anything but lurk in their snowy wastes and plot vengeance against mankind. For a moment the depth of what he did not know, the incomprehensible vastness of history, almost made him dizzy. He looked to the other riders nearby, some Rimmersmen, some southerners like himself, and wondered if the rest thought like he did. By their faces, whatever thoughts they had were just as grim.

Isgrimnur had already grown weary of staring at the mountain, but it had become hard to look at anything else. The great dark cone of Stormspike seemed to swell and spread as they approached until it covered most of the horizon and threatened to pierce the low sky with its sharp peak. Wispy clouds of steam drifted up from crevices in the mountain's flank, then twined upward until the winds of the upper heights snatched them away, leaving only a few faint wisps to wreathe Stormspike's head.

Despite the white wisps at its brow, the mountain was not enfeebled; it towered over the smaller peaks nearby like a great thane among his kneeling housecarls. The stripes of snow trailing down from the moun-tain's white cap only made its black stone immensity loom larger, as though Nature had sought to restrain it and failed. Yet Isgrimnur and a few thousand mortals planned to bring it under their sway.

"We are fools," said Sludig from just behind him.

Isgrimnur turned and looked at him. "Fools? Why?"

"Why? By the good God, my lord, look at that. That is no tower or crumbling wall. That is the Lord's own work, set down in the first days of Creation and still burning with His fires. How can we think to conquer it?"

Isgrimnur was disquieted by how closely Sludig's doubts echoed his own, but he only said, "If we do God's work, we need not fear God's creations, however mighty. Besides, we do not seek to conquer the moun-tain, old friend, just the creatures hiding within it. All that holds us back is a gate, made by the work of hands, not God."

"Fairy hands," said Sludig glumly. "Fairy magic."

Isgrimnur spotted the Sitha-woman on her white horse just a short distance behind them, her soft gray garments fluttering in the wind. Un-like the rest of the riders, huddled deep in their saddles with hoods pulled close against the flying snow, she seemed utterly unconcerned about such trivialities as wind and weather. "Ho, Lady Ayaminu!" he called. "Will you talk with me?"

She made no discernible movement but her horse sped its pace until she was riding between Isgrimnur and Sludig. "I am here," she said.

"What of the gate?" He did not trust her forbearance toward the Norns, but she had not yet told him anything false and was the best re-source they had until they could send out scouts. "Is it as strong as stories tell? Are there spells or some other Norn trickery protecting it?"

She gave him a look that had a small edge of amusement. "You do not really understand the ways of our people, Duke Isgrimnur. The two great doors of the gate were forged of bronze and witchwood long ago. What you call 'spells,' the tools used in making them, are a *part* of them, not something that has been put on like a coat of whitewash on a mud hut."

"Are you saying that we cannot knock them down, even if we rebuild the great Bear? Our weapons are iron—we can smash through any bronze. But this witchwood . . ." He shook his head. "That is something I do not understand, a magical wood as strong as forged metal."

Ayaminu made a swift gesture with one hand, as though catching a bird in mid-flight and then letting it go. "Anything can be knocked down. And even witchwood can be broken. Surely you have shattered a few Hikeda'ya swords in battle, so you know that it can be destroyed. But the older it is—the closer it is to its roots in the Garden and the purer its preparation—the more difficult it is to destroy. The gates are old. They have stood for thousands of years. Can you defeat them with a single iron ram? Only the Dance will tell."

"The dance?" Isgrimnur saw that Sludig was glaring. His liegeman did not like talk of spells and magic even in the context of preparing for a fight.

"The Dance of Time," the Sitha said, weaving her fingers in a swift pattern the duke could not follow. "The Dance of What Will Be. It is going on all around us and inside us. It seems to follow a set course of steps, but in truth there is no fixed pattern."

Isgrimnur scowled. "In other words, you don't know if we can knock the gate down."

"Of course not." This time she actually smiled. "But the tide seems to be with you. If there is ever a time when the gates might fall, that time is now. But many things still remain to be seen, and many steps must still be danced." Before Isgrimnur could protest the uselessness of her answers, Ayaminu pointed to a tall ring of standing rocks at the nearest edge of the ruined outer city. "There," she said. "Do you see that vast jumble of unroofed stone? That was once the great Sky Palace, the observatory where the Queen's Celebrants watched the stars."

"What happened to it? And why do you point it out?"

"What happened was that it was abandoned when men became too many and too fierce, as was all the rest of Nakkiga-That-Was, the city outside the mountain we are approaching. The reason I show it to you is because it would make a good place for camp. You do not wish to get too close to the mountain before you are ready, I think."

"Of course not. We will need to send out our scouts."

"Then I think the Sky Palace will make a good camp. There are still some cells that have roofs, where men and horses can sleep out of the cold, and it is far from Stormspike itself and spying eyes."

"This tumbledown Sky Palace of yours looks more like a trap than a refuge," Isgrimnur said, "or at least like a spot where I would plan an ambush if I were the White Foxes."

"I do not think you need fear an ambush. The Hikeda'ya are down to only a few fighters. They have not tried to stop you since you crossed into their lands because the mountain itself is their greatest defense. Their mistress Queen Utuk'ku is deep in what is called 'the dangerous sleep'—the Hikeda'ya have never been so weak as at this moment. As to camping in the Sky Palace, Isgrimnur, though you may not understand me, I promise you the ancient observatory has a . . . spirit of its own. That is the best I can explain it, and that spirit is not at all warlike, which is why it became a spot to contemplate the mysteries of the Sky Dance. I think your army will be safe there. The true danger is farther ahead, at the foot of the mountain itself. At the gates."

Isgrimnur looked from Ayaminu to Sludig, then at the array of titan stones before them, a few still suggesting the vague shapes of walls and arches and other structures, but far more of them toppled. The summer days were cold in these northern reaches but very long, and the men had been riding and marching for at least an hour or two longer than they normally would have.

"Well, then. I will take your advice," the duke said at last. "Sludig, ride to Jarl Vigri and tell him we will make camp in the Sky Palace there, as the lady names it."

Sludig, chewing on unspoken words, gave him a look that Isgrimnur thought bordered on insubordination; Sludig did not like magic, and he had good reason to fear it. Isgrimnur thought he might say something, but instead he only nodded and rode off to find Vigri.

Isgrimnur turned back to the great shadow of Stormspike, a spearhead jutting from the rocky ground and aimed at Heaven, a mute threat that could not be ignored however much he might have wished to turn back toward the lands he understood.

This is a lonely place, he thought. *This is a cold, lonely place we've come to.*

"Husband, come back to bed," said Khimabu. "The bell has not yet sounded."

It was true, the great stone bell in the Temple of the Martyrs had not rung the first hour of morning, but Viyeki had been awake for some time, sleepless and full of buzzing thoughts. "I must go, my wife. There is a meeting of the War Council."

She threw a slender arm across her eyes as he lit a taper. "You are not a member of the War Council, husband. Why must you go? Will you leave me to stand outside the council hall with the commoners and slaves, waiting for news? Yaarike will name you as his successor, will he not?"

"That is not for me to say. All I know is that he wants me there."

Khimabu sat up, the cover falling away. For a moment, as always, Viyeki was stunned by his wife's beauty, her graceful limbs and perfect, narrow face. His mouth dried as he looked at her. How much more astounding that she, a member of venerable Clan Daesa, should have let herself be joined to him. "You have been gone for months. Surely you will not desert me so soon?" She swung her long legs out of the bed and stood up, as unconcerned with her nakedness as a forest creature.

Looking at her—staring at her—as she began to dress, Viyeki was seized by contrasting moods. He was astonished to realize that this flawless scion of one of the oldest Nakkiga clans was his, but that was quickly followed, as it usually was, with the nagging question of why her parents and clansfolk had chosen him as the recipient of this great gift. Certainly few others except High Magister Yaarike had seen much potential in him, and Viyeki had labored long in thankless, middling obscurity for the Order of Builders before being lifted up.

"My wife," he said, and hesitated. She turned and saw him looking at her.

"Ah," she said. "Is there something else on your mind beyond the honor the old man is giving you? Would you perhaps like to see if this is the day we create an heir?" Her morning gown was not yet fastened, and she let it fall open to reveal her body of shadowed ivory. "I would not be unwilling . . ."

"My wife, we cannot celebrate, and we cannot make an heir—not this morning." He was surprised at how little he wanted her at this moment, when he should have been feeling triumphant and powerful. "This is the War Council. We are besieged. I cannot let my own selfish concerns keep me from attending Magister Yaarike. Leaders of all the orders will be there. How could I be the last to enter the Council Hall?"

In an instant the cold look that he so dreaded swept over her like a sudden storm around the mountain's peak. "No, how could you? And do you think you alone have tasks to do, husband? It is war, after all, as you said." She stared at him now as though he were not her mate but only a lowly servant. "I have my own work maintaining this household that you have so seldom visited lately, but I have also to feed and find places for all our workers and slaves whose homes near the gates have been sealed off at your own magister's orders."

"So that it can be better defended," he said with a calmness he did not feel. His wife's sudden angers always left him surprised and unprepared. "What else can be done? We are at war and that is where the enemy will attack."

"Of course, husband. But apparently your beloved master will not even allow you and your household the simple pleasure of celebrating your return and your long-deserved advancement."

"Khimabu, this is not the way . . ."

"I understand." She turned from him with a definite air of dismissal. "Your wife can wait. Making an heir can wait. Do you even *desire* an heir, Viyeki sey-Enduya, or have the mortals at our doorstep changed your mind about that, too?"

"Don't be foolish," he said, but seeing her expression he softened his tone. "You know that I do. If the Garden desires it and fate permits it, yes, my wife, of course I wish to make an heir with you." But after many Great Years without one, he wondered whether they would ever succeed, war or no.

"Then go to your council," she said as if that were something of little import, an amusement. "I will do my own work and think of how best to announce your rise to my kin and your underlings."

"No word of that can be spoken yet, Khimabu! Until my master informs the Celebrants, he still might change his mind."

"Is old Yaarike a fool?"

Even in the privacy of their bedchamber, such talk worried him. "No, of course he is not a fool."

"Then he will not change his mind. He will give my husband what my husband so richly deserves. And if my husband remembers what is important, so will I." She had banished the fury from her face, and now moved toward him, stopping just short. She took his hand and placed it on her breast through the thin fabric of the morning gown. He could feel her heart beating slowly and steadily. "So will I."

Outside the Council Hall, the Martyrs' Temple bell tolled again to mark the middle hour of morning, a deep, flat sound that always made Viyeki think of a heavy door falling shut. It was time for the council to begin.

He was surprised at how sparsely attended it was, how empty the huge, columned hall. Looking across the archaic witchwood table and its centerpiece, an arrangement of stones and living plants meant to symbolize the Garden that had birthed their race, Viyeki could not help wondering why so many of the other orders were not present—not Luk'kaya, High Gatherer of the Order of Harvesters, nor any representatives of other powerful orders like the Echoes.

Zuniyabe, chief of the Celebrants, was of course at the table with several lesser nobles of his order, but it could not have been a Queen's War Council without him, since he was the ultimate authority on tradition and the governing principles of the people.

Lord Akhenabi was absent, but his chief lieutenant Jikkyo, whose blind, white eyes belied his knowledge of all that concerned the Singers' order, had come in his master's place with underlings of his own, explaining that the Lord of Song was busy tending the slumbers of Queen Utuk'ku.

The Order of Sacrifice was doubly represented, both by General Suno'ku and the order's leader, Muyare, who had replaced dead Ekisuno as high marshal. Broad, stern-faced Muyare was Suno'ku's distant cousin, her senior, and—despite her fame and growing popularity among the lesser castes of Nakkiga—her commander.

When High Celebrant Zuniyabe indicated that they could start, Viyeki's master Yaarike extended his fingers in a gesture of polite inquiry. "What of the Harvesters, the Summoners, and the Echoes?" he asked. "I do not see any of them. Have they nothing to say to this council?"

"We thought it best to keep this small, so that we might talk as openly as possible." Suno'ku spoke before Zuniyabe or her superior had even opened their mouths. Viyeki thought Marshal Muyare looked a little regretful when he finally spoke.

"General Suno'ku is correct," he said. "We need only the orders who are already present to discuss the things that must occupy us today. And of course, that which concerns us most are the mortals who even now gather outside our door."

"And thus we strike the most important vein," said Zuniyabe. "Magister Yaarike, what news do you have on your order's preparations?"

Yaarike took a moment to consider the string of tally-beads before him. "Forgive me. In my age, I do not remember every detail as I should. That is why I have brought Host Foreman Viyeki. You all know him, I think."

The others nodded. The Singer Jikkyo turned a bland smile in Viyeki's direction. "We have not met, but I have heard his name. You are welcome to our deliberations, Host Foreman." Viyeki made a ritual gesture of gratitude, but he felt as though he had been greeted by a serpent who had not yet warmed enough to bite, but might soon feel up to it.

Formalities finished, Magister Yaarike went on to detail the various works in which the Order of Builders was occupied—shoring up defenses around and above the gate, clearing old tunnels which had fallen out of use but might be important in the days to come, and a dozen other such unsurprising tasks. Viyeki prompted him once or twice, but he doubted that his master had truly forgotten anything: it was Yaarike's way to seem more distracted and forgetful than he truly was, at least in public meetings.

"And our brave Sacrifices?" Zuniyabe asked when Yaarike had finished. "How do your preparations go, Marshal?"

Muyare made a sign of acceptance, acknowledging the question. High Celebrant Zuniyabe held no more power than the leader of any other order, and certainly was not as feared as Akhenabi, but as keepers of tradition the Celebrants gave shape to gatherings like these.

"As well as can be expected." Muyare glanced briefly at the scroll he had unrolled on the tabletop. "We suffered terrible losses in the south, as all know. Barely half a thousand trained Sacrifices remain here in Nakkiga, and even if others are still trying to return, they will not be able to pass the ring of mortals and their siege. We are desperately outnumbered."

The moment of silence that followed this did not last long. "Our danger is great, but we cannot only dwell on this present struggle," said General Suno'ku. "We need to think also of the future." Even though she did not speak loudly, the strong, clear tones of her voice drew their attention away from the marshal as if he had suddenly disappeared.

"And what does that mean, General?" asked Jikkyo. The blind Singer's hands were folded before him, his face toward the table as though in deep meditation, but it was impossible to ignore the sharpness in his voice. "If we do not succeed in the present, there *is* no future—or am I being unduly pessimistic?"

"I wish you were, Lord Jikkyo," said Suno'ku. "But the problems of tomorrow must not be ignored even in the midst of today's terrors."

"Enlighten us, then, please," said Yaarike, and anyone who did not know the man would have thought him brusque, but Viyeki recognized a hidden edge of mischief in his master's words. Surrounded by such venerable and powerful nobles, there were currents too deep for Viyeki to understand; he could not help admiring the way Suno'ku waded without hesitation into the dangerous waters.

"Yes, I will speak," she said, "but first my master Muyare would finish telling you of the preparations the Order of Sacrifice has made." She turned to him. "High Marshal?"

Suno'ku, despite her youth and rank, was all but giving orders to her superior, her own clansman. But instead of the cold indignation Viyeki expected, the marshal only nodded and then calmly outlined the various efforts his order was making to spread their thin troops over as many potential danger spots as possible. He answered the questions from the other councillors with a sort of numb honesty, as if he could not be bothered at this late date to pretend that their position was anything but hopeless.

"And the gate itself, Lord Jikkyo, Lord Yaarike?" Muyare asked when he had finished his recitation. "How long can it hold?"

Jikkyo unfolded his fingers and made a complicated sign that Viyeki did not understand, part of the Singers' own private language, never shared with other orders. "The gate, as well as many of our other most important measures of defense, has always been guarded by the queen's will. As she grew stronger, she was determined to keep her people safe. Health and long life to the Mother of All!"

The rest dutifully repeated it.

"But that is our greatest problem," Jikkyo continued in his soft voice. He seemed so much the gentle old man that it was hard to reconcile his appearance and manner with the dark tales Viyeki had heard about him, of disturbing exhibitions behind the closed doors of his ancient mansion and the terrifying fates of several of his rivals. But Viyeki did not doubt those rumors: only a creature of unbreakable will and great power could ever rise so high in the Order of Song.

"As you know," said Jikkyo, "after the disaster at Asu'a, the queen sleeps so deeply that it may be a long time until she awakens. We at this table are not children or slaves to be fed reassuring tales, so let us not chop our words too fine—our defeat in the south was terrible, and the queen suffered greatly from it. My master Akhenabi says that she will return to us, but even he in his awesome wisdom cannot say when, and we all doubt it will be soon. So the gate is weak. Yes, it is still a thing of stout witch-wood wound with the powerful songs of its making, but without the will of the waking queen behind it, it is but a *thing*. A mighty thing, but a thing nonetheless, and things can be broken."

Finished, he folded his fingers again and turned his sightless eyes toward the ceiling, as if in contemplation of something above and beyond the mountain itself.

"I can only echo what Lord Jikkyo has told us," Yaarike said. "My Builders will give their all to strengthen the mountain's defenses, including the gates, but our resources and time are limited."

A melancholy silence fell over the Council Hall.

"And the thing *you* wished to discuss, General Suno'ku?" asked Zuniyabe. "It seems it is now time to hear your idea. May the Garden grant it brings us some hope."

"I cannot speak to hope, which is an elusive and often false friend," she said. "What I suggest is simply this. If the gate is breached, then every dweller in our city must be armed, high caste or low, because there are not enough Sacrifices left to defend Nakkiga should the mortals enter."

Several voices spoke at once, but the High Celebrant gestured for silence. "Arm our slaves?" Zuniyabe asked, his legendary calm clearly taxed to its limit. "Are you truly suggesting we arm the lower castes and the slaves, General? To what point? If the Sacrifices fall and the high houses and orders are undefended, then even if the mortals were driven out again what would be left? A disorderly, armed rabble finally able to give vent to their mindless rage?"

"Better the chance of reestablishing order, I would think," said Suno'ku, "than the mortals left to murder, rape, and enslave as they wish."

All the nobles present had questions, although some of the remarks were closer to denunciations, and the argument quickly grew heated. It soon became clear that Marshal Muyare was not entirely in favor of such a scheme himself but seemed resigned to his younger relative having her way. "If we arm them, then they will be fighting the mortals alongside the Order of Sacrifice," Muyare said. "They will be commanded by trained warriors of our order. It will be up to us to maintain discipline. And as General Suno'ku says, we do not have the numbers otherwise to resist an invasion if the gates fail."

Zuniyabe spread his hands in a gesture of frustration. "I do not understand this. Like Lord Jikkyo, I see only evil coming from such a wild, unprecedented action."

"These are wild, unprecedented times," Suno'ku responded. "And before you finish expressing your disgust with my plan, there is more—as I said, we must think not just for today but for the future."

Yaarike, silent through most of the argument, now smiled. "It seems it is our day to entertain interesting ideas, General. Please do not stop now."

She looked at him hard for a moment, as though trying to decide where the Magister of Builders stood in the pantheon of allies and enemies gathered around the great witchwood table. "Very well. I suggest something that was mooted in the past, in the season when our queen sent the great nobles Sutekhi and Ommu and the others to the aid of Ineluki, the king in Asu'a, several Great Years ago. We must breed with the mortals."

Her words fell into utter silence. Even Muyare looked ashamed, though he did not gainsay her, and Viyeki could not help wondering what strange negotiations between the marshal and his younger relative had preceded the council.

"I cannot believe that I heard you correctly, General," said Zuniyabe. "Mortals? Breed with mortals? What blasphemy . . . ?"

"Please, High Celebrant, do not confuse exigency with blasphemy." Suno'ku had clearly come to the part of the gathering she had been anticipating since the start, and Viyeki watched as she began to assert control both over herself and the gathering by sheer force of will. Again, he was astonished that such a prodigy should have appeared at such a time, as if war and chaos were indeed the foundry of change. "As I said, this was spoken of before, in the days of High Celebrant Hikhi, good Zuniyabe's predecessor."

"And roundly rejected!" said Zuniyabe. "The queen herself said it would not be—could not be."

"Of course our queen is always correct," said Suno'ku. "But I think that if she were awake now, she would see that what was bad then has become worse. Think, fellow nobles, think! Our numbers were already dwindling. Long ago we began using mortal slaves to oversee other mortal slaves, and low-caste Hikeda'ya to keep peace among their fellows, because we nobles were too few and our children born too infrequently. But the mortals, both inside and outside our mountain, breed swiftly. If we do not change we will perish, if not by mortals storming our gates then by rebellion here in Nakkiga. All of us—your spouses and children and clansfolk, too—will die in our beds, or be paraded like the scorned losers of the mortals' wars before being torn to pieces by a baying mob." She leaned forward, and her voice became lower, less demanding. "Think on what I say. Only five hundred blooded, death-sung Sacrifices remain! And after the siege, even if we survive it, how many will still live then? Half that number? Fewer? My lords, we feed more than ten thousand peasants and mortal slaves here in Nakkiga. We of the ruling orders are already so few that, after two costly, failed wars, if our underlings did not fear the mortals beyond our mountain more than their own rulers, we nobles would all be in terrible danger."

Again, silence fell, although Viyeki thought it felt like the agitated air just before a storm. But before Zuniyabe could walk out of the council, or someone else say something that would turn the talk from argument into deadly insult, Yaarike let out a strange sound—a whistle, a snatch of melody that Viyeki recognized as an old song from Tumet'ai called "The Musician and the Soldier." The others in the room turned to him, as surprised as Viyeki.

Instead of explaining, Yaarike continued the tune until he had finished the refrain, then said, "I am curious, General Suno'ku, how such matings would be regulated. Would all the noble houses descend to the streets and rut with the lower creatures, or would there be fairs or games of honor so that we could choose the least disgusting?"

Suno'ku did a poor job of hiding her irritation. "Please, High Magister, give me some credit for sense. You know as well as I that many of our high nobility, male and female, already take mortals for lovers, and that sometimes children are born of these unions, however distasteful you find that fact."

Yaarike smiled again. "I find nothing distasteful but death, General, and even that has begun to look more friendly in recent days. But the children of slaves have always been slaves. You would change that?"

Suno'ku shook her head. "Unusual and unprecedented as it may seem, I suggest that noble parents must adopt those children, despite their mongrel blood. They will grow more swiftly than our own children—much more swiftly, as we know from watching the mortals increase through all the lands we once ruled. If these halfblood children are raised by the noble caste and schooled in the orders, who is to say that they will not be just as loyal subjects of the queen as any others?"

"You claimed that *I* confused blasphemy with exigency," said High Celebrant Zuniyabe, sounding more astonished now than angry. "But I think it is you who are confused, General. How can halfbloods feel what true Hikeda'ya feel?"

She shrugged, a very broad gesture for one of her caste and rank. "Test them. Like all entrants into the orders, they will enter into Yedade's Box. Nothing says we must take them all. In fact, the harder they must work to achieve what the true-born receive as their due, I think the more they will value it. And we will birth thousands of Sacrifices for the Queen."

"Tell me what you think of this madness, Jikkyo?" Zuniyabe demanded. "I am astonished beyond reply. What will Lord Akhenabi make of it?"

Jikkyo took a long time to speak. "I do not know. My master is subtle, and there may be branches and twigs to this plan that I cannot see, although I am much of your mind, Zuniyabe. I could not make such a decision on my own. I will let you know his thought."

Across the table, Suno'ku made a gesture of "patience agreed." It was as clear to Viyeki as it was to the rest that even if the Order of Sacrifice and all the others present supported it, no such policy was possible without the agreement of the Lord of Song.

"One last question," said Yaarike. "Marshal Muyare, even if we all agree to consider such an unprecedented and perilous change of policy, many questions remain. What would we do with so many new Hikeda'ya? If we breed halfbloods anywhere near as fast as mortals breed more mortals, surely the time will come when our sacred mountain is too small to shelter us all."

Muyare spread his hands; he still seemed reluctant to argue on his relative's behalf. "Perhaps. But it would be good to have our order at strength again."

"Esteemed Magister Yaarike, you forget something," said Suno'ku. "With the ranks of Sacrifices replenished and our other orders strengthened, we could again turn our hearts to what we all desire—taking back the lands the mortals have stolen from us. Then we would have as much room as we need."

"Another war?" asked Yaarike, but mildly.

"Our enemies' final destruction," said Suno'ku, and for a moment Viyeki saw the hard stone of which she was made, the unbending determination of her blood and upbringing. "We cannot share this land with them—surely we all agree on that. Eventually, one of our races must perish. On my oath as a Queen's Sacrifice, I will make sure it is the mortals."

Porto's father, dead these nine years, had been a carpenter. Porto spent much of his childhood in the Rocks, scrambling up and down ladders, fetching tools, and holding boards in place, so he volunteered to shore up the ranks of army carpenters in cutting and preparing a new pole to hold up the head of the great Bear.

The ram's iron head was immense, but Isgrimnur's men had found an ancient grove of trees at one end of the abandoned city before the mountain, and some of the older trunks there were almost unbelievably large. The leader of the duke's carpenters, a quiet but short-tempered man named Brenyar, chose a peppered birch over sixty cubits tall, a fit size to use for the battering ram's shaft. The wood was very hard, but Porto and a dozen others ax-wielders brought it down in less than a day and began to trim away the largest branches while other workers chopped down smaller trees to make rollers, which would let the great ram smash against the gates at greater speed.

Porto liked the work, but he had asked to join the carpenters in large part because he so badly needed to get away from Endri, at least for a short time. Since arriving at the mountain he had spent much of every day taking care of the younger man, cleaning his wound, giving him water, and trying to keep him warm and fed. He also had listened, and listened, and listened, because despite his weakness, Endri almost never stopped talking. Half the time he was inaudible, his speech little more than murmured sighs, but other times he wept with pain and begged his mother to come and take him home. After days of this, Porto was beginning to feel as though it might turn him mad.

Before leaving to help the woodcutters and carpenters with the day's work, he had managed to get Endri to take a little broth from their thin morning stew, made from a few tiny potatoes and an even smaller handful of soft-footed mushrooms he had gathered. The boy had not only eaten some but also managed to keep it down as well. That had heartened Porto, and as he wrapped Endri up in his own cloak, thinking that the active work in the ancient grove would be enough to keep himself warm, Porto promised the youth he would find something better for their pot that evening. But as it turned out, by the time his work was finished he had little strength left to hunt rabbits or squirrels, so he traded a tiny handful of potatoes to one of the other woodcutters for a bit of salt beef. It would take a while for the dried meat to soften and flavor the stew, Porto knew, but what else did he have here at the cold, gray end of the earth but time?

Endri was asleep when Porto got back to the camp. He made no attempt to wake him but added wood to the fire and put the dented pot on it to boil, which took much longer here than at home. He had chosen a spot separate from the rest of Duke Isgrimnur's troops so that Endri's moaning and mumbling would not keep the other soldiers awake, and now he scoured his tiny fiefdom in search of herbs for the pot. He found something that looked like white onion grass, and when he cautiously nibbled it he found to his delight that it tasted like the stuff as well. He pulled up a large handful and returned. The pot was just beginning to bubble.

"Ah, you'll like tonight's meal," he said as he squatted beside the fire. "Endri, are you awake yet? You won't taste a finer one even in the duke's tent."

Endri said nothing, so Porto leaned over and gave him a gentle shake. "Come on, lad. If you don't get up, you'll miss the feast." But something felt wrong, as though someone had stolen Endri away and replaced him with something solid and immobile.

Porto turned the youth over. Endri's face was slack; his eyes were open, but already they had filmed over. He did not look peaceful, but he did not look pained, either, and that was a small solace. He had been dead for hours.

The meal forgotten and the water boiling away to nothing, Porto slumped down beside the body and wept until the wind made his cold, wet cheeks burn.

He did not want to bury his friend in direct sight of the looming mountain, so he dragged the body to a clearing in a stand of young evergreens at the outer edge of the grove where he had been working. As the long northern twilight waned he scraped and hacked at the hard ground with his axe until he had made a trench deep enough to keep Endri safe from scavengers. Porto reluctantly took back his cloak but felt like a robber for doing it, so he made a bed of pine branches and then cut more branches to make a blanket to cover the body. He briefly considered taking the young man's prized Harborside scarf to return it to the lad's mother, but in the end he could not do it. Never once had Endri taken it off, and his pride in his old *setro* had been one of the most notable things about him. Buried in this bleak, foreign land, without a tombstone, he could at least go into the next life with something he prized, something that had reminded him of his home.

As it grew darker and the stars, like shy children, came out to watch him, Porto laid his friend in the grave and covered him over with fragrant pine boughs, then carefully filled the hole with earth. As he piled heavy stones on top to protect Endri's resting place he could hear other soldiers camped just a short way from him, their quiet conversations beyond his hearing but their voices murmurous as a river, and he wondered in a strange, empty way how many of them would also lie cold beneath these skies before all was done. At last, as night settled onto the north, he kneeled beside the mound and recited the few prayers he could remember.

"So began the Siege of Nakkiga.

"The mortals in their thousands swarmed across the plain at the mountain's foot, making their camp in the fallen houses of our ancestors like snakes in an ancient wall, bringing their great ram and other engines to attack our city's gates. At first the queen's Sacrifices and other orders were in disarray, but Marshal Muyare of the Iyora clan and his descendant-cousin General Suno'ku took the remnants of the Sacrifice army and began to train all Hikeda'ya, male and female, old and young, for a desperate defense of Nakkiga.

"Nor were the other orders idle, and many deeds of unsung heroism were done by the Builders of Lord Yaarike to shore up the city's defenses, and by the Harvesters of Lady Luk'kaya, who labored long and hard in the mountain's deep gardens to feed the people after a long era of war and its hardships.

"The Celebrants and the Echoes bound the other orders together in a web of shared thought. In the midst of all these measures, Akhenabi, the Lord of Song, prepared his order for a great strike against the mortal enemy, to weaken their hearts and turn the taste of their presumed triumph to ashes in their mouths.

"At first all that our people could do to fight the invaders was to attack them from above the gate, tunnels, and emplacements dug in centuries past by the Builders of old. Hikeda'ya struck from secret places along the mountainside, which had long fallen out of use and had to be cleared anew. From these hidden places the finest archers of the Order of Sacrifice rained death on the Northmen, killing many more than they lost.

"Yaarike's Builders, working with the masters of both the Singers

and the Caster engineers, created machines which could throw fire and flaming bolts down on the attackers from these high places, and at first these new engines found great success. Three times did the Northmen try to bring their great ram to the mountain's gates, and three times were they driven back, their hoardings in flame, and many of the ram's wielders dead or terribly burned.

"But the Northmen were determined not to lose their chance to destroy the Hikeda'ya, and so they chose the best climbers from their ranks and set them to scale our great mountain and silence its defenders. Terrible battles took place along the steep mountain tracks, in its darker places, even before the steaming vents that gave forth from Nakkiga's flaming heart. And though our Sacrifices fought bravely, they were greatly outnumbered by the mortals, who could spend men like cheap coins, and at last the Northmen were able to bring their great war engine to the gates. Soon the Northmen had found nearly all of our tunnels along the mountainside, and many pitched battles were fought where the mountain's precious interior touched the outer air. Those passages that had been secret but now were found out were quickly sealed by the queen's Order of Builders, sometimes even as those defending it still remained on the far side, so that the mortals could not come at Nakkiga from those ways. Then the Northerners in turn buried the outside of those passages beneath stone so that we could not use them again even if we chose, and began to find and destroy the few hidden passages still left to us from which our Sacrifices could harry the mortals. The ways into and out of the mountain now nearly all made useless, the battle narrowed to the ground around the great gates themselves.

"The mortals' rebuilt ram was covered with plates of hammered black iron to repel arrows and spears, and its body was the trunk of a great birch tree, the oldest that had stood in the old city's Sacred Grove, which had once been our Garden on this faulty earth, the hallowed spot where traitors and unruly slaves had been sacrificed at the turning of every Great Year, until the Well of Eternity was discovered in the depths of the mountain.

"The gates of Nakkiga themselves had been set up before the days of

the Parting, even before the queen first came into possession of the city, and they were strongly built and full of old songs. Even the mortals' mighty ram with its iron head in the shape of a savage bear could not cast it down, but the Northmen had the scent of blood in their nostrils and would not turn away from their purpose.

"Hour after hour, day after day, the ram crashed against the gate's witchwood timbers, and each blow echoed through Nakkiga's squares and across the houses of the city like the tread of some fearsome creature. It seemed that even the gate must fall at last if the Northmen could not be driven back.

"In that terrible hour, one of our nobles took it upon himself to save the city. General Nekhaneyo of Clan Shudra, the greatest warrior of his illustrious family, gathered three score of brave Sacrifices, each one a hero many times over in the Wars of Return, and after consulting with the Celebrants and other loremasters, led his troop into perhaps the last passage still hidden from the mortals, a secret track through the roots of the mountain, untraveled since the days of Ur-Nakkiga's first conquest by our people.

"We will never know what horrors they found there, or what terrors they faced, but when the brave ones emerged once more into the light of day from a forgotten cavern at the mountain's base near the shores of Lake Rumiya, their numbers had been almost halved, and many of those who remained bore dreadful wounds and burns.

"But with the hourly battering of the mighty gates bringing disaster ever nearer, their leader would not give them rest. Nekhaneyo told his warriors, "We are already dead and our ends sung! Let what we have already lost bring freedom to those we loved! For the Queen and the Garden!"

"Their heroic charge will be talked of as long as the Hikeda'ya live and as long as our Garden is remembered. Nekhaneyo led his survivors by cover of darkness around the mountain's foot, riding so fast that it is said their horses' hooves struck sparks from the stones in their path. They came upon the Northmen at the gate just before dawn. With surprise on their side, they slaughtered the sleeping mortals by the hundreds, and would have laid fire to the ram itself had not the mortals' leader, Duke

Isgrimnur of Elvritshalla, rallied his startled troops and led them in counterattack.

"The mortals swarmed like rats, and though Nekhaneyo fought his way through their unending numbers until he had almost reached the Northmen's leader, he fell at last, hacked and almost bloodless, a few scant steps from the mortal duke. The rest of his brave Sacrifices were soon surrounded and pulled down. So ended Nekhaneyo's Ride, and it seemed at that moment that Nakkiga's doom was sealed.

"When they heard of Nekhaneyo's fall the people surrounded the Council Hall, crying out that all was lost and demanding that the sleeping queen be taken down into the mountain's depths so that at least the Mother of All would be saved. But Host General Suno'ku, a great favorite of the people, stood on the steps of the hall and called them all cowards, shaming them, and asking how Nakkiga could fail when so many of them yet lived.

" 'Are there no stones to be cast?' " she demanded. " 'Are there no sticks to be sharpened into spears, no ancient witchwood blades of our ancestors hanging on walls to be taken down and given the chance once more to drink mortal blood? Have all the Hikeda'ya been destroyed already, leaving only ghosts who wail and lament?'

"When she had silenced them, Suno'ku gave them heart again, saying that it was better to die standing than to kneel to a conqueror and still receive death, or worse, to be made a slave. She reminded them of great Hamakho himself, who had walked all the way through Tzo with a dozen fatal arrows in him, and she called out the names of her own ancestors, including Ekimeniso himself.

" 'Do you think when we meet someday in the Garden that I could face the shade of my great foreparent, our queen's consort, if I laid down my arms and let the mortals have their way? Do you think I could bear his gaze if I knew that I had let fear make me a weak thing? Eight hundred seasons gone I killed a mortal slave in combat to win my rank in the Order of Sacrifice. Why should I not rejoice to think that I may yet kill dozens more in defense of my homeland?'

"Their spirit restored by her words, the people dispersed back to their houses and living quarters, determined to fight to their last breath and last

*drop of blood. And some said that in that hour Suno'ku became as great
a hero as her legendary foreparent, Ekimeniso of the Brooding Eye."*

—Lady Miga seyt-Jinnata of the Order of Chroniclers

Aerling Surefoot was a wiry, dark-bearded Rimmersman with hands that looked too big for his arms. When Porto offered his services, the frowning man asked only two questions.

"Can you climb?"

"I was raised on housetops. My father was a carpenter."

"Not quite the same, falling off a house and falling off a mountain. But we'll see. Can you follow orders?"

"Yes, sir."

Aerling looked him up and down. "You're a bit tall for scrambling in some of the small spaces we have to use, but at least you're thin. 'Twill help." He narrowed his eyes. "You're not scared of these whiteskins, are you?"

"No. I hate them." Endri's empty face still came to him every night in his dreams, his friend's ghost silent and sad. "I want to see them all dead."

"You'll get no argument here." Aerling finished sharpening his knife, wiped the whetstone on his breeks and slid it into his pack. "Just remember, they may look like dead 'uns but they're as alive as you or me. Full of tricks, yes, but when you cut them, the same red blood comes out. When you kill them, they're as dead as any ordinary man."

"Did you fight them at the Hayholt?"

Aerling shook his head. "Not me. I was here in the north, where we had battles of our own. When Skali Sharp-Nose fell in Hernystir we marched on Kaldskryke to take it back for Duke Isgrimnur. The people opened the gates for us—they'd had enough of Sharp-Nose long before— but Skali's son Geli, that scheming little coward, wouldn't surrender. He took his remaining men and climbed up to the top of St. Asla's church tower. Sealed the stairs with rubble, they did, then sat up there shooting arrows at any of the duke's men who dared to show themselves in the center of town. Thane Unnar sent me and a number of my men up there."

"I thought you said the stairway was blocked."

"We didn't take the stairs, you tall lummox, we climbed it the way we climb the cliffs back home in Ostheim. Ropes, man, ropes. And if you don't know your knots, you'd better learn quick, because you don't want to be fumbling with an overhand bend while someone's trying to put an arrow in your eye." He stared at Porto for another long moment, then reached into his pack and pulled out a looped coil of strong cord. "Here. See that man with half his beard burned off? No, don't ask him why or he'll tell you the whole bloody, boring story. That's Old Dragi. Tell him I said he should show you how to tie an overhand bend and a few other useful things—and how to *untie* them, too, for that's sometimes just as important. Come back to me tomorrow evening and show me what you've learned."

"What happened in the tower?"

"What's that?"

"The tower of St. Asla's. You said you climbed it."

"Of course we bloody well climbed it."

"Well . . . what happened?"

Aerling snorted. "Put it this way. Being Skali's son, young Geli may have had a beak on him like a bird, but he couldn't fly like one."

It was becoming very clear to Viyeki that the informality he had enjoyed with Lord Yaarike during their flight from the southern lands was now truly gone. He had to wait in the antechamber for his master's time just like any other high official of the Builders' order.

Viyeki noticed other high officials looking at him more than they generally did, some curiously, some with scarcely hidden resentment. He wondered whether Yaarike had already told some of them about his plan to make Viyeki his successor. Whatever the case, the magister seemed in no hurry to see him; Viyeki spent a long time waiting in the antechamber.

At last the door to the inner sanctum swung open and several figures emerged. General Suno'ku was in the lead, her pale hair bound in tight military braids, her owl helmet under her arm. As she and the other Sacrifices walked past, faces resolutely empty, she saw Viyeki and slowed long enough to nod formally to him.

"Try and talk sense into your high magister," she said quietly as she passed, and in that instant he suddenly perceived the force of her contained anger and had to resist the urge to step back, as if from an open flame.

Yaarike sat behind the wide table in the middle of his sanctum, almost hidden behind mounds of maps and building plans. Viyeki's first thought was that his master had aged tremendously in the last months. Yaarike's back was as straight as ever, and the hands holding the documents were steady, but there was something in his eyes and face that Viyeki had not seen before, a suggestion of weakness that he could not quite identify but could not ignore. Was it despair, or something more complicated? The continual pounding of the Northmen at the gates had become a drumbeat of approaching doom, and the entire city seemed to shuffle to its rhythm. Only the rigorous training of their orders—or the active threat of overseers with whips—kept both the high and low castes at their work.

"Come in, Viyeki-*tza*," Yaarike said when he saw him. "Close the door. Have you been to the Singers' order-house?"

"I have been there, yes, but that is all. I told my name and my commission to the speakstone in the courtyard but they did not open the doors or even answer." Scorned and ignored, Viyeki had felt like a mere messenger instead of a magister's heir.

Yaarike slowly shook his head. "Lord Akhenabi is determined to win the war by himself."

"But why, Master? Why will he not work with you?"

"Oh, he sends his minions when it is necessary. And it is not me he resists, but cooperation with the Order of Sacrifice."

Yaarike seemed to be doing Viyeki the honor of speaking to him as an equal again, or nearly, and that eased the host-foreman's mind. "It is a bad time for rivalry," was all he said. "The mortals are at our door."

"The queen is asleep," said the high magister, shaking his head. He lifted an ornament from the table, the skull of a *witiko'ya*, one of the long-toothed, wolflike creatures who had made the lands around Ur-Nakkiga their home before the Hikeda'ya came. Carvings all over the city portrayed the great hunts of yore, of Ekimeniso and even Queen Utuk'ku herself riding in pursuit of the deadly beasts, carrying no weapon but hunting spears. "The queen is asleep and the mortals, as you correctly observe, are at the door. Now is *precisely* the time for rivalry. When our revered Utuk'ku is awake, all of the ambitious lords and ladies are bottled in a jar like flies and can only buzz in circles, gaining small advantages here or there. No, now is the time for those who want it to grab for power." Yaarike laughed sourly. "In fact, there may never be another chance like this, Host Foreman. They are playing for high stakes in the very shadow of destruction."

"I saw General Suno'ku in the antechamber," Viyeki said. "She told me, 'Try and talk sense into your master.' If I may be so bold, Magister, what did she mean?"

Yaarike set down the long-toothed skull and flicked a bit of dust from its low crown. "She wants my help to force Lord Akhenabi into line, because I am one of the eldest of the order-magisters—almost as august as Akhenabi himself." He showed a wry smile that had little warmth. "She thinks the Lord of Song unwilling to bend himself to the greater good."

"And is she right?"

"Of course she is, as she defines it. But Akhenabi has always considered the greater good to mean what is best for the Order of Song. And for himself."

"So there is nothing you can do."

"Oh, there are things I may yet accomplish before I leave this world. Important things for the survival of our race. But these are not your concerns, Viyeki-*tza*. You will follow me to the magister's chair, if I have my way. But you will not *be* me, nor should you. There may yet be some great calamity in my future, and I wish you to remain separate from me in the thoughts of those outside our order. We will have to stop meeting, at least in the open."

Viyeki felt something like a blow against his heart. "Stop meeting . . . ?"

"I have my reasons."

"Magister, surely nothing you could do . . ."

"I have my reasons."

Viyeki had not heard his master's voice so stern and unyielding toward him since his earliest time in the order. His hands moved rapidly: *I am admonished*, followed by a second sign that meant *silent as the stone*.

In a flat tone Yaarike said, "And yet I can see you still have questions."

It was true, Viyeki's heart was full of pain that he had thought was hidden. He was unhappy to know he had revealed himself so easily. "Yes,

High Magister, I fear that I do. Why is Host Foreman Naji appointed to the greatest task?"

Yaarike eyed him expressionlessly. "What greatest task is that?"

"The work around the mountain's gates, Magister. The work to improve our only protection against the Northmen." Viyeki looked down at the stone flags instead of at his master and tried to find an appropriate composure.

"Ah," said Yaarike after a long moment. "I wondered what was troubling you. I could see it behind your movements." The High Magister pushed his chair back from the table and stood, showing his age in the deliberate way he did it. For a moment Viyeki spotted a bright flash of firelight at Yaarike's throat, or so it seemed. Seeing the Heart of What Was Lost again, even for a brief instant, made him think of the proud moment when Yaarike had trusted him with the safety of his family treasure. But the news of Naji's appointment had made that triumph seem hollow.

"I will walk you to the door," the magister said. "Yes, it is time for you to go, Host Foreman. Learn to measure yourself. Excess of anything is hard to hide—joy, anger, sorrow. And when you reveal yourself, you reveal yourself to your enemies as well as your allies."

"Yes, Master. But I still do not fully understand."

"That may change."

Viyeki took a deep breath. "I beg pardon, High Magister, but even if you cast me from the order, I cannot be silent. The work at the gates is by far the most important task we have. All our lives rest on it. Host Foreman Naji is not up to this challenge. He is a solid workman, but he has not the skill for such a task."

The older man looked at him for a long time, long enough that Viyeki could feel his own heart beat more swiftly at the length of his master's silence. It generally augured either fury or amusement, but little in between.

"I have met no finer Builder's sensibility than yours in all my years in the order," Yaarike finally said. "Your grasp of figures and your imagination, which has startled even me—" He broke off. "But I must take more into account than simply skill, Host Foreman. Or ambition. I must make the decisions I think best for all. And this is my decision. Do your work in the deep tunnels, and do it well. If you fear Naji's abilities are not sufficient, all the more reason for you to prepare a final refuge for our queen and people."

Viyeki did not speak until he felt himself in strict control once more. "If that is your desire, High Magister, of course I will do as you wish."

"Learn to mask your feelings better, Viyeki." Yaarike came forward and took his arm as if in companionship, though it might also have been a sign of the magister's weakness. "In that at least you are definitely Naji's inferior—he is as stolid as the stones he piles. Do not let your emotions blow you like the wind. And do not brood. This is not your fault, but mine. I should not have told you so soon that I wanted you as my successor."

"You have changed your mind, then."

"Young fool!" said Yaarike. "It was not necessary for anyone else to know it yet, and it has made you an object of interest. We must do our best to quell that interest."

"But if you have not informed the Celebrants, how does anyone know? I saw how the others looked at me."

Yaarike ignored the question. "From now on, you will come to me only when summoned, Viyeki. You will confine your correspondence with me to the facts of your work in the deeps. You will answer all questions about your future role in this order with polite evasion. Do you understand?"

"I do." But still his heart was beating wildly.

His master seemed remote now. "The days ahead will be difficult and dangerous, not just for the Order of Builders but for all the Hikeda'ya. General Suno'ku is on the rise. Akhenabi will not give in, although he may make a show of doing so. The dance is barely begun, yet already disaster waits at every step, every turn. And if the mortals break down the gates, nothing else will matter anyway. We will disappear like one of those stars that lights the whole sky and then burns to a cinder and is forgotten. Now you are dismissed."

As Viyeki turned for the doorway, Yaarike reached out and touched his sleeve. "One last thing."

Startled by even such a small, informal contact, Viyeki stopped short. "Yes, Master?"

"I do not wish to interfere in the domain of your home, Viyeki-*tza*, but I strongly advise you to stop your wife from crowing to her relatives in the orders of Sacrifice and Song about your good fortune. No good will come of it. Is that clear?"

Something cold settled in the pit of his stomach. Khimabu, despite his warnings, had told her family. "Yes, Master. Very clear."

The door swung shut. Viyeki had just enough time as he turned to compose his face into a mask of perfect placidity before he walked out past the other supplicants gathered in the high magister's antechamber.

Porto's days merged into what seemed an endless succession of climbing and huddling out of the wind interspersed with moments of sheer terror. He did his best not to think about his home and his wife and child, because what good would that do? He was stuck here at the end of the world, in the most foreign of foreign lands, and he had no more control over whether he would ever return to Perdruin than he did over the stars wheeling through the night sky.

He had plenty of time to watch those stars because, despite exhaustion, most nights he could not easily fall asleep, haunted by ghosts old and new. And since a few of their tunnels still lay undiscovered, the mountainside belonged to the Norns after dark; any mortal rash enough to tread in their domain, or even make himself unnecessarily visible, would usually be found dead in the morning with a single black arrow lodged in a vital spot.

But during the daytime the mortals' greater numbers gave the Mountain Goats, as Porto's troop dubbed itself, an advantage that they pressed as hard as they could, overwhelming the small groups of Norn bowmen they encountered on the mountain's rocky sides—although seldom without a pitched and often deadly struggle. The fairies seemed to have run out of magical tricks, but that only meant they fought more fiercely; one of the White Foxes, already disarmed and all but dismembered, had still managed to drag a comrade of Porto's to the ground and sink teeth into the man's neck before any of the others could help him. Porto and the others had pulled the Norn off him and stabbed the pale creature until it stopped moving, but the man it had attacked bled to death.

Porto could not have hated the White Foxes more, their unnatural quickness, their near-identical faces, their utter refusal to surrender, but he also recognized their bravery. Outnumbered and driven to ground like badly wounded animals, they fought to the last breath for their land. He hated these things that had killed Endri, Brindur's son, Floki, and so many others, but he also had to respect their courage.

Would I do the same, if it were my home and my wife in danger—my sweet Sida? Or little Tinio? He believed he would. He prayed that he would, but only God knew with certainty what a man would do when such a time came.

Hours became days, each day with its mountainside patrol, and virtually every patrol with its ration of sudden danger and death. Days became sennights, and the grave trenches the Northmen had dug were filled and covered over and more trenches started, but still the Nakkiga Gates held—still the mountain would not yield. The air, always cold, began to turn colder. The sleet that blew into their faces as the Mountain Goats clambered over the treacherous high slopes felt as hard and sharp as daggers.

Summer was waning and autumn was coming down across the north. The winter—the true, deadly winter that even the hardiest Rimmersmen feared—was on the way. And Porto and his fellows were trapped in its path like beetles exposed in a shattered log.

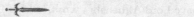

Troop Governor Ruho'o looked up from his position of supplication as though ready for execution. He held up his hands in the gesture commonly called *release to the parent*, something taught to children that apparently still remained even after all the training the Builders' order gave its officers.

"They will not go farther, Host Foreman," the governor said without meeting Viyeki's eye. "The shame is on me and my house. I should execute them all, but I cannot."

Viyeki generally did not believe in executing balky workers, especially at a time when trained Builders were in short supply, but he was tempted to make an exception now, starting with the Troop Governor himself.

"Do they not understand their people's need?" Viyeki added an appropriate edge of contempt to his words. "We are preparing a place for our folk to shelter if the gates fall. If there is no water close to that shelter, not even the Order of Song can save us—they cannot sing it up out of pure stone. Our people will all die gasping from thirst, like the proud walking fish in the ancient stories. Like animals. Even the queen herself!" He narrowed his eyes. "I should have these shirkers dig a pit and cast themselves in. You too, though live burial is better than you deserve."

The governor fell forward, sprawled on his face at Viyeki's feet, and moaned. "Take the head from my shoulders, Host Foreman!" he begged. "I have failed you, the Garden, and the Mother of All."

"And what good would your head do me?" Viyeki fought to keep his peevishness in check. "It is too ugly to make much of a trophy. Get up and tell me why your charges are willing to die instead of obeying orders that come not just from me, but from High Magister Yaarike himself."

Ruho'o backed slowly into a crouching position. "The workers are frightened, Lord Viyeki. Nobody but the Order of Song ever goes into those depths by choice, and only the Singers ever come back out again. The workers say . . . they say they cannot help themselves. They take a few steps into the downward tunnels and their hearts squeeze like a fist in their chests until they almost swoon. Something is down there."

"Of course something is down there. Many things are down there. The mountain is ours, though, and nothing down there is to be feared. We have Lord Akhenabi's word."

"All the same, there are still four of our engineers missing, Lord, the ones you sent first into the lower tunnels. They did not return. But some of the men say they heard those engineers' voices. Pleading for someone . . ." The foreman hesitated. "Pleading for someone to come and wake them. That is what I have heard."

"But you did not hear this yourself." Viyeki scowled. Perhaps a few executions would be necessary after all.

"No. But one of them, old Sasigi, appeared to me in a dream. I swear it is true! He said that they were all lost in the darkness. A darkness that *breathed*. And that he feared if he did not find his way out again, it would find him and chew him and swallow him down, and he would never awaken again."

"Superstition," said Viyeki, but that did not keep superstitious fear from tickling the nape of his own neck. "A dream, only. I expect more of you than to spread this kind of thing, Governor Ruho'o." He composed himself. "How many of the men are refusing to do their duty?"

The governor looked at him with something like wonder. "Why, all of them, Lord. I would not trouble you otherwise."

It was an impossible situation. Viyeki could not help imagining what his master Yaarike would think when he failed at even this less glorious task after complaining about Naji being given the work around the great gates. But short of killing enough valuable workers to frighten the rest into compliance, what could he do? The caverns known as the Forbidden Deeps cut right across the path of the new canal, and it seemed impossible to dig around them swiftly enough to make a refuge ready before the Northmen broke down the gates. Nor was Viyeki such a fool as to completely discount the men's fears. He knew they had good reasons to dislike the deepest places.

Even after the Hikeda'ya had held Nakkiga for close to fifty Great Years—three long millennia as mortals would reckon it—the mountain still held many secrets. The Order of Song knew some of them, which was part of what gave them such power in the queen's city, but the mountain had hidden depths that even Akhenabi and perhaps even Queen Utuk'ku herself might hesitate to plumb. Viyeki had felt the terror of those deep places himself in his early years, the freezing claw that gripped the heart and turned all one's thoughts into leaves swept up in a howling gale. He had even once seen Yaarike himself turn back from a place that he said was "too dark to enter," though the high magister had held a brightly burning torch. How to force mere laborers?

He could see no other choice. "Go back and keep the men quiet, Troop Governor Ruho'o. Occupy them with some of the finishing work in the tunnels that are already completed. I will devise a solution. And spread no more tales, nor let others spread them!"

"Go back?" For an instant the governor, who had come prepared to be executed for his failure, did not look overwhelmingly grateful that he was being sent back, but he quickly smoothed his expression into blankness. "Yes, my lord. You are very wise. I will do just as you say."

Though he could hear the sounds of hammers striking stone in many other parts of the city, Viyeki thought the Street of Eight Ships, usually bustling with workers and their overseers, was strangely quiet today. It made the constant shuddering boom of the mortals' mighty ram even more dreadful. The Builders' order-house was all but empty, and the functionary outside the High Magister's sanctum told him that Yaarike was out somewhere, supervising one of the many sites where the Builders were laboring to protect the city. Viyeki was frustrated, but since the functionary could not or would not tell him precisely where Yaarike was, Viyeki had already turned to leave when he met High Foreman Naji in the doorway.

Naji, always correctly courteous, made the appropriate gesture of greeting to an approximate equal, reminding Viyeki that whatever he might have been promised, at this point he was only one among several Host Foremen that Yaarike commanded.

"Is the old man in a good mood?" Naji asked.

"He is not here." Viyeki was suddenly curious. "Is he not at your site at the gates?"

"He has scarcely been there—not for days. Perhaps we have earned his confidence, and so he chooses to spend his time elsewhere." Naji was an unemotional type, generally uninterested in things he had not already learned, but he was no fool, as his look of deliberately bland inquiry demonstrated. "Why do you seek him?"

The last thing Viyeki wished to do was to talk about his unruly workers—it would have been hard enough to admit it to the high magister. "Nothing—a trifle. How goes your work on the gate?"

Naji made a gesture of sufficiency. "It still stands. But the great bolts are slowly shaking free of the surrounding stone, of course. With all the weight above it, if the gate is not flush, that will put great strain on the lintel." For a moment he seemed ready to talk about their shared profession, but a sudden look of distrust flashed across his face, and his posture became more rigid. "But are you not in charge of the refuge down in the deeps? What brings you back up to the city?"

"As I said, a trifle—just an idea I wished to discuss with the High Magister." Viyeki wanted to end this conversation. If word of his troubles with his workers filtered back up to the city, the other High Foremen would see his visit to the order-house for what it truly was—desperation. "If you see our master, tell him I will find him another time."

Naji looked mollified and his posture became less formal. "As I said, I scarcely see him—he is here, then he is there, as swift and hard to track as a rumor. He communicates with us mostly by messenger. The High Magister complains about his years, but should I ever reach such an age I pray I have even a fraction of his vigor."

Age does not always weaken its victims, Viyeki thought. Sometimes, as with Lord Akhenabi, it made them more cruel, more dangerous, and more powerful. "These are deadly times," was what he said to Naji. "Our master gives his all. We can do no less." Viyeki felt the hypocrisy of his words even as he uttered them and abruptly changed the subject. "And what of the fighting outside the mountain? What do you hear from the Order of Sacrifice?"

Naji shook his head. "Grim things, I fear. The Marshal and General Suno'ku must conserve their forces in case we fail and the gate is breached. So the numbers of those fighting the Northmen are small, yet more of them fall every day, though we can ill-afford to lose even one Sacrifice. But Suno'ku inspires them to keep fighting, and the gates have held for far longer than most thought they would."

"What do you think of her? Of the general?"

For the first time, Naji's mask of formality slipped entirely. "I think she is the greatest of us—saving only the Mother of All, of course. We are blessed by the Garden to have her in this dark time. Such courage! But even more, it is a courage that she can lend to others when their own has fled."

"She is brave, yes. And fierce. I saw her at Tangleroot Castle. And at Three Ravens Tower." There were moments when Viyeki remembered the bright-haired warrior as he had first seen her there, and he could almost believe that she *could* save them all. But they were only moments. "I must go now. I dare not leave my governors in charge too long."

"I know what you mean," said Naji. "The unsaddled goat quickly begins to bite." And then he did a strange thing, extending his arm and hand for the other to clasp. "May we both bring credit on our order in this evil time, Host Foreman Viyeki. Who knows when we will see each other again?"

And Viyeki, who had spoken truthfully but spitefully about Naji's shortcomings many times of late, was shamed. He put out his own hand

and clasped Naji's arm just below the elbow. "Yes, order-brother. May we both make our master proud. And if we do not see each other again in this world, we will meet in the Garden."

They parted, Naji to his other business, Viyeki back to the depths and his workmen who would not work. And if the High Magister's wisdom was not available to him, he knew he must solve the problem himself. He owed it to his queen and his people.

As he walked down the front steps of the order-house, the iron ram crashed against the outside of the gates once more, shaking all that was not solid bedrock. Even the bells of the temple towers swayed from the shock and uttered softly, like the moans of frightened children.

Isgrimnur never slept well in the field. Part of it was the absence of Gutrun, of course, of his wife's familiar, soothing shape in the bed next to him, of her voice that calmed him in the night and reminded him that there was more to life than his worries. On this night he had been slipping in and out of thin sleep for hours, and also in and out of a dream in which Isorn his eldest son—his dead son—rushed at a gate that broke and gave way. Behind it lay the darkness of an endless pit. As Isorn struggled at the edge of this terrible fall, his father tried to call to him but could not make any kind of warning cry. Then, as his dream-self flailed, speechless and helpless, something hit the side of Isgrimnur's tent with a loud enough noise to send him tumbling out of the dream and onto the floor.

He shouted for his house-carls as he scrabbled in the darkness for his sword. *"Haddi—Kár! To me!"* Again something struck the tent, this time scratching and clawing so that the wall bulged first in one place, then another. Some heavy shape was trying to rip its way in—a bear, perhaps, or worse, a troop of murderous, white-skinned Norns. "To me!" he shouted. "Where are you all?" At last he found Kvalnir. His fingers closed on the sword's hilt, and in a moment, he had worked it out of the scabbard.

"Duke Isgrimnur!" Haddi was just outside the tent. He sounded like a terrified child. *"We are . . . there are . . . !"*

Isgrimnur kicked off the blankets still tangling his legs and staggered upright, then pushed his way out the tent flap. He had only a moment to stare at Haddi, a trained killer who looked like a terrified child, then the bustling, thumping noise started again behind him, but this time the tent yawed and then collapsed beneath the assault. Isgrimnur could see only the dim outlines of something struggling in the midst of the poles and bunched hides. "What in the Holy Name of the Aedon is happening?" the duke bellowed.

Haddi, bizarrely, had fallen to his knees on the snowy ground and was now praying. All around, other shapes moved between the tents of the duke's commanders, some running, others limping or even crawling. Isgrimnur could make no sense of what had happened, only that it must be some terrible disaster. Had the earth shaken? Had a great tree fallen?

A muted noise of something being torn dragged his attention back to his fallen tent, where a dark shape rose from the wreckage. For a brief moment the duke thought he had been right in his first guess, that it was a bear or some other large animal: the thing was crouched and hard to make out except for a gleam of broken teeth. Then it struggled upright and he could see it full in the starlight. It was man-shaped, draped in rags dusted with snow and tattered until they were little more than cobwebs, but the eyes above the grinning jaws were empty black holes.

Duke Isgrimnur had only a moment to gape at this incomprehensible apparition before it lurched toward him, muddy hand grabbing at the empty air. The duke lifted Kvalnir and moved crabways, keeping the great blade between him and the dismal thing. The night was full of despairing cries, but when Isgrimnur called he heard no answering shouts, and he felt a moment of utter terror thinking all his men might have been attacked and killed in their sleep.

The thing with no eyes stumbled toward him like a drunkard, head wagging, jaws snapping loosely. Only as Isgrimnur drew back his sword to ward it off did he see and recognize the bracelet on the thing's clawing hand. It was gold that Isgrimnur himself had given out as war-booty after the battle for the Hayholt, a reward to his brave soldiers. This dead thing had been one of his own men.

The creature moved as crookedly as a wagon with a broken wheel but showed little fear of his sword, so instead of poking at it Isgrimnur strode forward, swinging Kvalnir in a broad arc to take the thing high in the neck. He felt the blow land, felt the bones beneath the rags snap, then the thing staggered to one side and toppled.

"Haddi! To me, curse you!" Isgrimnur called, but before he could find Haddi or any of his other liegemen, the thing the duke had just killed dragged itself back onto its feet.

"Damnation," was all Isgrimnur could say.

With its neck cut mostly through, the dead man's head hung limply to one side, bobbing and swinging as it staggered toward him. The duke cursed again and kept cursing as he lifted his sword and shoved it into the thing's guts, or at least where its guts should be, then put all his weight into it so he could drive the living corpse back into the wreckage of the tent.

Even tangled in the tent's hides, the eyeless thing still did not stop trying to get up, but by luck the duke had sliced through its backbone with his last thrust; now the struggling figure looked like two men huddled in a single costume for some holiday merriment, neither half able to get the other to cooperate. Isgrimnur swore again and hacked with broad Kvalnir until the head finally came off and the dead thing stopped moving.

Haddi had vanished, and none of Isgrimnur's other servants were close by. The camp was in chaos, and now that his eyes had adjusted to the dark, the duke was unsettled to see how many of the shadowy shapes around him were not his living soldiers but corpses animated by witchcraft. He began shouting again for his men, but before any of them reached him he had to kill two more of the terrible things, including one that had only one leg but still hopped slowly after him with intent to murder. Using Kvalnir more like an axe than a sword, he managed to take off the heads of both revenants while sustaining only a few scratches, but already he was winded and seeing sparks at the edge of his vision. Terror was stealing his breath, making him feel as though he fought uphill at a fierce angle. Some terrible Norn magicks were at work, that seemed certain. How many of these creatures were there?

How many have we buried? he thought bleakly. *That's the answer.*

Some of the duke's men finally found him, their eyes bulging with horror as they begged him for answers he could not give. He took a moment to look up to the slope above the camp where they had buried most of the dead, a spot that received more sun than most, which had made the frozen ground easier to dig. A swarm of clumsy shapes were clambering from the burial trenches there, slipping and tumbling but always moving downhill toward the living.

"Take their heads off," he told his men. "Without a head they fall and stay down. Take their heads!"

He was relieved to see a bulky shape he felt sure was Brindur gathering men of his own, and beyond that, like a single tree still standing after a great windstorm, Vigri's banner had been raised and someone was waving it in the air, drawing more survivors.

As Duke Isgrimnur's own small troop set about cutting down the dead that surrounded them, he saw others doing the same. The rout was halted, the men recovering, and the tide of battle finally seemed to be turning, or at least he hoped so. But many of the Rimmersmen had realized what they fought and were weeping even as they cut and hacked at the clumsy dead things.

More cursed Norn tricks, Isgrimnur thought, *and this one the foulest of all. Still, they could not hope to defeat our greater numbers with such slow-moving foes, even if they are our dead comrades.* Something tugged at his thoughts, something beyond the moment's struggle. *But wait, what followed the last time they created such a horror? The White Foxes always have more than one purpose—*

His mind suddenly clear, Isgrimnur began to bellow, *"'Ware the gate, men! 'Ware the mountain! All eyes watch for the White Foxes!"*

Other voices picked up the duke's call and added their own, lifting their warnings above the shouts and curses of those fighting the dead. As Isgrimnur hacked the head from a stumbling thing that would have pulled down one of his soldiers from behind, a sentry's horn sounded raggedly from the base of the mountain near the gates. He heard some of his men shouting, "The gate!" and "The mountain!" and "The gates are open!" Another screamed, "The whiteskins are coming!"

Isgrimnur cursed himself for being right, and also for not being right swiftly enough. "That is the real danger!" he bellowed. "Men, close up. Fight your way toward the Nakkiga Gate. We are attacked! The Norns are trying to flee the mountain!"

But that did not make sense, he realized even as he shouted it. Where would the Norns flee *to?* The mountain was surely their last refuge. Still, it was clear now from the eddying shapes moonlight made of the battling men that those nearest the gate, the sentries and the engineers tending the siege weapons, were bearing the main brunt of a wave of attackers.

"It's the ram, damn it!" the duke cried out as he finally understood. "Hurry to the ram! Vigri! Brindur! They mean to destroy the ram!"

His men could replace the great tree that was its body, he knew, but if the Norns managed to ruin or make off with the mighty iron head of the bear, it could not be replaced before winter came. There was not enough iron left in the camp to forge another without leaving the army weaponless.

"Leave the dead where they are and cut your way toward the gates!" he shouted. It was like a dream, like his dream, like falling helplessly into darkness. "By all that is holy, does no one hear me? *Protect the ram!*"

Porto would never forget that night—the night the dead woke up. He and the rest of Aerling Surefoot's men had found a new tunnel on the mountain, killed its single guard after an exchange of arrows, then blocked the passage at the end of the cavern with heavy stones and logs. With so much to do, they had not returned from the mountainside until after dark. It had been a fearful task, clambering down those icy, treacherous slopes when they did not dare light a torch for fear of lurking Norn bowmen, so by the time they reached the bottom the Mountain Goats had collapsed into sleep in a great huddle without bothering to find their way back to their designated fires.

Porto woke at the first shouts, but in his weariness he took the cries for something less fearful—men brawling among themselves perhaps, a common thing during this long, bone-chilling siege. It was only when he heard the great, creaking noise of the Nakkiga gates swinging open and the nearest sentries shouting their alarms, that Porto realized something dire was happening.

Mounted shadows swept outward from the gate, cutting down all before them in an unnatural near-silence. Even the cries of their victims were louder than the muffled hooves of the attackers' mounts. Then, as Porto hurried forward, trying to find one of the scattered groups of soldiers to join, he saw that the duke's camp was being attacked not just from the front, but from the rear as well, creating terrible confusion.

A man-shaped figure came staggering toward him out of the dark. At first he thought it was some hideously wounded Northman—which, in a way, it was, although this one's wounds had killed him days or weeks earlier. The thing barely had eyes, just gleaming wetness deep in the sockets, and its rotting shroud exposed gaping, bloodless wounds in its face and chest.

The dead, he realized, terrified but also strangely unsurprised. *The Norns have raised the dead. Our dead.*

He dodged the thing's clumsy reach but was almost caught by a swipe from the rusting knife clutched in its other hand. The thing did not even seem to realize it was armed, swinging both arms aimlessly, and Porto thanked God and all the saints that the things were slow as he leaped past it and brought his sword around hard enough to slice the dead man's neck to the bone. The corpse stumbled, then slowly turned toward him as if its head were not half severed. Porto dragged his sword free and this time hacked at the corpse's legs until he smashed its shin into a ragged white pulp of bone and unbleeding flesh and the thing finally toppled. Meanwhile he could hear the cries of his fellows as the shadowy White Foxes from the gate darted in and out among the Northmen, dealing death and terrible wounds, seemingly at will.

Porto finally severed the corpse's head from its shoulders, stilling its movements, but he had been driven away from the nearest group of his fellow soldiers and now stood by himself in a swirling chaos of men and shadows. Some of the dark shapes seemed impossibly swift, others slow as dying insects. He called out for Aerling and the rest of the Mountain Goats but he might as well have been shouting in an empty forest.

Something careened toward him, a huge dark shape that, only at the last instant, he saw was a horse and rider. He had only time to throw himself flat on the snowy ground before he felt the wind of the rider's stroke pass just above him. When he rolled over the Norn had vanished into the dark again.

Porto did not know how long he had been fighting, or even whether many of his fellows still lived. His greatest fear, though, had not come to pass: he had destroyed half a dozen walking corpses and crippled several others, but none of the dead faces had been Endri's. He hoped that if the demon-spell had roused the dead boy, the stones piled on his grave had kept him in the ground.

As he stood for a moment, head bowed, fighting for breath, he heard a shout of something like triumph. It didn't sound like the poisonous cry of one of the Norns but like that of a good, hoarse mortal man, and he felt a sudden hope. What had happened?

The greatest knot of fighting was down by the gates, where Porto could see a large number of living men surrounding a single pale rider, who was slashing away on all sides with a blade that was invisible in the darkness but clearly swift and deadly. Then one of the mortal spearmen got in a lucky thrust and knocked off the rider's helmet. The Norn's horse reared, and Porto saw a gleam of moon-pale hair. It was the female Norn-warrior he had seen at Tangleroot Castle, he felt certain, the woman who had brought reinforcements to save her kin trapped in the ruins. Half a dozen Northmen's bodies lay beneath her horse's hooves, but she was fighting defensively, and even as he admired her speed and skill, Porto headed toward the fight to help his fellows. Thane Brindur and a few of his men were still trying to bring her down with hand-axes, swords, and jabbing spears, but the Norn woman made her horse spin so swiftly it seemed like magic, and each time her arm swung a man reeled back with a fountaining wound or collapsed where he stood.

Somebody called from the gate. This time it was no mortal voice, but a high, birdlike screech, and the Norn woman immediately wheeled her mount toward the sound, her sword cutting the air so swiftly that the soldiers she had been keeping at bay could only throw themselves on the ground and then crawl away to avoid being trampled or decapitated. The pale-haired warrior galloped back toward the gate and the shadows waiting for her there. The Northmen got to their feet and chased her, shouting in triumph.

We've driven them back, Porto realized. He had never really thought he would survive this storm of death and madness, but the Norn horde was retreating into the open gate, fleeing back into the mountain. Brindur led the chase, but he was on foot and the Norns moved like wind itself, seeming to glide across the uneven ground. The Northmen could not catch them.

Porto slumped to his knees. The massive sally-gate groaned as it began to swing inward, then slammed thunderously shut behind the last of the Norns. A dozen or so Northmen leaped and shouted and pounded on the gates with their weapons, still seized by battle madness, as if they could conquer the entire mountain by themselves if only they might pass the threshold.

Porto could feel all his new wounds, the sharp cuts the shadowy Norns had dealt him and the scrapes and bloody weals left by dead fingernails. He was so tired that he almost lay down among his dead and wounded comrades to sleep, but feared he would be buried by mistake.

As he stood trying to get his breath back, his legs shaky as a newborn colt's, he saw something crawling toward him. It was so low to the ground he wanted to believe it some scavenging animal that had crept out onto the field in search of human flesh, but it did not move like any natural thing.

He lifted his sword. The blade felt heavy as a chestnut-wood beam.

His terror that the dead thing would prove to be Endri, or some other comrade, ended when the crawling shape lifted its face to the starlight. He did not recognize its agonized mouth or staring eyes, but there was some-thing strange about it that still caught his attention. He stood all but un-moving as the thing kept crawling toward his feet, his blade quivering with the effort of his aching arms to keep it upright. The slick wetness of the blood trail left on the snowy earth behind it caught his eye. As it drew near, it raised a wavering hand toward him; then, when the effort was apparently too much, it let its pale hand drop onto Porto's boot.

"Help . . . me," it gasped.

The terrible thing was not a moving corpse, Porto realized in shock, but a living man. This was one of his fellow soldiers, a mortally wounded Rimmersman leaving his blood smeared behind him.

Then, as if merely saying those two words had exhausted his last strength, the dying man collapsed to the churned earth. Porto shouted out for help, his voice cracking, but nobody came. In the gray before dawn, the mountainside looked like some mad artist's depiction of Hell itself—a cold hell, not a lake of fire but a place of corpses and near-corpses slowly whitening beneath drifting snow. The man who had collapsed at his feet let out a last, rattling wheeze of breath, then lay still.

Porto crawled a little way off from the dead soldier and sank into a crouch, rocking himself back and forth. The rising sun was just beginning to warm the sky but the new light only made the charnel wreckage around him more horrible, the bodies more pitiful. At last, strengthless and exhausted, he fell back onto the cold ground and wept.

"Before discussing this fateful hour of the siege, when Akhenabi and his Singers raised the mortal dead and General Suno'ku led a sally out of the gates in an effort to destroy the Northmen's great ram, your chronicler must speak with her own voice for a moment, to tell something of the difficulties our order faces when trying to relate the tales of such times.

"It is not for poetry alone that we name our queen's restorative slumbers the keta-yi'indra—"dangerous sleep." The word keta's origins date back to the Garden itself, and it contains in its meaning not just the idea of "dangerous" but also "chaotic" and "unknowable."

We Cloud Children do not use keta to describe other perils. A wounded giant or thousands of Northmen besieging Nakkiga are both dangerous to our folk, but they are not unknowable. But our queen's sleep of recovery brings a special kind of threat to our race—chaos and the unknown— simply because she is not present to guide us. The order of things is compromised, as if the stars themselves left their celestial tracks and made for themselves new and random ways across the sky. When the queen sleeps, instead of her loved and trusted voice, many voices speak to us, and many hands strive for mastery of the People's fate. Nothing is in its proper place.

" 'In the season of keta-yi'indra,' Kusayu the Fourth Celebrant once declared, 'the sky and earth change places and the mountain stands on its peak.' It was in Kusayu's day that Drukhi the Martyr, the queen's son, was murdered by mortals. In her grief, Utuk'ku slept even longer than she has in our present time, and during that sleep many things changed in Nakkiga. The people were lost as though in a great darkness and all was uncertain.

"And so it was on that more recent day we speak of here, during the Northmen's siege of Nakkiga, when sudden victory and sudden defeat were both in our reach at the same moment. But in the end, both possibilities vanished.

"The risk of opening the gates for General Suno'ku's attack on the black iron ram did not end in disaster, as some feared, but neither was the weapon destroyed before the general and her surviving Sacrifices were forced to retreat.

"And Lord Akhenabi sang a song of such power that hundreds upon hundreds of mortal corpses rose from their burial places and walked beneath the sky, slaying many of our enemy and striking terror into them all. But it was not enough to drive the Northmen out of our lands again.

"The uncertainty of those days also spawned many tales and rumors that are still told, and which make the work of a humble chronicler much more difficult. In such times, truth is always elusive. Some might even say that when the queen sleeps there are suddenly many truths, precisely because it is our great queen herself in her wisdom, power, and ubiquity who determines the order of all things. In her absence, facts are no longer trustworthy. In her absence, authority is diffused or even lost entirely. How can we know what is real? And how can a mere chronicler discern the truth of such moments after the fact, even less than a Great Year later?

"All that seems to be certain about that night is that Lord Akhenabi raised the mortal dead and General Suno'ku did her best to cripple the mortals' siege engine. One succeeded and one failed, but still the siege dragged on. Even today many tales are told about that hour of the open gates, of folk slipping out of Nakkiga in the confusion, or (as some claim) spies from outside sneaking into the city itself, but these are whispers from a time when what was real was not fixed, when our queen slept and nothing was certain except chaos and the unknown. No one can say precisely what happened, least of all a mere chronicler, because truth itself was sleeping."

—Lady Miga seyt-Jinnata of the Order of Chroniclers

Isgrimnur was so tired he could barely put one foot in front of the other, but the long day was not quite over yet. He thanked almighty God that at least the risen dead seemed to be staying dead now that the sun had come up. Now the bodies that had risen would have to be burned after appropriate prayers. The duke decided on his way back to his tent that he would let the army's chief priest lead the ritual this time. Wasn't that the fellow's calling, anyway? Isgrimnur had run out of things to say.

Someone was waiting for him inside his tent, silent and unmoving in the shadows. Isgrimnur snatched at his dagger, raging at himself for his inattention, but when he took a menacing step forward, the figure made no move to resist.

"Send your carls away, Duke Isgrimnur. I would speak for your ears only."

"Ayaminu?" Isgrimnur's heart was pounding. "By the Aedon, woman, what are you doing waiting in the dark like that? I might have killed you!"

The Sitha inclined her head. "You might." She did not sound as if she thought it likely.

"Where have you been?" he demanded, the shock making him bluster louder than he might have otherwise. "I called for you many times during the rising of the dead, but you did not answer."

"No," she said. "I did not. And that is all I can safely tell you."

Isgrimnur could not help wondering whether she had done something to betray him but could not imagine a reason why she would. "What is it you want, fairy woman?" he asked at last. "I have dead men to burn and a siege to finish."

Ayaminu nodded. "I told you before, that you could not understand the deeps inside the mountain and the veins of what you might call madness among the Hikeda'ya. Before you plan the rest of your battle, I believe there are other deeps you must plumb. One of them is the history of our folk, which extends far beyond the arrival of mortal men in these lands."

Isgrimnur poured himself a bowl of ale from a pitcher. It was colder than he liked, but he had cursed the weather enough already. He offered some to the Sitha-woman but she shook her head. "So speak," he told her.

"I think you know a little of what is called The Parting, when the Hikeda'ya and my clan, the Zida'ya, went their separate ways," Ayaminu told him. "The Hikeda'ya—the Norns or White Foxes, as you call them—have long declared that it was you mortals who drove our two tribes apart, the Hikeda'ya wanting revenge for the death of Queen Utuk'ku's son but the Zida'ya unwilling to join them in destroying another race."

Isgrimnur had heard something of this from young Simon, but he could remember very little of what their young king had told him of fairy history. Isgrimnur's father had converted from the old faith to the Church of Usires Aedon when Isgrimnur was young, and it had been hard enough to learn all the new Usirean lore. He still swore by the wrong gods sometimes: he had scant room to carry around Sithi stories as well. "Treat me like an ignorant mortal," he suggested.

Ayaminu actually smiled, a sight so rare Isgrimnur was a little startled. He generally thought of her as old, in part because of her snowy white hair and her slow, cautious speech, but by any mortal standard she was quite beautiful, and at this moment he felt almost captivated by her. *Fairy glamours*, he told himself. *Don't ever tell Gutrun or she'll make you regret it.*

"I am not the oldest of my people," Ayaminu said, "but I am by no means the youngest. I was born well before the Parting, and lived the first part of my life in Hikehikayo, in the snowy Whitefells far to the west of here. I see the look in your eyes, Duke—do not be impatient. I have been patient with you, and even though my work here is finished, I have remained to tell you things you need to know."

"What do you mean, your work is finished?"

"What I say. I never claimed my people wanted the same thing yours do. I have done all that was asked of me."

"And what was that work?"

She gave him a solemn stare. "It is possible you will never know—these are strange times, and they have spawned many strange enmities and alliances which cannot yet be divulged. And it may come to nothing in any case—only the Dance of Years will tell. But I have done what I came to do, and I promise I have not interfered in your war."

"*Our* war?" He felt a rising surge of anger. "You call it ours?"

She raised a hand. "Peace, Duke Isgrimnur. I have things to tell you, and we are wasting time. War is like a skein of wool. Does the wool begin with the skein, or the sheep from which it came, or even from the person who first conceived of weaving with it? Does it end when the skein is finished, or when the garment is woven, or does it exist until the garment itself finally falls to tatters? What about those who remember that garment? It is still alive in their memory."

"I don't understand you. This seems like scholar-talk to little point!"

"Perhaps. But whoever's war this is, I have done what was asked of me, and now it is finished. It is time for me to return to my people. If a day comes when I am allowed to speak of my part in things, I promise I will tell you. But before I go, I will speak to you from my own heart and tell you something that I think you should know, so heed me, Duke. There are some inside the mountain—some Norns, as you call them—who wish to end the fighting."

Isgrimnur felt himself turning red. "Are you mad? Did you see what they did? Did your work, as you call it, whatever it was, prevent you from seeing how our own dead were summoned out of their graves and set against us?"

"That was by the hand of Akhenabi, Lord of Song. But he is not the only one defending the mountain, and while the queen of the Hikeda'ya sleeps, he is not the only voice and hand that matters."

The duke shook his head in angry confusion. "What are you suggesting? That we bargain to lift the siege? Even if I believed you, why would I do such a thing? My men want blood for blood and death for death."

"Of course they do. That is the nature of anger, of pain. But both your people and mine choose the most clear-headed among them to consider all possibilities when the rest are mad for destruction. Your people have chosen you, Duke Isgrimnur."

"Tell me straightly what you're saying, Ayaminu. I am tired, and my heart is cursed heavy with all that's happened." He poured himself more ale, drank it off this time in a swallow. "What are you telling me?"

"I did not finish my own history, Duke Isgrimnur," she said, still standing in shadow. "Be patient with me yet a while. As I said, I was born in Hikehikayo before the Parting. In that city in those days there was no great separation between the Norns and the Sithi. All lived together and were much alike, and all gave their loyalty to the whole people. But that changed, and not just because of the death of the queen's son. Long before Prince Drukhi's death, a certain envy had already crept into Utuk'ku's heart. I will not muddle you with the tangled details, but when Utuk'ku and her husband left my folk to lead their loyal clans on a different road, it was more to do with past grievances and perceived slights than anything else. The death of Drukhi was only the excuse."

"I am already muddled."

"Then I will make it simpler, Duke Isgrimnur. Just as there are Sithi who do not love mortals, there are a few Norns who do not entirely hate mortals. I grew up in Hikehikayo when those you call Norns and those you call Sithi, like me, still lived together in peace. And despite all the seasons that have swirled by since that time, I still know some among the Hikeda'ya, and know their hearts."

"Are you saying you could convince them to surrender?"

She made a noise he couldn't unpuzzle, a little burst of breath. "Me? No. As long as the queen lives, they will not surrender, especially the Order of Sacrifice. But that does not mean that the end of this struggle cannot be made less bloody, less vicious."

Isgrimnur groaned. "For the love of the Lord God, no more clans, orders, or history, I beg you! Just tell me what you mean!"

"Only this. Speak to them, as you would any besieged mortal enemy. Give them your terms and let the less bloody-minded of Nakkiga hope for something other than complete destruction. It could be that the results will be better than you can now foresee."

"How do you know? Perhaps like Brindur I have come to feel that only destroying every last one of those murdering creatures will satisfy me."

"I know little of mortals, although I have long studied them, Isgrimnur—but I think I know something about you. I will say no more. I cannot say more. And this suggestion of mine may come to nothing, but I would not rest easily when my own song finally ends if I had not made the attempt."

He did not like the implication that this strange, ageless female creature might know him better than he did himself. "A parley, then? All of this is to get me to parley with our enemies? The same white-skinned beasts who butchered my son Isorn and thousands upon thousands more?"

"To consider it, Duke, yes. To consider what such a parley might bring. To think about other ways of solving this problem. And it is a problem, Isgrimnur—mark me well. Even when you knock down the ancient gates, your work will only have begun. Do you think Akhenabi's tricks were the worst thing you will ever see? I promise you, there are things waiting for you in the darkness of Ur-Nakkiga that will make you wish yourself deaf and blind from birth." Her voice had risen a little, and although it was still not loud, it was all he could do not to step away from her. "Utuk'ku did not conquer an empty mountain. And the Norns have not stayed free for so long without learning something of their conquest and its secrets."

"Is that a warning or a threat?"

"What warning does not contain some threat in it? But I promise I do not threaten you on the Hikeda'ya's behalf. I say these things because, though I still find your people as dangerous as wild animals—but, sadly, without the innocence of beasts—I think there is more to you. The end of every battle is the beginning of something else, often something too large to understand at that moment, inside the Dance of Time." Ayaminu now did something even more surprising than her smile: she bowed. "I must take my leave. I doubt we will see each other again, Isgrimnur, or that I will ever have the chance to explain more of what I have done here, and why. The world does not spin that way yet, and may never do so. But I wish you well."

She slipped out of the tent while the duke was still trying to make sense of her last words, and by the time he pushed out through the door a few moments later he saw no sign of her, but only the frozen, muddy camp and the soldiers dragging bodies in the flurrying snow.

Part
Four

The Fatal Mountain

After long hours studying old charts and making his own painful and occasionally dangerous explorations, Viyeki had found a course for his men that would allow them to skirt the Forbidden Deeps in their continued excavation of a refuge. Still, solving that problem did not much improve his mood: even the most blinkered foreman in the order would have recognized the doom that hung over them, which might render even a completed refuge pointless. And that grim knowledge was not limited to the nobility. Every Hikeda'ya in Nakkiga knew what was coming, although some, by reason of their responsibilities or simple stubbornness, would not admit it.

Viyeki had long ago given up his family litter so that its parts could be used in repairs to the gate and other important things. Thus, on this day of the council meeting that might determine the fate of his entire race, the host foreman walked to the great Council Palace. His sacrifice was a minor one, he knew, compared to most—the sight of so many starving folk in the streets made that clear. Many of the slaves and lower-caste Hikeda'ya seemed to have simply run out of strength even to finish their errands or return home, and sat slumped in the streets wherever they had stopped. But although Viyeki's household still had food enough to maintain life, they did not have enough to share, especially with so many sufferers. More than half of the houses in Nakkiga's lowest tier were now shuttered and dark, some because the residents had not returned from the war in the south, or had died from illness or starvation, but in many others the occupants were alive but staying almost motionless, hour after hour, to preserve their dying strength.

In the low-caste district close to the foot of the thundering Tearfall something had corrupted a warehouse full of black rye, sickening many of the already hungry residents and driving them to acts of madness so disturbing that the Queen's Teeth, Utuk'ku's private guard, had been dispatched by the War Council to close off the entire neighborhood. The queen's elite guard sealed many houses with the howling tenants still inside; even after the noises finally ceased, nobody went near them. Viyeki had passed through the district once after the madness struck. Now he went no small distance out of his way to avoid it.

But even on the second tier, site of Viyeki's own house and the mansions of other noble families, the distress of his people had become all too evident. Even the privileged clerics and Celebrant officials employed in the queen's palace were growing emaciated, the skin of their faces almost transparent over the bones. Fear was everywhere, hanging over the city like smoke. Akhenabi's great casting and Suno'ku's raid had failed. The Northmen had not fled, the queen slept on, and the Order of Sacrifice had dwindled to a few hundred. And hour after hour, the pounding of the great ram thundered through Nakkiga's silent streets.

But for the Tearfall and the temple bells, the city has gone completely silent, Viyeki noted. *But that is our nature.* He felt both despair and a kind of helpless love for his people. *When we are threatened, we turn inward. We close ourselves in, we sink into the dark. We survive. But when survival is the only goal, what do the survivors become?*

This city of Nakkiga, he reflected, was like one of the cave-borers—blind, cattle-sized crustaceans that made their home in the deepest, dark parts of the mountain, seldom seeing any light. As with all their kind, the cave-borers carried their skeletons on the outsides of their bodies, and even when they were dying they gave no outward sign: the many-legged things would stagger onward, still acting out the patterns of life, until they simply stopped in place, like a wagon with a broken axle, and never moved again—apparently whole on the outside, but utterly dead within.

Is that to be the fate of our city, the lights going out one by one, never to be lit again? The fate of our entire people? To stumble blindly forward, dying with every step, until at last we simply cease to move?

Viyeki made his way across Nakkiga's third tier, toward the arching entrance of the Maze and the dark facade of the Council Hall behind it, as lost in his grim thoughts as a man wandering in heavy mist.

The last guard finished examining Viyeki's summoning-stone, then bowed and ushered him into the great chamber of the Council Hall. Once inside, he was surprised to discover several newcomers around the witch-wood table, including several nobles from the Order of Echoes and their partners from the Maze Palace, the Queen's Whisperers.

The new face beside Lord Jikkyo of the Singers was a female member of his order too young to wear the mask of one of the Eldest, those born in the first years after the escape from the Garden. Her face was marked all over with strange runes, so that from a distance her skin looked almost black.

As Viyeki entered the vast, high-ceilinged room and seated himself, Magister Yaarike gave him a brief glance and nod but otherwise showed him no particular attention. As if to underscore this new distance between them, two other high foremen were seated on the magister's far side. One of them was Viyeki's rival, Naji. Viyeki put on a face as expressionless as a bowl of still water, but it was painful to have his diminished importance displayed to all in the War Council, even if it was, as Yaarike had suggested, only for show.

I am dying but still walking like a thing alive, he thought, then chided himself for such self-indulgent brooding. He was the scion of Clan Enduya, his family old in the service to the queen, even if not as exalted as some of the other clans represented around the table. Viyeki too was Hikeda'ya nobility: he would be true to his blood.

"So," said High Celebrant Zuniyabe after the Invocation of the Garden and other preliminaries had been finished, "for today's gathering, we welcome Magister Kuju-Vayo of the Echoes and Lord Mimiti of the Queen's Whisperers to our number. And, unless I miss my guess, you have brought someone new to our deliberations as well, Lord Jikkyo."

The blind Singer nodded. "Our great master Akhenabi, like our revered queen, has exhausted himself in defense of the Hikeda'ya. Like her, he is also deep in the slumber of renewal. As acting leader of the Order of Singers, I have brought Host Singer Nijika to be my second."

The younger Singer looked around the council table, her wide, dark eyes almost indistinguishable from the black runes tattooed on her face, but she gave no other sign of greeting or even acknowledgement. The others at the table exchanged grim looks at the loss of Akhenabi, the most powerful of their number.

"I am sorry to hear Lord Akhenabi is unable to join us," Yaarike said. "There are many questions he might have answered. As it is, we must examine the failure of our efforts outside the gates without his wisdom to guide us."

General Suno'ku spoke up, and Viyeki thought he heard a tremble of anger in her voice. "My Sacrifices and I did what we could, High Magister. We were informed of what was happening only a bell-hour before Akhenabi's resurrection song began, and also the distraction of the dead rising did not serve as well as we had hoped—the mortals regrouped quickly." Her relative the High Marshal now made a sign and Suno'ku fell silent, but it was clear she would have said more.

"I hope I am not hearing people blaming my master, who nearly gave his life to sing that song." Jikkyo spoke with deceptive mildness. "Such great shapings are not conjured from nowhere. They take time and they take strength—nearly all the strength the Lord of Song possessed, as it happened. He only narrowly escaped death. Also, the hour of the song's effect cannot always be accurately anticipated. Tell me, please, does the Order of Sacrifice truly blame Lord Akhenabi for the failure of the sortie?"

Before the disagreement worsened, High Celebrant Zuniyabe raised his hand, demanding the council's attention. His ivory mask did not hide the narrowing of his eyes. "I pray that at such a moment we will remember that dissension among us only serves our enemies. We have more important matters to talk about than affixing blame. The mortal commander has asked to parley."

For those who had not heard this request—a number that most definitely included Viyeki—the revelation was like a lightning strike. Faces turned as members of the council tried to ascertain who was surprised and who was not. The first to ask the question that was on most tongues was Kuju-Vayo, the immensely tall and slender master of the Order of Echoes.

"How did this come about?" he demanded. "And why would the mortals want such a thing in the first place? They have overwhelming numbers on their side. It is a trap or a trick."

It would be strange indeed, Viyeki thought, if Kuju-Vayo and his officers had in truth been unaware of the request for parley, since their task was to pass the thoughts and demands of Nakkiga's ruling elite to the other royal orders by use of the sacred objects called "Witnesses," mirrors said to have been fashioned from dragon's scales. It was axiomatic that the Echoes knew their people's great secrets before anyone else, yet the Lord of Echoes seemed to have been caught by surprise.

"Perhaps my master's Song of the Dancing Dead has shocked the mortals more than all of you suspected," said Jikkyo. "Perhaps they are frightened and this King Isgrimnur wants only a face-saving excuse to retreat."

"He is not a king," said Yaarike. "He is the leader of his own nation, Rimmersgard, but he is not the king of all the mortal lands. Those are his masters in Erkynland, and this Northman duke can only speak with them by sending written messages." He nodded slowly. "But it could still be a trick, of course."

"One of the Zida'ya accompanies them," said Suno'ku. "We have seen her. She carries a Witness."

"But that one is gone," Jikkyo countered. "She left their camp days ago and has departed our lands entirely. We know this beyond doubt."

"Perhaps a falling-out between allies," said Marshal Muyare, all heavy satisfaction. "They could never understand each other, the Year-Dancers and the mortals. It is another proof that the Zida'ya have chosen the wrong side, and another reason our weakling kin must go the same way as the mortals."

"I will slit the throats of every member of Year-Dancing House myself," said Suno'ku in perfect seriousness. "They have been traitors to the Keida'ya race since before the Parting."

Zuniyabe held up his hand for attention. The great hall did not become quiet as swiftly as it had the first time he had done it. "The Song has become muddled between many voices, as the old saying goes," he said when the gathering had finally gone silent. "No, we must speak now about what *is*, not what we believe or guess. The facts are that a message from the mortals stamped with this Duke Isgrimnur's seal was left in our last spy-tunnel on the mountainside—a tunnel we thought was still undiscovered." His gaze darted briefly to Muyare and Suno'ku. "Clearly, we were wrong."

"If it was found by one of my Sacrifices, I should have seen it first," protested Muyare. "This is a breach of our oldest traditions—!"

"Nevertheless, it came to me." Zuniyabe lowered his voice, which for a moment had become loud. "Let us worry about protocol and tradition another day, High Marshal. This secret was too great to risk until it could be revealed to you all, in this room." He looked around. "The message asked for one of our number to come out of the gate unarmed to speak with their commander, who swears he will also come open-handed. His troops will be withdrawn far enough from the gate that we can see there is no treachery intended."

"This is nonsense," declared Kuju-Vayo of the Echoes. "Who could we send to speak for all? Only the queen, and she sleeps!"

"This is not meant to be a negotiation, I suspect, but only the presentation of demands," said Zuniyabe. "And there is another thing. The mortals have asked particularly that we send General Suno'ku—or, as they put it, 'the great she-warrior with the war-braided hair.'"

Now several spoke at once, in tones that ranged from questioning to open fury.

"No," said Viyeki's colleague Naji, and seemed surprised to discover he had spoken. "That is, surely it is a trick. They wish to take our beloved general from us. The people will not stand for it."

"Ha! Let the people do what they please—I will go, yes!" said Suno'ku, and slammed her fist against the tabletop. "By the sacred walls of Tzo, I will go to the gates, then before the mortal chieftain speaks a word I will pull out his heart with my bare hand and show it to him. Let his liegemen kill me then. It will not matter. We will have given the only answer we can give!"

Competing voices rose louder and louder, until Zuniyabe reached out his hand in the gesture demanding immediate silence.

Even the Chief Celebrant cannot make us behave well, thought Viyeki in something like despair. *With the queen gone and Akhenabi now sleeping too, we are a hair's breadth from chaos. It would take only a mistake, a single hot word, to have the orders at swords-point with one another.*

"You will not harm the mortal leader, Suno'ku," said Zuniyabe, making a sign of displeasure. "At parley, it would be beneath us. We will hear their demands." The High Celebrant turned to Muyare. "Marshal? Will you make certain your cousin-descendant understands?"

For long moments Muyare stared back at him, his handsome face unreadable. "I will vouch for the general's understanding," he said at last. "And, if need be, her willingness to do what the council decides."

"Good. We want to know what the mortals think and plan. There must be no attack from us during the parley, unless they show treachery." Zuniyabe now turned to Jikkyo the Singer. "I do not think even so illustrious a hero as General Suno'ku should go by herself, however. What do you think, Host Singer?"

Jikkyo also waited long moments before replying. "I agree. Some of the other orders should also be represented, that we may all feel comfortable we have heard the mortals' demands correctly."

"Do you doubt my honesty?" Suno'ku asked him. "Or my loyalty to our queen?"

"Neither, but I do admit to doubting your restraint, General." Jikkyo folded his long hands, which—like his subordinate Nijika's face—were covered with intricate black designs. "I think one of each of the orders who make up this war council should accompany General Suno'ku. Since there is to be no negotiating during this parley, Host Singer Nijika is capable of representing our order on my behalf."

The masters of the other orders agreed and also chose subordinates to attend the parley, promising that nothing would be decided until the news of the Northman's words had been brought back to Nakkiga.

Viyeki's master Yaarike was the last to speak. "I agree that my order should be represented as well," he said. "But I have an urge to see these mortal creatures face to face. Sadly, I was only able to show them my back as we returned from the South. I myself will go to the parley on behalf of the Order of Builders."

This seemed to cause only a little surprise among the other orders—Yaarike was known for his unconventional ideas and general stubbornness—but it startled Viyeki, and the words were out of his mouth before he realized. "Master, you cannot go! Please forgive my forwardness, but short of only the leaders of the Sacrifices, you are crucial to the defense of the city. What if it is a trick by the mortals, as some fear? Bad enough we lose important leaders from the other orders, but at least their magisters remain behind. We cannot afford to risk you on such a dangerous task, my lord."

Yaarike turned toward Viyeki, an uncharacteristic anger pulling at the magister's lean face, but General Suno'ku spoke up from the far side of the table. "I think the Host Foreman is right. At best, the mortal vermin will honor their promise, and we will hear their terms for our surrender—a demand that the Order of Sacrifice will never accept. At worst, it is a trap, and the city will still need to protect itself and prepare to deal with the mortals should they breach the gate. Send your second-in-command, High Magister Yaarike."

Viyeki's master tried to argue, but it was clear that with Akhenabi still recovering, the possibility of losing the lord of the Builders as well, worried everyone present. Viyeki could sense the fear behind the array of careful faces. At last Yaarike appealed to Zuniyabe, but the High Celebrant only shook his head. "Your whims cannot win out this time, caste-brother. You have heard the will of the entire Council of War. Host-Singer Viyeki will go in your stead."

There was still much to discuss, both about the parley and the larger matters of the siege and the city, and so the meeting went on and on until the evening bells finally began ringing in the Temple of the Martyrs.

From the moment Viyeki had gainsaid him before the council, Yaarike would not even look at him. Viyeki did his best to remain outwardly unmoved, but inside he was hollow. *I have ended my career, it seems. But I did it because I knew it was right for our people.* Still, he could not escape the idea that it might have been his own jealousy and hurt as much as fear for his master's safety that had driven him to speak up.

He would have to tell his wife Khimabu that he was going out unarmed to face the enemy. Why did he fear that more than the blades of the Northmen?

I wonder if all of history was as muddled as this? Viyeki was filled with the weary hopelessness of one who had lived for a long time under siege. *The chroniclers of future years, if there are any, will only be able to guess at what a mass of contradictions we were, who lived in such times.* He had a moment of sour amusement. *If the lives and deaths of such small creatures as myself ever reach their notice at all.*

News had spread through Duke Isgrimnur's army that there was to be a parley with the White Foxes. The troops were to withdraw back down the line of the valley before twilight came, but first the duke wanted to make sure no nests of Norn bowmen remained in undiscovered holes on the heights above the gate, and a task like that was work for the Mountain Goats. They had already labored long to find and seal all the Norns' escape routes, but the immortals were as crafty and determined as they were hateful.

As the cold afternoon faded, Aerling Surefoot led Porto and four others on a patrol across the lower slopes. For the first hours of the gray day they found nothing but traces of earlier skirmishes, broken Norn arrows, and remnants of their own camps. The Norns never left the bodies of their fallen behind, so even places where the Mountain Goats had killed some of the mountain's defenders only days before now seemed to have been deserted for years, and the brooding sky seemed to hang low over their heads.

"Make no mistake," said Aerling as they rested on an outcrop and scanned the dark slopes above, "the whiteskins won't give up. As well expect a nest of snakes to surrender. We'll have to kill every cursed one of them."

Porto had already had his fill of tunnel-fighting in the Norn passages which they had found and cleared during the weeks of siege. Even when the Mountain Goats outnumbered the pale things by a dozen to one, the silent, swift Norns were horribly difficult to kill. The idea of trying to clear an entire underground city made him feel sick at his stomach.

When they had all caught their breath Aerling led them farther up the mountain. They followed the faint tracks they had made in earlier forays, and if Porto did not quite have the confidence of some of the veterans, his long legs had become strong, and he could move uphill and leap from one perilous spot to another as well as any of his comrades. Thus it was that he was near the front of their small line, just behind Aerling, when he saw something flash in a thick copse of trees above and a little toward the southern side of the mountain. Porto tugged at the leg of Aerling's breeks to get his attention. The Goats following behind took note and wordlessly crouched to wait.

When Porto whispered to Aerling about what he'd seen, the leader nodded, then motioned to the group to split into two parts. Aerling chose Porto to accompany him, along with a whippet-fast young fellow from

Vestvennby named Kolbjorn, who despite his name—he had proudly informed Porto it meant "black bear"—was so pale and slender that he looked more Norn than Rimmersman. Aerling sent the other two with the old campaigner Dragi, to make their way up behind the trees while Porto and the other two approached from the front.

They climbed toward the copse as slowly and as silently as they could manage, crawling on their bellies through snow and over rocks until they had reached the trees. Unlike his fellows, Porto did not carry a bow—several attempts to teach him to shoot had failed to convinced him it was worth tripping over it—so he unsheathed his sword and stayed as low as he could behind Aerling and Kolbjorn. They paused frequently to listen and look for any sign of movement where Porto had seen something gleaming, but when the wind slowed, the mountainside seemed utterly silent.

At last they reached an overhang of stone just below their target where they sheltered for long moments, waiting for the wind to rise again. When it did, Aerling motioned to them both, then scrambled up over the top and charged into the clearing with Porto and Kolbjorn just behind him.

The open space between the pines was empty, nothing but muddy scrapes on the ground, half covered by snow, to show anyone had ever been there. But something shiny hung from a tree branch about chest-high. Aerling lifted it from the place it had caught, then brought it back to show the other two. It was a necklace of some kind, a piece of pale blue crystal about the size of a finger, carved crudely in the shape of a woman. Its slender chain was broken. Porto guessed that it had caught on the branch as one of the Norns had retreated from a skirmish. He leaned nearer and saw that what had at first appeared plain and even crude was instead beautifully simple: each angle was perfectly shaped, and the closer he looked the less he could make out what it was supposed to be.

Aerling held his hand out, proffering the necklace. "You saw it, Southerner. It's yours."

Porto's first desire was to step back. Although in some ways the thing was beautiful—how brightly it would glimmer against Sida's breast when he brought it home to her!—it was alien, too; just looking at it filled him with a sudden, fierce pain of homesickness.

Someone shouted in alarm from beyond the trees, a ragged, rising cry that ended abruptly. Even as Porto and his two companions turned from side to side, trying to judge the direction it had come from, another voice shrieked out a single word: *"Hunë!"*

It took Porto a moment to understand, but then terror came: it was a Rimmersgard word he had heard before and always to his sorrow. *Giant.* It meant giant.

A terrible crash, loud as thunder but far closer, then suddenly trees were falling everywhere around them. A moment later, even as Kolbjorn turned and dashed out of the clearing, Porto realized that the trees were all falling from one direction, and that Kolbjorn had sensibly, if not bravely, gone the other way. Porto had only a moment to lament his own slow reflexes, then something hurtled out of the mass of broken, sagging trees and landed at Aerling's feet. It was the headless corpse of Dragi, recognizable only by the boots the old soldier always cared for so lovingly.

More trees fell, making the ground jump; one of them nearly crushed Porto, but he threw himself to one side. Then the monster emerged out of the fog, striding over the felled trunks, sweeping smaller trees out of its path as if they were reeds.

Porto had seen giants before, when the troops had crossed over into the Nornfells, and he had watched from a grateful distance as the Rimmersmen had killed them, usually by sheer force of numbers. A dozen or more soldiers would pierce the huge beasts with arrows then keep them at bay with long spears until they finally fell bleeding to the ground, where they could be finished. But he had never seen one so close, and it all but stopped his heart.

The monstrous creature was half again the height of a man, with long arms and a face as ugly and full of rage as a demon's from another world. Its shaggy fur was as white as the snow itself, which meant it was still young, and unlike those Porto had seen in battle, it did not wear the leather harness that the Norns put on those who fought for them. As the giant pulled itself loose from the last fallen tree and advanced on Aerling, it bared its huge, yellow fangs. The stench of rotting flesh made Porto gag even as he stumbled back.

But Aerling was wedged between two fallen trees, branches tangling him from all sides. The Mountain Goat leader tried to work his bow free and could not, so he let go of it and pulled his sword instead. The giant growled, a rumble Porto could feel deep in the bones of his chest, then slapped at Aerling with a hand the size of a serving platter. The Rimmersman lunged at the massive paw and managed to sink his blade into the creature's wrist, but the heavy hand knocked him loose from the trees that had held him. Aerling flew half a dozen steps across the clearing and landed like a mealsack among the broken trunks.

Porto's blood was thundering so loudly in his brain that he could not think. He wanted to pray, wanted to tell his wife goodbye, but all he could see was that red, dripping mouth and the creature's deep-set eyes as it moved toward him, splintering fallen wood beneath its feet. Porto turned and ran. Snagged by branches, stumbling across toppled trees, his retreat seemed impossibly, fatally slow, but he dared not look back. At last he reached the center of the clearing where Aerling lay motionless, only a few steps away from the edge of the outcrop they had climbed. Porto knew that if he jumped off the stony shelf the giant would be on him before he could rise, and that would be the end.

He set his back foot, dodged a swipe from a huge, hairy hand, and swung at the thing's legs, but he caught his sword on the spiky branch of a fallen tree and barely creased the giant's fur. In a heartbeat, the beast had lurched forward and snatched him up into the air. Porto's sword fell from his fingers as the breath whistled out of him.

Yellow teeth grimaced only inches from his face. Tiny eyes peered out at him from under the bony shelf of the monster's brow, and in that moment of ultimate, dreamlike terror, he could see something looking back at him, a mocking intelligence in the giant's inhuman gaze that was almost worse than anything else.

Then the creature's hot, putrid breath blasted him as it let out a sudden, deafening roar. Porto was flung to the side so hard he bounced, the world turning up and down, whirling around him until it seemed almost like a dream. At last he stopped rolling and lay flat. Airless, he gasped and choked, struggling to fill his burning lungs and to rise before the monster seized him again. But the giant was doing some kind of bizarre dance and seemed not even to notice him; instead it whirled in place, flailing its huge arms and roaring so loudly that the branches on the remaining trees shook and rattled.

Something was dangling from the giant's neck, though Porto could make little sense of any of it. His air was out, his sight was going black, and no matter what he did he could not seem to suck anything into his straining chest. Still, he could not help thinking that it looked almost like the giant's throat was pulsing blood.

Another shape joined the dance, tiny, slender, and swift. It was Kolbjorn, and he held a long, crooked spear in his hand. As a little air began to creep back into Porto's starving lungs, and his vision cleared, he saw that the thing wagging in the monster's gorge was also a crude spear. As the monster spun and contorted, trying to dislodge that weapon, Kolbjorn kept stabbing at him with his other spear. The young Vestiman had not run away after all, but had found fallen branches and hastily carved the ends into sharp points.

Porto could not leave Kolbjorn to fight and die alone. He pulled himself up onto his hands and knees but could barely feel his limbs, and still could not breathe deeply enough to snuff the spangles of light floating before his eyes. Something inside him was cracked, broken. He crawled to his sword, narrowly avoiding the giant's ponderous feet as the beast finally dislodged the makeshift spear and turned to face the attacker.

Porto curled his hand around his sword hilt and kept crawling forward. Kolbjorn thrust again, and this time his spear went high into the giant's belly, but was stopped from sinking in too far by a cross-branch left on the shaft. Now Kolbjorn could only hold grimly onto the end of his weapon as the giant tried to reach him, the broken branch like the haft on a boar spear. Then the monster reached down and snapped the spear in half with a twist of its massive hand. Red blood was blooming in the white fur where the spear had entered, but only a trickle compared to the larger wound in its throat.

As the giant lurched toward Kolbjorn, its roars now ragged at the edges with fury and pain, it turned its back on Porto. He heaved himself onto his feet and staggered toward it. His chest seemed to be on fire, but he set his feet as well as he could and swung his sword through a hard, flat arc into the back of the creature's leg just above the knee. The giant staggered, then threw back its head and howled, and in the monster's moment of inattention Kolbjorn snatched up the spear that had first wounded the creature's neck and drove it as hard as he could into the hairy white stomach. The roar changed pitch once more, growing higher and even angrier, but as the creature staggered toward Kolbjorn with arms spread, yet another shape rose from the broken trunks.

Porto had thought Aerling killed by the giant's terrible blow, but now the leader of the Mountain Goats climbed unsteadily onto his feet, supporting himself on a fallen tree, then stepped under the giant's reaching arms to ram his own sword into the creature's groin. The iron blade was yanked from Aerling's hand as the giant staggered backward, but blood now fountained from the monster's inner thigh.

Growling, moaning, the creature raised both arms above its head, as though in its rage it wished to pull down the whole wide sky. It took a single step toward Aerling, spraying blood over the broken trees and snow, then it tottered, took another step, and fell.

Porto crawled toward it, his thoughts so disordered he could not even remember where he was or how such a madness had come to be. As he climbed onto the creature's back he could still feel its hitching breath. The feeling of the huge, warm thing beneath him was so disgusting, so maddening, that Porto plunged his sword into its back, then pulled it out despite the shrieking pain of his own ribs and rammed it into the giant's back over and over until the pain finally took all his senses away.

The afternoon had all but gone by the time they had found what was left of the other Mountain Goats and buried them in the clearing near the blood-matted body of the Hunë. Dragi's head had rolled or been flung a hundred paces down the mountainside. When they found it, the old soldier's face wore an expression closer to surprise than fear.

"A head for a head," said Aerling, and began to hack through the giant's shaggy neck, a butchery that took a long time. Porto knew he would never forget the noise it made. Then the last of the Mountain Goats stumbled back down the mountain as the gray day waned, Aerling carrying the monster's heavy, bloody head cradled against his chest as though it were something precious.

The duke's army had already begun their withdrawal from the gate for the parley, but several sentries rushed toward Porto and the rest when they appeared out of the heights of the mountain. Porto simply stood and stared at the faces around them and the bustle of activity across the camp as though he had never been there before.

The sentries escorted them back to the remains of the camp with no little ceremony, and a crowd soon formed around them. He and Aerling and Kolbjorn could muster only a few words for their comrades, but Aerling's bloody trophy quickly made the main details clear. Porto met his second nearly mythical creature of the day only a short time later, when Duke Isgrimnur himself came to see them. The duke was almost as tall as Porto but twice his girth, and although Isgrimnur was clearly distracted by the approaching parley, he clasped each Mountain Goat's hand and thanked them.

"By God, you have done a hero's work today, each of you," he said. "If that thing had come down from the mountain and caught me and the others unarmed at the parley . . ." He shook his head. "But look at you, wounded and still bleeding! God's Suffering, why hasn't anyone seen to these men?" He called for a surgeon.

Porto watched the duke and the others as though from the bottom of a deep well. He could hear what was said but it seemed mostly nonsense, and his thoughts kept wandering away.

"Why do you stand so, fellow?" Isgrimnur demanded of him. "Oh, aye, you're the Perdruin-man. What is your name—is it Porto? Here, what are you hiding under that cloak?"

"Nothing," said Porto, finding his tongue at last. "My ribs, I think . . . might be broken."

"Can you kneel?" Isgrimnur asked him, but Porto did not understand his meaning, nor much of anything else. "See, Sludig? He's almost dead on his feet, the poor devil," the duke fumed. "Frayja's Garters, where is that surgeon?"

"His Grace wants you to kneel if you can," said Isgrimnur's yellow-bearded lieutenant, not unkindly.

Will they put us to death? Porto wondered, and at that moment it did not seem a strange thing. He felt as though he and Aerling and Kolbjorn were all steeped in blood and destruction, that they had become something apart from all these ordinary soldiers—something terrible.

Young Kolbjorn looked up at the duke. The young man's gaze was distant and almost sleepy, his hands red with dried blood. "It killed Dragi. Tore his head off."

"I heard, lad," said Isgrimnur, "and I am sorrier than you can guess. But you have done a brave thing, the three of you."

"We were six when we went up," said Aerling, still clutching the giant's head like a treasured heirloom.

"And we will say prayers for your brave brothers tonight, I promise," the duke said. "But I have the authority of the king and queen of all the High Ward, and you will be knights for this."

Porto tried to lower himself to his knees, but the pain was so fierce in his chest that he swayed.

"Sludig, help that man," the duke said, and the yellow-bearded one clasped a strong hand around Porto's arm and let him down slowly.

Isgrimnur began to speak words that Porto could only partly hear, because a red noise was rising in his skull that seemed loud as a rushing river. He heard the names of King Seoman and Queen Miriamele and wondered why he did not entirely remember who they were. In his weary mind he imagined them as Isgrimnur's masters, monarchs of the far north sitting on thrones of ice, both swaddled in furs and jewels.

Something touched him. It was Isgrimnur's great sword Kvalnir, and it moved gently from one side of his head to the other, tapping each shoulder. "Then I name you champions of the High Ward," the duke said, "and lay on you the charges of knighthood. Arise, Sir Aerling, Sir Kolbjorn, Sir Porto."

But Porto could not manage to get up until the yellow-bearded one named Sludig helped him. He felt like a newborn colt, his legs shuddering sticks that could barely hold his weight. The duke was already being called away to other duties. A surgeon had arrived, his pack full of linen bandages and salves.

Aerling was still clutching the giant's bloody head and would not let anyone take it from him.

Is it an honor, his wife had demanded, *or does your master mean to see you killed?*

Even now, as he approached the crowd waiting at the ancient gatehouse, Viyeki could not guess at the true answer. He had not admitted to

Khimabu that he had probably destroyed any chance of succeeding Yaarike as magister. Viyeki had the courage to face the Northman hordes—just barely—but not enough to admit his foolishness to his wife. As it was, she had bidden farewell to him at the door of their house stone-faced and dry-eyed, as though she had already been widowed for many seasons.

General Suno'ku was at the gatehouse before them, pacing back and forth, a display of impatience and vigor seldom seen among the impassive Hikeda'ya. She did not wear her white armor, but only what was called a house uniform of the same color, as if she did not fear the barbs of the enemy at all. As usual, Viyeki was torn between his admiration of her spirit and concern for her stubborn, heedless bravery. As the day had worn on and this hour had come ever closer, he had found himself hoping that something would arise to change the plan. It was not a fear of being injured or killed he felt, but a sort of deeper, more formless dread, like a man in the wilderness watching an approaching storm as it turned the skies black.

You're a fool, he told himself. *Nothing will happen today. The Northmen will give their terms, and we will take them back to our masters. There will be no great deeds. Suno'ku has sworn to abide by the council's will, and whatever else she may be—however uncommon she may be in our dark, quiet world—she is no traitor.*

Viyeki joined the other two legates, rune-faced Nijika of the Singers' order and a thin, small-statured Celebrant named Yayano of the Pointing Finger, kin to Zuniyabe and a powerful noble in his own right. Together, they followed Suno'ku through the echoing gatehouse. The general seemed to want to waste no time. Before they had even reached the gates—which were heavily patched and barricaded on the inside, the hasty work of High Foreman Naji's crew of Builders—Suno'ku was already signaling to the guards to open them. As the bars and bolts were drawn from the sally-gate and the Sacrifice guards moved into close order to prevent mortal trickery, Viyeki and the other legates all stood silently. At last the pulleys creaked, the heavy witchwood timbers groaned, and the tall but narrow salley-gate swung open.

Even under dim twilight, it seemed bizarre to see the sky again. Viyeki had been back inside Nakkiga long enough to regain the feeling that stone above his head was the natural order of things. The great gray expanse of clouds outside the mountain seemed almost too vast to bear, as if something monstrous had torn off the top of the world. The rocky slopes on either side of the gate seemed to stretch out forever.

A dozen Northmen waited in the no-man's-land beyond the gates, behind and a bit to the side of their great ram, which had been left in place—as a reminder, Viyeki did not doubt. He turned to look back at the gates and saw the great dints in their stony timbers, as well as all the places the metal bracings had buckled under the repeated pounding. Most of the ornamentation had long since been smashed into fragments. The gates now looked, not like the symbol of power and protection they had always been, but like something old and frail and long forgotten. Seeing the damage made Viyeki's guts churn, and he turned to discover what expression Suno'ku wore. But if she had seen what he had, the general had not stopped to dwell on it; she faced the mortals squarely and began to walk toward them.

"But there are only supposed to be four," said Yayano. "Four of them, four of us!"

"The others are merely guards. They will make sure we have not brought weapons," Suno'ku called sharply over her shoulder. "By the Garden that made you, show the mortals no fear!"

She stopped a few steps away from the bearded Northmen, who stared back at the Hikeda'ya as though they were something entirely unknowable. Suno'ku spread her arms and stood with her feet wide apart; it took a moment before the guards realized she was waiting for them. Half a dozen burly Northmen now came toward her, creatures Viyeki thought more like stubby mountain giants than people. These gross mortals ran their hands over Suno'ku's body and one of them said something to his fellows, which provoked a nervous laugh from a few of the others.

"I speak your tongue well enough," Suno'ku said. "And in any case, you should know that I do not need any weapon to end you. I could do it with my hands alone, and you would be dead before you fell."

The Rimmersmen were war-hardened killers who gave no obvious sign of having heard what she said, but Viyeki's keen eyes saw the tightening of their muscles, the narrowing of their eyes.

When the Hikeda'ya legates had all been searched, the mortal guards retreated to one side. The biggest of the waiting Northmen waved them back even farther. They obeyed him, but with the unhappy look of dogs kept on too short a rope. Viyeki thought the large one must be their leader, Duke Isgrimnur. His beard was not quite so long or full as the others—the shortest of the mortal captains had a trail of whiskers so lengthy it was tucked into his belt—but everything else about the duke seemed over-sized. His chest was broad, his belly even more so, and Viyeki thought he looked like a creature who could not control his appetites. His face was broad too, with a tinge of choleric red, but the man's eyes were shrewd and strangely calm.

"Well, my lady, we meet at last," said the duke in a deep, rumbling voice. "I fear none of us can speak your tongue. Can we trust you to trans-late our words fairly to your people?"

"As I said, I use your tongue well enough for this day," said Suno'ku. "And though I do not know all its twistings and turnings, I do not think in any case that I am anyone's *lady*. I am Suno'ku seyt-Iyora, Host General of the Queen's Sacrifices, and I speak for my lord Muyare, the Queen's High Marshal. Speak your terms so that we may get on with this."

Isgrimnur's mouth curled in what might have been a smile. "Very well. You see that we have come in good faith, as we promised on our love for our God. Neither my companions nor myself are armed. We wish only to talk straightly with you."

"There has already been more than enough talk," she said. "State your terms."

"You are as abrupt in diplomacy as in battle," the duke said almost approvingly. "Very well. You must know that your position is hopeless. We have cleared the mountainside of your soldiers, sealed your burrows, and now you are trapped in this place with your backs against stone. Your people crossed into our lands and attacked us, and aided the Storm King in trying to destroy us. But we are not animals. If you surrender and open your mountain fortress to us, we will not harm any innocent women or children. In fact, they may go freely and we will give them passage, as long as they do not try to cross back into the lands of men."

Several of the duke's men stared open-mouthed, as though this were something they had not heard before. The short one with the long beard said, "Let them go free? Even if it is only women and children, that is madness, my lord!"

"Quiet, Vigri. The king and queen in Erkynland gave me the power to dispose of this struggle as I deem fitting." Isgrimnur had never taken his eyes off General Suno'ku. "Do you understand me?"

Do the rest of us not even exist? Viyeki wondered. *Are we no more than court musicians, while Suno'ku is the dancer who all watch?* But as he looked at the pale-haired warrior standing so straight and unconcerned before the burly mortals, he was content to let her stand for them all.

"Truly?" Suno'ku asked. "I am female, Duke, as you may have noticed. Will you let me walk free? And many of my Sacrifices are women too. Shall they all go free?" She shook her head. "You do not know anything about us, mortal. Children? Even our children are twice your age—thrice, even ten times!—and, I doubt not, many times wiser as well."

The yellow-bearded mortal beside the duke said something quiet but angry into Isgrimnur's ear.

"Peace, Sludig," the duke said. "She is more fighter than diplomat, but we guessed that already. I said 'innocent,' General. I understand your women fight too. I meant those who had not raised arms against us."

"Are those your only terms, then?" Suno'ku demanded, her disgust very plain. "Surrender our home and our females and children can go free?"

The duke shook his head. "Your warriors—Sacrifices, do you call them?—must all lay down their arms. When they do, we will decide their fate, male or female. And your leaders must surrender to us as well. But for the rest, I will be merciful. You have my word as a man and as an Aedonite."

For the first time one of the other legates spoke. "Our leaders?" demanded Yayano of the Celebrants. Viyeki thought his astonishment and fury must have been clear to even the most obtuse of the mortals. "You say we must surrender our leaders? Do you mean the queen herself, too—the Mother of All?"

Isgrimnur looked uncomfortable. "We will treat her with respect, you have my word. But yes, she must surrender to us along with her advisors. Your queen is no innocent. She was a great force behind the Storm King's wrongful war on our people and lands."

Viyeki was as shocked as the rest. He had been curious what the mortals intended to gain from this seemingly pointless meeting, but not in his wildest imaginings had he thought they would ask for the queen to be handed over. He felt as though he were on fire inside, and when Suno'ku raised her hand to forbid Yayano more angry questions, he was relieved. Now the general would curse the mortals and refuse them, then he and the others would return to the mountain so they could all prepare to die in a way that was fitting. If that was all they had left, the decision of how to make a proper end to the great song of their race, it was still better than surrender to this pack of hairy animals.

But to Viyeki's astonishment, Suno'ku merely said, "If you are finished, we will take your words to our leaders. You will have our reply by dawn tomorrow." She turned on her heel and began to march back toward the gates. Viyeki fell in behind her with the rest of the legates, so stunned that his thoughts seemed barren, like a high mountain pass scoured by gale winds.

As the mountain's face loomed above them, Suno'ku abruptly stopped. The salley-gate was opening, but at her sharp order the guards inside let it grind to a halt.

"Wait for me there," she told Viyeki and the others. "I have one last word for the duke."

"Do not throw yourself away," said Yayano. He looked to Nijika, legate from the Order of Song, but it was impossible to tell from her expression whether the tattooed Singer agreed or disagreed with him.

Viyeki felt the ominous mood drop over him again like a chilly fog. "Stay with us, General," he begged. "There is nothing to dispute. Their surrender terms are no terms at all."

"I did not ask you, Builder," Suno'ku said, not even glancing in his direction. "You have the words to take back to our masters. Those shameful words." Her face was like something carved on an old temple, the expression something that no one alive could read and properly understand. "I have now fulfilled my task, and thus am no longer a legate."

"But, General . . . !" Viyeki began.

"Silence." She fixed him with a stare so hard and cold that it almost made him stagger. "Go back to your drawings and tools, although they will avail you little. Mere stones cannot save us now." And so saying, she left them in the shadow of the gate and marched toward the mortals.

Duke Isgrimnur and his men had turned away to return to their lines, but a cry of warning from one of the guards made them face around.

Viyeki could see the duke talking angrily to his men as he tried to get free of them and turn back to meet Suno'ku.

Here is the flaw in the stone, Viyeki thought with sudden apprehension but could not say why. All he knew was that in that instant, as he watched the two walk toward each other, the slender Hikeda'ya and the broad, shaggy mortal, he felt he stood before a weak place in the world and time, a flaw that had been there for countless years but had only now worked its way to the surface. He did not know precisely what had come before or what would come after, but he knew nothing would be the same. Without thinking, he took a few steps after Suno'ku, but the other legates grabbed at him and held him back.

"Damn you, Sludig, I love you like a son, but if you lay your hand on me again you will lose it."

"My lord, Duke Isgrimnur, please—"

"By Heaven's bloody hammer, *I will speak to her!*" Isgrimnur knew it was what his young king and queen back in Erkynland would want. And even though he had to swallow his own hatred to do it, he knew that it was what his God wanted, too, or his faith was all sham.

He turned to face the Norn warrior. Even as a trickle of fear made its way through his innards, he could not help admiring her. Her walk was purposefully martial, yet her every movement was that of a sleek predator, a cat or wolf. The duke was twice her size, but Isgrimnur had seen the Norns fight hand to hand, and he knew that if it abruptly came to blows, he would be hard-pressed to keep himself alive until his men could help him.

"I wait for you, General," he called. "Do you think to kill me? I warn you, Jarl Vigri is small but his heart is that of a giant's. It is also full of hate for your people. And there are others of my nobles I could not even bring to the parley because I could not trust their fury."

"I do not come to kill you, Duke Isgrimnur." She stopped in front of him. "I come to tell you something you should know. The Hikeda'ya will never surrender either our mountain or our queen. Never."

"Then why the hurry to inform me? Tomorrow at dawn would be soon enough. Our task will still be the same."

The fairy woman stared at him for long moments. Isgrimnur did his best to hold her eye calmly, marveling that he should have to steady his knees in the face of a slender woman more than a head shorter than himself.

"I think your kind are little better than animals," she said at last, "But I think you are an honest mortal. That does not mean I would not happily kill you and tie your head to my saddle by that bristling beard."

"Of course not. Is that why you returned—to flatter me?"

She smirked—it could be called nothing else. The duke had never seen a Norn smile. It was an unsettling experience.

"I said before that you do not understand us. I will tell you once more, and then the Garden itself will witness I have behaved honorably. We will not surrender, mortal. Even if you batter down our ancient gates and bring all your numbers into our mountain, still we will not surrender. You said that the women and children could flee, but you understand nothing about us. Not even the lowliest caste-servants or slaves will give in, even if you kill every Sacrifice." She pointed toward the mountain. "Those Hikeda'ya you dismiss as mere women and children will lie in wait for your warriors in every dark place of our home, at every bend in every tunnel, with stones and sharp sticks. And eventually there will come a moment desperate enough that the Order of Singers will call up some of the older, darker inhabitants of our mountain. Those of your brutes who are not slaughtered will stumble in waking nightmare through the dark places until they die. You cannot conceive of the terrors you will face, Duke of Elvritshalla. Victory? That is no word for what the survivors of your army will take away from Nakkiga—those few who escape. Madness will be their reward. Madness and death."

Something rumbled as she finished. Isgrimnur looked up at the sky, but the low gray firmament was so full of darkly knotted clouds that the thunder might have come from any direction.

"I thank you for your honesty, General. I will not make the mistake of calling you 'Lady' again." He folded his arms across his chest. "But do not mistake my troops, either. They are fierce fighters all, hard men. They have faced your kind many times already and do not fear them. And they have many losses to avenge."

Suno'ku looked at him again. The duke thought he could see

something moving behind the bland face, a hint of what almost looked like surprise.

"Losses?" she said, her voice cold as the sky. "Losses, you say? I saw a hundred of my best Sacrifices die before my eyes at Asu'a. I saw my foreparent, our greatest general, pulled down and swarmed by your rabble. I found his body in pieces."

"Asu'a. You mean the Hayholt." Isgrimnur fought down his own anger. "My son and heir died there at your people's hands. *My son.* And Thane Brindur's son was burned alive by your troops only a short time ago, remember? We could hear his screams all over the battlefield." The sky rumbled again, and this time even the ground seemed to shudder. Isgrimnur wondered if the Norns were working some foul new weathermagic. Was he being stalled? What other reason could this hard-faced killer have to trade words with him after their business was plainly finished?

"Then we both have little reason to speak more," she said. Strangely, she seemed almost relieved. "We are finished here."

"I suppose we are," said Isgrimnur. "But I would ask one more question. You are brave, General—maybe even more than the rest of your fierce race. I knew that from the first moment I saw you. I do not expect any pity from you for my kind, but is there no pity in you for your own people? Would your pride condemn every one of them to death?"

"It is not pride, Duke Isgrimnur. My people are everything to me," she said. "I would die for them a thousand times, but they would do the same for their queen and their land without question." She said it so simply that he knew for her it was an utter truth. It also meant that she was right: the time for talk was over.

This time the rumble came not just from the sky but all around. Isgrimnur looked up, surprised. Sludig was running toward him.

"The gate!" he shouted. "The White Foxes are opening the gate! Treachery! The Norns are attacking!"

But the gate was still closed, Isgrimnur saw, nothing open but the salley-port, and that barely, with the other three Norn legates still standing before it, watching. He looked to Suno'ku, but she seemed as puzzled as he was. She stared up into the sky for a long, searching moment before turning toward the great bulk of the mountain.

Sludig reached Isgrimnur, grabbed his arm, and yanked so hard that the duke almost fell. Another guard reached him too, and the two of them began to wrestle him back toward the Rimmersgard lines. "Hurry!" Sludig cried.

But no force of Norns were issuing from the gate; it was still closed, though the noise was growing louder all around, deafeningly loud, like the hooves of ten thousand mounted riders or more.

Stumbling backward as his men pulled at him, Isgrimnur looked up at the mountainside and saw a massive cornice of stone, far above the gate, abruptly break loose from the slope's evening-darkened face with a crack louder than a thunderclap. It began to shudder and slide downward, breaking into pieces as it came.

"The mountain," Isgrimnur cried. "By Dror's Mallet, the mountain itself is falling!"

The first great pieces of stone smashed down around the gate, digging huge gouges in the snowy ground, throwing up splatters of mud. A massive length of stone had come loose from the mountain face directly above the gate, a piece of rock big enough to hold a good-sized Rimmersgard town; it broke into pieces as it shuddered and scraped its way downward. Men were screaming and shouting all around. Isgrimnur himself might have been one of them, but the roar was growing louder by the instant and he could not tell. The rumble became a deep, rasping growl that seemed to shake every bone in his body until he thought they would shatter—and yet, astonishingly, his feet were still under him.

Isgrimnur was half-running, half-staggering toward his troops when suddenly his legs were swept from beneath him and he fell heavily, face down into the mud. Then something shook the ground so brutally that he was bounced up into the air and flipped over onto his back. He saw a black boulder the size of a house cartwheel toward him down the sloping side of the valley, but he could not move because Sludig was clutching his legs.

The great oblong stone bounded past them. It hit the looser soil of the valley floor and teetered up on one end for a moment, then fell back, crashing to the ground in an eruption of snowy earth and small stones just a scant dozen yards from where the duke and his rescuer Sludig lay. Shards of rock as big as Isgrimnur himself rained down around them, but the duke could only cover his head and stare back at the mountain.

As the last and largest chunks of stone tumbled down the steep mountain face, some of them a hundred cubits or more in length, Isgrimnur thought he saw the pale form of the Norn general Suno'ku still standing in the same spot where they had last spoken, facing the mountain, as unmoving as if she had been god-struck. Then the great sliding mass of stone came down where she stood, grinding and crashing, and she was gone.

For long moments afterward the noise echoed along the valley like the groan of a retreating storm. Then, at last, it was silent.

The ancient gate and the entire lower front of the mountain had vanished from view, buried under uncountable tons of black stone, a monstrous mass of ship-sized boulders and crushed and broken rock piled far up the mountain's slope.

Isgrimnur wiped his face. His hand came away bloody, although he felt no pain. Sludig crawled up beside him. The duke could hear screams from the troops who had been crushed beneath the outer edge of the rockfall but had not been lucky enough to die. But from the mountain, from the city of the Norns, there was only the near-silence of settling stone and the occasional patter as a rock bounced down the piled rubble until it found a resting place.

"Duke Isgrimnur," Sludig asked, pulling at his arm. Isgrimnur could barely hear him, his ears still deafened. "Do you live? Are you badly hurt?"

Isgrimnur stared at the blood on his fingers as though it were something he had never seen before, then lifted his eyes to the grave, silent stillness of the mountain, which stood wreathed in stone dust and swirling snow.

"It's over," Isgrimnur said, though his mouth was so choked with dirt he could barely form the words. Despite everything else, he could only think of the pale shape of the warrior Suno'ku, her back straight as a sword blade while she waited for death. He spat to clear his tongue. "God save us all, Sludig, we will never clear that . . . and they will never escape. The war is over."

Part
Five

The Long Way Back

"The thoroughfares of Nakkiga's first tier were hung with snowy mourning banners, and even the poorest of the poor had some white token tied at arm or neck. The general's own Sacrifice host formed an honor guard for their fallen leader, lining up along both sides of the Glinting Passage so that all who came to Black Water Field to honor her walked between them.

"Suno'ku seyt-Iyora's coffin was empty, of course, but the people of Nakkiga still turned out in great numbers to bid the beloved warrior farewell. Despite the loss of such a figure, some even sensed an air of triumph to the ceremony: after all—and against all expectations—the mortals' siege had ended, the enemy was leaving, and Nakkiga still stood.

"Except for the queen herself and Lord Akhenabi, both still under the veil of the yi'indra, all the highest nobles of our race attended Suno'ku's funeral. Prince-Templar Pratiki of the queen's own Hamakha clan placed a sacred witchwood crown upon the empty coffin, and the general's commander and relative, High Marshal Muyare sey-Iyora, honored her with a wreath of yew branches. And as a further tribute to Suno'ku's bravery and the esteem in which she was held by all, High Magister Yaarike of the Builders brought his family's greatest heirloom, a jeweled necklace called The Heart of What Was Lost, and placed it beside the other offerings.

"When the ceremony was ended, the coffin and tributes were carried *in a slow march through the crowds and then deposited in the Iyora clan vault. In a time of great danger to our race, Suno'ku had become the spirit of the Hikeda'ya. The people would never forget her."*

—Lady Miga seyt-Jinnata, the Order of Chroniclers

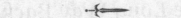

"Come, husband, why can I not tempt you? The smoked blind-fish is exquisite, the best we have had in an age. Even better, it comes from your lake."

"It is not *my* lake," Viyeki said, but even he thought he sounded unconvincing.

"Of course it is." Khimabu gestured for one of the new servants to take him the platter. "Who else's would it be?"

One of the strangest and most fortuitous things that had happened when the stones fell and sealed off the gates was that the great throbbing and shifting of the mountain's substance had also caused a collapse at the site deep in the mountain where Viyeki's Builder host had begun digging around the Forbidden Deeps. This great rupture of stone had exposed an entrance into another part of the lower depths, revealing a heretofore unknown lake that had lain hidden in the darkness of Nakkiga's roots since Time itself began. The new body of water, which a surprised Viyeki named Dark Garden Lake when he was summoned there by his workers the day after the collapse, proved to be rich with eyeless fish and other edible creatures and mosses, easing at a stroke the city's fears of starvation. Although it seemed certain that public sentiment would rename it Lake Suno'ku, in all other ways Viyeki had received the credit for the momentous discovery. And if he was uncomfortable with his newfound acclaim, his wife was not.

"Why will you not eat?" she asked. "If you will not try the fish, at least have a little porcupine moss. The cook has outdone himself." Porcupine moss was a bristly sort of lichen, hard to find, but when boiled and spiced it was a favorite of the old noble families.

"I cannot help thinking it all too convenient," Viyeki said. "Magister Yaarike knows more of the deep places than anyone else in Nakkiga. He must have known there was a chance we would find a lake there."

"It is of no matter," said Khimabu in frustration. "Yaarike favors you, as he should. Despite all your worries, he has now announced to the Maze that you will be his successor as high magister! Is it so strange or wrong that he might have hoped you would find such a place?"

Viyeki put down his fork with the untasted fish still on it. "Forgive me, wife," he said. "I am troubled by many things. I am poor company."

"You are, it is true," she said. "But I forgive you." She brightened. Her features might have been those of a girl just emerged into womanhood. "My cousin Jasiyo says he thinks the Maze will honor you on the queen's behalf. Think of that!"

He rose, trying not to seem too hasty, but his stomach had suddenly gone sour and the smell of the meal was making him queasy. "Yes, we are honored, of course," he said. "And I am grateful. Please excuse me, my wife. My head is aching, and I feel the need of some air."

It was not air he needed, or even freedom of movement. As he paced the streets of the second tier, Viyeki knew that what he really needed was certainty, or at least understanding. What he needed was for all his painful, confused thoughts to give him some peace.

The Hikeda'ya of Nakkiga had always lived with the shaking and crumbling of the earth. Thus, when the great stones had fallen upon the gates, most of the people had thought it only another example of the mountain's uneasy sleep. But Viyeki had been outside the mountain during the first moments, before the others had dragged him through the sally-gate. He had seen the twilight suddenly turn black and the sky turn to falling stone. He had seen dozens of Rimmersmen obliterated beneath the tumbling rocks in an instant. He had watched General Suno'ku wait calmly for death, then saw her snuffed like a candle. He still awoke several times each night, gasping, trying in vain to shield himself from a thundershower of stone.

But his continuing disquiet was not caused simply by what he had experienced when the mountain fell. What was troubling him far more was Yaarike's strange gesture at the general's funeral.

Like the rest of the Hikeda'ya who were present, serfs and nobles, Viyeki had applauded Yaarike's generous tribute to the fallen warrior, his tomb-gift of Clan Kijada's treasured relic, The Heart of What Was Lost; unlike the others, though, Viyeki's approval had not even lasted until the coffin had been slid into its niche. And the more he considered it the less sense it made, until now the question tormented him through all his waking hours.

Why would his master do such a thing? Many of the Hikeda'ya had genuinely loved and admired Suno'ku, but Yaarike had not been one of them. If any other high official had spoken of her so slightingly, then put a magnificent and treasured family heirloom—an heirloom of the Garden itself!—on her coffin, Viyeki would have thought it merely cynical, a political gesture to buy favor with the common herd who had revered the general and almost come to believe that she had fought off the Northmen and saved them single-handedly. But Viyeki's master was famous for his dismissal of mere gestures, of his refusal to court popularity by appeasing either the masses or the powerful elite. In any case, Yaarike had no need to appease anyone. Even after the great rockfall, the work of the Builders during the siege and Viyeki's own discovery made the high magister nearly unassailable.

So why should Lord Yaarike do such a strange thing? Why had Viyeki's unsentimental old master felt moved enough to seal away his family's greatest prize in someone else's grave?

At a moment when his own fortunes were at their height, the puzzle of it would not let him be. And so, churning inside, Viyeki walked the dark streets, barely seeing the other nobles when they saluted him or the servants and low-caste workers who scurried out of his path.

"I have been the besieger and also the besieged," Isgrimnur said as he sipped his bowl of ale. "But I have never seen anything as damnably strange as this."

He was sitting on a wooden chest in front of his tent while his carls cooked supper over the fire. The skies had cleared, and despite the afternoon shadow of the mountain stretching over the valley, it was not terribly cold. Sludig, still done up in his furs, held out his own bowl to be refilled.

"Rocks fall," Sludig said. "Even mountains. God has His own plans."

"It is not that." Isgrimnur wiped his lips with the back of his hand. "It's knowing that the White Foxes are *still there*. It's as if they went into a house and closed the door and shuttered the windows, leaving us to stand help-lessly in the street. The murdering creatures are *there*, only a few steps from us, but we can do nothing! If I had twice the number of men it still would take me half a year or more to clear all that stone."

Sludig shrugged. "Let the fairies starve in their hole, my lord. We can't get in, but they can't get out, either."

"They will not stay in there forever," said Isgrimnur. "I cannot believe they will be unable to find their way out again. They tunnel like moles, those Norns."

"Then we will come back and finish the job," said Sludig, and drank deeply.

Isgrimnur watched his men beginning the long process of breaking down the camp and preparing for the trip south. They were in no hurry, nor should they be: many of the wounded were still too weak to walk, and it would be a long march home to Rimmersgard—even farther for most of the mercenary troops. He thought for a moment of the tall fellow he had knighted for helping kill a giant. Nabbanai, was he? Or Perdruinese? Something southern. That one likely wouldn't reach home until Aedon-tide, poor devil. But perhaps his new rank would help speed his way. "Did we give those fellows who killed the giant anything? Some gold?"

"I will see to it, my lord." Sludig stretched. "But not being a knight myself, I don't know exactly how much to give them."

Isgrimnur showed him a sour grin. "You need not fear I'll forget your long, hard service, Sludig. In any case, you will be recognized and re-warded by the king and queen, too. So these men—reward them well. It takes courage as well as luck to kill one of those monsters."

"Courage is always in supply," Sludig said. "Luck, not so often, so let's offer our thanks to the mountain for coming down on our enemies. The good Lord alone knows how many men we would have lost if we'd had to take the city inside it."

"Shall we drink to the mountain? That seems strange, somehow." Is-grimnur looked up at the great jagged cone. Steam and smoke still wreathed its upper reaches, as if to show that no matter what had hap-pened, a scattering of stones here or there, the great peak still remained above such mundane things as even a war between mortals and fairies.

"Why not?" Sludig waved his bowl for more and one of the carls dutifully came forward with the jug. "We have drunk to defeated enemies before this, if they were brave or noble. The mountain ended the war, and because of that many of our men will see their homes and families again. That strikes me as noble enough to warrant a salute." He lifted his bowl. "To the mountain! Long may she keep her secrets hidden from God-fearing men. Long may she keep the Norns out of the light and away from our lands."

"Yes, I can drink to that, my friend," said Isgrimnur as he lifted his own. "To the mountain, and to the end of killing."

"And to all our brave dead."

Isgrimnur, thinking of Isorn his son, suddenly could not find words and only nodded.

When they finished their toast Sludig sat silently, regarding the shadow-darkened peak. "At any rate," he said suddenly, "now perhaps we can put our swords away for a time. The war is over. The Storm King and the Norns have been destroyed or driven back into the darkness." He looked at the duke, slightly shamefaced. "In truth, I think I would like to buy a farm."

Isgrimnur laughed so hard he spilled the last of his ale. "By the Ransomer, I wager that never in a thousand, thousand years, will such a thing come to pass—my brave, bloody-handed Sludig turned farmer! But thank you for amusing me when I thought I was beyond it."

Sludig smiled. "Perhaps it will not happen, my lord. I have been wrong erenow, and changed my mind a hundred times about other things. But at this moment, after all we've seen and done, I think it would be nice to watch things grow."

The Order of Builders had repair work underway almost everywhere in Nakkiga; with his noble blood, rank, and especially his new importance, it was easy for Viyeki to go where he pleased, see what he wished, and ask whatever questions he wanted. But the thing he was seeking did not appear on any of the official schemes, so it took some time before he tracked down the gang chief who had led the small crew.

The chief, a slender, older Hikeda'ya with hands so callused they were yellow, led Viyeki into the highest tunnels behind the mountain's face, far above most of the work that had been done to shore up the gates and defend the heights of Ur-Nakkiga, to a place many hundreds of cubits above the starting point of the rockfall.

"Here it is, my lord Host Foreman," said the underling. "The work was done in the very first days of the siege and then abandoned."

Viyeki looked around. The natural cavern had been hastily and crudely enlarged, but that was not what caught his attention. A row of a dozen or more tunnels had been gouged in the cavern's rough floor nearest the outside of the mountain, each tunnel as wide as Viyeki's waist. Somewhat strangely, the rough chamber had its own well.

"Where does this water come from?" he asked, looking down into the blackness. He dropped a pebble, heard it splash not far below.

"From one of the meltwater rivulets that run down from the peak," the chief told him. "All thanks to the Garden, the mountain itself makes certain we will never die of thirst."

"And what was the purpose of your task here? What need was this digging so high above the gates meant to serve?"

"We were never told, Lord Viyeki."

Finished with his inspection of the well, he examined the crude tunnels that had been sunk into the cavern floor. Their endings were beyond what he could see with his torch but they seemed unexceptional. When he had first discovered a passing mention of this place in the order's records chamber, Viyeki had felt sure he had found something important, but now that he was here it was hard to see it as anything more than another abandoned project from the confusion of the siege's early days. "Do you know who ended the digging here?"

The gang-foreman looked at him in surprise. Underlings were seldom told much about their work, and they almost never, ever asked. "No, Host Foreman. But the high magister himself came to see it in the beginning. Perhaps he was displeased with the location chosen."

So Yaarike had been here to inspect the digging. "And did he say anything about the project being abandoned?"

Again the look of incomprehension. "No, lord. The order came to us some eight or nine bells later. There was much to do and it was a muddled time. I'm sorry I cannot tell you more."

Viyeki nodded. "No matter. I am only correcting some of our records back at the order-house. Your assistance has been appreciated."

The gang chief looked cautiously pleased, but still maintained his stance of extreme humility. "It is an honor to serve you, Lord Viyeki," he said. "Everyone knows that you saved our people from starvation."

He waved his hand, dismissing the praise. "The spirit of the Garden was watching out for us all."

As he followed his guide back down the steep tunnels to the lower levels of the works, he felt compelled to ask, "Did anyone visit this site during the last days of the siege, after the work was abandoned?"

"I don't think so, Lord Viyeki. Why would they?"

"Of course," Viyeki said. "Why indeed?"

The temple bells rang to mark the passage of the days, and the life of Nak-kiga continued as it had since the siege's end, the city both mourning its dead and rejoicing at its unexpected salvation. But Viyeki found he could not do either with any comfort: the questions of what had happened before the collapse of the mountainside still worried at his thoughts like a canker. Even his wife Khimabu, who was otherwise very contented with the state of affairs, noticed his distraction.

"It would be one thing if you mourned the dead properly, dressing in white and paying the priests for bells to be rung on feast days," she told him. "But instead you go about with a long face and your robes covered in dust like a common laborer. My family wonders what is wrong with you—and so do I."

But on the few occasions he tried to explain, she did not want to hear.

"Why would you act this way? Can you not understand that we have been very fortunate? Why would you wish to trouble your people, who have had enough of suffering, with questions about something that is over and done with?"

Thus, when Viyeki discovered several more similarly abandoned projects above the failure line of the collapse, each one with its own well, all strung along the face of the mountain like gems on a necklace, he told no one. There was only one he wished to speak with about it in any case, and Viyeki was not quite ready for that conversation.

"*We come now to the end of this particular tale of the Wars of Return, and to a necessary apology from your chronicler. Because these words were written less than half a Great Year after the events described, and because your scribe lived through the siege of the city and felt the mountain fall it has been more difficult than usual to keep this chronicler's flawed perceptions from affecting the proper recounting of fact.*

"*The only true history is that which has survived for generations and provided edification to our people, history that gives us an understanding of the past which holds firmly to the eternal truths of who we are—the undeniable truths of our martyrs, our sacred home, and our beloved monarch.*

"*But since Queen Utuk'ku slept the keta-yi'indra throughout the siege, and even as of this writing has still not returned to us from her healing exile on the Road of Dreams, this telling of our history can only be flawed and incomplete, full of the errors that come when one humble chronicler tries to tell the tale without the necessary perspective of time and the corrections of her superiors. Still, it was this scribe's duty to do so, and she performed it as best she could.*

"*A great tragedy in the south was nearly followed by an even greater tragedy, the loss of our longtime home and the destruction of our people. But by the virtue of the nobles of our most important orders, the Sacrifices, the Singers, and the Builders, we survived. A lesson is here for all: Do not trust in what seem to be the truths of the moment. Put your faith instead in the things that are eternal. Love our queen and love our mountain, love and remember the Garden That Was Lost, and the song of our race will find its proper melody.*

"*Here this telling ends. The humble chronicler begs pardon for her failings and hopes that her efforts have brought at least something of use to those who read this.*"

—Lady Miga seyt-Jinnata, Order of Chroniclers,
in the Eighth Great Year of High Celebrant Zuniyabe,
16th magister of that order

Viyeki's Builders were digging out a blocked main tunnel to the outside. As he returned from an inspection of the workers' progress, making his way down a narrow, nameless alley on the main tier of Nakkiga, he suddenly felt the hairs on his neck rise. It took a moment longer before he heard the muffled sound of soft boots. Instead of waiting to discover whether any of those coming behind him even approached his own rank, Viyeki heeded the warning of his lifted hackles and stepped to the side to allow those behind him to pass.

It was a line of Singers in robes the color of dried blood, a dozen or more, and the four at the back were carrying a litter. As the procession went by, some silent signal was passed. The litter stopped and its curtains parted. Viyeki could see nothing of the face in the deep-shadowed hood that appeared there, but he knew that unmusical voice the instant he heard it.

"Hold, there! I see a face I believe I know. Is that Viyeki sey-Enduya of the Builders?"

Surprised and perhaps even a bit frightened at the unexpected recognition, Viyeki made all the proper gestures of respect as he bowed low. "It is, great Lord Akhenabi, and it is flattering that you remember me. I only heard of your recovery a few bells ago, but I have already lit several candles in the temples in gratitude for your return to us. I'm sure all of Nakkiga feels the same." Despite his fear of the powerful Lord of Song, Viyeki was not exaggerating: the people of Nakkiga might all tremble before the magician, but Akhenabi had been a familiar part of all their lives since before any but the queen and a few of her eldest councilors could remember. The news of his reawakening had been greeted by most as a reassuring return to the way things had been.

As befitted one of his stature, the great Singer gave no sign he had heard the flattering words. "I have been told that Lord Yaarike has named you his successor, Host Foreman. I hope that when you ascend to Yaarike's title you will be as cooperative with the important work of our order as your master has been."

Without another word or any sort of sign, Akhenabi's litter rose back onto the shoulders of his carriers. The hooded procession abruptly moved off down the street, vanishing into the darkness and leaving Viyeki to ponder all the meanings that could lurk in the Lord of Song's words.

Cooperative. He hopes I will be as cooperative as Lord Yaarike. That innocuous phrase, which ordinarily would have seemed only a bit of obvious politicking, seemed in present circumstances something more sinister. *Of course our orders worked together during the siege for the good of all Nakkiga. But does Akhenabi mean some other cooperation with the Order of Song? Something darker and more secret?*

After a long day spent breathing stone-dust in the sweltering depths of the mountain, Viyeki wanted nothing more than to return to his house, to order and quiet. But Akhenabi's cryptic words gnawed at him, and he knew rest would be as elusive as it had been for many nights now. The only thing that might quiet his mind was finding answers to the questions that tormented him, though he knew hearing them might destroy his world.

But even if he could not put off the confrontation any longer, he still had to return to his house first. He had something there that he needed.

"Southerner! Porto! Over here!"

It was Kolbjorn, waving from the other side of a group of men hitching oxen to carts. "Hoy! Over here!" the Northman called.

Porto went to join him, stepping over the quantities of dung that decorated the muddy road. The wind had a freezing bite to it today, and the drovers and others were struggling to work while keeping their backs to the icy breeze.

"I've been looking all over for you," the young Rimmersman said. "One of the duke's men is waiting for us back at the campfire."

Porto pulled his cloak tighter. "Why? By the Good God, they're not going to keep us here any longer, are they? I have five hundred leagues to ride home. I will be fortunate if I am back before the Elysiamansa festival."

"You will be fortunate indeed if snakes don't eat you," said Kolbjorn. "I hear the southern lands are fierce with snakes."

Porto rolled his eyes. The Rimmersmen all seemed to think he had

spent his life in a steaming jungle like the swampy Wran instead of a perfectly civilized city. "Oh, yes, the snakes are common as kittens where I
come from. They crawl into your bed at night to stay warm and then lick
your nose to wake you when they're hungry."

Kolbjorn stared at him for a moment, sensing the other might be
having fun at his expense. "Well, I'd rather fight giants every day than
have those Devil's creatures under my feet all the time."

Porto laughed. "You are a braver man than I, Kolbjorn, but we already
knew that. What does the duke's man want?"

"Ask him. There he stands."

The yellow-bearded Rimmersman was the only figure beside the
fire—the one they called Sludig Two-Axes, one of Isgrimnur's fiercest
fighters. At the moment he looked distracted but otherwise approach-
able.

"You were looking for me, my lord?"

Sludig lifted his head. "Ah, yes. Porto of Perdruin, am I right? And
don't call me "my lord." You're a knight and I'm not." He showed his teeth
in a hard grin. "Yes, I've been looking for you. The duke sent this." He
lifted his broad hand. It held a purse.

When he was sure it was really meant for him, Porto reached out. "What
is it?" He loosened the string and looked inside. "Sweet Mother of the Aedon, this is for me? Three gold imperators? And look at all this silver!"

Kolbjorn was smirking. "I already got mine. Counted it, too. Five
gold's worth all together."

"But why?"

"Because it is traditional when a man has been knighted that he be
given land or wealth," Sludig said, grinning. "Duke Isgrimnur asked me
to tell you he is short of land these days until all the new king's and queen's
business is dealt with, but he can at least give you something to make your
homeward trip a little easier. Do you accept it?"

"Accept it? My wife would skin me if I didn't. Please thank the duke—
he is very generous."

"More than generous," said Kolbjorn. "Was there one for Aerling as
well? The man who led us?"

"He has had it already," said Sludig. "Barely seemed to notice, I have
to say. Busy polishing that giant's skull."

Porto shook his head. "He has not been entirely right since . . . the day the mountain fell."

Sludig nodded. "In truth, none of us have been. Now I must be going. There is much to do before we break camp tomorrow and start back. Before your road parts from ours, Southerner, you and this young Vestiman should come and take a cup with me."

"Seems a nice enough fellow," Kolbjorn said when Sludig was gone. "He strangled one of the White Foxes with his bare hands, did you know that?"

Porto shrugged. "We have all done strange things here at the ends of the earth."

The magister's chamber on the highest floor of the order-house was chilly, as Yaarike always kept it, with a small oil lamp on his table providing the only light and heat. They had been working together for hours bringing the master lists up to date on the order's many current tasks, but Viyeki was so full of disquiet he had spoken very little.

"You seem remote, Viyeki-*tza*," Yaarike finally said. "You have scarcely attended to a word I've said, forcing me to repeat myself many times. That is not like you. You were always my most eager student."

Viyeki took a breath, then another. "That is because something is troubling me, High Magister."

Yaarike's sharp eyes watched him closely. "Speak, then. I hope it is not that thing we spoke of before. You deserve all that has come to you from finding the hidden lake. It does not harm your fitting modesty."

"That is not what troubles me now. May I share my thoughts, Master?"

"I think you should."

Now that the time had come he found it hard to speak. The basalt walls of the order-house pressed in on him, their great age a silent reproof. How dare he stand beneath that arched ceiling, which had seen hundreds of foremen like Viyeki come and go, and harbor such thoughts about a high magister, let alone one who had been so generous to him? He felt he stood on sliding ground, being carried toward a precipice.

Better to jump than to fall.

"I have been thinking about how you showed me the Heart of What Was Lost when you thought you might not survive to return to Nakkiga, and wished to make certain it would reach your family. That was a great honor, High Magister."

"I have trusted few who are not my blood as I trust you, Viyeki-*tza*."

"But then you gave your sacred family treasure to be buried with General Suno'ku, to honor her. Putting the happiness of the people above your own desires."

Yaarike looked at him evenly, but his tone had a question in it. "Yes. That is always a magister's duty."

"I do my best to understand all your lessons, Master. Because of that, I have been thinking, and I have decided that I need to show you something of my own family heritage. May I?"

"Of course."

Viyeki withdrew the bundle of cloth from his robe and placed it on the table in front of his master. Then he carefully unwrapped it until the gray thing lay revealed.

For long moments Yaarike only looked down at the witchwood dagger, at its long, thin blade and its pommel in the shape of a flower, the petals made of milky crystal. "It is a beautiful thing," the magister said at last. "How old?"

"Nothing like the Heart of What Was Lost," said Viyeki. "This snow rose dagger did not come from the Lost Garden, but was made here in this land—in our old city of Kementari before it fell. It was given to my foreparent Enduyo in the era of the fifth Celebrant, as a token of gratitude from the queen. In some ways it is the foundation of our clan."

"Your foreparent was greatly honored indeed, if this gift came from the queen's own hand. May I hold it?" Now Yaarike glanced up to meet Viyeki's gaze, his questioning look almost aggressive.

Viyeki spread his hands. "Of course, Master."

Still cradling it in its wrappings, the magister tilted the slender blade to study it more carefully in the unsteady lamplight. *Dark*, thought Viyeki. *It is always so dark inside the mountain and inside the hearts of the Hikeda'ya.* For a moment, with the end of all things familiar pressing on his mind and speeding his heart, he again felt himself to be a creature that lived its life in secret, some sightless, burrowing thing of the dark depths. If the race of Hikeda'ya all died here beneath the mountain, the world outside might never know.

Nor care if they did know, except to breathe a sigh of relief, Viyeki decided, and in that instant nothing seemed to matter at all—not his honor, not his painful, complicated feelings about his master, not his marriage nor his clan nor any of the things that he had thought important.

Suddenly he felt too weak to stand. Without asking permission, he let himself sag into the chair opposite his master's seat. Yaarike glanced up briefly from the snow rose dagger but said nothing. After a moment's more inspection, the magister held out the knife. Viyeki took it back.

"I seem to remember some controversy surrounding Enduyo," said Yaarike, "but I never knew the details."

"Forgive me, Master, but I do not believe you." Viyeki found himself growing bolder, as though he had let go of something that had previously kept him tethered to the known, the comfortable. "No, I cannot believe one of your wisdom would have offered someone like me the chance to succeed you unless you knew every detail of my ancestry back to the Eight Ships—if not all the way back to the Garden itself. And the controversy, as you call it, happened during your lifetime, when you were already a young foreman in this order. Surely you remember? After all, it ended my ancestor's life."

Yaarike actually smiled, a wintry twitch of his thin lips. "Ah, but I am old and have much to recall. Perhaps you could remind me, Viyeki-*tza*."

"My ancestor Enduyo of Kementari was an official of the palace, a master cleric. He was ordered by the queen's Oathbound to confirm the treachery of two Maze clerics with whom he often worked. He had no personal proof of their guilt, but the palace believed them guilty so he was ordered to testify against them. To refuse would have meant the disgrace and destruction of his entire family. Given no honorable choice, he elected instead to use this dagger and end himself. Like so." Viyeki pulled his robe aside and let the knife slide forward a little until the tip of the narrow gray blade rested against his chest. "Even the clerics he had been ordered to incriminate attended his funeral, out of respect. Of course, they were still found guilty—still went to the executioner." He looked up at his master. "So you see, this blade is schooled at solving difficult problems."

"And is there a reason you brought it here to show me?" the magister asked. "I certainly hope you are not planning to use it to take a life today . . . yours or anyone else's." Yaarike poured himself a cup from the ewer on the table, then without asking filled another cup for Viyeki and pushed it toward him. "Here. This cloudberry wine is a very old vintage. It is said there is a trace of *kei-mi* in every barrel."

Viyeki had never tasted the witchwood extract and knew he might never have another chance. He took the cup and drank deep. The wine was tart, almost too sour, with a taste that lingered on his tongue for long moments, as arresting as a memory both strong and bittersweet. "Thank you, my lord." But he would not let himself be distracted. "So you see, I find myself in a dilemma today, High Magister. Only you of all others can help me to resolve it."

"And this dilemma is . . . ?"

"Two choices. One is to denounce someone who has been my teacher and guide much of my life, one whom I have loved like a grandfather."

"A truly dreadful possibility. And your alternative?"

"To remain silent about a terrible crime—not just the murder of a beloved hero but an attack on truth and history itself. So it seems I am trapped between betraying my mentor or my queen." He touched the dagger lying in his lap. "You can see that following my ancestor's course seems the only honorable alternative to those two unthinkable acts."

His master drank deeply, then carefully wiped his upper lip with the back of his hand. "I think you had better tell me what has led you to this perilous situation, High Foreman."

"The death of General Suno'ku, Magister. And the collapse of the mountainside. I have come to believe that neither were accidents."

Yaarike's eyes narrowed ever so slightly, but he only signaled for Viyeki to continue.

He marveled at the calm in his own voice as he described the row of diggings he had found above the gate inside the mountain, all of them listed in the order's records as abandoned projects, all of them exactly the same.

"And what do you guess the purpose of these diggings, as you call them, to have been?" Yaarike asked.

"To make the mountain fall."

"And how would that be accomplished—and kept secret, no less?" He sounded as if he was challenging a bright pupil to think harder, not arguing against a foolish impossibility.

Now that he was committed to speaking what he had so long kept secret and silent, Viyeki felt as though his gut had been tied into a cruel knot. "The hard part would be the secrecy, because it would not be a simple or swift task. After all, it took nearly two score of our Builders working for days to bring down a much smaller weight of stone at Three Ravens Tower."

"True enough. But who could undertake such a complicated and dangerous task here in Nakkiga without anyone knowing? And why hide it? The collapse of the mountainside saved our city and our people, after all."

Every word from his master's mouth pulled at the ends of the knot inside him, tightening it. "The deed was hidden because defense of our mountain was not its only purpose, I would guess. As to the other question, the person or persons responsible would need both knowledge of such things and the power make to make it happen and keep it secret from the people of Nakkiga."

Yaarike nodded slowly. "That makes sense, at least. Please continue, Host Foreman. Tell me the rest of how this astounding trick could be accomplished from inside the mountain."

"The set of tunnels in each digging would have been excavated by workmen who would not know what they were doing—tunnels leading down to a place where the rock of the mountain's face was weakest. Then the workers would be sent away and the diggings declared useless. But each of those places also had a source of water close at hand. Could not someone repeatedly fill those new tunnels with water, which would then run down and into the cracks behind that weak spot in the mountain's face? Even the youngest scholar in our order knows that once such water reached the end of its journey it would freeze because of the chill of the outside air. When the ice expanded, pushing the rock outward around it, more water could be poured in, beginning the process again. Eventually, enough of such careful, secret work could weaken the entire rock face until it split loose from the mountain's surface and fell, destroying our enemies below and sealing the gates off from invaders for a long time. And only the most skillful of Builders could even hope to make such a thing happen at the proper time. Even so, it must have been very difficult."

"I hear many interesting ideas in what you say, Viyeki-*tza*, but not much in the way of proof. And although it caused the tragedy of Suno'ku's death, the collapse also saved our city—perhaps our entire race. It would be a hard thing to accuse an official of high family of such a strange and userful crime."

"I know, Master. That is one of many reasons why I brought this." He patted the blade in his lap. "Because with it I can solve that problem without bringing the official's family or my own into disrepute."

"Solve what problem, exactly?"

"The problem of not being able to let it go. I need to *know*, High Magister. I need to know what happened, and the truth about someone I admired beyond any other."

His master looked from the knife in Viyeki's hands to his own hands, graceful and strong, roughened by the handling of innumerable stones. "Let me then hasten you toward your solution." Abruptly, Yaarike pulled open his heavy robes, exposing the thin tunic he wore beneath. "You are right in your suspicions, Viyeki-*tza*—all of them. It was my idea to bring the mountain down. And I also caused Suno'ku's death, although that was not as I wished it. Now strike, then fold my hands around the blade so it will seem I pierced my own heart. Otherwise my clan will hound you, and you should not take the punishment for my mistakes."

Viyeki shook his head. "No. This blade is not for you, Master—it is for me to end my own life. I cannot live in a world where one who means so much to me, who has shaped my being more than my own parents, could do such a thing." His hand closed around the hilt and he lifted the needle-sharp dagger to his breast. "Just tell me why first, Master. Why did you kill the general? She seemed brave and honorable to me. Why did you hate her so?"

Yaarike seemed surprised. "I did not hate her. I said what I believed at her tomb—she was the best of us."

"But you killed her!"

The Lord of Builders sighed. "Not by choice—I for one hoped she would escape to the Northmen's side of the rockfall, but the collapse took longer to begin than I'd guessed. Why do you suppose I tried to take on the role of legate—the role you infuriatingly stole back from me? I did not want to see you killed or made a prisoner of the mortals. If things went awry, I wanted you to replace me as leader of this order."

But Viyeki was fixed on one word. "What do you mean, 'we,' Magister? Did you take Naji into your confidence when you would not trust me?"

Yaarike shook his head. "Ah, Viyeki, how can you be so clever and yet such a fool? Host Foreman Naji is of no importance. He knew nothing of any of this. I gave him the task of supervising the gate only because I wanted no blame to adhere to *you* if my plan went awry."

"But you said *we*, Master. Who else planned this with you?"

"You spoke of the need for secrecy. That is what Lord Akhenabi brought to the conspiracy. Who better to undertake a task like that, to undermine the mountain under the very nose of a hundred Builders, than his Singers? They can walk the between-spaces when they must. They can be all but invisible."

"But . . . Akhenabi was asleep!" The idea that his master had planned this with the Lord of Song was the most disturbing thing he had heard.

"So it was told to all Nakkiga. It made his work—our work—easier. But he was not the only one who took part in the plan. Again, why do you think I pushed you away, made it clear that you were not privy to my inmost counsels? Because that inner circle was myself, Akhenabi, and Marshal Muyare."

"The marshal? Sunoku's own relative conspired against her?" Viyeki let the hand holding the blade fall back into his lap. He had thought himself a cynic, but now was revealed as childishly naive. "Her own clansman wished our greatest general dead?"

"If our people could also be saved, yes," Yaarike said. "Few reach the highest circles in Nakkiga if they are crippled by too much sentiment, and Muyare knew it was only a matter of time until she supplanted him. But Muyare's price for joining the conspiracy was that Akhenabi and I had to agree to support Suno'ku's plan to rebuild our people through interbreeding with slaves. Muyare saw the wisdom in growing a new army, so there will be half-mortals in the houses of our nobles one day soon—half-mortals in the orders themselves."

"So you all joined together to murder her?"

"I did not want to, but it was Akhenabi's price, and if he was willing to gamble with the survival of our people, I was not. As I said, I hoped Suno'ku would only be exiled—that she would become a prisoner of the mortals, along with those who accompanied her. I did not lie when I said she was the best of us. It grieves me still that she was the last casualty of the war against the Northmen."

"This is serpent-talk—truth and lies mixed." Viyeki felt something like a storm boiling inside him now. How simple it would be to end all the confusion, all the disillusionment, with one swift thrust of the knife into his own breast. "Do you tell me you and all the others admired your victim?"

"I cannot speak for Muyare. As for Akhenabi, no. He saw only a rival for power, one who could best his reign of fear with something more genuine—the belief of the people."

"And yet you helped him kill her."

"As I said, I admired her, but I also saw her for what she would become—the end of our race. I did not want her dead, but I did want her gone from Nakkiga."

The tip of the blade had actually pierced the cloth and pricked the skin of his chest; Viyeki could feel the pain like a tiny star burning a mere hand's-breadth from his heart. But as much as he wanted an end to the agony of his thoughts, he wanted answers more. "I do not understand you, Yaarike."

"Suno'ku *was* the heart of what was lost, but made flesh—one who believed the old truths with all her spirit, and could make them real to others by the force of her own belief. But the old truths, I fear, are no longer true, Viyeki-*tza*. That is why the next generation will require different minds, different truths. General Suno'ku, in the burning purity of her heart, would never have given up the struggle against the mortals. She would have waited only until we had bred enough new soldiers to be fit for war again, then led our people into first one disastrous fight against the swarming mortals, then another. Again and again, until nothing of our people and our orginal bloodline was left." Yaarike reached out his hand and gently touched Viyeki's where it held the dagger. "Do you not understand? I have chosen you because you always look at and consider what the others do not, my young pupil. I said once that you could see around corners. Look ahead now. Let your heart tell you if I am wrong or not. Let your heart tell you if what I did was wrong for our people. If your answer is different than mine, then I was wrong about you—wrong about everything—and you must denounce me."

Viyeki closed his eyes. How could the deepest wishes of his people be wrong? How could Suno'ku, that bright, brave flame, have been a danger? One might as easily say that the queen herself had betrayed them. "You are far wiser than I am, Master, but you cannot change me with words. I have already made my peace with death before I came here today," he said. "Like our Sacrifices, I am dead already."

A sudden movement; the magister, moving more quickly than Viyeki could have supposed, knocked the witchwood knife from his hand and sent it clattering to the floor. "By the Garden and all who escaped it, we do not need more Sacrifices!" Yaarike put a hand on him again, his grip surprisingly strong for his great age, holding Viyeki in the chair when he would have scrambled after the fallen blade. "Listen. We have always had Sacrifices and they have always done their duty without question. But in the days and years ahead, we need something different. We need Builders."

Yaarike straightened up, then bent and retrieved the knife, placing it on the table before Viyeki with a deliberateness that was almost like ritual. "Here. It is yours. But do not hasten to end yourself. Think first and think carefully. Suno'ku and Akhenabi and Marshal Muyare—all of them are what we have always been. Even I am too old to change, though I can see the consequences. No, if you choose to live, it will be left to you and those still to come to find a new way, so that our people can survive in this world and still honor the Garden and those who have gone before."

Viyeki could only stare at the knife. His master's voice seemed to come from a long way away.

"I am leaving now," Yaarike said. "Back to my house and my servants and my family, to return here tomorrow and continue with rebuilding our Nakkiga. If you choose to live, you may also choose to denounce me. So be it. My crime is greater than any punishment the palace could devise, so whatever happens, be assured I am already my own torturer. The loss of a family jewel, however precious, is nothing to that. As for you, Viyeki-*tza* . . . what you will become is still an unanswered question." And then, surprisingly, Yaarike bowed with the deep courtesy given from one of high standing to an equal before turning and walking toward the door.

Viyeki sat in the chair, staring at the knife. Enough time passed that it became clear no guards had been summoned, that his master had done just as he had said he would. But Viyeki, his thoughts now weary, dull, and bruised like over-disciplined slaves, did not know what to do next. He had come to the order-house prepared to die. But what if he did not? How could he live each day from now on knowing that all he had thought simple and true was instead as tangled and foul as the roots of a rotting tree?

The lamp burned down until only a flicker lit the room, and still he sat.

When he walked through the front door, his wife and the servants were waiting. When Khimabu saw him she made a gesture of respect that had both fright and anger in it. "Husband! I feared something had happened to you!"

"Nothing has happened to me." He walked past her and placed the wrapped snow rose dagger back in its box upon the fireplace mantel. "Nothing is different. Nothing will change." But as he said it, he knew it was not true. Whatever might follow from this moment, everything had changed.

"I thought you might have been hurt or even killed in some accident," she said, but her tone suggested that she was almost disappointed that nothing had happened to be worth so much worrying.

He shook his head. He had left the house empty, a man who thought himself already dead. Now he was something else—a man who, as his master had said, could see around corners. A man who could think about the days still to come.

"Do not make a few hours of absence sound so dreadful, my wife," he said, and stood patiently while the servants hurried to remove his robes. "What terrible things could happen to me? I will get up tomorrow like all days, and go to work for my master and my people. After all, I am no Sacrifice, am I? No, I am a Builder."

Aerling, busy as always with his grisly task, scarcely looked up when Porto asked permission to leave the camp and bid Endri goodbye. Porto could scarcely remember the last time Aerling had put down the giant's head. He had removed its flesh and cleaned the skull with rock dust and snow until it almost gleamed, even in the dull northern light. It seemed a strange way to honor fallen comrades, but since he had been in the north, Porto had seen the same look Aerling wore on many other faces and had learned not to ask. If he had possessed a mirror, he suspected he would have seen it on his own face as well.

"We won't have time in the morning," Aerling said. "Go and do what you must now." And then he looked up, and there was something else on his face this time beside mere emptiness. "We have to *remember*. We all have to remember. So go and do your remembering."

Porto nodded.

Aerling looked from Porto down to the grinning, fanged skull. "I need to remember, too." He held up the skull with both hands, tilted it, then lowered it to his lap again and began scraping with his knife at a remaining lump of dried flesh where the neck had joined the head. "I'm going to take it home," he said. "I'm going to put it by the fireplace," he said. "That way I'll remember."

"I'll remember the men too, Thane," Porto said after a moment of silence. "Old Dragi and the rest. They died bravely. You can tell their families that."

Aerling shook his head. "No. I'm going to take this home so that when I wake up in the night sweating cold and my heart beating too fast, remembering that creature staring down at me, I'll look at this instead and I'll remember that it's dead. Dead." He nodded, as though he had proved a point, and went back to his scraping.

As Porto walked out of camp and back into the mountain's long shadow he could not help wondering that everything in the valley now looked so ordinary, so harmless. But for the immense tailing of boulders and broken stones that seemed to have been dumped against the mountain's base, there was no sign anything had happened here for centuries. The gate was buried, the monsters inside now invisible. The trees dripped with melting snow. Even the sounds of his comrades readying for departure seemed to fade away.

He made his way through the abandoned grove, past trees so tall he thought they must have grown before men came to Osten Ard. It was even more quiet here, like an empty church. He hoped the winter would remain at bay until he had at least made his way out of cold Rimmersgard. Porto had a fierce longing for the true southern sun, for the sound of the ocean and the smell of the harbor. He might have been knighted by the duke of Elvritshalla, but he had never felt so Perdruinese as he did now, surrounded by Northmen and the great cold mountains. He could not imagine that, once home, he would ever leave Ansis Pelippé again. Not to fight, that was certain. Not to see friends and comrades die.

Porto saw from the edge of the clearing that something was wrong with Endri's grave. As he neared it he made out that it had been torn open and his heart dropped—the stone cairn he had built had clearly not been enough to keep the scavengers away. Then another thought crept into his mind and his innards went icy cold. He stood at the edge of the pit and looked at the way the stones had been pushed outward around the mound and the way the earth itself had fallen in.

He had prayed Endri's grave had been beyond the Norns' terrible spells, but the marks in the earth of hands digging upward like the claws of a mole told him otherwise. The hole had been emptied, but not from outside. The chances were good that if he had risen, Endri had been burned with the others.

Porto was turning to go when he glanced to the southern side of the clearing. In a knot of young trees, none of them much more than twice the height of a man, leaned an upright, unmoving man-shape, sagging like a scarecrow in a Nabbanai field.

"Oh, dear God," Porto moaned softly, and made the sign of the Tree on his breast. "Sweet Usires preserve us."

As he drew closer to the body he saw that the garments did indeed look like Endri's, stained with earth and blotched with melted snow. But when he was only a yard or so away he saw what had stopped the dead man here, so far from everyone else, so far from both the living and the other spell-raised dead. Endri's red Harborside scarf was tangled in low branches and had pulled tight around the corpse's throat like a hangman's noose. The young man's head hung down, hiding his face, but the skin Porto could see was mottled and black.

He reached out toward the body, doing his best to ignore the terrible stench, disgust and pity fighting in his trembling hands. Endri was facing south. He had not been moving toward the Norn summons, or even toward his living fellows, Porto realized, and tears sprang into his eyes as he understood. The dead man had been trying to go home.

Then Endri moved.

Porto jumped back in horror, and when he made the Tree this time it was as though he stabbed at his own breast. The dead fingers twitched and the corpse tried to take a stumbling step, but it was held fast. Porto could not move either, though no scarf held him.

The corpse lifted its head, revealing the full horror of weeks in the ground. Something in the ruined eyes seemed to recognize Porto, because the dead hand rose as though trying to touch him.

"God in His mercy, what did they do to you?" Porto whispered.

He could not stand to look at the corrupted, collapsing face a moment longer. He drew his sword and hacked as hard as he could at the thing's neck, but was unable to swing his blade cleanly among the encroaching trees. After many more clumsy swipes, the head at last parted from the neck and thumped to the ground. The body slipped from the restraining scarf and tumbled down beside it.

"Now you can go home," he said as he stood over the corpse, though it was hard for him to speak. "Go in peace."

Porto carried first the body and then the head back to its grave, fighting down the urge to retch at the ripe smell of death, trying to remember that this was Endri his friend, who deserved better than he had been given. Then he went back for the scarf, untangling it carefully from the branches. At the grave, he placed the head atop the body and then carefully wrapped the scarf around Endri's neck again, the beloved scarf the boy's mother had woven, to hide the raw and ragged wounds Porto's sword had made.

When he had filled in the grave, and had again piled the heavy stones atop it, he kneeled to pray, then said farewell to his friend for the second and last time. When he was done, Porto climbed to his feet and walked slowly back to camp.

Appendices

An Explanation . . .

An Explanation of the Fairy People Known as Sithi, and their Cousins the Norns, as well as their sometime Servants, the Ocean Children.

Excerpted from *A History of the Erkynlandish People and Their Great Capital, the Hayholt* by Tiamak of Erchester, Counselor to the High Throne

Despite appearing to be of two quite separate races, the golden-skinned Sithi and the Norns with their faces and limbs as pale as snow both belong to a single fairy race which was once called the Keida'ya, which in their tongue means "Children of the Witchwood Trees."

Long before men recorded history, the ancient Keida'ya lived (or so we are told and must believe, for no mortal man was there to see it) in a far-away land called *Venyha Do'sae*, the Garden that was Lost. And although the reasons for the Keida'ya leaving that place and coming here are mostly unknown to us, stories told to our own High King Seoman when he lived among the Sithi, and to ancient travelers like Caias Sterna of Nabban, help us to know something of those elder days before the immortals came to Osten Ard. The Keida'ya lived in a city on the shore of a great sea, and by their own account lived there for a hundred centuries or more in peace and prosperity. But then something came to break that peace, a foe or plague known only as Unbeing. The Keida'ya fought against it, but the power of this Unbeing was too great, and at last they were forced, with the help of their magical servants the Tinukeda'ya, to build eight great ships and escape the Garden that they had lost to Unbeing.

So they came to our land of Osten Ard. The immortals claim they came here long before the first of our own ancestors arrived, but since that goes flatly against the teaching of the Aedonite Church, few scholars accept this as truth. Still, it is known from writings that survived the fall of Khand that even in the days of that impossibly remote empire the *Hyan,* or "Immortal Ones" as they were named by the Khandians, had already built great cities across the world, from the distant north Trollfells to the southern islands.

What also is known beyond doubt is that the Keida'ya saw the growth of the Nabbanai Imperium from the earliest confederations of tiny fiefdoms to its world-spanning heights. The co-existence of the two empires, mortal and immortal, was not without strife, but the Keida'ya, even after they divided themselves into two great clans, the *Zida'ya* and *Hikeda'ya,* their names for Sithi and Norn, respectively, largely kept their attention fixed upon their own domains and ceded all the lands and mortal men that did not interest them to the expanding Imperium.

Like the long-vanished Khandians, we of the current age call the Keida'ya and their component clans "immortals," but believe from what we have learned that they are merely long-lived, not truly undying. They can be killed, of course, or else the great war just ended would have gone against us, and it seems that at last, after many centuries, a form of old age finally overtakes them. Eventually even these ancient creatures die, although at an age hard for men to believe.

King Seoman met the revered matriarch of the Sithi, Amerasu, called Ship-Born, and the king tells that despite her birth on one of the crafts that brought her people to Osten Ard countless centuries ago, she seemed no older than a woman of handsome and healthy middle age. She died violently, so how long she might have otherwise lived is unknown, but it is agreed by all that Queen Utuk'ku, mistress of the Norns, is older still—she might have been Amerasu's great-grandmother—and that Utuk'ku once lived in the legendary Garden itself before her people fled. The Norn Queen at least does appear to be immortal, or as close to it as any of her kind have yet come . . .

[material excised here]

. . . At some time between the rise of the mortal empire of Khand and the later dominion of the Nabbanai Imperators, some conflict split the immortal Keida'ya into two races, the golden creatures we know as the Sithi, or *Zida'ya*—in their tongue the name means "Dawn Children"—and the pale, deadly *Hikeda'ya*, which seems to translate to "Cloud Children," the enemies men call "Norns" because of their home in the far north.

In the years since the Rimmersmen came across the western oceans with their iron weapons and destroyed the peace of both men and fairies and captured the immortals' palace of Asu'a (which now exists only as ruins beneath the castle called Hayholt in Erkynland) the Sithi deserted their great cities and retreated to the forests and wastelands and other remote places of Osten Ard. The Norns, still ruled by their deathless queen, Utuk'ku, also fled before the violence of the newly-arrived Rimmersmen, and the last of that fairy-clan survives in the hidden fastness of their northern mountain fortress, Nakkiga, the last of the great cities built by the immortals . . .

[material excised here]

. . . One last race must be spoken of, because the Keida'ya did not come to these lands alone, but brought with them their servants and slaves, the Tinukeda'ya, or "Ocean Children," who because of their many forms are sometimes considered together by mortal scholars under the name "Changelings." The Tinukeda'ya, though they share an origin in the Garden with the Sithi and Norns, are not all of one general appearance, as is true with the golden and white clans of the Keida'ya, who are almost uniformly slender and manlike, with large, upturned eyes and narrow faces. But some Tinukeda'ya are as big as mountain giants, and seem to serve only as beasts of burden. Others are small, fitted for work in narrow underground tunnels, as though Heaven itself had crafted them with that purpose in mind. In truth, many of the Tinukeda'ya grew skilled not just in delving but in crafting stone and other arts, and served the Keida'ya by building their great cities. Some even say that the Eight Great Ships that sailed away from the dying Garden and brought the immortals here were largely built by their Tinukeda'ya servitors, but that is not known for certain. However, High King Seoman was told by a noble of the highest Sithi clan that holding the Tinukeda'ya in slavery and bringing them to our lands against their will, was his people's greatest shame. In time many of these "Ocean Children" escaped their masters, and it is said that like the

Sithi and the Norns, many still survive in places remote from mankind. Others live among us, like the Niskies of Nabban, who use their songs to protect the ships they serve.

So it is that three tribes of immortals share this world with mankind, the Hikeda'ya pale as death, the Zida'ya as golden as the sun, and the Tinukeda'ya in all their manifold sizes and shapes. Perhaps someday these fairy-folk will be gone, and remain only as a memory among our kind, a dim, partial tale like The Lion-Fighter of Old Khand. Or perhaps it is too soon to write their epitaph, and they will rise again one day from the shadowed places to contend with us once more. We know little of them for certain, but we do know that none of them love men, and some despise us utterly.

Glossary of Terms

PEOPLE

RIMMERSMEN

Aerling Surefoot—leader of the Mountain Goats

Alfwer—Rimmersgard thane (baron) of Heitskeld

Brenyar—leader of the army's carpenters

Brindur—thane (baron) of Norskog

Dragi—the oldest Mountain Goat

Elvrit—founder of Rimmersgard

Fani—one of Brindur's Skoggeymen

Fanngrun—a Rimmersgard noble of Vattinland, cousin to former King Jormgrun

Fingil Red-Hand—king of Rimmersgard, descendant of Elvrit, conqueror of Asu'a

Finnbogi—a Rimmersgard thane (baron) killed at the Hayholt

Floki—son of Brindur

Isbeorn—thane (baron) of Hargres Dale, later Duke of Elvritshalla and Isgrimnur's father

Geli—son of Skali Sharpnose of Kaldskryke, late enemy of Isgrimnur

Gutrun—Duchess of Elvritshalla, Isgrimnur's wife

Haddi—one of Isgrimnur's house-carls

Helgrimnur Stonehand—Rimmersgard thane (baron)

Helvnur—nephew of Helgrimnur Stonehand

Hjortur—in charge of the Donkey (catapult)

Isgrimnur—Duke of Elvritshalla, ruler (beneath the High Throne) of all Rimmersgard

Isorn—Isgrimnur's son, killed in the Storm King's War

Jormgrun—King of Rimmersgard, overthrown by John of Erkynland

Kár—one of Isgrimnur's house-carls

Kolbjorn—a Vestiman

Marri Ironbeard—one of Brindur's Skoggeymen

Sludig (aka Sludig Two-Axes)—one of Isgrimnur's most loyal men, a veteran of the Storm King's War

Unnar—a Rimmersgard thane (baron)

Vigri—jarl (earl) of Enggidal

HIKEDA'YA (NORNS)

Ekimeniso of the Brooding Eye—late husband of Queen Utuk'ku, leader of Clan Iyora

Enduyo of Kementari—Viyeki's ancestor, a palace functionary, founder of Clan Enduya

Hamakho Wormslayer—founder of the Hamakha Clan and ancestor of Queen Utuk'ku

Hayyano—League Commander of the Order of Sacrifice

Hiki—High Celebrant, Zuniyabe's predecessor."

Jasiyo—Khimabu's gossipy cousin

Jikkyo, Lord, a high noble of the Order of Song

Khimabu—Viyeki's wife, of Clan Daesa

Kuju-Vayo—an official of the Order of Echoes

Mimiti—one of the Queen's Whisperers

Kusayu—eleventh High Celebrant

Luk'kaya—High Gatherer, Magister of the Harvesters

Miga Seyt-Jinnata, Lady—a High Scribe of the Order of Chroniclers

Muyare—Marshal of Sacrifices, Suno'ku's relative, replaces Ekisuno as leader of armies

Nekhaneyo—a noble of Clan Shudra

Nijika—a Host Singer of the Order of Song

Pratiki—a "prince-templar" of Clan Hamakha, Queen Utuk'ku's clan

Ruho'o—a Governor of the Order of Builders

Ruzayo Falcon's Eye—famous Hikeda'ya hero of the Giant Wars

Sasigi—member of the Order of Builders

Sulen—the thirteenth High Celebrant

Suno'ku, General—an important leader of the Order of Sacrifice, member of Clan Iyora

Twenty-Four, The—famous heroes who fought at Ruzayo's side

Tzayin-Kha—a Host Singer of the Order of Song

Viyeki—Host Foreman of the Order of Builders, member of Clan Enduyo

Yaarike—High Magister of the Order of Builders, leader of Clan Kijada

Yaaro-Mon—Yaarike's great-grandfather, a fugitive from the Garden

Yayano of the Pointing Finger—a noble Celebrant, kin to Zuniyabe

Zuniyabe—the sixteenth High Celebrant

OTHERS

Andoro—Porto's brother

Ayaminu—a Sitha, originally from Hikehikayo

Crexis, Imperator—the ruler of Nabban at the time of the execution of Usires Aedon

Endri—a soldier from Harborside in Ansis Pelippé in Perdruin

Halawe, Lord—Perdruinese noble who went to fight at the Hayholt, killed by bukken. Endri was one of his "recruits

Miriamele, Queen—at the time of this story the High Queen of Osten Ard

Porto—a soldier from The Rocks in Ansis Pelippé

Sida—Porto's wife

Simon, King—aka "Seoman Snowlock," at the time of this story the High King of Osten Ard

Tinio (short for "Portinio")—Sida and Porto's son

Usires Aedon—the martyr who was executed on The Holy Tree in Nabban but came back to life, celebrated as the child of God

PLACES, CREATURES, THINGS

Asu'a—the Sithi and Norn name for their ancient city, currently buried beneath the mortal's castle called the Hayholt

Avenue of Triumph—a processional road leading to the Sancellan Mahistrevis in Nabban

Black Water Field—a great common square in Nakkiga, at the foot of the Tearfall

Bridge of Exodus—a structure in Nakkiga-That-Was

Cold Root—Suno'ku's sword

Cold Leaf—Suno'ku's dagger

Dirt Goblins—informal name for "Bukken" (Rimmersgard name) or "diggers"—burrowing, manlike creatures

Elder Halls—older cemeteries

Field of Banners—the muster-place of the Hikeda'ya armies outside of the mountain, now a bare spot in Nakkiga-That-Was

Field of Stone Flowers—memorial to Queen Utuk'ku's most beloved dead

Gatherer's Temple—a building at the heart of Tzo, in the Lost Garden

Glittering Passage—the great main boulevard on the first tier of Nakkiga

Grayflame—sword of the Hikeda'ya hero, Hamakho

Green Angel Tower—mortal name for the last Sithi structure at the Hay-holt; the tower collapsed at the end of the Storm King's War

Gyrfalcon Castles—fortresses built on the side of Ur-Nakkiga Moon Festival Canal—one of several canals, now dry and obscured, that once crisscrossed Nakkiga-That-Was

"The Musician and the Soldier"—an old Keida'ya song from Tumet'ai

Hall of Sleeping Sacrifices—a tomb

Hikehikayo—once a city inhabited by both Sithi and Norn, now deserted, located in the Whitefell Mountains west of Nakkiga

House of Sleep—places where the dead are prepared for entombment

Hringholt—a province of Rimmersgard

Kei-mi—an extract of witchwood bark

Kementari—a Keida'ya city, now ruined, on the island of Warinsten

keta-yi'indra—a deep, deathlike, rejuvenative sleep utilized by very old, very skilled immortals

Kraki's Field—battle site in Rimmersgard near Hernystiri border

Kvalnir—Isgrimnur's sword

Lake Rumiya—lake on the northeastern side of the mountain Ur-Nakkiga (or Stormspike, as the Rimmersmen call it)

Nakkiga-That-Was—the ruined city outside the mountain, once also inhabited by the Hikeda'ya

Norskog—Brindur's home, next to Skoggey

Ostheim—Aerling's home city in Rimmersgard

Queen's Gallery—a structure in Nakkiga-That-Was

Royal Way—ancient ceremonial road through Nakkiga-That-Was, now ruined

Silent Palace—the complex containing the Elder Halls

Skuggi Pass—near the border of Northern Rimmersgard and the Norn lands

Castle Tangleroot—a ruined Hikeda'ya border fort

Sky Palace—an observatory in Nakkiga-That-Was where the Hikeda'ya once watched the stars

Sky Dance—Hikeda'ya term for the changing constellations

St. Asla's church—Rimmersgard church where Geli, Skali's son, took sanctuary

Street of Eight Ships—a wide avenue in Nakkiga

Temple of the Martyrs.—building at the heart of Nakkiga, famous for its water clock and bells

The Cold, Slow Halls—a place of punishment in the depths of Nakkiga

The Heart of What Was Lost—a gem brought out of the Garden by Yaaro-Mon

Saint Tunato's Day—known in the north as St. Tunath's Day, Decander the 21st

Three Ravens Tower—a fortress built into the wall guarding the inner Norn lands

Well of Eternity—also known as The Well of the Breathing Harp, at the heart of Nakkiga

White Bear and Stars—Duke Isgrimnur's family standard

Witiko'ya—a ferocious, wolflike creature

Yedade's Box—a device by which Hikeda'ya children are sorted

WORDS

Hikeda'yei!—literally, "You Hikeda'ya people!"

Ogu Minurato—Hikeda'ya name for "Tangleroot Castle"

Sturmrspeik—Rimmerspakk name for "Stormspike"

Venga Do'tzae—Hikeda'ya version of Zida'ya name meaning "The Lost Garden" or "The Blessed Garden"—the abandoned ancient home of the Keida'ya (the combined race)

Shu'do-tkzayha—Hikeda'ya version of Zida'ya name for mortals, "Sudhoda'ya," meaning "Sunset-children"

Not ready to leave Osten Ard?

Turn the page for an extract from the first book in Tad
Williams' new series The Last King of Osten Ard

The Witchwood CROWN

Available now in print and eBook

Foreword

Rider and mount glided down the slope through stands of Kynswood trees, larches, shiny-leaved beeches, and oaks festooned with dangling catkins. Silent and surprising, the pair appeared first in one beam of bright sunlight then another at a speed that would have startled any merely mortal eye. The rider's pale cloak seemed to catch and reflect the colors all around, so that an idle or distracted glance would have seen only a hint of movement, imagined only wind.

The warmth of the day pleased Tanahaya. The music of forest insects pleased her too, the whirring of grasshoppers and the hum of busy honeymakers. Even though the smell of the mortal habitation was strong and this patch of forest only a momentary refuge, she spoke silent words of gratitude for an interlude of happiness.

Praises, Mother Sun. Praises for the growing-scents. Praise for the bees and their goldendance.

She was young by the standards of her people, with only a few centuries upon the broad earth. Tanahaya of Shisae'ron had spent many of those years in the saddle, first as messenger for her clan's leader, Himano of the Flowering Hills, then later, after she had made her worth known to the House of Year-Dancing, performing tasks for her friends in that clan. But this errand to the mortals' capital seemed as if it might be the most perilous of all her journeys, and was certainly the strangest. She hoped she was strong and clever enough to fulfill the trust of those who had sent her.

Tanahaya had been described as wise beyond her years, but she still could not understand the importance her friends placed on the affairs of mortals—especially the short-lived creatures who inhabited this particular part of the world. That was even more inexplicable now, when it seemed clear to her that the Zida'ya could no longer trust any mortals at all.

Still, there was the castle she had been seeking, its highest roofs just visible through the trees. Looking at its squat towers and heavy stone walls, it was hard for Tanahaya to believe that Asu'a, the greatest and most beautiful city of her people, had once stood here. Could anything of their old home be left in this pile of clumsy stone that men called the Hayholt?

I must not think of what might be true, of what I fear or what I hope. Horse and rider moved down the slope. *I must see only what* is. *Otherwise I fail my oath and I fail my friends.*

She stopped at the edge of the trees. "*Tsa*, Spidersilk," she whispered, and the horse stood in silence as Tanahaya listened. New noises wafted up the slope to her, as well as a new and not entirely welcome scent, the animal tang of unwashed mortals. Tanahaya clicked her tongue and Spidersilk stepped aside into shadow.

She had a hand on the hilt of her sword when a golden-haired girl dashed into the sunlight, a basket of winter flowers swinging in one hand, daffodils and snowdrops and royal purple crocuses. Tanahaya's senses told her the child was not alone, so she stayed hidden in the shadows between trees as a half-dozen armed soldiers followed the child in gasping, clanking pursuit. After a moment, Tanahaya relaxed: it was clear the mortals did not mean to harm the little one. Still, she was surprised that mortal soldiers were so heedless of danger: she could have put arrows in most of them before they even realized they were not alone in the Kynswood.

A mortal woman in a hat with a brim as wide as a wagon's wheel followed the armored men into the clearing. "Lillia!" the woman cried, then stopped and bent to catch her breath. "Do not run, child! Oh, you are wicked! Wicked to make us chase you!"

The child stopped, eyes wide. "But Auntie Rhoner, look! Berries!"

"Berries! In Marris-month? You little mad thing." The woman, still trying to catch her breath, was handsome by mortal standards, or so Tanahaya guessed—tall, with fine, strong bones in her face. By the name the child had given her, Tanahaya guessed this must be Countess Rhona of Nad Glehs, one of the mortal queen's closest friends. Tanahaya did not find it strange that a noble of high standing should be minding a child, though others might have. "No, you come back with me, honey-lamb," the countess said. "Those are owlberries and they'll make you sick."

"No they won't," the child declared. "Because they're forest berries. And forest berries have lots of magic. *Fairy* magic."

"Magic." The woman in the hat sounded disgusted, but even from such a distance Tanahaya's sharp eyes could see the smile that played across her face. "I'll give you fairy magic, *mu' harcha*! You wanted to search for early flowers, and I brought you. We have been out for hours—and by Deanagha's spotless skirts, look at me. I am filthy and bepricked with nettles!"

"They're not nettles, they're berry bushes," said the golden-haired girl. "That's why they have thorns. So nobody will eat the berries."

"Nobody wants to eat those berries but birds. Not even the deer will go near them!"

The heavily armored soldiers, still struggling for breath in their heavy mail, faces gleaming with sweat, began to straighten up. The girl had clearly led them a long, wearying chase over the hillside. "Should we grab her, your ladyship?" asked one.

The countess frowned. "Lillia, it is time to go back. I want my midday meal."

"I don't have to do anything unless you call me 'Princess' or 'Your Highness'."

"What silliness! Your grandparents are away and I am your keeper, little lion cub. Come now. Don't make me cross."

"I wish Uncle Timo was here. He lets me do things."

"Uncle Timo is your sworn bondsman. No, he is your helpless slave and lets you get away with everything. I am made of harder stuff. Come along."

The girl called Lillia looked from the countess to all the dark bushes full of pale, blue-white fruit, then sighed and slowly walked back down the slope. If its handle had been any longer, her basket would have dragged in the loamy soil. "When Queen Grandmother and King Grandfather come back, I'm going to tell on you," she warned.

"Tell what?" The countess frowned. "That I wouldn't let you run away by yourself in the forest to be eaten by wolves and bears?"

"I could give them berries. Then they wouldn't eat me."

The woman took her hand. "Even hungry bears won't eat owlberries. And the wolves would rather eat *you*."

As the small party vanished back down the deer trail into a thick copse of oak and ash trees farther down the slope, Tanahaya watched with a kind of wonder. To think that little creature named Lillia would reach womanhood, perhaps marry and become a mother and grandmother, grow old and even die—all in not much more than one of her people's Great Years! It seemed to Tanahaya that being mortal must be like trying to live a full life in the space between falling from a high place and hitting the ground, a rush through wind and confusion to death. How did the poor creatures manage?

For the first time it occurred to Tanahaya of Shisae'ron that perhaps she might learn something from this task. It was an unexpected thought.

So this young creature was Lillia, she told herself, the granddaughter of Queen Miriamele and King Seoman—the objects of Tanahaya's embassy. She would be seeing that proud little bumblebee of a girl again.

Bumblebee? No, butterfly, she thought with a sudden pang. *A flash of color and glory beneath the sky, and then, like all mortals, too soon she will become dust.*

But if the fears of Tanahaya's friends proved accurate, she knew, then the end for that butterfly child and all the rest of the Hayholt's mortals might come even sooner than any of them could guess.

As she reined up again to examine the castle, she could still hear the faint rattle of the retreating soldiers and the golden girl's voice, no words now but just a musical burble rising from the forest below. The wind changed, and the stink of mortals, of unwashed bodies and unchanged garments abruptly deepened; it was all she could do not to turn around and retreat. She would have to accustom herself, she knew.

Tanahaya had never liked the squat, cheerless look of men's buildings any more than she cared for men's odor, and the Hayholt, this great castle of theirs, was no different. Despite its size, it seemed nothing more than a collection of carelessly built dwellings hiding behind brutish stone walls, one wall set inside another like a succession of mushroom rings. The entire awkward structure perched on a high headland above the wide bay known as Kynslagh, as though it were the nest of some slovenly seabird. Even the red tiles that roofed many of the buildings seemed dull to her as dried blood, and Tanahaya thought the famous castle looked more like a place to be imprisoned than anything else. It was astounding to realize that a few mortal decades earlier—an eyeblink of time to her people—the Storm King's attack on the living had ended just here, only moments from success. She thought she could still hear the great crying-out of that day and feel the countless shadows that would not disperse, the torment and terror of so many. Even Time itself had almost been overthrown here. How could the mortals continue to live in such a place? Could they not feel the uneasy dead all around them?

Watching the girl had brought her a moment of good cheer, but now it blew away like dust on a hot, dry wind. For a moment Tanahaya's hand strayed to the Witness in her belt-pouch, the sacred, timeworn mirror that would allow her to speak across great earthly distances to those who had sent her. She didn't belong here—it was hard to believe that any of her race could in these fallen times. It was not too late, after all: she could beg her loved ones in Jao é-Tinukai'i to find someone else for this task.

Tanahaya's impulse did not last. It was not her place to judge these short-lived creatures, but to do what she had been bid for the good of her own people.

After all, she reminded herself, *a year does not dance itself into being. Everything is sacrifice.*

She lifted her hand from the hidden mirror and caught up the reins once more. Even from this distance, the stench of mortals seemed unbearably strong, so fierce she could barely stand it. How much worse would it be when she was out of the heights and riding through their cramped streets?

Something struck her hard in the back. Tanahaya gasped, but could not get her breath. She tried to turn to see what had hit her, simultaneously reaching to draw her sword, but before it cleared the scabbard another arrow struck her, this time in the chest.

The Sitha tried to crouch low in the saddle but that only pressed the second arrow more agonizingly into her body. She could feel something like a cool breath on her back and knew it must be blood soaking her jerkin. She reached down and broke the second shaft off close to her ribs. Free of that obstruction but still pulsing blood around the broken shaft, she threw herself against Spidersilk's neck and clung tightly, aiming now only for escape. But even as she clapped her heels against the horse's side a new arrow hissed into the animal's neck just a handspan from Tanahaya's fingers. The horse reared, shrilling in pain and terror. As Tanahaya struggled to hang on, a fourth arrow took her high in her back and spun her out of the saddle. She fell into air, and for a mad moment it seemed almost like flight. Then something struck her all over and at once, a great, flat blow, and a soundless darkness rushed over her like a river.

PART ONE

Widows

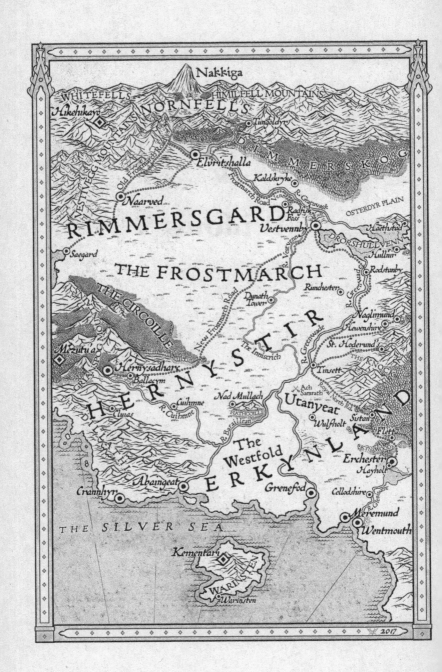

Locusts laid their eggs in the corpse
Of a soldier. When the worms were
Mature, they took wing. Their drone
Was ominous, their shells hard.
Anyone could tell they had hatched
From an unsatisfied anger.
They flew swiftly toward the North.
They hid the sky like a curtain.
When the wife of the soldier
Saw them, she turned pale, her breath
Failed her. She knew he was dead
In battle, his corpse lost in the desert.
That night she dreamed
She rode a white horse, so swift
It left no footprints, and came
To where he lay in the sand.
She looked at his face, eaten
By the locusts, and tears of
Blood filled her eyes. Ever after
She would not let her children
Injure any insect that
Might have fed on the dead. She
Would lift her face to the sky
And say, "O locusts, if you
Are seeking a place to winter,
You can find shelter in my heart."

—HSU CHAO
"The Locust Swarm"

1

The Glorious

The pavilion walls billowed and snapped as the winds rose. Tiamak thought it was like being inside a large drum. Many people in the tent were trying to be heard, but the clear voice of a young minstrel floated above it all, singing a song of heroism:

> *"Sing ye loud his royal name*
> *Seoman the Glorious!*
> *Spread it far, his royal fame*
> *Seoman the Glorious!"*

The king did not look glorious. He looked tired. Tiamak could see it in the lines of Simon's face, the way his shoulders hunched as if he awaited a blow. But that blow had already fallen. Today was only the grim anniversary.

Limping more than usual because of the cold day, little Tiamak made his way among all the larger men. These courtiers and important officials were gathered around the king, who sat on one of two high-backed wooden chairs at the center of the tent, both draped in the royal colors. A banner with the twin drakes, the red and the white, hung above them. The other chair was empty.

As a makeshift throne room in the middle of a Hernystir field, Tiamak thought, it was more than adequate, but it was also clearly the one place King Seoman did not want to be. Not today.

> *"With hero's sword in his right hand*
> *And nought but courage in his heart*
> *Did Seoman make his gallant stand*
> *Though cowards fled apart*
>
> *"When the hellspawned Norns did bring*
> *Foul war upon the innocent*
> *And giants beat upon the gates*
> *And Norn sails filled the Gleniwent . . ."*

"I don't understand," said the king loudly to one of the courtiers. "In truth, my good man, I haven't understood a thing you've said, what with all this shouting and caterwauling. Why should they have to lime the bridges? Do they think we are birds that need catching?"

"*Line* the bridges, sire."

The king scowled. "I know, Sir Murtach. It was meant as a jest. But it still doesn't make any sense."

The courtier's determined smile faltered. "It is the tradition for the people to line up along the bridges as well as the roads, but King Hugh is concerned that the bridges might not stand under the weight of so many."

"And so *we* must give up our wagons and come on foot? All of us?"

Sir Murtach flinched. "It is what King Hugh requests, Your Majesty."

> *"When armies of the Stormlord came*
> *Unto the very Swertclif plain*
> *Who stood on Hayholt's battlements*
> *And bade them all turn back again?*
>
> *"Sing ye loud his royal name*
> *Seoman the Glorious!*
> *Spread it far, his royal fame*
> *Seoman the Glorious!"*

King Simon's head had tipped to one side. It was *not* the side from which he was being urgently addressed by another messenger, who had finally worked his way to a place beside the makeshift throne. Something had distracted Simon. Tiamak thought that seeing the king's temper fray was like watching a swamp flatboat beginning to draw water. It was plain that if someone didn't do something soon, the whole craft would sink.

> *"He slew the dragon fierce and cold*
> *And banished winter by his hand*
> *He tamed the Sithi proud and old*
> *And saved the blighted, threatened land . . ."*

Murtach was still talking in one royal ear, and the other messenger had started his speech for the third time when Simon suddenly stood. The courtiers fell back swiftly, like hunting hounds when the bear turns at bay. The king's beard was still partly red, but he had enough gray in it now, as well as the broad white stripe where he had once been splashed by dragon's blood, that when his anger was up he looked a bit like an Aedonite prophet from the old days.

"That! That!" Simon shouted. "It's bad enough that I cannot hear myself think, that every man in camp wants me to do something or . . . or not do something . . . but must I listen to such terrible lies and exaggerations as well?" He turned and pointed his finger at the miscreant. "Well? Must I?"

At the far end of the king's finger, the young minstrel stared back with the round eyes of a quiet, nighttime grazer caught in the sudden glare of a torch. He swallowed. It seemed to take a long time. "Beg pardon, Majesty?" he squeaked.

"That song! That preposterous song! *He slew the dragon fierce and cold'*—a palpable lie!" The king strode forward until he towered over the thin, dark-haired singer, who seemed to be melting and shrinking like a snowflake caught in a warm hand. "By the Bloody Tree, I never killed that dragon, I just wounded it a bit. I was terrified. And I didn't tame the Sithi either, for the love of our lord Usires!"

The minstrel looked at up at him, mouth working but without sound.

"And the rest of the song is even more mad. Banished the winter? You might as well say I make the sun rise every day!"

"B–But . . . but it is only a song, Majesty," the minstrel finally said. "It is a well-known and well-loved one—all the people sing it . . ."

"Pfah." But Simon was no longer shouting. His anger was like a swift storm—the thunder had boomed, now all that was left was cold rain. "Then go sing it to all the people. Or better yet, when we return to the Hayholt, ask old Sangfugol what really happened. Ask him what it was truly like when the Storm King's darkness came down on us and we all pissed ourselves in fear."

A moment of confused bravery showed itself on the young man's face. "But it was Sangfugol who *made* that song, Your Majesty. And he was the one who taught it to me."

Simon growled. "So, then all bards are liars. Go on, boy. Get away from me."

The minstrel looked quite forlorn as he pushed his way toward the door of the pavilion. Tiamak caught at his sleeve as he went by. "Wait outside," he told the singer. "Wait for me."

The young man was so full of anguish he had not truly heard. "I beg pardon?"

"Just wait outside for a few moments. I will come for you."

The youth looked at the little Wrannaman oddly, but everyone in the court knew Tiamak and how close he was to the king and queen. The harper blinked his eyes, doing his best to compose himself. "If you say so, my lord."

Simon was already driving the rest of the courtiers from the pavilion. "Enough! Leave me be now, all of you. I cannot do everything, and certainly not in one day! Give me peace!"

Tiamak waited until the wave of humanity had swept past him and out of the tent, then he waited a bit longer until the king finished pacing and dropped back onto his chair. Simon looked up at his councilor and his face sagged with unhappiness and useless anger. "Don't look at me that way, Tiamak."

The king seldom lost his temper with those who served him, and was much loved for it. Back home in Erkynland many called him "the Commoner King" or even "the Scullion King" because of his youthful days as a Hayholt dogsbody. Generally Simon remembered very well indeed what it felt like to be ignored or blamed by those with power. But sometimes, especially when he was in the grip of such heartache as he was today, he fell into foul moods.

Tiamak, of course, knew that the moods seldom lasted long and were followed quickly by regret. "I am not looking at you in any particular way, Majesty."

"Don't mock me. You are. It's that sad, wise expression you put on when you're thinking about what a dunderhead one of your monarchs is. And that monarch is nearly always me."

"You need rest, Majesty." It was a privilege to speak as old friends, one that Tiamak would never have presumed on with others in the room. "You are weary and your temper is short."

The king opened his mouth, then shook his head. "This is a bad day," he said at last. "A very bad day. Where is Miriamele?"

"The queen declined any audiences today. She is out walking."

"I am glad for her. I hope she is being left alone."

"As much as she wishes to be. Her ladies are with her. She likes company more than you do on days like this."

"Days like this, I would like to be on the top of a mountain in the Trollfells with Binabik and his folk, with nothing but snow to look at and nothing but wind to hear."

"We have plenty of wind for you here in this meadow," Tiamak said. "But not too much snow, considering that there is still almost a fortnight of winter left."

"Oh, I know what day it is, what month," Simon said. "I need no reminding."

Tiamak cleared his throat. "Of course not. But will you take my advice? Rest yourself for a while. Let your unhappiness cool."

"It was just . . . hearing that nonsense, over and over . . . Simon the hero, all of that. I did not seem such a hero when my son . . ."

"Please, Majesty."

"But I should not have taken it out on the harper." Again, the storm had blown over quickly, and now Simon was shaking his head. "He has given me many a sweet hour of song before. It is not his fault that lies become history so quickly. Perhaps I should tell him that I was unfair, and I am sorry."

Tiamak hid his smile. A king who apologized! No wonder he was tied to his two monarchs with bonds stronger than iron. "I will confess, it was not like you, Majesty."

"Well, find him for me, would you?"

"In truth, I think he is just outside the tent, Majesty."

"Oh, for the love of St. Tunath and St. Rhiap, Tiamak, would you please stop calling me 'Majesty' when we're alone? You said he was nearby?"

"I'll go see, Simon."

The minstrel was indeed near, cowering from the brisk Marris winds in a fold of tent wall beside the doorway. He followed Tiamak back into the pavilion like a man expecting a death sentence.

"There you are," the king said. "Come. Your name is Rinan, yes?"

The eyes, already wide, grew wider still. "Yes, Majesty."

"I was harsh to you, Rinan. Today . . . I am not a happy man today."

Tiamak thought that the harper, like everyone else in the royal court, knew only too well what day it was, but was wise enough to stay quiet while the king struggled to find words.

"In any case, I am sorry for it," the king said. "Come back to me tomorrow, and I will be in a better humor for songs. But have that old scoundrel Sangfugol teach you a few lays that at least approach the truth, if not actually wrestle with it."

"Yes, sire."

"Go on then. You have a fine voice. Remember that music is a noble charge, even a dangerous charge, because it can pierce a man's heart when a spear or arrow cannot."

As the young man hurried out of the pavilion, Simon looked up at his old friend. "I suppose now I must bring back all the others and make amends to them as well?"

"I see no reason why you should," Tiamak told him. "You have already given them all the hours since you broke your fast. I think it might be good for you to eat and rest."

"But I have to reply to King Hugh and his damned 'suggestions,' as he calls them." Simon tugged at his beard. "What is he about, Tiamak? You would think with all these nonsensical conditions, he would rather not have us come to Hernysadharc at all. Does he resent having to feed and house even this fairly small royal progress?"

"Oh, I'm sure that's not so. The Hernystiri are always finicky with their rituals." But secretly Tiamak did not like it either. It was one thing to insist on proper arrangements, another thing to keep the High King and High Queen waiting in a field for two days over issues of ceremony that should have been settled weeks ago. After all, the king of Hernystir would not have a throne at all were it not for the High Ward that Simon and Miriamele represented. Hernystir only had a king because Miri's grandfather, King John, had permitted it under his own overarching rule. Still, Tiamak thought, Hugh was a comparatively young king: perhaps this rudeness was nothing more than a new monarch's inexperience. "I am certain Sir Murtach, Count Eolair, and I will have everything set to rights soon," he said aloud.

"Well, I hope you're right, Tiamak. Tell them we agree to everything and to send us the be-damned invitation tomorrow morning. It's a sad errand that brings us this way in the first place, and today is a sad anniversary. It seems pointless to dicker about such things—how many banners, how high the thrones, the procession route . . ." He wagged his hand in disgust. "If Hugh wishes to make himself look important, let him. He can act like a child if he wants, but Miri and I don't need to."

"You may be doing the king of Hernystir a disservice," said Tiamak mildly, but in his heart of hearts he didn't think so. He truly didn't think so.

"Can we swim in it, Papa?"

The black river was fast and silent. "I don't think so, son."

"And what's on the other side?" the child asked.

"Nobody knows."

It was a mixture of Simon's dreams and memories, made partly from the time he had taken young John Josua down to Grenburn Town near the river to see the flooding. In the wake of the Storm King's defeat the winters had grown warmer, and in the years after the fall of the tower, spring thaws had swollen the rivers of Erkynland until they overflowed their banks, turning fields on both sides of the Gleniwent into a great plain of water, with islands of floating debris that had once been houses and barns. John Josua had been nearly five years of age when Simon took him to Grenburn, and full of questions. Not that he had ever stopped being full of questions.

"Don't cross the river, Papa," his dream-son told him.

"I won't." Simon didn't laugh, but in life he had, amused by the boy's solemn warning. "It's too wide, John Josua. I'm a grown man but I don't think I could swim so far." He pointed to the far side, a place where the fields were higher. It was farther than Simon could have shot an arrow.

"If I went across, would you come after me?" the child asked. "Or if I fell in?"

"Of course." He remembered saying it with such certainty. "I would jump in and pull you out. Of course I would!"

But something was distracting him, some dream noise that he knew he should ignore, but it was hard not to notice the hard-edged baying of hounds. All his life since the weird white Stormspike pack had chased him, Simon had found that the noise of howling dogs chilled his blood.

"Papa?" The boy sounded farther away than he had a moment before, but Simon had turned his back on the river to look out across fields that were darkening as the sun disappeared behind the clouds. Somewhere in the distance a shape moved across the ground, but it moved like a single thing—no hunting pack, but a single hunting *thing* . . .

"Papa?"

So faint! And the little prince was no longer holding his hand—how had that happened? Even though it was only a dream, though Simon half-knew he was in bed and sleeping, he felt a dreadful cold terror rush through him, as if the very blood was freezing in his brains. His son was no longer beside him.

He looked around wildly but at first saw nothing. In the distance the mournful, scraping noise of the hounds grew louder. Then he saw the little head bobbing on the dark river, the small hands lifted as if to greet some friend—a false friend, a lying friend—and his heart shuddered as though it would stop. He ran, he was running, he had been running forever but still he came no closer. The clouds thickened overhead and the sunlight all but vanished. He thought he could hear a terrible, thin cry and the sound of splashing, but although he threw himself toward the place he had last seen the child, he could get no closer.

He screamed, then, and leaped, as if he could cross all that uncrossable difference by the sheer strength of his need . . . of his regret.

"Simon!"

A cool hand was on his forehead, not so much soothing him as holding him back, prisoning him. For a moment he was so maddened with terror that he reached up to strike the obstacle out of his way, then he heard her gasp, surprised by his sudden movement, and he remembered where he was.

"M-Miri?"

"A bad dream, Simon. You're having a bad dream." When she felt his muscles unknot, she took her hand from his head. She also had an arm around his chest, which she loosed before letting herself back down beside him in the disordered bed. "Shall I call for someone to bring you something?"

He shook his head, but of course she couldn't see him. "No. I'll . . ."

"Was it the same dream as last time? The dragon?"

"No. It was about John Josua when he was little. Of course—I haven't been able to think of anything else for days."

Simon lay staring up into the darkness for a long time. He could tell by her breathing she had not gone back to sleep either. "I dreamed of him," he said at last. "He got away from me. I chased him but I couldn't reach him."

She still didn't speak, but she put a hand against his cheek and left it there.

"Seven years gone, Miri, seven years since that cursed fever took him, and still I can't stop."

She stirred. "Do you think it is any different for me? I miss him every moment!"

He could tell by her voice that she was angry, although he did not know exactly why. How could the priests say that death came as the great friend when instead it came like an army, taking what it wished and destroying peace even years after it had withdrawn? "I know, dear one. I know."

After a while, she said, "And think—we have the ninth of Marris every year from now until the end of time. It was such a happy day once. When he was born."

"It still should be, my dear wife. God takes everyone back, but our son gave us an heir before we lost him. He gave us a great deal."

"An heir." The edge in her voice was brittle. "All I want is *him*. All I want is John Josua. Instead we are lumbered with *her* for the rest of our lives."

"You said yourself that the Widow is a small price to pay for our grand-daughter, not to mention our grandson and heir."

"I said that before Morgan became a young man."

"Hah!" Simon wasn't actually amused, but it was better than cursing. "Scarcely a man yet."

Miriamele took a careful breath before speaking. "Our grandson is seven-teen years old. Much the same age that you were when we were first wed. Man enough to be taking his fill of the ladies. Man enough to spend his days drink-ing and dicing and doing whatever takes his fancy. You did not do the same at that age!"

"I was washing dishes, and peeling potatoes and onions, and sweeping the castle, my dear—but not by choice. And then I fought for Josua—but that was not really by choice, either."

"Still. With ne'er-do-well companions like the ones he has, how will Mor-gan grow? He will bend to their shape."

"He will grow out of this foolishness, Miri. He must." But Simon didn't entirely believe it. Their living grandson sometimes seemed as lost to him as the son who had been swept away into the black river of death.

After another silent time in the dark, she said, "And I miss our little one, too. I mean our granddaughter." Miriamele put her arm across her husband's belly, moving closer. He could feel the tightness in her muscles. "I wish we hadn't left her home. Do you think she's being good for Rhona?"

"Never." He actually laughed a little. "You worry too much, my love. You know we could not bring Lillia. It's still winter in Rimmersgard and the air will be full of ice and fever. We brought the grandchild who would benefit from being with us."

"Benefit. How could anyone who has already lost a parent benefit from watching a good old man die?"

"Prince Morgan needs to learn that he is not just himself. He is the hope of many people." Simon felt sleep pulling at him again, finally. "As are you and I, my wife." He meant it kindly, but he felt her stiffen again. "I must sleep. You, too. Don't lie there and fret, Miri. Come closer—put your head on my chest. There." Sometimes, especially when she was unhappy, he missed her badly, even though she was only a short distance away.

Just as she began to settle her head on his chest, she stiffened. "His grave!" she whispered. "We didn't . . ."

Simon stroked her hair. "We did. Or at least Pasevalles promised in his last letter that he would take flowers, and also that he would make certain Arch-bishop Gervis performs John Josua's *mansa*."

"Ah." He felt her stiff muscles loosen. "Pasevalles is a good man. We're lucky to have him."

"We are indeed. Now we should both sleep, Miri. It will be a busy day to-morrow."

"Why? Is Hugh finally going to let us in?"

"He'd better. I'm losing my patience."

"I never liked him. Not from the first."

"Yes, but you don't like many people at the first, dear one." He let his head roll sideways until it touched hers.

"That's not true. I used to." She pushed a little closer. The wind was rising again, making the tent ropes hum outside. "I had more love in me, I think. Sometimes now I fear I have used it all."

"Except for me and your grandchildren, yes?"

She waited an instant too long for Simon's liking. "Of course," she said. "Of course." But this anniversary had always been blighted since their son had died. Small wonder that she was bitter.

Somewhere during the wind's song, Simon fell asleep again.

2

The Finest Tent
on the Frostmarch

He had been following his father for a long time, it seemed, although he did not remember when or where they had begun. The sky had grown dark and the familiar tall shape was only a shadow in front of him now, sometimes barely visible as the path twisted through the deepening twilight. He wished he wasn't too old to hold his father's hand. Or was he?

He did not know how old he was.

"Papa, wait!" he cried.

His father said something, but Morgan couldn't understand him. Something seemed to be muffling his father's voice, doors or distance or simply distraction. He hurried after, out of breath, short legs aching, trying not to notice the sounds in the trees that seemed to follow him, the strange voices hooting as softly as the ghosts of doves. Where was this place? How had they come here? So many trees! Were they in the forest of Grandfather's stories, that dark, unknowable place full of odd sounds and watching eyes?

"Papa?" He raised his voice almost to a scream. "Where are you? Wait for me!"

The trees were everywhere and the moonlight was so faint that he could hardly see the path. As he hurried around each bend in pursuit of his father's ever-dwindling figure the roots seemed to writhe in the mud beneath his feet like moon-silvery snakes, grabbing at him and tripping him. Several times he stumbled and nearly fell, but forced himself on. The entire forest seemed to be twisting around him now, the trees spinning and drooping like exhausted dancers. He stopped to listen, but heard only the ghastly, breathless hoots from above.

"Papa! Where did you go? Come back!"

He thought he heard his father's measured voice float back to him from somewhere far ahead, but he could not tell if he was saying "I'm here!" or "I fear . . . !"

But fathers were never afraid. They stayed with you. They protected you. They weren't afraid themselves.

"Papa?"

The path was gone. He could feel the roots moving beneath his feet as the branches reached down to enfold him and smother the light.

"Papa? Don't leave me!"

He was alone—abandoned and crying. He was just another orphan, a stray.

"Papa!"

No answer. Never an answer. He fought to get free, but the trees still clung.

It was the same every time . . .

Morgan, Prince of Erkynland and heir to the High Throne of Prester John's empire, tumbled off his cot and onto the ground, fighting with the cloak that tangled him. Half lost in the dream-forest, he lay for long moments on the damp rugs, his heart thundering in his chest. At last he sat up, trying to make sense of where he was and what had happened. He was cold even with the blanket still clinging to his neck like a spurned lover, and something nearby was making a nasty, rasping noise. Morgan peered worriedly into the darkness, but after a moment realized the sound was only the snoring of his squire, Melkin.

Well, praise be to God that somebody can sleep.

Memory came slouching back. He was on the royal progress with his grand-father and grandmother. He and Melkin were in his tent in the middle of some field outside Hernysadharc, the capital, and it was cold because spring was still a fortnight away. Tonight there had been a meal and too much talk. Also too much wine, although now he was wishing he had drunk more of it—a great deal more, to chase the chill from his bones, the deep, feverish body-cold of another foul dream.

His eyes were wet, he realized, his cheeks damp. He'd been crying in his sleep.

Papa. I couldn't catch up to him . . . There seemed to be a hole where his heart should be, as though the wind were blowing right through him. Angry, he wiped his face with his sleeve.

Weeping like a child. Idiot! Coward! What if someone saw me?

Wine was what he needed. Morgan knew from experience that a large cup of sour, reliable red would warm the cold hole in his vitals and push the dream out of his thoughts. But he had no wine. He had drunk all that had been offered while he dined with the king and queen, but it hadn't been enough to give him a dreamless night.

For a moment he considered simply trying to go back to sleep. The wind was blowing chill outside, and the camp was full of people who would gladly scurry to his grandparents with the tale if they saw him out staggering around at this hour of the night. But the memory of that endless forest track, of the horror of never being able to catch up to his father, was too much.

Wine. Yes, it would be good to hear the foolish arguments of his friends, an ordinary, reassuring thing. And it would be even better to be drunk again, drunk enough this time that he would not hear the voices in the forest, would not feel the chill of being left behind, perhaps would not even dream.

Morgan dragged himself to his feet and pushed his way out of the tent in search of accommodating oblivion. He had a good idea of where to look.

No royal proclamation or official announcement of any kind designated the tent shared by the Nabbanai knights Sir Astrian and Sir Olveris as the home of the makeshift tavern. The presence of seasoned drinker Sir Porto and a reasonably constant supply of wine was enough.

The sprawling royal camp was dark, but a pair of lanterns made the tent seem nearly festive. Old Sir Porto stared down into his cup and nodded. "Bless us when we are weak, O Lord," he said in his most doleful tones. "And save some blessings, if You please, because soon we will be weak again." He took a long swallow, then wiped his damp mouth and scruffy white beard with the back of his hand. "That is the last," he said. "God be kind, what I wouldn't give for a little of that red stuff from Onestris they keep back at the *Maid*. A man's vintage, that is. This . . . this grape water is scarcely old enough to know of the existence of sin."

"One does not need to know about sin to enjoy it," said Sir Astrian.

"Please, my lord," said the young woman on Astrian's lap. She was struggling hard to stand, but having no success. "I will be punished if I don't get back to my work! Let me go."

Astrian did not loosen his grip, and kept her on his knee with small adjustments of balance. "What?" he demanded. "Would you return to the shocking boredom of the ostler's wagons?" He reached up and pulled at the girl's bodice until her bosom threatened to overspill.

"My lord!" She snatched to hold up the fabric, and his hands, unchecked, strayed elsewhere.

The tent flap jiggled but did not open. Something good-sized was caught in it, and the poles of the tent swayed as though in a gale.

"The heir to all the lands of Osten Ard appears to be tangled," said Sir Astrian. "Somebody set him free and be rewarded with a sizeable estate."

"I will give you a sizeable boot in your arse," said the voice whose owner was writhing in the flap like a butterfly trying to escape its cocoon. "As soon as I find you."

"Someone go to our noble prince's aid—make haste!" cried Astrian. "I would myself, but at the moment I am engaged in fierce battle." He finally managed to pull down hard enough to overcome the young woman's resistance and her bare breasts sprang into view. Instead of surrendering and trying to cover herself, though, the girl redoubled her efforts to escape, cursing and flailing.

"The bubs, the bubs!" sang Sir Astrian. *"The bubs, the bubs, in all Nabban did ring! On the day they hanged our Redeemer, though no hands did pull the cord, The bubs in every tower tolled, to prove Aedon our lord!"*

With help from dour, black-haired Sir Olveris, Prince Morgan finally emerged from the tent flap. Morgan's hair, a shade too brown for golden, clung in strands across his face, damp with melting snowflakes. His brows, a shade darker and thicker than his hair, rose in slow, slightly distracted dismay as he saw the serving girl fighting to free herself. "God's Eyes, Astrian, what are you doing? Let the poor girl go. And someone pour me a cup of something strong." He looked around. "What? No succor for your lord? I call you traitors."

"We have finished the last, Highness," said Porto, guiltily wiping his upper lip. "The place is as dry as the dunes of Nascadu."

"God curse it!" Morgan seemed genuinely upset. "Nothing to drown a night of foul dreams? Ah, well—distract me, then, Astrian. You owe me another game and I am ready to take my money back. And this time we are not using your dice, you cunning near-dwarf."

"Cruel words," said Astrian, grinning. The ostler's maid was still trying to get off his lap and looked ready to weep. "I am not the tallest man in this kingdom, true, but I am not so low as you make me. My head reaches Olveris's neck, and since there is nothing of much use above that point, he and I are as good as even."

"Sweet Aedon!" Morgan lowered himself carefully onto a wooden stool, scowling ferociously. "Are you still mauling her? I said let the girl go, Astrian! If she doesn't want to be here, let her be on her way." He kicked at Astrian's leg, then folded away his frown to show the young woman a smile made slightly less courtly by the extreme redness of his face. "He begs your pardon, lass."

"Of course I do, my prince." Astrian released his prey just as she was straining away from him, so that she would have fallen to the ground if Olveris had not caught her and held her up until she gained her balance. The tall knight said nothing, as was his wont, but rolled his eyes at Astrian as he returned to his own seat atop a wooden chest.

"My apologies for Sir Astrian," Morgan said to the girl. "He is a rude fellow. And what is your name, my dear?"

She was as red-faced with exertion as the prince was with drink and her eyes were wide as a frightened horse's, but when she had pushed herself back into her bodice she did her best to curtsey to Morgan. "Thank you, your Highness. I am Goda, and I only came here to tell these . . . men that Lord Jeremias said they were to have no more wine. As it is, he said, they have already drunk much of what was meant for the return journey." Despite the angry force of her words she was near tears.

"It is a good thing that there will be mead in Hernysadharc, then." Morgan waved permission for her to go. She lifted her skirts and almost ran from the tent.

"If they ever let us into the city." Porto's voice was doleful as a funeral bell. "Soon, we will die of thirst here in this field."

"I must say, Highness," Astrian said, "*you* look as though you've already found a bit of something to ease this sad journey. Did you bring it back to share with your brothers of the road?"

"Share?" Morgan shook his head. "I had to spend the longest evening of my life at the royal table with my grandmother and grandfather, having my sins . . .

my sins and yours, that is . . . listed for me in exis . . . excu . . . exquisite detail. Then I tried to sleep, and . . ." He scowled and waved the idea away with his hand. "It matters not. I deserved every drop I could guzzle, and it was still nowhere near enough." He sighed. "Still, if there's nothing left to drink, we might as well gamble." With the young woman now long gone, Morgan let himself slump, revealing what he truly was—a very young man who had drunk too much.

"So you bring us nothing, Highness?" asked Porto.

"I swallowed everything I could reach at my grandparents' table. But it wasn't enough. No, they all just kept *talking*. And it was about nothing—the bloody Hernystiri king, and the royal blacksmith's need for scrap to turn into horse nails, and the complaints of the local Hernystiri farmers that their lands are being pillaged by the royal progress. And after putting up with that all evening, I am beginning to be sober again. I do not favor sobriety." He looked to Astrian. "By the way, speaking of pillagers, I cannot help noticing a haunch of something on the spit over your fire. It looks rather like the remains of a fat farm pig."

"No, no, a free wild boar of the hills, Highness," Astrian said. "Isn't that right, Porto? He led us a fierce chase."

Porto looked more than a bit shamefaced. "Oh, aye, he did."

"All over his pen, I have no doubt." Morgan frowned. "God save us, the boredom!" But the prince looked more haunted than bored. "Oh, and there was a messenger arrived from Elvritshalla right in the middle of it all. The Rimmersmen beg us to make good speed after we leave Hernystir. It seems the duke is not dead yet."

"But those are excellent tidings!" said Porto, sitting a little straighter. "Old Isgrimnur still lives? Excellent news."

"Yes. Huzzah, I suppose." Morgan gave Astrian a hard look. "Why are we not dicing, fellow? Why is my money still in your pocket?"

"My lord," said Porto, "I do not mean to scold, but Duke Isgrimnur has been one of your grandparents' greatest allies. I fought with him for the Hayholt more than thirty years ago, and again at the cursed Nakkiga Gate."

"You still call it 'fighting'?" Astrian smirked. "I believe the name for what you did was 'hiding'."

Porto scowled. "My dignity does not allow me to respond to such wretched untruths. Were you there, sir? No. You were a mere imp of a child then, vexing your nursemaid, while I was risking my life against the Norns."

Astrian's loud laugh was his only reply.

Porto struggled to his feet, scraping his head against the top of the tent. It was said that of all the knights who had ever fought to uphold the High Ward, only the great Camaris had been taller than Porto. However, that was where the comparison ceased. "What is this, then—laughter?" the old soldier demanded. "Shall I call you Sir Mockery? What is this?" He pulled a pendant out of his collar, a smooth female shape carved in rounded blue crystal. "Did I not take this from one of the fairies after I slew him? This is Norn stuff, the true article. Go ahead, mock—you have no such prize."

Sir Olveris said, "I doubt not that you took it from one who was face-down and dying, old man. And then finished him off with your sword in his back."

Prince Morgan jumped in surprise. "By the bloody Tree, Olveris, you are silent so long, then you speak from the shadows without warning. I thought for a moment we were haunted!"

The black-haired man did not reply. He had exhausted himself with such a long speech.

"Enough with tormenting Porto," the prince said. "Come now, Astrian, is it to be Caster's Call or Hyrka? I will not let this day end without some good result, and beggaring you would make me very happy. I have not had a good day with the bones since we crossed the border into Hernystir."

"There are no borders out here," said Astrian as he gave the prince's dice a good, long look, weighing them on his palm and then letting his fingers probe the pips for boar's bristles or painted lead. "These will do," he said, handing them back.

"What do you mean by that nonsense?" the prince asked. "No borders?" He rolled his first number. "A ten, sir—two hands. You may bid as you explain your remark."

"It is only this, Highness," said Astrian. "We crossed into Hernystir days ago. Rimmersgard is still twenty leagues away. Who do you suppose lives in Ballydun, the walled city just to the east?"

Morgan shrugged, watching Astrian make his point with a six and a four. Everything the knight did had a compact grace to it, most definitely including his use of a sword, where his speed and nimbleness more than made up for his small stature. He was frequently named—and not least by himself—one of the best swordsmen in any land. "Hernystirmen, I suppose," Morgan said. "Knights, nobles, peasants, all the regular sorts of people."

"Rimmersmen, your Highness. They settled there after some war hundreds of years ago and never moved again. Most of the folk there are of northern blood." Now it was Astrian's turn, and he immediately rolled stones—"ballocks" as soldiers termed it, a pair of ones. He swept the small pot from the chest serving as a table. "I *do* like your dice, my prince. Now, did you notice that village we passed this morning? Not that you looked as if you were seeing much."

"My head was pounding and ringing like your damn Nabbanai bells. Yes, I suppose I saw it. Some children and others came out to wave at us, yes?"

"Exactly. And do you know what language they speak there?"

"No, by the eternal Aedon, how would I know that?"

"They speak Hernystiri, of course—we are in Hernystir, after all." Astrian grinned. "But *their* blood is that of Erkynland, just like yours, and there are many Erkynlandish words in their speech. Do you see?"

"Do I see what?" Morgan had lost the second throw as well, and his improved mood was beginning to fail again. "That nobody here seems to know what language they should speak? 'S'bloody Tree, man, how is that my concern?"

"Because it shows that borders are nonsense, at least most of the time. There are a few—such as the boundaries between Northern Rimmersgard and the Nornfells—that mean something real, because they are fiercely defended on both sides. But here on the Frostmarch all are mixed up together—Hernystiri, Rimmersmen, Erkynlanders. The people here speak a jumble of different tongues. They remember feuds that go back hundreds of years, but they speak in a way that would make their ancestors see blood before their eyes."

"Do not jest about the Nornfells," said Sir Porto. "You were not there at Nakkiga. You did not see those . . . things, or hear them singing with voices like sweet children, even as they killed and died."

"I do not jest at all," said Astrian. "God grant the White Foxes stay in the north where they belong. But the rest of the peoples of Osten Ard are mixing like the wax of different colored candles, melted and swirled together. Soon there will be no difference between a Rimmersman and a Hernystirman, or between a Nabbanai lord and a Thrithings barbarian. That is the curse of peace."

"Peace is no curse," said old Porto.

"I would love to do some deeds worthy of a prince," said Morgan sadly as he watched another pile of coins disappear into Astrian's purse. "Not a large war, perhaps but it has been more than a score of years since we fought the Thrithings-men and I see no threat to hope for. It is a bad time to be young."

"Porto would say it is never a bad time to be young," said Olveris from the back of the tent. "He would also say it is never a good time to be old."

"I can speak for myself, sir," said the tall knight. "I am not so ancient, nor so drunk, that I must be interpreted like a Naraxi island-man." His face drooped a little. "Nevertheless, Olveris is not wrong."

"Will there ever be another war?" Morgan asked.

"Oh, I rather think so," said Astrian. "Men do not manage well with too much peace. Someone will find a quarrel."

"I can only pray that you're right," said Morgan. "Hah! Look at those beauties—a pair of ale wagons! *This* pot is mine." He swept the coins toward him, but one slid off the chest and onto the dark ground. He got down on his knees to search for it.

"To be honest, Highness, I grow a little bored with dicing," said Astrian.

"Of course you do, now that I am beginning to win my money back!" Morgan straightened up in triumph, the wayward coin in his fist. "What else have we to do, in any case? It must be rising midnight, and you told me the wine is all gone."

"Perhaps," said Astrian.

"Perhaps?" Morgan grimaced. "Anything but 'yes' has an ugly sound, for I could happily drink more."

Sir Porto stirred. "I marvel at your stomach, young master. It must be from your mother's side. Your late father, I recall, never drank anything stronger than the weakest, most watered wine . . ." His eyes widened in distress. "Oh, Highness, forgive me. I forgot what day it is."

"Fool," said Olveris.

Morgan shook his head as though in anger, but said, "Don't chide old Porto. What should I care? The dead are dead—it does no good to think on them too much."

Porto still looked shaken, but now a little surprised as well. "Ah, but I am sure he watches you from Heaven, Prince Morgan. If it were me . . ." He fell silent, caught up by a sudden thought of his own.

"Only you could so deftly crush a conversation, ancient fool," Astrian told him. "We speak of wine, then you chime in with death *and* Heaven, the two chief foes of a man's drinking pleasure."

Morgan shook his head again. "I said leave him be, both of you. If my father is watching over me, it would be the first time. No, truly—I will tell you a story. Once when I was but young, I went to his chambers to tell him I had saddled and rode my horse all by myself. When he came to the door, he said I must tell my master he was not to be disturbed."

"I do not understand," said Porto, frowning.

"He thought I was some page boy sent by Count Eolair." Morgan smiled at the joke but did not seem to find it truly funny.

"Perhaps he had the sun in his eyes," Porto said. "I am all but blind when the sun shines in my face . . ."

"It wasn't the first time he did not know his own son, nor the last." Morgan looked down for a moment, then turned to Astrian. "We were talking about wine. Why? Do we have some left after all?"

Sir Astrian smiled. "As it happens, a few local girls we met promised they would meet us tonight in the birch grove at the edge of the field. I told them if they brought wine they might even meet the true prince of all Osten Ard."

For a moment Morgan brightened, but then an unhappy shadow passed over his face. "I can't do it, Astrian. My grandparents want to be ready to ride into Hernysadharc tomorrow morning as soon as the invitation is received. They told me to be in my tent by the end of the second watch."

"They want you rested, am I not right? So you may present yourself to the Hernystiri as befits a prince?"

"I suppose."

"Then what do you think would be better, to go sourly and soberly to bed after I have finished taking more money from you, or to have an enjoyable time with some local wenches and to wet your dry throat enough to allow you a happy, peaceful sleep?"

Morgan laughed despite himself. "By God, you could argue the Ransomer down off the Holy Tree, Astrian. Well, perhaps I will go along for a little while, then. But you must promise to help me get back to the royal tents. My grandfather is already furious with me." He made a face. "*He* had adventures. *He* slew dragons. But what does he expect of me? Endless, horrid ceremonies. Sitting still all day while fools drone on about justice and taxes and hides of land, like the buzzing of bees on a hot day. It is enough to send anyone to sleep, whether they have drunk any wine or not." He stood, brushing the worst of the dry grass and dirt from his clothes, although it was hard to tell by lamplight whether he had improved his appearance much. The sleeve of his jerkin had a woeful tatter, and the knees of his hose were both now damp and darkened with mud. "Olveris, Porto, are you coming?"

Olveris appeared suddenly from the shadows like something lifted from a box. Porto only shook his head. "I am too old for this foolishness, night after night," he said. "I will remain here and think about my soul."

"That is the part of you least worth exercising, old man." Astrian rose and stretched. "And now, Highness, if you'll follow me, I believe some ladies await us."

"It amazes me how such a short fellow cuts such a figure with the women," the prince said, looking on his friend with more than a little pride.

"Huh," said Olveris, looking down at the prince, who was in truth less than a handspan taller than Sir Astrian. "I see *two* short fellows."

"Silence, beanpole," said Morgan.

"There is no need for amazement, Highness." Astrian was grinning. "As with swordplay, the weapon must only be well-employed and long enough to reach its target." He made a mocking bow and swaggered out, pointedly leaving Prince Morgan and Sir Olveris to follow him.

After they had gone, Porto rose with a series of pained grunts and began to look around in case someone had left something to drink. After long moments of fruitless search, he sighed, then followed his comrades out between the tents and toward the distant birch grove.

The prince knew he had waved to the guards standing watch. That much was certain. Everything had been fine up until then. But now he seemed caught like a fish in a net, and it had happened quite by surprise.

He was having a particularly difficult time with tent flaps today—that much, at least, was beyond argument.

Morgan pawed at the heavy cloth, turning, trying to find the edge. No luck. He took another step forward, but now there seemed to be fabric on both sides of him. What madman would make a tent with two flaps? And when had they substituted it for the perfectly good tent he'd already had? The prince cursed and pawed again, then picked up as much of the flap as he could reach and lifted it, staggering forward with the weight of the heavy fabric on his head and shoulders. The stars appeared above him.

For just a brief moment he wondered why there were stars inside his tent, but then realized that he had somehow worked his way back outside. He had an overwhelming need to piss, so he undid his breeks and sent forth a mighty stream. He watched it feather in the stiff breeze until it dwindled and died. He decided he should try the flap again.

Ah, yes. I have been drinking. It explained a great deal.

This time he solved the puzzle after only a short interval of grunting and fumbling, and made it two steps into the tent before he smashed his shin against some obstacle. The pain was so fierce that he was still hopping on one foot swearing like a Meremund riverman when somebody flipped open a hooded lantern, bathing the interior of the tent in light.

"Where have you been?" demanded his grandmother, the queen. Morgan almost fell down before remembering two feet on the ground made for better balance. The shock of the sudden light and Queen Miriamele's voice had not yet passed when she added, "And what are you thinking, child? Fasten your clothes, please."

He scrabbled to pull his breeks closed. Drink had made his fingers as clumsy as raw sausages. "I . . . Majesty, I . . ."

"Oh, for the love of all that is good, sit down before you trip on something else and kill yourself."

He sank onto the chest that had so recently and cruelly attacked him. His shin still throbbed. "Am I . . . is this . . . I thought . . ."

"Yes, you young fool, this is your tent. I was waiting for you. God, you are stinking drunk. And stinking is the word."

He tried to smile, but it didn't feel like he was getting it right. "Not my fault. Astr'n. Astr'n challenged Baron Colfer's men to contest." For a long time Morgan had thought that the man he was matching cup for cup was Baron Colfer himself. He had been surprised that the baron was so young and so muscular, and that he had the Holy Tree tattooed on his forehead. It hadn't been until Morgan had fallen to his knees vomiting and the baron's men had been cheering loudly for someone called "Ox" that he had realized the baron himself was not present.

He wouldn't have felt so bad at this moment if he had managed to win. That would have made the scolding worthwhile.

"You have no idea how lucky you are that it was me waiting for you, not your grandfather. He already thinks you are becoming an embarrassment."

" 'M not an em . . . embearsamint. 'M a prince."

His grandmother rolled her eyes to the heavens. "Oh, spare me. Is this what a prince does to honor the day of his father's birth? Drinks until the morning hours? Stumbles back in, half-dressed, smelling of vomit and cheap sachet? Could you not at least spend your time with women who can afford a decent pomander? You stink like the end of Market Day."

Yes, there had been a few girls. He remembered that now. He and Astrian had been walking them back to their village, for their protection—Olveris was off protecting an older woman he'd met—but then things had become a bit confusing, as the walk turned into a game of hide and seek. Then there had been wet grass. Somebody had been named "Sofra," he thought—a very friendly someone. After that he had been back in camp, trying to get past the demon tent-flap. Waiting for his lazy squire to wake up and help him . . . which reminded him. "Where's Melkin?"

"If you mean your squire, I sent him out a short while ago to get me a blanket—a clean blanket. I didn't expect to be waiting so long, and I was getting cold."

She sounded very, very unhappy. "Please, Majesty. Gra'mother. I know you're angry, but . . . but I can explain."

Queen Miriamele rose. "There is nothing to explain, Morgan. There is nothing interesting or unusual about anything you have been doing, except for the fact that you are heir to the High Throne." She moved to the tent flap. "We will only be a day or two in Hernysadharc—where the people are already whispering about you and your friends, I am told—then we must travel to Elvritshalla in Rimmersgard to say farewell to one of the finest men your grandfather and I have ever known. You will not simply be a visitor there, you will be all they will see and remember for years of the man who will one day lead them—the man to whom even the king of Hernystir and the duke of Rimmersgard must kneel. Will you make yourself an ugly joke as you have done in Erchester and all during this journey? Will you earn the people's loyalty or their scorn?" She flipped shut the hood on the lantern, leaving only her voice to share the darkened tent with him. "We leave early tomorrow. Isgrimnur still lives, but for how long no one knows. You will be on your horse at first light. If you are timely and presentable, I will not tell your grandfather about this. Remember, first light."

Morgan groaned despite himself. "Too early! Why so early?" He tried to remember what Astrian had said, because it had made sense at the time. "I only drank wine so I could sleep better and not . . . I mean, so I could be a good prince. A better prince."

There was a long silence. The queen's voice was cold as a blade. "Your grandfather and I are tired of this foolishness, Morgan. Very, very tired."

The queen seemed to have no trouble with the flap, passing through and out into the night without a sound. Morgan sat on the chest in darkness and wondered why things were always so much easier for everyone else.